A MATTER OF RANGE:
THE COMPLETE ADVENTURES
OF THE MAJOR, VOLUME 2

A MATTER OF RANGE
The Complete
Adventures of the

Major

VOLUME 2

BY

L. PATRICK
GREENE

ALTUS
PRESS

2017

© 2017 Altus Press • First Edition—2017

EDITED AND DESIGNED BY
Matthew Moring

ASSOCIATE EDITOR
Ray Riethmeier

THANKS TO
Gordon Dymowski, Richard Hall, Everard P. Digges LaTouche & Walker Martin

TABLE OF CONTENTS

PAROLE

"**OF COURSE,** Don," said the girl, "I would marry you tomorrow. I have faith in you and in your ability to make good."

Donald Barton, wearing the smart uniform of a sergeant of the Mounted Police, reached over and took the girl's hand.

"I know, dear. Still, I can't help thinking that your father's right. It wouldn't be playing the game to ask you to share the rough quarters of a sergeant stationed at an outpost tucked away in some remote part of the veldt; no chance for social intercourse with white folks; and loneliness! No, I can't take you to that."

"I'm no child, Don. I know just what it would mean. Didn't I go through it all when father first come up here? We were the first settlers and the land around here for miles and miles was nothing but thick jungle growth. Now look at it."

From the porch of the Martin homestead a bird's-eye view could be obtained of the valley below, where acre after acre of corn rippled before the soft evening breeze. Large herds of cattle grazed in well-fenced pasture land, and, nearer to the homestead, was a smaller pasture where many horses frolicked.

Through the thickly leaved trees a glimpse could be obtained of the slow moving, sluggish African river, which formed the boundary between the Transvaal and Portuguese East Africa; along the river bank were several windmills pumping into a large reservoir, the water for use in the dry season.

The whole was a monument to the adaptability of the white man; to his indomitable spirit; to his victory over the vagaries of nature.

From the beginning Marjorie Martin had worked side by side with her father, encouraging him when things went wrong; dreaming, suggesting, planning, until the dream became a reality, and settled prosperity arose from disordered chaos.

She was essentially a man's woman; she could handle horses and firearms better than many men; was reliant, direct of speech, with a frankness that sometimes hurt. Generally she loved to dress in the unconventional riding costume, and there were few who had seen her attired—as now—in a fluffy white dress, making a picture which conjured up visions of an English spring. Still fewer knew the tenderness and the lovable womanly qualities she possessed.

The wives of new settlers to the district said that Marjorie was mannish, unsexed. But her father knew better—her mother had died when Marjorie was born—and so did Donald Barton, and as long as she had their good opinion, Marjorie cared not what others thought of her.

"I would go through it all again, Donald, if you asked me," she continued. "But I love you all the more, if that were possible for refusing to ask me."

"We won't have much longer to wait, Marje. I'm next on the list for promotion to commissioned rank."

"How long, do you think, Don?"

"A year at the outside; sooner, if I could get to work on some case which would bring my name before the chief."

The arrival of a native runner with the mail put an end to further conversation.

In the outlands letters from home are of first importance. Other things are forgotten until the letters are read and re-read, and the newspapers devoured down to the last advertisement in the "Help wanted" column.

Barton's English mail consisted merely of a catalogue from a mail order house and, with an expression of disgust, he opened an official looking envelope stamped with the seal of the Transvaal Government.

It was from the captain of his troop.

"Listen to this, Marje," he said, and read:

"I've just received official notice that the Major, our old and tried friend, has been on the war-path once again. This time it seems to be serious, as the enclosed clippings and police circular will show.

"The chief asks us to make a special effort to get the Major, as the Diamond Mining Syndicate is yelling blue murder.

"It is probable that the Major will make a break for Portuguese

Territory—he always has—so I'm going to appoint you for special duty. I know you are on leave of absence, but when I tell you that your leave is indefinitely extended—until the Major is caught or we get reliable information that he has entered Portuguese Territory—I feel sure that you will not mind this appointment.

"You can make your headquarters at the Martin's and you had better get into plain clothes. Keep your ears open, and your eyes peeled. It may mean your commission if you succeed in landing the Major.

"(Signed) Jas. Johnson.

Officer Commanding 'K' Troop."

The enclosed clippings were from the weekly paper of the Diamond Mining township. They told of how the Major had been engaged in the nefarious crime of I.D.B.—illicit diamond buying. The De Beers Company at Kimberley, controlled the diamond trade, and part of the year they closed down their mines for fear of flooding the market. Having done a great deal to build up the trade of South Africa, that grateful country protects the monopoly by a special statute against I.D.B. which imposes imprisonment for ten years for illicit diamond buying. The Major had, according to the clipping, cunningly escaped from the trap prepared for him by the police, much to the merriment of the colony, for the Major was a popular character, and the chagrin of the police.

Barton chuckled loudly as he read, for, possessed of a lively imagination and a first hand knowledge of the Major, he was able to supplement the meagre newspaper report.

He unfolded the police circulars. A photograph of the wanted man stared from the center of the lithographed sheet.

Across the top of the paper in bold, black lettering were the words:

"Five Thousand Pounds Reward for information leading to the arrest of the above, generally known as 'the Major.' Has many aliases. Last seen heading toward the Portuguese Territory, by way of Barberton."

There followed a brief, but succulent, description of the Major:

"Well-built man, about six feet in height, and weighing close to two hundred pounds. Fair complexion; light hair; gray eyes. Always immaculately dressed; wears a monocle and speaks with a pronounced drawl."

Marjorie's eyes glistened with excitement. "Why it's wonderful, Don," she cried. "It's your big chance. With the five thousand you can leave the police, buy a farm near here and still have enough to stock it properly. We'll get father to—"

"Not so fast, Marje," Barton interrupted with a smile. "First catch the Major, and then we'll spend the five thousand."

"Oh! You're going to catch him, Don," she said in confident tones. "If he's heading this way he'll have to cross the river at our ford, or at Simkin's place ten miles up the valley. The river's in flood, you know, and he just can't cross anywhere else. You mustn't post those circulars, Don."

"No? Of course I hate to do it. The Major's such a good sport he's no criminal. But—why don't you want me to put up the circulars? Do you want him to get away?"

"Don't be silly, Don." Marjorie made a gesture of impatience. "Don't you see that if you post the circulars, one of the settlers might catch him, claim the reward and all the credit?"

"That's a risk I've got to take."

Marjorie was thoughtful a moment.

"Don," she said, "this Major chap is supposed to be pretty crafty, isn't he?"

Barton laughed. "He's all of that," he said, and told her of some of the Major's exploits: notably of the attempt of one police officer to trap him into buying a diamond. The Major had bought the diamond and got away but the police officer had himself been arrested for illegally offering diamonds for sale!

"Do you think a man like that would be likely to be trapped by any of the farmers round here? Why, he could even fool father."

"That's true," Barton said ruefully. "I'd never be sure of the Major, myself, until I had him handcuffed and leg ironed."

"Then don't you see," exclaimed Marjorie triumphantly, "that to post those circulars would put an end to all chance of arresting him? We're way off the beaten track here in the valley, and the chances are that he will make an open break for the border, relying on the fact that no one knows him. He wouldn't expect a policemen to be stationed here. But if you post those circulars he would be sure to hear of it, and he'd be on his guard."

"By Jove, I think you're right."

"I know I am."

"Do you know," said Barton slowly, "I wouldn't like to make good at the expense of the Major. You see, dear, he's such a decent sort of chap. This I.D.B. is really his protest against what he considers an unjust law. I happen to know that he was once imprisoned simply because he bought, in good faith, a diamond from a native. He was new to the country then, and didn't know the law. He's never done anything really wrong and we of the police look upon him as a political offender rather than a criminal."

"You're hopeless, Don. He's broken the laws of the country; that makes him a criminal, doesn't it? Every bit as much as though he picked my pocket. Just because he has a colorful personality, that doesn't make him any less a law breaker."

Barton was silent. He was thinking of the Major's character, of his courage, his generosity, of his essential cleanness.

"Bring the horses round," said Marjorie, jumping up suddenly, "I'm going to change."

"Where are we going?"

"You are going to Simkin's place to warn him to be on the look out for the Major; only I wouldn't tell him too much. I'll go a little way with you. If you ride hard you ought to be back in time for scoff at seven."

AN HOUR or so later as Marjorie was returning along the winding, dusty road which led past the homestead, she suddenly caught sight of a rapidly moving cloud of dust, rising high above the *mapani* bush. A moment later the beating of a horse's hoofs came to her ears.

"Someone's in a hurry," she thought, pulling her mount, a coal black Arab, into the shade of a Kaffir orange tree. "I wonder who?"

She stood up in her saddle and from this eminence she could follow the winding course of the road for some distance. Soon horse and rider came into her field of vision, and her keen eyes detected the rolling gait of the horse, the drooping figure of the man.

"Whoever it is," she mused, "he's ridden far and fast."

The stranger was rapidly coming nearer. He had almost reached the bend in the road, the turning of which would bring him into a straight stretch of road leading directly by Marjorie.

"It must be the Major," she exclaimed and the next moment reproached herself for being unarmed. If it was indeed the Major, she had no means to stop him. He could get by her, reach the ford and security from arrest in the Portuguese Territory which lay beyond. A quick glance around assured her that there was no one within hail to lend her assistance, and for a moment she tasted the bitterness of defeat.

With a sudden resolve she dropped lightly into her saddle and leaning forward, quickly removed the horse's bridle and cast it behind her into the bush.

"Home, Satan," she whispered, and brought her spurs with a sharp thrust into the blooded stallion's side.

With a snort, half amazement, half rage, the powerful animal, bolted down the road at a breakneck speed.

The stranger at that moment turned the bend in the road and saw, coming toward him, at a thunderous gallop, a perfect fury of a horse. Its rider swayed grotesquely from side to side.

The man pulled up his horse to watch.

"It's a girl," he said with a gasp. Marjorie's hair floated out behind her like a silken cloud. "And her mount's bridleless."

"Stop him!" called a voice, heard faintly above the thudding of hoofs. "He's running away."

The man wheeled his horse and urged it to a canter. The runaway came nearer and nearer. Now it was up to his horse's crupper; its black nostrils were level with his knee: then for one moment the two horses raced neck and neck and in that moment the man leaned over and swept the girl from the saddle, and the runaway galloped on, riderless.

The man's horse, unable to sustain the double load, faltered in his stride and nearly fell. Pulling him up, the man lowered the girl gently to the ground, and jumped down quickly beside her.

"Are you all right? Not hurt at all, are you?"

"No," she said breathlessly. "I'm not hurt a bit, thanks to you. A little shaken, that's all. I don't know how Satan managed to—"

She stopped abruptly—unable to explain to her own satisfaction the fact that her horse was bridleless. She looked keenly at the man. He was, she saw, without doubt, the Major. She wondered if he would see through her ruse.

He nodded absently. "If you think," he said, "that you can manage to make the homestead alone—it's quite near, isn't it?— I'll go on. I'm in a deuce of a hurry."

"But you can't go like that," she cried impetuously. "You must come up and stay overnight. Father would never forgive me if you were to go without giving him a chance to thank you."

He shook his head. "Thanks! But I must go on."

"How can you? Look at your horse: he's all tuckered out; you look ready to drop yourself. Besides—" She hesitated. A wave of self-disgust swept over her. She did not relish the part she had forced herself to play.

She reeled faintly and would have fallen had not the man caught her.

"The shock was greater than you thought," he said with a smile.

He lifted her on to the horse and walked back beside her to the homestead.

"Sixpence," she called to the horse boy who came running with the news that Satan had returned riderless, "take the *Baas's* horse and give him a good rubdown and feed. That, and a rest, will put new life into him," she said, turning to the Major. "Now, you must come in; for a little while at least."

The Major hesitated, looked at his tired mount being slowly led away by Sixpence, shook his head doubtfully, then followed the girl into the house.

"I must be on my way in half an hour," he said. "I want to make the ford before sundown."

Marjorie clapped her hands. "Tom," she said to the white-clad house boy, "show the *Baas* where he can wash up. I'll have some scoff waiting for you when you come down," she added to the Major.

Ten minutes later, feeling greatly refreshed, the man reentered the cool, airy room, where he found an appetizing meal awaiting him.

"It is rare, dear lady," he said to Marjorie, who attended to his wants, "that a rover such as I am sits down to such a meal, and in such charming company."

"It is such a little you will let me do," she murmured.

A large clock in the hall chimed the half hour.

"I must be moving on," he said.

"Oh!" She made a gesture of impatience. "I do wish you would stay and meet father."

"I am sorry, and all that, but—it's quite impossible. Quite."

He pushed back his chair and rose to his feet.

"Good-bye, dear lady. I shall always remember your kindness and thank the Devil—or is it Satan?—for being the means of my meeting you and sharing your hospitality."

Again Marjorie's determination almost failed her as the Major, with a courtly bow, turned to leave the room. He was almost at the door when she called,

"Stop!"

There was something in her voice which made him wheel around and face her quizzically.

"You must not go."

She rose from her chair, her right hand hidden behind her.

"No?" he said lightly. "You have a reason?"

"A very good reason," she said curtly. "It is this, Major."

He looked blankly at the revolver which she leveled at him.

"What do you mean Major?" his tone was one of innocent amazement.

With her left hand she shook out a police circular and threw it toward him.

He took it up and looked at it.

"Who is the handsome-looking Johnny? Oh, I see, you think it's me?"

"It is you."

"Didn't think I was so good looking."

To tell the truth the Major was baffled. His situation was not desperate. There were many cunning tricks by which he could make a safe getaway, and if a man had held him up thus he would, without doubt, have resorted to one of them. For instance, the floor of the dining room was highly polished and was carpeted by several small rugs. Marjorie was standing on one of them and, when he had stooped down to pick up the circular she tossed him, he was within easy reach of a corner of the rug. A quick strong jerk of it would have thrown the girl to the floor and— But the Major always seemed witless when dealing with a woman.

"Then it was all a sell," he said abruptly. "The runaway, and everything?"

Marjorie allowed herself a little smile of triumph.

"Yes. I've ridden Satan lots of times without a bridle. I guessed you were the Major when I first saw your dust; but I was unarmed and that seemed the only way to prevent you from crossing the border."

"You mean that you banked on my—er—chivalry. A maiden in distress and all that sort of thing?"

Marjorie flushed.

"And yet I can't see," went on the Major, "why you did it. You seem to be well-fixed here; quite prosperous, I should say."

"It was for Don," she said, and told him the whole story.

"You don't mean Donald Barton?"

"Yes."

"And he's here? Why, that's simply priceless. I'm so charmed at the idea of meeting the old fellow again, that I can almost forgive you everything. The last time I saw him he told me all about you. 'She's a regular good sport, Major!' he said. 'Plays the game like a man.' He'll be tickled when he hears how well you played the game today."

"You won't tell him how I trapped you, will you?"

The look the Major gave her made Marjorie feel like a small child.

"Really, you misjudge me, Miss Marjorie. That's not done, you know. But what are you going to do with me? I'm afraid your hand will get tired pointing that bally popper at me for another hour or so. Why don't you ask for my parole?"

"Will you give it?"

"Yes, to you, and until Barton takes me away under arrest."

"Then I'll accept it."

She tossed the revolver into an open drawer.

"That's bully," said the Major.

"I'll join you on the porch in a little while," said Marjorie wanly. "I'm going to change."

As she ran upstairs she felt herself half wishing that the Major would break his parole.

"But of course he won't," she sighed. "He's a gentleman." And then she fell to wondering if Donald would approve of the part she had played that day.

"MARGE," BARTON called gaily, three hours later, as he ran up the porch steps, "your father says we are not to wait scoff for him. He's going over to the Graham's place and may stay all night."

"All right, Don. There's someone up here to see you. I'll go and hurry up scoff. You must be starved."

Marjorie ran into the house.

"By Jove, Barton, old fellow. I'm glad to see you again," drawled a well remembered voice from the depths of a lounge chair. "I'd rise to greet you, but I'm so comfortable here that I know you'll forgive me."

"The Major!" gasped Barton, and his hand leaped to his revolver. "You darned fool! What did you hang around here for?"

" 'Mine not to reason why,' as the poet says. And please don't bother with your shooter. I am handcuffed—so to speak—and quite harmless. You see, I gave Miss Marjorie my parole."

Barton dropped into a nearby chair.

"You know I'm glad to see you, Major; but the Lord knows I could almost wish you were the other side of the river. Of course I'll have to take you in and—"

The Major waved his hand airily. "Let there be no regrets, old boy. It's all in the game. You know," he added confidentially, "I've always wondered why they didn't put a price on my head long ago. I felt rather neglected. But they've made up for it at last. Just think! Five thousand pounds. Why, I must be as famous as Deadwood Dick and the James brothers. I feel quite perked up about it, I assure you."

"You always were a good sport, Major, but how—?"

"Yes; of course you want to know all about it. Miss Marjorie is a girl to be proud of. I congratulate you. You see, my horse was about played out and when I saw a girl riding a powerfully built stallion, I decided that I wanted it. So I divorced Miss Marjorie from her horse and I found that I had caught a Tartar. She pulled a gun on me, and I was arrested neatly and efficiently. Damned efficiently, I should say."

Marjorie, who was standing just inside the doorway listening to the conversation, breathed a sigh of relief, and sent a mental message of thanks to the Major.

NEXT MORNING, before Marjorie was up, the two men, the "criminal" and the policeman, started on the journey back to the mining settlement.

Jail awaited one; for the other, a big reward and, perhaps, a commission.

"Will you give me your parole, Major?" asked Barton as they left the house.

The Major laughed shortly.

"Not by a long sight, old chap! We've a long way to go, and there's many a slip between the veldt and the jail."

"I'm sorry," Barton said slowly. "Because I'll have to take all the precautions possible."

He reached for his handcuffs apologetically.

"That's all right," the Major reassured him.

He held them up and gazed at them in admiration. The polished steel reflected the rays of the early morning sun.

"By Jove!" he exclaimed. "I do believe that it would be possible to heliograph with them!"

Barton looked at him quickly and the Major burst into a roar of laughter.

"I foresee, old man, that you're going to have gray hairs before we reach the *'dorp.'* That is," he added as an afterthought, "if we ever do get there."

"It won't be your fault, if we do, Major. Well, let's go. I want to reach the Big Tree water hole before the sun gets too high up."

He waited until the Major had climbed clumsily into his saddle before mounting himself; then, taking the bridle reins of the Major's horse, he led the way down the dusty road at a sharp canter.

Save for the handcuffs on the Major's wrists, there was nothing in the bearing of either of the two men, that suggested that one was a policeman and the other his prisoner, a man with a price on his head. They conversed merrily as they rode along; chiefly uniting in damning the administration of the late chief of police, and praising the activities of the new one.

"You speak as if you had met the new chief, Major."

"I have," replied the Major. "He wanted me to join the police last time I saw him. And, 'pon my soul, it would not be half bad if I did. I must think it over."

After passing through the gate in the fence which encircled the Martin property, Barton left the dusty roadway, setting his course due south through the veldt.

"We can cut off about ten miles going this way," explained Barton. "The road winds like a drunken snake."

The Major nodded. "Wish I'd known that yesterday; I might have made the ford and got clean away; but I'm new to this country."

He sighed, then ducked quickly to avoid being swept from his saddle by the low bough of a tree under which they were passing.

"You nearly lost your prisoner then, Barton. You must really be more careful. The reward wouldn't be given, I fancy, if you took me in dead."

"I'm sorry, Major," Barton apologized, and pulled up to a walk. "The going is pretty rough here, and will be until we get out of the valley."

Soon the luxuriant growth became thinner and thinner until, finally, they left it far behind them and there was nothing to turn them aside from a straight course but an occasional thick clump of *mapani*, a group of anthills, or a "wait a minute" thorn bush.

On topping a slight rise, after four hours' steady riding, Barton pointed to a large baobab tree about three hundred yards away. "The water hole is there, Major," he said. "We can have a good rest in the—"

At that moment, the Major's horse swerved suddenly, throwing its rider with force to the ground.

Barton's horse also became unmanageable and he was obliged to release the other mount which galloped away, head flung back, and nostrils distended with terror.

Having succeeded somewhat in soothing his horse, Barton's first impulse was to ride after the runaway. Then, seeing that the Major had not moved, he rode up to him, fearing that he was hurt.

The next thing he knew was the vision of a lion hurtling through the air toward him. He pulled his horse sharply to the left, causing the tawny beast partially to miss its mark. But the claws tore down the horse's hind quarters and the terrified animal made a desperate lunge forward, throwing Barton straight into the jaws of a second lion which had come up on the other side.

The horse made off at full speed, leaping over the prostrated Major, followed closely by the first lion.

Barton barely touched the ground at all but was caught in mid-air by the lion, which started to carry him toward the bushes from whence it had emerged.

It was at this moment that the Major, recovering from the shock of his fall, lifted his head. His first reaction was one of despair, for there seemed no way out of the predicament. Handcuffed as he was, there seemed little he could do even should he succeed in reaching Barton's rifle which was lying on the ground some twenty yards away. There was a chance, a slim one, it is true, if he could get the rifle before the other lion returned, and without attracting the attention of the lion which had the policeman in its grip. With that end in view he started to crawl on his belly slowly toward the gun.

Barton was held by the right shoulder, his face on a level with the lion's neck, while his legs were dragging on the ground under its belly. But his mind was alert and he at once cast about for some means of saving himself.

Feeling carefully with his left hand he discovered, to his joy, that his large hunting knife had not been jarred out of its sheath by the fall and the subsequent dragging. Pulling it out, he held on to it firmly as a man clutches to his last hope of life, and waited for an opportunity to use it.

It soon came. The Major, who was now only ten yards from the rifle, suddenly decided to cast discretion to the winds and make a run for it. He half rose to his feet. This movement attracted the attention of the lion to him, and it laid Barton down and glared savagely at the Major.

This brief respite afforded the policeman the opportunity he looked for.

Feeling carefully behind the shoulder for a vital spot he struck a couple of back-handed blows with the knife he held in his left hand. The lion remained stock still for a second, and Barton then plunged the knife upward into the throat.

At this the animal, now streaming with blood, sprang back several yards and remained facing him. Slowly, half dazed Barton rose to his feet, and concentrated his efforts in trying to keep the lion from charging the Major, who had recovered the rifle and was endeavoring to release the magazine catch and permit a bullet to enter the chamber.

In a calm, dispassionate tone, Barton cursed the lion; casting reflections on the morals of its mother and the ancestry of its father.

Then, when it seemed to Barton that his strength could hold out no longer, for he was badly mangled, a shot rang out and the lion with a strangled cough, toppled over dead.

The world revolved dizzily around Barton and he heard a dim, far-off voice say:

"It's all right now, old man." Then the sun went out and he fell forward in a faint.

The Major ran swiftly to him and fumbling in Barton's pocket, discovered, with an exclamation of triumph, the keys to the handcuffs.

Working quickly, the Major soon managed to get rid of the handcuffs, but not a moment too soon, for the other lion, returning from his fruitless chase of the horses, was coming forward at express speed.

Dropping on one knee, the Major fired three shots in rapid succession, stopping the oncoming fury dead in its tracks.

Taking the still unconscious policeman on his back, the Major carried him to the water hole and there bathed his wounds.

"Hullo," said Barton, wearily opening his eyes. "Haven't you gone yet, Major?" Then he lapsed once again into unconsciousness.

"I don't see how I can leave him here," mused the Major. "On the other hand—"

His conjectures were interrupted.

The Major's horse, dreading the terrors of the veldt, had come to the water hole to seek the companionship of man.

Without further ado the Major carefully lifted Barton on to the horse and mounted behind him.

"I'm sorry, old chap," he said, as though apologizing to the horse for the double burden he had to bear, "but this Johnny would fall off if I didn't hold him on. Besides we've got to go faster than a walk."

"HOW IS the dear old invalid, Miss Marjorie?" the Major asked.

Barton had been put to bed; his wounds skillfully dressed by the girl, who, as is the case with the women folk of pioneers, had no mean knowledge of surgery.

"He's sleeping calmly, and I don't think there is any cause for alarm. The wounds are clean, and, as you say the lion was young and healthy, there's not much danger of blood poisoning."

"Oh, yes, please believe me, Miss Marjorie, he was decidedly healthy, I assure you."

"But you?" the girl looked up suddenly with a smile on her face. "What are you doing here? I thought you had gone, after you had helped carry Don upstairs."

The Major coughed deprecatingly and, for the first time in many days, felt for his eye glass.

"I couldn't go, you know. Really I couldn't until I heard how old Don was. Besides, when I came into this house I automatically, so to speak, was under parole to you."

"I told Don all about the rotten trick I played yesterday, Major; and it was a rotten trick," the girl said slowly.

"Yes?"

His tone was one of mild interest.

"Sixpence," she called, and as the horse boy came running to her cry, ordered: "Saddle Satan and bring him here."

"You are going for a ride, Miss Marjorie?"

She made no reply, but when Sixpence brought round the horse she held out her hand to the Major.

"Your horse was all in, so you must take Satan. I will send some food across the river to you tonight. Good-bye, Major, and good luck."

"But my parole, Miss Marjorie?"

"I release you from that."

"That's bully of you. But how about Don? How about your plans, your—"

"We are both young. A year will soon pass."

"Marjorie!" Barton's voice called faintly.

"There's Don calling me," she said hurriedly. "Good night, Major. Take good care of Satan."

He watched her as, humming a cheerful little tune, she ran up the steps into the house.

"She played the game after all," murmured the Major, and leaping lightly into the saddle he galloped swiftly down the road which led to the ford and freedom.

A MATTER OF RANGE

THE STEEP sides of the boulder-strewn *kopje* swarmed with the people of Thuso's *kraal*—men, women and children. At the base of the *kopje* stood Thuso, surrounded by his councilors.

Among the latter was a man dressed in the regalia of a witch-doctor—the living symbol of Africa's darkness. On his head the horns of an ox, fantastically curved, were fastened; a leopard skin hung from his shoulders; charms of snakes' fangs and human teeth were strung on a cord about his neck, and his face and body were daubed with ash-paint. Here and there his skin showed through the gray daub of ashes, and it gleamed white!

His face was in no particular negroid. His wide-spaced eyes were blue—cold blue, always shifting; his nose was arched, aquiline; his lips were thin and firmly compressed.

In his hands he held a rifle.

"All is ready, white man," Thuso said. "Make good now your boast, or—" He paused significantly.

The white man spat in contempt.

"I shall not fail, O Chief." He barely opened his lips when he spoke. The words seemed to trickle out of the corner of his mouth.

"Two hundred spear lengths from us," he continued, "the fastest riding-bull of your herd is tethered so that he can not move to the right or to the left, forward or back. Your young men saw to that."

Thuso made a gesture of impatience, but the white man proceeded deliberately.

"Two hundred spear lengths beyond the bull, and in a line with us and it, bound to a stake, is Marka—the man who would set himself up against me, the man who says my counsel is evil, my magic a thing to be mocked.

"We shall see. I have cast my magic upon the bull. Nothing can harm it. The death that is in this—" he patted the rifle with a long, claw-like hand—"shall pass through it, harming it not. But upon Marka I have cast no charm. So watch!"

The chief raised his *assegai;* indunnas shouted angry commands and the black swarm upon the *kopje* ceased its noisy clamor.

All was still. It seemed as if the vast horde had suddenly stopped breathing. Not a thing moved; no fitful breeze was present to stir the wan grass of the veldt.

The white man stepped a few paces forward, stopped, examined the sights of his weapon, adjusted the sling, slipped a cartridge into the breech and then slowly brought the rifle up to his shoulder.

And now the eyes of the watchers turned from him to the tethered bull five hundred yards away; beyond that to the black dot, which was Marka, on the level, sand-colored plain.

Then, when it seemed that the limit of human patience had been reached, the vast silence was broken by a vicious crack and a coil of blue smoke floated lazily from the muzzle of the rifle.

The report unloosened the voices so long silent.

The first awed exclamation, *"Auka!"* was followed by a babel of sounds.

"See!" exclaimed one of the indunnas, voicing the thoughts of many of the watchers. "The bull lives. He still lives. He lashes at the flies with his tail. The white man's magic has passed through him, harming him not, because of the charm."

"Aye. The bull lives," said another, "but is Marka dead?"

The white man took a powerful spyglass from the case which he had worn concealed under the leopard skin and, focusing it on the distant spot, gazed through it long and earnestly.

At length a sneering smile of satisfaction crossed his face.

Turning to the chief he said, "My magic was greater than Marka's, Thuso. You will not forget your promise?"

"I am not wont to retrace my footprints," Thuso answered with the pompous dignity of a petty autocrat. "What I have said, I have said. But not yet am I sure Marka is dead."

"*Tchat!* There is no need to doubt. See!" He pointed to two tiny specks—almost invisible in the deep blue of the sky.

As the chief watched, the two were joined by two others and all four dropped, stone-like, to the veldt.

"Vultures, come to the kill," continued the white man. "But if you still doubt send a warrior out there and bid him bring you word of what he sees."

"It is well thought of," muttered Thuso, and so ordered one of his young men.

"If Marka is indeed dead," he said to the warrior, "hold your shield high above your head."

From mouth to mouth the chief's order spread, and again the people were silent, waiting for the signal that would tell them which magic was the greater—Marka's, or the white man's.

The minutes passed slowly. To the waiting throng the pace of the warrior was that of the snail, yet they called him the Springbok.

The white man sat down on a nearby boulder, his back to the speeding messenger, his attitude one of contemptuous indifference.

At last a mighty shout went up from the watchers. The messenger had reached his goal, and he was waving his shield above his head.

"Your magic is indeed great, white man," said Thuso in awed tones. "The death that is in your fire-stick has passed through the bull, harming it not. But Marka is dead. *Au-a!*"

The white man rose to his feet.

"Then let us go to the Council Place. There is much I would say to your people. I have spoken."

Then he turned and led the way to the *kraal* which nestled at the foot of the *kopje,* but on the other side from where they were now standing.

As he walked he covertly wiped the sweat from his face—for he had been under a severe mental strain—and muttered in English, "It was a hard shot, the hardest I've ever made. But I knew I couldn't miss."

That night there was much beer drinking and merriment at the *kraal* of Thuso. But some few men there were, who sat apart and refused the beer pots when offered them. These—Marka's sons—were noted by the white man and, when one of them, thinking to take advantage of the darkness and the drunkenness of the warriors, left the *kraal,* he was followed by four warriors into whose ears the white man had whispered evil commands.

IT WAS just a matter of pure luck that the officials of the Anton Diamond Mining Syndicate discovered that the man who had staked a claim close to their holdings, and had commenced mining operations, was a famous Illicit Diamond Buyer. That in itself would have made them suspicious and uncomfortable—it savored too much of their own first mining venture. When a further trick of fate put into their hands the definite knowledge that the I.D.B. was buying stones smuggled out of *their* diggings by native laborers, and burying the stones on his claim with the intention of later "finding" them and registering them as by law ordained, why then the Anton officials were greatly incensed. The fact that they owed their present wealth to earlier illegalities of a like nature did not mitigate their wrath— added to it, rather.

As Satans rebuking sin, they at once lodged complaints with the police authorities and, because the Anton officials were powerful politically, the police lost no time in getting into action.

But, proving that Lady Luck sometimes plays fair, the I.D.B. discovered, just by chance, that he was "discovered" and that an elaborate plan was afoot which would surely be the means of sending him to labor on the Breakwater at Cape Town for the rest of his natural life.

So he stood not on the order of his going, but under cover of darkness fled in great haste. He left the diamonds behind him, fearing that, if captured, he would be in a much worse plight should the stones be found on him. Albeit he did set off several sticks of dynamite which caused his diggings to cave in and thus make the rediscovery of the pilfered stones that much harder.

He and his native servant who fled with him were pursued, of course, but the police were unable to pick up the spoor until the morning. So with the eight hours' start, an uncanny knowledge of the country, good riding and superlative horses, the fugitives made good their escape.

About the same time that the four pursuing troopers—after five days of hard trekking—lost the spoor and were ready to admit defeat, the I.D.B. and his servant were camped by a small spruit nearly a hundred miles to the north of them.

Each was chewing meditatively on a piece of biltong, washing down the salty stuff with muddy coffee.

"If the *baas* had shot the buck this morning," the native, a squat, but powerful Hottentot, said presently, "we would be eating now instead of fattening our thirst."

The white man smiled.

"Yes, Jim. And the mounted police might have heard the shot and we would be riding hard now instead of resting."

"That's true, *Baas*. And I'm tired of running. We go no further today?"

"Nay. In a little while the sun will have set and there is no danger. They cannot follow our spoor to this place. Tomorrow we will go on at our own pace seeking a *kraal* where, perchance, the people will be glad to feed and shelter us for a time in payment for a lion shot, or—"

But Jim, the Hottentot, did not hear. He had turned over on his side and was snoring lustily.

The white man rose to his feet and, catching the two horses—one a Basutu stallion, the other a rangy, flea-bitten gray—which had been turned loose to graze, tethered them to a nearby tree.

That done he returned to the fire and, sitting down on a large boulder, prepared to keep watch through the night.

It was typical of the man that despite the hard riding of the past days, and the fact that he was a half-starved fugitive from the law of the diamond monopolists, he still presented an immaculate appearance. His white drill riding breeches and his khaki tunic were slightly dust-stained, it is true, but his face was clean-shaven, his monocle glittered dazzlingly in his eye, and his brown riding-boots were highly polished. His hair, jet black save for graying patches over the temples, looked as if the man had just risen from a barber's chair, and certainly not as if he were on the African veldt—and in a very precarious position.

But that was always the Major's way. In addition to a normal man's desire for cleanliness he had for so long acted a pose, that it is doubtful if he would consider himself entirely dressed without his monocle.

But those who knew him well knew that the affected drawl, the air of helplessness, the air of innocence, and the inane, vacuous expression of his face, merely masked an extraordinarily keen brain. It was all this which made him the most successful I.D.B. in South Africa; the despair—and because he was such a real sportsman and a "damned good sort," the pride—of the police.

"I wish I knew where the deuce we are," he muttered aloud. "I'm not quite sure of this bally country. I think, perhaps, it's Portuguese territory. If so, we're safe—from arrest, that is. I wonder how those bally blighters got on to my game? But what's the use of wondering about that? I've been doing nothin' else these past few days. That's all past now, anyway. It means I'm through in the Transvaal and the colony; I'll never be permitted to go back. Trod on the toes of high-muckamucks too hard. And poor old Jim, he's exiled too—and we're both stony broke. Total wealth: two horses, saddles and bridles; a billy can, rifle and fifty cartridges; one revolver and twenty cartridges, and a cigarette case—empty! That's all. But wait—I forgot the monocle! I must not forget that, oh, dear me, no. Well, we'll see what the morning brings."

He put an armful of wood on the fire; the sun had set and already the night air was growing chill.

The bush veldt began to echo with the cries of the night creatures.

The horses neighed in fear and lashed at some fancied—or real—danger. The Major whistled softly. The low notes calmed their fears, and they playfully nibbled each other.

There were heavy crashings in the thick undergrowth; a cock ostrich boomed; the ground reverberated to the roar of a distant lion; a grass snake slithered over Jim's leg and coiled itself up close to the fire; a bell-bird *tonked* dismally.

There followed a period of silence.

And then Jim's eyes opened.

From the deep sleep of exhaustion he became instantly wide awake, every faculty alert. There was no intermediate stage, no yawning or stretching, no rubbing of eyes or collecting of wits. Neither did he move, but waited, eyes fixed on the Major, concentrating, sending out a silent call for his master's attention.

A few minutes passed.

"What is it, Jim?" the Major suddenly asked softly. Yet he had not looked up. He was apparently absorbed in polishing his monocle.

"Someone comes, *Baas.*"

"A friend, Jim?"

"Who knows, *Baas?* But would a friend come crawling on hands and knees?"

"You have been dreaming, Jim," the Major scoffed. But he placed the monocle carefully in his breast-pocket, and without any waste motions drew his revolver.

A stealthy rustling sound came from the bush just beyond the range of the firelight, followed by a groan as of a man in pain.

The Major jumped to his feet and started in the direction of the noise.

"No! *Baas.* Don't go!" cried Jim, and he, too, rose to his feet. "Or if you must," he continued, "I go with you."

He snatched a blazing brand from the fire and, holding it before him, followed his *baas.*

Soon they came upon the form of a man lying supine. He was evidently in poor shape, at the point of total exhaustion.

Picking him up, they carried him to the fire, and by its fitful light examined him carefully.

He was a native of powerful build and wore the head-ring of a man of affairs, but his tribal marks were strange to Jim. In the lobes of his ears he wore brass cartridge-cases.

Blood had clotted about a wound in his scalp—made by a glancing blow with a knobkerrie, the Major judged—and the fleshy part of both thighs had been pierced by *assegai.* As if that were not enough, his whole body seemed to be one big bruise. "Better that we take him back where we found him, *Baas,*" Jim muttered. "Undoubtedly this man has offended a powerful witch-doctor, and this is his punishment. If we aid him, we, too, will be punished."

"And is that indeed your true desire? To let him die?"

Jim smiled shamefacedly.

"That would be the wise thing to do, *Baas.* But we are fools. Methinks that sometimes the spirits look kindly on fools. See if you can make him swallow some coffee, *Baas,* and I will make a strong medicine that will heal his wounds."

Jim took from his saddle wallet a bag containing dried herbs. Some of these he put in the cook-pot and covered them with water. He put the pot on the fire, and squatting nearby, muttered charms and supplications to the Great Spirits to look favorably upon his medicine making.

Soon the water began to boil and strong, pungent odors came from the pot.

"He can't drink the coffee, Jim. He's too far gone. He breathes with difficulty."

"No matter, *Baas.* My magic is ready now."

Jim took the pot from the fire. It contained now a thick, sticky and evil smelling ointment which, after it had cooled a little, he rubbed into the body of the wounded man. He smeared still more all over him and allowed it to dry.

"He will be better in the morning, *Baas.* Warriors are not women to die for so little. Look you; the wounds are of no moment. It is only that he is tired in spirit as well as of body. Even now my magic is beginning to work. See! He sleeps as a man should."

"It is true, Jim," the Major said in wondering tones. "I have seen you work many wonders, but none to equal this."

"Yet I have worked this wonder before. But then you were sick and did not know."

"Not all the wisdom of medical schools," the Major muttered in English, "could equal this. 'Out of the mouths of babes,' and all that. You are a babe, Jim, you know, and full of wisdom, you old sinner."

"Damme, yes," chuckled Jim, who spoke English like a sailor's parrot. "Me a bloody babe—damme, yes."

THE MAJOR and Jim were about early next morning. The Major was roasting two guinea fowls which he had knocked down with a stick, and Jim was busily grooming the horses.

The stranger was still asleep and, judging by the loudness of his snores, had recuperated a great deal from his weakness of the night.

Just at the moment that the coffee boiled over and the Major announced to Jim that the fowls were ready for the eating, the sleeper awoke with a yell. Jim and his *baas* hurried over to him and, noting the fear in the wounded man's eyes, quickly assured him that he was with friends.

Partly reassured, he attempted to rise to his feet, but they restrained him.

"You must help me, white man," he cried, "and you, too, oh, black one. There is much to be done and the time is short."

"First eat and drink," commanded the Major quietly, "then you shall tell us the story."

With a gesture of resignation the man assented and greedily tore the flesh off the bones of the fowl Jim brought to him.

"Two days have passed since I last ate," he said when, the bones picked clean, he flung the carcass into the bush behind him.

"So? Then let the tale of your hunger be told."

"I am of the tribe of Thuso. Matiswa, my name. Marka—the greatest of all witch-doctors—my father."

"To the meat of the story," growled Jim. "You said there was need of great haste."

"It is necessary that you know all things from the beginning," Matiswa retorted chidingly. "Because of the wise counsel of Marka, Thuso was enabled to rule us long; neither did we acknowledge any overlord."

"Not even the great white queen?" the Major interposed quietly.

"No. Not to her or to the big chief of the Portuguese, do my people pay homage. We are a people set apart, a law unto ourselves. And this because of the wise counsel of Marka, who let it be known among the white men that our country was a poor country; that gold and the stones for which white men lie and kill do not exist within our borders. And so, because we in no way interfered with the whites, and because we had nothing they counted precious, they have up to this time suffered us to go our own way.

"But always, understand, Marka told us that it was not fear that kept the white men from our borders. We know too well of the white man's power. Not a few of us know of the gun of many voices. '*Tot tot tot tot,*' it says, and at each word a man dies. We knew that, and Marka ever kept the matter fresh in our minds, that the white men could take us to themselves whenever they so desired.

"Now pay heed to the evil that has come to us. A certain white man came to live among us. A trader he said he was, and of a truth he built a store and exchanged beads and gaily colored cloth in exchange for our corn and cattle. And he won the friendship of Thuso, the chief. Thuso gave him a place among the councilors of the people. A strong *mouti* the white man had, stronger than the beer brewed by our women. Much of this he gave to Thuso, so the chief's tongue was loosened, and he spoke of many things which Marka would have had him keep secret."

"Did he speak of gold and the stones for which white men lie and kill?"

Matiswa looked at the Major suspiciously.

"What matter?" he asked, then continued hurriedly. "There came a time when the white man set himself up as a greater witch-doctor than Marka, my father. Aye, he had many cunning tricks and, belike, he was in league with the evil spirits. Of a surety he was a servant of the evil ones. But so it was. Thuso and many of the indunnas gave heed to his council. Yet there were still certain things which Thuso— because of the curse laid upon him by Marka—kept secret from the white man; certain things which he would not permit him to do. *Au-a!* Woe is me."

"You are long-winded," Jim exclaimed irritably. "The day grows old."

"Not in a breath can the shame of a race be told, black one. Four nights ago the white man urged Thuso to march at the head of his *impi* and kill the white men wherever he found them. 'Nothing shall harm your warriors,' he said, 'and you'll be a bigger chief than was Chaka, at whose name the hills shook.' At this we warriors laughed and mocked the white man. 'I have a magic,' he cried, 'to turn aside the bullets of the white men; not even the gun of many voices will be able to hurt you.'

"Then Marka urged the chief that the white man's magic be put to the test, and it was so ordered.

"On the morrow, in the sight of all the people, the white man sent 'the voice which kills' through the body of a bull, harming it not, and killed my father, who was on the far side of the bull and a great distance beyond it. A great wonder making, and my people doubted no longer."

"Clever Johnny, that," murmured the Major in English. "Worked off a simple matter of trajectory as a great magic. I must make his acquaintance."

Matiswa looked inquiringly at the Hottentot.

"My *baas* makes a charm," Jim explained. "He is in all things wonderful and I—I am his servant. Continue."

"That night a great feast was held at the *kraal*. But first the white man—Inyorka, the Snake, we call him—told Thuso that he needed much of the yellow stone before he could make enough magic to preserve the warriors all through the long trek which was before them. Perhaps Thuso still doubted; perhaps he remembered at that moment somewhat of the wisdom of my father.

" 'After I have seen my warriors,' he said, 'go up against the guns of the white men, unharmed, then shall all things be made known to you.'

"And with that the white man had to be content.

" 'In four days,' he said, 'I will lead a party of your young men against the Dutchman, Peters, and you shall see that my charm is indeed all powerful.' Now this white man Peters lives just beyond our borders and he has at all times been a good friend to us—he and his women folk. So I endeavored to get to them that I might warn them. But warriors were sent by Inyorka to intercept me. They beat me sorely and left me for dead. When I came to I knew that it would be folly to attempt to reach the Dutchman, for his house would be watched. And so I came this way, praying that the spirits would bring me deliverance."

"The spirits have not failed you," said the Major. "Now tell me the things I ask you—and tell me in few words.

"How many spears follow the lead of Thuso?"

"Five hundred—no more."

"How far to his *kraal?*"

"Two days, traveling as I traveled; one day for a man suffering no hurt, fearing no evil; a forenoon's trek on horseback.

"And the place of Peters'? Where is that?"

"A four hours' trek beyond the *kraal* of Thuso. And there is no way to it save past the *kraal*."

"And think you that Peters knows nothing of the evil that is afoot?"

"Nay! Since the coming of the trader he has been at enmity with Thuso."

"So? And what think you of this magic of the white man's? What think you of his purpose?"

"Is it not plain, *Baas?*" interposed Jim.

"He wants to find where the stones and gold are. After that—"

"That is my thought, too," said Matiswa. "As for the magic—that is trickery. But how shall my people know before it is too late?"

The Major made no immediate reply. He was busy writing a message on a page torn from his notebook.

When it was finished he asked, "Can you ride?"

"Aye, white man."

"Then take the black horse and ride toward the setting sun. It may be that by noon tomorrow you will see before you four *Nonquai*. Give them this talking magic. That is all. Now go."

Matiswa rose to his feet, strengthened by the food and embued with a new confidence and, mounting the black stallion which Jim had hastily saddled, was soon lost to sight in the bush which masked the trail.

"And now, Jim," said the Major, "we, too, will trek."

"But whither, *Baas?*" the Hottentot answered mournfully.

"To the *kraal* of Thuso. Where else?"

"Au-a! If we go there we die."

"If we stay here the *Nonquai* will come and, taking us, will send us to labor on the Breakwater. If we stay here the people of Thuso will go out against the white men; there will be much killing of men, women and children."

"And it is in your mind, *Baas,* that we two can stop them?"

"Some thought I had of that."

"The *Baas* is all-powerful," Jim waxed sarcastic. "He holds up his hand and dams a mighty river."

The Major rose to his feet.

"The sun is hastening on its journey, Jim. Let us be going."

But Jim was still argumentative.

"But why, *Baas?* It is all folly. Suppose the people of Thuso go out against the white men, believing that they have a charm that will turn aside the bullets. What then? It will soon be brought home to them that their charm is a thing of no account. The end will soon come, and no harm will have been done. Why must we die because five hundred warriors are fools?"

"Yes. Those five hundred warriors are fools, and some of them will be killed, and they will kill white men—but they are led by an evil white man. The fault is not theirs. And true it is, also, that in but a little while they will be defeated and their villages will be burned as a warning to others.

"But what is this?"

The Major indicated a cartridge which hung suspended from the lobe of Jim's right ear.

Jim grinned—a sickly, self-conscious grin.

"The man Matiswa had empty ones in his ears, *Baas,* and it came to me that it was a charm to strengthen the heart of man. And so I took a cartridge from your belt and—the *Baas* will pardon?"

"Aye," the Major replied absently. "For truly the man Matiswa was brave. Beaten, bruised, he forgot all his hurt, hoping only to prevent his people from committing a folly. But what use of further words? You know the thing he intended to do, and if we fail him perchance he will succeed elsewhere. Yes, keep the cartridge, Jim. You have need of a charm to bolster up your woman heart."

The Major mounted and rode slowly away.

But Jim ran after him, crying for him to stop.

He reined in his horse and waited for the Hottentot to catch up with him.

"Well, Jim?"

"The *Baas* did not understand. It is not that I fear death—that comes to us all—but the thought of walking to my death was distasteful. That was all, *Baas.*"

The Major started to dismount.

"Then Jim, the Hottentot, shall ride, and his *Baas* shall walk."

Again Jim checked him.

"No! Not that either, *Baas.* Let me take hold of a stirrup and all will be well. I can run, yes, but I will not walk."

The Major's chuckle was one of relief, and he slipped his foot out of the stirrup.

"After a while," he said, "you shall ride and I will run. Now we must waste no more time."

He pricked the horse with his spur and set off at a hand gallop and Jim, with effortless, machine-like stride, ran at his side.

IT WAS nearly sundown when they reached Thuso's *kraal.* All three—the Major, Jim, and the horse—were tuckered out. Having missed the trail, they had traveled much further than the "forenoon's trek" of Matiswa's estimate.

At the gate in the stockade encircling the *kraal* they were taken in charge by a party of warriors and led to a large hut built close to a tin shack which was evidently the store.

There, after helping themselves to the Major's rifle, revolver, and cartridges, the warriors left them.

"This is funny," the Major exclaimed. "Wonder why they've gone away and left us all to ourselves. Oh, I see. This must be a white man's place, and it's probably bad form to hang around uninvited."

Then to Jim in the vile "kitchen Kaffir" which newcomers use and think they are speaking the vernacular, he added, "Mena's going inside *lo ivinkel. Wena slala* here. See?"

Jim responded with a string of lurid curses and invectives.

"White men are all fools," he concluded, "and I'm a fool, too, to serve a man of this sort."

"What's that you say, dog?"

Jim turned with a start to face a lean, hungry-looking white man who had come up behind him.

The Major hurried to greet the speaker.

"I say, old top, I'm deuced glad to see you—" he began.

The other ignored him half-contemptuously.

"Well, dog?" he said to Jim, and the *sjambok* in his hand twitched suggestively.

"Your pardon, boss," Jim said humbly, cringingly. "I did not know a white man—other than the one I serve—was in this place. And truly, he is a fool, and the child of fools."

The white man smiled—not a pleasant smile—and turned to the Major.

"Your servant is cheeky. He needs a whipping. Shall I—?"

He raised his *sjambok.*

"Oh, no! Please don't. He's not half bad, really."

The other leered.

"You're too damned soft," he said, then, throwing back his head, began to laugh.

"Why, what is it?" the Major exclaimed wonderingly. "The sun, perhaps?"

"No. It's not that. I was just thinkin' that back in England I'd be touching my hat to men like you, an' bowin' and scrapin' and sayin', 'Yes, sir,' and 'No, sir!' You, with your bleedin' monocle and your dude, fool ways. But here, I'm the top man. You, and the likes of you, you ain't nothing. Even your nigger laughs at you. But it's men like me that do things out here.

"Sit down, you!" he growled to Jim in the vernacular.

"I'm afraid I don't understand you, old top," the Major said in grieved tones. "I think you're very rude to treat a traveler like this. I'm most deucedly hungry."

"You are? Well, come in and have scoff. It's all ready. Been ready for the last half hour, or more, waitin' for you."

"Waitin' for me? But how?"

"Of course. I've got eyes, haven't I? Saw you coming over the veldt."

He led the way inside the hut and motioned the Major to sit down on one of the chairs drawn up to a cheap deal table. He clapped his hands, and a native entered and set two plates heaped with food on the table.

"My name's Aubrey St. John," began the Major.

"Eat," growled the other. "We'll talk afterward."

"But how about my servant—he must be hungry. You'll pardon my importunity, I hope?"

"He's been taken care of already. My boy's lookin' out for him."

The trader eyed his guest sarcastically. "And to think," he muttered, "I once touched my hat to the likes of him."

If the Major heard the remark he evinced no outward sign of having done so. He was too busy obeying the injunction, "Eat!"

"That's the best chicken," he said after a while, as he pushed his plate from him with a sigh, "I've ever eaten. Your cook must have worked under the Savoy chef. And now, Mr.—er—"

"Dowson's my name, Aubrey. Just plain Bill Dowson."

"Well, Mr. Dowson, if you had a cigarette I'd be quite happy."

"Yes, you would. Haven't any. Sell you a chunk of chewing tobacco, though."

The Major held up his hands in horror.

"Just who are you," Dowson continued, "and what are you doing here?"

"I've already told you my name, old top. Just out from England on a little huntin' trip. Wanted to do it the right way, you know. Anyone can kill lions and elephants, if they have lots of native gentlemen as beaters, camp followers and what not. But it takes quite a huntsman to go out accompanied by only one native trekker—is that what you call them? Well, alas an' dear me, my guide doesn't seem quite up to snuff. Yesterday he lost my wagon and mules as we were crossing a river; the current was too strong and washed them away. Yet I'm sure I crossed exactly where he told me to, though he did get me quite rattled when I was about half-way across by shoutin' something at me in his heathenish language. I may have driven a little bit off the course. We spent until nearly dark trying to fish out some of our provisions, but it was no go. So supperless to bed. Then this morning he sets out to guide me to a *kraal* nearby, as well as I could understand him, where there was a store and I could buy provisions. After ridin' all day, we get here."

Dowson nodded.

"I suppose you're tired," he said.

"By Jove, yes. You won't have to sing me a lullaby."

"All right. You can go to bed right away. Sleep on the skins in the corner, there. It's the best I can offer you. I'll take you to a better place in the morning. Good night!"

"Good night, old chap. Oh, but I say, my—"

"Well?"

"The natives took my rifle and revolver and cartridges. Why did they do that? They'll let me have them back, won't they?"

"Yes, of course. I'll give them to you in the morning. It's against their law for white men to carry guns about the *kraal*."

"Ah! I see. I'm quite safe here, do you think?"

"Yes. You're quite safe here. Good night."

"There's just one other thing. Will you send my servant in to me? He helps me undress, you know. He's a perfectly priceless valet."

Dowson sneered.

"I'll send him in to you."

Jim was seated outside the hut. An empty beer pot was on the ground beside him.

"How did you know there was a store at this *kraal?*" Dowson asked him suddenly.

"I didn't, *Baas*. I told the fool who pays me there was a store here, yes. But that was in order to hearten him. After he had lost the mules and wagon in the river and was forced to sleep on an empty belly, he wept the tears of a woman. In the morning I climbed a nearby *kopje* and saw the smoke of the cook-fires of this *kraal*. So I brought him hither. There were no other *kraals* near."

"But you have been all day trekking!"

"Au-a! That was the fault of that fool. We crossed over the spoor of an elephant. It was an old spoor—older than last month's moon—but the fool must follow it, his gun at the ready. Nothing I could say would turn him from his purpose. Thus we lost much time."

"How did he lose the wagon and mules? What manner of trekker are you?"

"The fault was not mine, *Baas*. I said, 'Do not cross over the river, the flood is too high.' But he paid no heed to me—perhaps he did not understand. When I sought to pull the mules up intending to make camp, he brushed me on one side and, climbing into the wagon, drove down the steep bank into the river."

Dowson chuckled.

"You speak a true thing," he said. "Your *Baas* is a fool. Go to him now. He has need of you." And with that he passed on.

Jim waited until the storekeeper had passed out of sight, then he entered the hut.

"How goes the game, *Baas?*" he asked softly.

"I am in a maze, Jim. I do not understand. I do not know how to set down my feet; I am fearful of breaking something."

"In such cases," Jim said, "it is well to jump hard with both feet at once."

"What do you make of the storekeeper, Jim?"

"He is a man of deep cunning, *Baas*. I fear him. He says little, but he knows much. A spear is silent, but it bites deep. He asked me many questions, trying to trap me. I do not think that he altogether believes the story we tell."

"It would be strange if he did. It is a queer story. Yet, for that same reason, I think he will believe. And if he does not, what matter? He will not have us killed, I think, before the affair with Peters, the Dutchman."

"One thing, *Baas*, I have learned. All the people of this *kraal* fear him. They have no love for him, but will obey him in all things because he can make mighty charms."

"If I can get a chance to speak to Thuso, the chief, in the morning I can make this magic a thing of no account."

"I do not think they will let you see the chief, *Baas*."

"No?"

"No, *Baas*. You may be all the things you say you are. But the storekeeper is not sure, and he is very wise. He will take no chances. He may think there are no crocodiles in the river, but he will not bathe in the river until he is sure there are no crocodiles."

"If I had not given up my rifle I would feel happier."

"If you had not given it up, *Baas*, we both would now be dead. The spears of the warriors are very sharp."

The Major sighed.

"That is true. But did you have food in plenty to eat, Jim?"

"Aye, *Baas*. And beer to drink! But I think they meant that to unloosen my tongue! *Baas*, I poured the beer on the ground. You will remember that to my credit? It was good beer and I was very thirsty."

"Yes. I'll remember, Jim. And now to sleep. I'll keep first watch."

Without further word Jim stretched himself out on the floor of the hut, and in a few minutes was fast asleep. He had traveled far that day, and in the first hour of sleep his legs twitched constantly as if he were still trekking.

The hours passed slowly, and in silence.

Once the Major, coming to a sudden conclusion, or rather suddenly determined to put a long considered plan into action, went to the door of the hut intending to make a survey of the *kraal*. But four warriors, armed with spears, barred his way.

"It would seem," he muttered as he returned to his chair and resumed his watch, "that I have put my head into a hornet's nest. There's nothing I can do. We are just two more sheep for the slaughter. But I wonder what Dowson's game is? He's not exactly antagonistic; a little surly, yes, but that's nothing against a man. And if he's plotting to wipe out the Dutchman, Peters, and lead these people against the whites, why does he take the trouble to be even half-way decent to me? Well, the morning will settle everything. I think I'm going to sleep now. Dear me, yes. It's nearly morning and it 'ud never do for Dowson to find me keeping watch. For the matter of that there is no sense in waking Jim. The poor old chap is deucedly tired."

But although the Major lay down on the heap of skins in the corner of the hut, he did not go to sleep. His brain was too active planning a speech which he hoped to make to Thuso and the warriors, a speech which would show them the folly of proclaiming war upon the whites and would effectively counteract the supposedly powerful charms of the man Dowson.

At last he had the points he would make all clearly arranged, and was well satisfied that the things he would say would succeed, at least, in making Thuso and his people hesitate before committing any definite act of aggression. And this feeling of satisfaction was no expression of conceit. He knew that he understood the psychology of Africa's black children better than most white men; he knew them as well as they knew themselves; almost as well as their witch-doctors knew them. And he spoke many dialects as if he had been born to the tribes. Even Jim, the Hottentot, could not master the clicks of the Bushman tribe as well as his *Baas*.

But this feeling of satisfaction was tempered by one of doubt. Suppose Dowson refused to give him the opportunity of speaking to the chief?

And with that thought came morning—and the storekeeper.

"Sleep well?" asked Dowson.

The Major sat up with a yawn, and stretched his arms wearily above his head.

"Famously. I'll have my bath and then I'll be ready for breakfast. Where's that lazy servant of mine? Ah! There he is. Snoring still, is he? Wake him up for me, there's a good fellow."

Dowson applied his boot to Jim's ribs, and not very gently.

Jim awoke with a yell and a curse. Then, rubbing his eyes, and seeing Dowson standing over him, he muttered confused apologies.

"Get out of here, you," Dowson ordered with a snarl, and Jim made a precipitous exit.

"I don't understand you," Dowson continued, turning to the Major. "No?"

"No. You seem to be a damned fool, but I don't know."

"Oh, but I'm not a fool, really. I'm most deucedly clever, 'pon my soul. A man has to get up very early indeed to pull wool in my eyes.

For instance, Jim, my servant, you know, tried to hold me up for ten quid a month. But I beat him down. I only pay him eight!"

"Eight! You could hire every man in this *kraal* for that sum."

"Then I've been bilked, after all?"

Dowson made a gesture of impatience.

"Never mind that. Thing I want to know is: Just what do you expect me to do?"

"First breakfast, old man, then fit me out with mules, a Cape cart, provisions and all the rest."

"You have money for this?"

"Oh, no; I make a practise of never carrying a lot of money around with me. Just enough to keep me goin' from day to day as it were. I keep all my funds in a bank at Diamondsville."

"And you expect me to fit you out?"

"Why not? You don't doubt my word, do you? But, of course, you do. You don't know me from Eve's better half, do you? Well, won't my note do?"

"No, it won't."

"Then what am I to do?" The Major made a helpless gesture.

"You can send your nigger to Diamondsville with a note."

"Oh, I couldn't do that. I'd be quite lost without him."

"Well, you can make the trip yourself."

"But how can I do that without a guide, and without provisions? Haven't you a runner—I think that's what you call 'em—you can send for me?"

"Yes," Dowson answered slowly. "But what are you going to do until you get an answer."

"Be your honored guest, sir."

"You have a damned nerve," Dowson exclaimed with heat. "I'm doing a lot when I say I'll send one of my boys with a message. I'm damned if I'll feed you until he returns on the chance that you may have money. I've been sold that way before."

"Did you say your name was Shylock, my man," the Major murmured. Then aloud, and in tones of dismay, "But surely you're not goin' to turn me out to starve on the veldt?"

"No, I won't do that. White men have to stick together. I'll take you to Dutch Peters' place. He'll put you up. He's a soft-hearted fool, is Peters."

"That'll be bully. When do we go?"

"Now."

"After breakfast you mean, don't you?"

"I've had my breakfast."

"You mean you won't give me any?"

Dowson made no reply.

"Then I'm going with my servant, Jim, and see if the natives of this *kraal* aren't whiter than you."

"The men have all gone on a hunt," Dowson said stolidly, "and the women won't give you food. They don't like strangers here. If it hadn't been for me they would have killed you last night."

"Really?" There was a note of fear in the Major's voice.

"Yes, really," Dowson mimicked. "Come on. We'll be at Peters' place by noon; you can eat there. Better write that note to your bank first. You'll need a hundred pounds."

He handed pencil and paper to the Major, who, tongue sticking out the corner of his mouth, indicted a letter to the Colonial Bank authorizing them to pay bearer the sum of one hundred pounds.

"What a damned fool you are," Dowson said as he took the paper from the Major. "Well, let's go."

Outside the hut the Major saw Jim in the custody of four armed natives.

"I thought you said the men had all gone on a hunt," said the Major.

"These men are my body-guard—and yours. The chief gave them to me, and while they are with us no one will harm you."

"But they told me all natives were friendly toward white men," the Major expostulated. "Aren't you just tryin' to frighten me?"

Dowson laughed. "Walk away from me, and make believe you are going into that hut opposite."

With hesitating feet the Major obeyed.

Just as he was stooping to enter the door an *assegai* whizzed past his ear and stuck quivering in the wooden upright. With a squeal of fear he ran back to the shelter of Dowson's authority.

"Let us get away from here," he stuttered excitedly. "I've had enough."

Dowson blew on a whistle and a boy brought up two horses. He and the Major mounted and followed, by Jim and the four warriors, moved off.

At the gate in the stockade the storekeeper halted with an impatient curse.

"I forgot to give you your rifle and revolver," he said. "You'll need them. We might see some game on the way."

He barked an order to one of the warriors, who ran back to the store, entered, and returned bearing the Major's rifle, revolver and cartridges. These he handed to the Major, who took them casually, buckled the cartridge belts about him, put the revolver in his holster, and swung the rifle by its sling over his shoulder. Apparently he had only given the weapons and ammunition a passing glance, yet he knew that the revolver was still loaded in all six chambers, that the rifle had not been tampered with, and that none of the cartridges was missing.

"I got them from the chief last night," Dowson explained. "It's lucky for you you gave them up without giving any trouble. A rifle or revolver isn't much good with these men at close quarters; not if there's a lot of them. You might kill five or six, but the rest'll keep coming. That's a good thing to know, Aubrey."

"Yes, thanks, Mr. Dowson," the Major answered timidly. "Then what is the best thing to do?"

"Run like hell."

"Like this?"

The Major dug his spurs into his horse and galloped madly across the veldt, Dowson in hot pursuit.

The Major's horse—it was Jim's, really—was fast, but Dowson's was faster and the storekeeper soon drew level.

"You damned fool," he cried, "pull up or I'll blow your brains out."

The Major quickly obeyed.

"Why all the heat?" he said with a laugh. "I was just having a joke."

"A hell of a joke. Look what they're doing to your nigger."

The Major looked back. He could not see Jim, but the four warriors were holding something which struggled upon the ground; their *assegais* were upraised.

Dowson blew his whistle. The four lowered their *assegais* and separated. The something which they had been holding down—it was Jim—rose to its feet.

"Let's go on to Peters'," said the Major with a sickly grin. "I'm afraid of this place."

THREE HOURS later the little party came within sight of a small homestead built, it seemed from a distance, at the base of a towering *kopje*. It was evidently the farm land of an industrious white man. Acres of land were under cultivation, and in a large corral were a lot of oxen.

"You can go the rest of the way yourself," said Dowson, drawing rein. "I'm not on good terms with Peters. He'll give you a better welcome if you go alone."

"All right, old man. It was good of you to take so much trouble, even if you wouldn't give me breakfast. You'll let me know when the messenger comes back from Diamondsville, won't you? Good-bye. I'll give your love to Mr. Peters. I hope he's a better tempered Johnny than you are. I wish, though, I had something to take him for a present."

"There's a buck. If you must take something, shoot that and give it to him. Peters is not much of a huntsman, and he'll be glad to get fresh meat."

Dowson pointed to a klipspringer that was grazing about two hundred yards away.

The Major dismounted, clumsily, and the buck bounded away a few paces.

Dowson whistled. The buck stopped, inquisitive like all timid animals, and stared back at its enemies.

The Major took careful aim, hesitated, lowered his rifle and—he could not afford to waste ammunition—said, "Won't you shoot it for me? I'm such a rotten shot; I'm afraid I'd miss."

Dowson sneered and clapped his hands. The buck bounded frantically away. When it was nearly four hundred yards distant Dowson, not troubling to dismount, put his rifle to his shoulder and, hardly seeming to take aim, fired.

The buck gave one convulsive leap into the air, then plunged forward on its nose and did not move again.

"Take that to Peters," he growled, "with my compliments."

With that he rode off, followed by the four warriors. As he rode he blew three loud blasts on his whistle.

The Major looked at Jim, and Jim at the Major, wonderingly.

"That white man is surely a thing of evil, *Baas!*"

"True, Jim. The spoors of my thought are crossed. There are many things I do not understand. Why does he do this? Why does he do that? If he is going to lead the people of Thuso against Peters, why does he permit me to come here? Why did he return my rifle and revolver?"

"I know nothing, *Baas,*" Jim replied, "save that I am very hungry; that over yonder is a dead buck, and over yonder is the place of a white man who may be friendly to us, and who may suffer us to eat."

"Then let us go there. You go on. I will get the buck and catch up with you."

The Major mounted and rode over to the klipspringer, lashed it to his saddle and then rode after Jim.

About ten minutes later they reached the homestead and were greeted by a tall, powerfully built Dutchman.

"Allehmahtig!" he exclaimed. "What make you here? Are you a friend of that son of Belial, Dowson? *Ach!* But I see you're not. You are clean. He is—" Peters spat expressively. "Come in," he continued. "Your boy will take your horse. I have no boys; they have all left me because of that *schelm* Dowson."

"My boy is hungry," said the Major in *Taal,* and the Dutchman's face lighted with joy. "Can he get food?"

"Surely. I, myself, will get it for him. It is long since I heard the speech of my fathers. My wife, she is English; and my daughter says the *Taal* is the language of barbarians. Go in. I will see to your boy, then we will eat, and talk. Oh, surely we must talk."

He went off with Jim, and the Major, standing in the doorway, was undecided what to do; whether to follow them, or enter the house unannounced. The fact that two womenfolk were present rather complicated matters. Had there been just Peters it would have been possible, he thought, to escape from the place before Dowson led the warriors to the attack. But now—

"Won't you come in, sir?"

He turned with a jump at the sound of the low, well modulated voice.

The owner of the voice laughed merrily at his discomfiture.

"I'm frightfully sorry I made you jump. But please come in, or are you too shy? And if you're too shy, won't you please put on your helmet. You'll get sunstroke if you don't."

"I'll come in, if I may," mumbled the Major. "But it's not fair, really, it's not."

"What's not fair?"

"For a beautiful young lady like you to pounce upon a man un-awares."

"I think you'd better see mother," she replied demurely, and led the way into a pleasant room.

"Mother, this is Mr.—er—" She looked inquiringly at the Major, her brown eyes twinkling.

"St. John. Aubrey St. John," the Major said hurriedly. "And, of course, you are Miss Peters and this is Mrs. Peters."

He bowed to the other occupant of the room and then ran out of the door, nearly knocking down Peters, who was just coming in.

"Man," he exclaimed, "I've got to see you at once. I want to talk to you where the womenfolk can't hear us."

"*Ach!* You have expressed my desires. Where the women can't hear us, eh? We will speak a great deal in the *Taal*—the language of barbar-ians! My daughter has little respect for her father, I think. That is the fault of an English mother. But I am content. I would not have things different. Yes. We will talk. But first we will eat. Not since yesterday sundown have you eaten, your boy tells me."

But the Major had him by the arm and, leading him into another room, shut the door.

"We will talk now," he said, and the Dutchman sobered instantly at the tone of his voice. "There is much to do, and little time in which to do it. Tell me, what has Dowson against you?"

"He wants this farm. I think that he has discovered gold veins here; I know he has. First he wanted me to sell the place, then he offered to show me where the gold was and go into partnership with me. But I refused. We love this place. Anyone can dig for gold, but what is it when they have it? We are content to live as we live, and I refused to go in with Dowson. So he is angry with me, has poisoned Thuso's men against me, and through some devil-working has caused all my laborers to leave. That was yesterday. Why do you ask?"

The Major told him briefly all he knew.

The Dutchman, his blue eyes blazing with wrath, listened in silence until the tale was all told.

"Yes," he said then. "He would do that, the devil! To gain his own ends he would commit murder—worse. He sets the blacks against men of his own color. And worse even than that, he seals the death warrant of Thuso's people. For the military—whether it be the soldiers of the English, or those of the Portuguese—won't spare them once they take the field. Once they are on the war-path the natives will fight until the last man is killed. And that won't be very long. But first they will kill me, and the good wife, and the little daughter, and you. The devil! Before he came, Thuso was a good chief, and his people were happy. We must die, yes, but I feel very sorry for Thuso and his people. It is not their fault."

"But why must we die? We can hold them off. You have rifles—"

The Major's eyes rested on the rifle rack at the end of the room—"and ammunition. You can shoot, and your wife and your daughter; yes?"

"They are better shots than most men," Peters said proudly.

"Well, then. I can shoot, and Jim, my servant, if he is bribed or in fear of his life, can squeeze a trigger. We can hold them off. Perhaps when they see that Dowson's charm doesn't work they'll give up."

The Dutchman's face lighted.

"You are right, man, I tell you. We will hold them off. They will attack soon, you think?"

"Yes. The warriors had all left the *kraal* this morning, and after Dowson left he blew some signals on his whistle. How many rooms have you upstairs?"

"One. It has windows on three sides."

"Good. We'll knock a hole in the other wall. From that room we ought to be able to do good shootin'. Given plenty of ammunition we can keep them at a safe distance as long as it is light, and they're not likely to attack us after dark. Better break the news to the ladies now. Oh, yes, and send Jim in here to me, will you, and some food? I'm deucedly hungry."

Peters left the room, and five minutes later Jim entered, grinning cheerfully, bearing a tray laden with food.

The Major fell to with great zest, earning Jim's ungrudging admiration.

"It is better to have a full belly and die, *Baas,*" he chuckled, "than to be empty and live."

"A man only says that when he is empty, Jim. When he is full, life is very pleasant. And now I am full; therefore I do not want to die; therefore I shall not die."

As he spoke the door opened and Peters, followed by his wife and daughter, entered. They were all very serious, but showed no trace of fear. The women went over to the rack and took down their rifles.

The Major joined them. "I see you have expresses. That is too bad. That means, I suppose, that you have no .303 ammunition?"

"No!" The girl scoffed. "The .303 is a ladies' gun."

"Hardly that, miss. It makes a frightful hole if you file down the bullet and make dum-dums. Your father tells me you can shoot?"

She smiled proudly.

"And you, too, Mrs. Peters?"

Mrs. Peters nodded, but her lips trembled slightly as she said, "I don't know how I'll shoot today. I've never shot at a man before."

"You're not going to shoot at a man, mother," the girl exclaimed hotly, "but at a snake. Let's show Mr. St. John what good shots we are. Look!"

She pointed out of the back window where, on the rocks at the base of the *kopje*—it was over six hundred yards away—targets were painted. Between the house and the targets were mounds which marked the various ranges: Two hundred, three hundred, four hundred, five hundred and six hundred yards.

"Five bulls out of ten shots at six hundred yards is mother's record. Not bad, eh, Mr. St. John?"

" 'Pon my soul, no! And you, what is your record?"

"You shall see. Get the cartridges out, Father. We always keep the cartridges locked up," she added, in explanation to the Major. "Some of the boys like to use them for earrings, and they're too precious to be used that way."

Peters knelt down before a large, iron-bound chest and raised the massive lid.

"Allehmahtig!" he roared. "The devils, the slim devils. They've taken the cartridges. Not one have they left!"

The others crowded around him in consternation. The chest was empty.

"It must have been Simeon, our houseboy, who took them," continued Peters. "I've always trusted him, I thought he was loyal. He's been with us for years, and now—"

"But you must have cartridges somewhere else. You didn't keep them all there, surely," expostulated the Major.

The Dutchman shook his head slowly.

"No. It was a rule I made. Never did we leave cartridges lying around. Always they must be in that chest. We used but few; we did not need them save when we went hunting, or shot at the targets. We had no fear of the natives, and so—but what use are words? The cartridges have gone."

"Well! Never mind," said the Major cheerfully. "At least my gun is all right, and I have—" he counted his rifle cartridges—"forty-nine shots in the locker. Perhaps that will be enough to stop them. It will be more than enough if I can get Dowson with my first shot—and I will."

But he was conscious of a feeling of doubt.

"I wonder—" he began slowly—

As he spoke a wild chanting was borne to their ears on the breeze, and the Major, rifle in hand, rushed to the window just in time to see the warriors, dressed in full war regalia, burst like a black wave of death from the quiet sea of corn.

At their head, dressed now as a witch-doctor of the tribe, was Dowson. Even at this distance the Major could recognize the man; could hear his sneering voice shout obscenities which brought a blush to the faces of the women and muttered curses to the lips of Peters.

Going down on one knee, resting his gun on the window sill, the Major covered the renegade and fired.

A loud yell of defiance greeted the shot which, to an accustomed ear, lacked the usual sharp crack of a high-powered rifle. Dowson leaped high into the air in satanic derision, and the horde came on.

"You missed," said the girl quietly.

"Yes, I missed," retorted the Major, "and now I know why Dowson dared to let me have my rifle and cartridges. That was only the percussion cap in the cartridge we heard."

"You mean?" She whispered the question, fearing that her mother might overhear and lose somewhat of her splendid courage.

"That he has taken all the powder out of my cartridges. Look!"

He held one of them toward her. It showed signs of having been *clamped in a vise*, evidently while the charge was removed and the projectile replaced.

"He's clever," the Major said bitterly. "He thinks of everything. Oh, he's deuced clever. And when the natives hear me firing and see that no one is killed or wounded, they think it is because of his charm. And every time I fire I strengthen his case. Listen to him. He's telling them we can't hurt him or them. And the beggar's right. Damn! Oh, damn!"

The girl looked round cautiously. Her father and mother were searching for stray cartridges.

"Don't let them know yet," she whispered. "It might discourage them, and we mustn't be discouraged." She put her firm, tanned hand on his. "I have it," she went on. "If we take the bullets out of all your cartridges we might find among them enough powder to make one full charge. Let's try."

"It's a happy thought—but look! Dowson's coming on alone."

As he spoke Dowson left the warriors and advanced until he was within fifty yards of the house. He carried a rifle in his right hand.

"I'm going to try a few shots at him," said the Major. "Perhaps he's miscalculated; perhaps he's left enough powder in one of the cartridges to carry that far."

He fired six shots in rapid succession and then six more, but the experiment was a vain one. The reports echoed mockingly, as the percussion caps exploded, but found no charge within the cartridges to speed the projectile on its way.

And now Dowson began to caper up and down, shouting rude taunts.

"In a little while," he cried in the vernacular, so that his followers could understand, "we will come and wipe you out. Then we will wipe out all the white men that dwell between here and the great waters. Nothing can harm my warriors, for I have cast a spell over them; the guns of the white men cannot harm them. In a little while we shall come for you. The young maiden and the woman shall be given to the young men; they shall be slaves in their huts. The old man and he-who-can-hold-his-eye-on-the-palm-of-his-hand shall be given to torture, they and the black one, their servant. Fires shall be lighted on their bellies; their eyelids shall be cut off. In a little while we will come. But first we will eat. Even now my warriors kill an ox. We will drink its blood, then we will drink your blood."

"Try your revolver," whispered the girl.

The Major shook his head.

"He's treated those cartridges the same way. The cunning devil has thought of everything."

"Down," she cried, and pulled him down with her hand.

Dowson had suddenly leveled his rifle and fired.

The bullet whistled viciously over their heads and struck Peters, who had risen to join them, in the right shoulder.

He dropped to the ground with a moan, but quickly recovering, waved them on one side as they sprang to assist him.

"It is nothing! *Ach Gott!* It is nothing, I tell you. Keep watch and kill that *schelm*. Why don't you fire?"

And the Major, not wishing to confess yet that his rifle was as useless in this emergency as a child's toy, obediently fired several rounds.

"He keeps under cover all the time," he said as if he wished to explain his lack of success.

Dowson gesticulated in derision and then swaggeringly rejoined the warriors, who greeted him with wild shouts of praise.

They were sure now that the white man's magic was infallible; that there was nothing to stop them from wiping out all white men, from becoming all powerful, giving only a choice of death or slavery to any who dared to stand before them.

And now they retreated some three or four hundred yards to where a huge pyre had been built. Twelve oxen stood nearby, waiting to be butchered. Torches were applied to the pyre; *assegais* gleamed in the sun, then showed again blood red. The lowing of dying oxen mingled with the savage shouts of blood-lustful men. Women brought large calabashes of beer which were greedily drained; the scent of cooking flesh filled the air. All was given over to revelry.

But always Dowson, the renegade, danced in front of the fire, encouraging the warriors to heartier drinking and promising them great wealth in the days to come. "We are safe for a little while, at least," said the Major, and he and the girl joined the others.

"You fired twelve and more shots," said the Dutchman, "but Dowson still lives. And it is not your fault; no. It is the cartridges, eh?"

"Hush, father. Mother—"

"Mother knows all about it, daughter," Mrs. Peters said softly. "Dowson has thought of everything, hasn't he?"

"No; not everything, mother. We are going to take the bullets from the cases and perhaps we'll find enough powder to make several good charges. I'm sure we will."

"Haw! Haw!" Peters laughed noisily. "My daughter is no bread-and-milk girl. She thinks beyond Dowson's cunning. Well! Let's to work."

They seated themselves at the table, the cartridges—rifle and re-volver—before them, and with feverish haste commenced to act on the girl's suggestion. As each bullet was extracted they carefully tapped the empty case, holding it over a sheet of white paper.

The women, Peters and the Major used pliers, but Jim, with his white, strong teeth, worked faster than any of them.

Frequently the girl would glance up at the Major and her eyes would sparkle, her lips part a little, disclosing even, pearly teeth. He was very good to look upon, and she had seen very few men.

Soon the task was finished. Upon the sheet of paper was a thin, black film—that was all. Dowson had left nothing but the caps in the cartridges.

"I'd have been satisfied," muttered Peters to the Major, "if we could have found enough for just two shots."

"It won't come to that," the Major replied uneasily. "Can't we escape now out that way?" He pointed to the hills at the back of the house.

"Had that been possible we would have gone long ago. Even if we weren't watched—and I take it we are—there's no way up that *kopje*. It rises up a sheer one hundred feet, man, and no foothold."

The Major turned to Jim.

"Well, what think you, O mighty warrior? Have we run our race?"

Jim looked up with a scowl from the long, wicked-looking knife he had discovered and was whetting on the sole of his foot.

"I don't like this, *Baas*. Are we women, we two, to sit here waiting for what may come to us? Let us go our way. Who is there to stop us?" He slashed viciously with the knife.

The Major chuckled.

"I do not see how that may be, warrior. My place is here—I cannot go. But you, you are a free man."

"*Baas,* listen, and you, too, O man with a lion's beard. I have a plan. You have failed. Those noise sticks of yours have failed—as I have always said they would, when you most need them. But this will not fail."

Again the gleaming blade slashed through the air.

"Those fools," he motioned toward the howling warriors, "are drunk; the watch they keep is poor. Who is to stop me if I wish to join them—to drink beer, and to eat the flesh of the ox? I shall be as one of them. I shall go and come as I please, and I shall please to be near the white man and once near him—"

Swish went the blade.

"And then, Jim," the Major questioned softly. "What then?"

"Then, *Baas,* the warriors will see that the things he has told them are nothing but lies, and they will go to their *kraal.* On the other hand they may be too drunk to perceive how greatly I have helped them. If that is so, I die. But if I stay here I surely die, slowly, without a chance to test this knife. It is a good blade; it has a sweet song."

The Major looked at the Dutchman and Peters nodded gravely. "He is a man. Let him go."

"Yes; go, Jim. I would be glad to die with you as I have lived with you. I have been a poor *Baas,* and now, because of me, you must die before your time rightly comes."

"And when does my time rightly come, *Baas?* When I am old and toothless; when I can no longer follow the spoor, or drink to fullness; when life is only a memory of the better things gone by; when I am fit only to herd goats, pitied and mocked? Nay, *Baas.* Then it is too late to die. The time to die is when the eye is still keen, the blood still strong and warm; when there are no regrets, no sighing for things gone by; when, as now, I can take my place—a man among men. As for the rest, *Baas,* what need of words between us two? Let me go now before the woman that is in me rises to the top."

He turned slowly away, but the Major caught him fiercely by the shoulder.

"Stay, Jim. What is that in your ear?"

Jim turned and put his hand wonderingly up to his ear, and took from the slit in its lobe a cartridge.

He looked at it in silence for a moment, then handed it to his *Baas.* "I always said I was a fool, *Baas!* Beat me!" he said.

But the Major ignored him, and his face was grave, although the others were elated. He did not dare encourage them to hope; he must be sure first.

"What distance, Peters," he asked, "is Dowson from here?"

The Dutchman crossed over to the window, wincing with pain as he did so.

"Four hundred and fifty, perhaps five hundred yards from here, perhaps more. It is a very deceiving light."

"I've got to know closer than that. Jim, give me my helmet."

Jim looked alarmed.

"Why? Is the *Baas* going out? The *Baas* will not forget that he said I might go."

"Give me my helmet. I am going to measure the distance from here to the man Dowson."

And now the others shared Jim's alarm and crowded round the Major.

"Man, you must have been hit. Sit down and let us bathe your head."

"It is the sun, perhaps," murmured Mrs. Peters.

The girl placed her cool, slim hand on his forehead.

"He has no fever," she announced gravely.

The Major laughingly waved them to one side.

"You are so funny," he exclaimed. "Here we are in the deuce of a hole, and you forget everything because you think I have a little fever. But see!"

He placed the white pith, broad-brimmed helmet on his head and, standing in the center of the room so that he could look out of the window toward the natives, he could see Dowson, who was seated now on the stump of a tree.

Always keeping his eyes on Dowson, the Major lowered has head until the focus of his eye, the brim of his hat, and the storekeeper were in one straight line.

Then, not raising his head or shifting his eyes, he slowly pivoted in his tracks until he was looking out of the window beyond which was the rifle range. An imaginary line, drawn from his eyes to the brim of his hat and extended, touched a boulder at a point about six feet from the ground, at exactly the two hundred yards range.

Three times he did this, while the others watched wonderingly, and each time his experiment worked out the same.

"Seven hundred yards from here to the targets, didn't you say, miss?"

"Yes, but—"

"And two from seven leaves exactly five. Five hundred yards! Why that's a nice easy range for target shooting. I think that even I can score a bull's-eye from here."

While he spoke he ran a pull-through through the barrel of his rifle, satisfied himself it was clean, loaded it with the one precious cartridge which Jim had taken for a charm—ages, it seemed, ago.

"Five hundred yards," he muttered, and pushed up his sights. "A gentle wind, not much. Better make a little allowance, just a very little." He adjusted the wind gage.

He brought the rifle up to his shoulder. His cheek cuddled lovingly into the butt, he exhaled deeply. The muzzle wavered slightly as, with wide-open eyes, he searched for his target. Then, getting the target aligned with his sights, his right forearm, strengthened by the sling, stiffened.

And then, when it seemed they must all scream aloud in protest against the frightful suspense, a sharp report broke the silence and the bullet was sped on its way.

The Major dropped his rifle and seemed to follow the course of the bullet with his eyes.

They all tried to do that!

And they saw the man Dowson, the man who had betrayed his race for the hope of gain, leap up into the air and fall in a huddled heap at the foot of the tree stump upon which he had been sitting; they saw the warriors of Thuso, then more warriors, run up to examine him; saw them pick him up and shake him; saw them drop him again—a huddled, lifeless heap—and run headlong from the place.

It was all over. The people of Thuso had learned their lesson. The charm had failed the man who made it; how then could they hope to profit by it?

THREE DAYS later four white men wearing the uniform of the great white queen came to the *kraal* of Thuso. Matiswa, the son of Marka, riding on a coal black stallion, was with them and he was greeted as one newly risen from the dead.

From Thuso they learned part of the story of what had happened at the Peters place and, desiring to know the whole of it, they rode on, taking the stallion with them.

And there they saw Jim, who told them much; and Peters and his wife, who told them more, and fed them well; and the girl, who told them everything.

At her request they decided to return at once to their headquarters—hoping that the Major would have the sense to keep out of the way until they had gone.

But they ran into him just beyond the last corn-patch, and immediately covered him with their revolvers.

"You're a damned fool, Major," said one.

"Why didn't you keep out of the way?"

"Now we've got to take you back with us."

"But everything will be all right, don't you fret, when we tell them at headquarters what you did here."

The Major, polishing his monocle, replied with a sweet smile. "But I don't want to go back. I've done nothing, really I haven't. You misjudge me when you hunt me down like a beastly criminal. But you brought Satan back for me, so I can forgive you a great deal."

He patted the satiny coat of his horse.

"They say that stallion of yours is fast, Major?" said the first trooper.

"He is."

"Betting man?"

"Sometimes. Why?"

"Bet you can't ride him out of rifle range in five minutes."

"That's too easy."

"Is it? Well, I've made me bet. Are you on?"

"Yes." With a quick leap the Major was in the saddle and the stallion was racing down the dusty trail at breakneck speed toward the homestead.

Gravely the four troopers waited until the first one said, "Time's up," then each pulled his rifle from its scabbard and fired shot after shot into the air.

"He's a bad man to bet with, is the Major," said the senior trooper. "He always wins."

HIS OWN PEOPLE

FROM THE tent came the sounds of splashing water and a voice, a pleasing barytone, raised in the rollicking "Song of the Freebooters." Jim, the Hottentot, ceased for a moment grooming the silky coat of a black stallion and, squatting on his haunches, listened. His thick lips parted in a wide grin; his eyes danced with excitement.

As the voice came to the end of a stanza, Jim jumped to his feet, made the clicking noise of happiness and danced a few shuffling steps before applying himself with renewed zest to his task.

Not that the stallion required grooming. Had his coat been rubbed all over with a lady's handkerchief, the dainty fabric would have come away unsoiled. Nor had Jim been commanded to perform this task—in things of that sort the Major, his *baas*, rarely commanded; there was no need. It was simply a manifestation of Jim's exuberant spirits.

It was not the words of the song that cheered Jim. They were English and, therefore, meaningless to him. Nor was it the tune which urged his feet to dancing steps. To Jim's savage ears it was discordant; the beat was a thing of no rhythm.

But—the Major was singing. Therefore the Major was happy; therefore Jim was happy. To the Hottentot, that song meant that the Major had successfully completed a deal, and whether that deal was within or without the law meant nothing to Jim. The fact that the Major was much sought after by various police officials was ignored by the Hottentot. It is doubtful, indeed, if he understood just what was his *baas's* profession, or in what way it was illegal. For the matter of that, many white men looked upon I.D.B. as a political offense rather than a criminal one. And the Major was an I.D.B. and a criminal in the eyes of the law.

And of all the I.D.B.s, the Major—not altogether a myth—was by far the cleverest—clever in that he was *known* to be an I.D.B. but had so far escaped conviction. Yet he was popular with the police. They sensed that beneath the bland, dudeish, almost effeminate exterior was a man, that the inane, almost vacuous expression of his face was but a mask to hide the keen working of his brain, that his drawl and "silly ass" turns of speech were but a pose.

"Yah!" Jim confided to the stallion. "The *baas* has made his play—or else he makes ready to play. Else why should he buy a new span of mules, foodstuffs in abundance and a wagon-load of trade goods. Yet that is strange. At all other times he has scorned to deal in trade. But what matter? A game is afoot, and with that I am content."

The singing stopped suddenly, and now from the tent sounded the purring, hissing noise of a man briskly toweling himself. A moment later—just as the sun was appearing above the distant horizon and the gray clouds of night swiftly changed through shades of pink and crimson, purple, lavender and glorious gold to fleecy white, to nothingness—the Major came to the opening of the tent.

He watched in silence until the kaleidoscope of colors had passed away. He drank the sweet freshness of the morning air in thirsty gulps, his nostrils dilated, catching each fragrant odor of the veldt. In these few moments he stored up the strength which enabled him to ignore the scorching, pitiless sun through the long African day.

Even as he watched, the sun rose perceptibly above the horizon, the last vestige of cloud disappeared, the drops of dew vanished from the herbage. Above was the electric blue of the sky; at his feet, showing between the straggling tufts of grass, was the red, hard-baked veldt, which stretched in all directions, unbroken by human habitations, as far as eye could reach.

The Major was naked save for a towel he wore about his loins, naked save for that—and a monocle. His hair, tousled from his bath, was streaked with gray. But the skin of his face was firm and smooth; his teeth were white and even.

The only suggestion of his body was one of perfect health, of strength well distributed and in the complete control of an active brain. When he moved, the muscles which rippled under his skin were not knotted, ugly things, but delicate yet powerful engines which obeyed the lever of his will.

JIM, AS his *baas* came out of the tent, left the stallion and, squatting close by, stared at the Major in open-eyed admiration. Jim—his own body squat and ugly but immensely powerful—always found cause to wonder in his *baas's* symmetrical proportions.

"Jim," said the Major, speaking in the vernacular, "after we have scoffed, we trek."

"That is good, *baas,*" Jim said complacently. "That I knew."

"Yes? Then perhaps you know, O man of wisdom, where we go?"

"Nay! That is not known to me. But what matter? We trek; that is sufficient. We see new country. We live as men should live, and not herded together like senseless cattle, fighting over the same grazing-grounds when there is plenty of fodder but a little way off. We hunt and, if we kill, we eat. If not—"

"We open a tin and eat just the same, old dear," the Major interposed in English.

"Oh, damme, yaas, *baas,*" Jim agreed.

"We will trek south, Jim," the Major said slowly.

"South, *baas?*" Jim moved uneasily. "Of what worth is the south? Should a man spit there, it will fall upon another's body. When one drinks, many gather to catch the drippings."

"Then do not spit—do not drink, Jim."

"What then, *baas?* Shall a man die?"

The Major laughed.

"You do not like the south, Jim."

"Nay, *baas.*" Jim was very emphatic.

"Yet your *kraal* is in the Southlands."

"That is true, *baas.* And a hyena is born in a hole in the ground— but he does not stay there."

"True, O knower of all things!" bantered the Major. "But the hyena will return to the hole when hard pressed by foes."

"It is not known to me that any seek to take me," Jim said simply.

"It cannot be answered." The Major laughed. Then: "But if the hyena has a mate, what, then, Jim? Will he not make a nest in that hole?"

"Of a truth—yes, *baas.* That is known to you. But we are dealing in words of no meaning." Jim seemed ill at ease.

"Two—or is it three?—wives await you in that *kraal* of yours, Jim."

"Four, *baas*," Jim said mournfully. "When a man is young, he is also a fool."

"Four reasons why we should trek south, Jim."

"Nay, *baas!* Four reasons why we should trek north."

The Major laughed softly.

"Without doubt they mourn for you, Jim. Four wives mourning a husband—many children lacking a father!"

"That may well be. But I think no children bear my name. As for the women—these ten years they have not seen me. Perchance they dwell in the huts of other men. If not, and they still mourn for me, they would resent my return, which would deprive them of their chief joy—women delight in tears. Is not that known to you, *baas?* Nay! Let well-be be. I am content, and so, doubtless, are they."

"And so"—the Major spoke English now, speaking his thoughts aloud as he often did when alone with the Hottentot. A lazy drawl, which was not in evidence when speaking the vernacular, crept into his voice—"and so," he said "the dear old fellow hasn't seen his bally people for ten years. That's the deuce and all of a time. I wonder why he hasn't gone back. If I know Jim—and I fancy I know him as well as I know myself—he is anxious to go back despite his bally protestations to the contrary. I have been selfish—beastly so. Ten years, I think—yes; ten years he has been with me, always at my beck and call. He's been a bally brick—never groused—always ready to follow where I led. By Jove, what a rotter I feel! I've kept him from his own kind all these years, and—well, he shall go back—and go back like a blooming duke. By Jove—yes! He's earned thousands, yes—thousands for me, and I've never paid him a blooming tikkey! I've even stopped him from getting jolly good and drunk—and how the old boy does enjoy getting blotto! He shall have all the trade stuff. But I'll have to go back with him or he'll drink himself stony broke on the way."

The Major lapsed into a thoughtful silence. After a few minutes he said abruptly to the Hottentot,

"How much did I promise to pay you when you first came to me, Jim?"

"Ten shilling a month, *baas.*"

"And how much *have* I paid, you?"

"Of what need to tell, *baas?* What is it between us two?"

"How much, Jim?"

"Nothing, *baas.*" Jim laughed. "But I have not wanted for food or clothes, nor have I found life a burden—living with you."

The Major's eyes gleamed.

"And you have found many stones for me, Jim?"

"Many, *baas.* And will doubtless find many more."

"And you have been beaten because you were the Major's boy?"

"And would have been beaten many times more had I *not* been the Major's servant," Jim countered happily.

Again the Major lapsed into a thoughtful silence, and Jim shuffled uneasily. Then,

"Is it permitted me to know why you left the *kraal,* Jim?"

"Of a truth, yes, *baas.* I would have told you before, but it seemed a matter of small moment.

"My father was the headman of the *kraal* and chief of all the *kraals* in the valley. When he died, I, his oldest son, was his lawful successor. But my brother, a man of great cunning although small of stature, sought my place. And so, *Baas,* the people of the valley were divided. The old men, the wise men of the *kraals* were on my side, but most of the warriors shouted the name of my brother.

"Perchance, had I desired to put the matter to a test, I could have defeated my brother. But to what end? Much blood would have been shed—and bloodshed always begets bloodshed. So I left the valley secretly; no man knew of my going. Only my wives knew. I bade them follow me, but they would not. They scorned me for a coward and a fool because I would not fight for the place that was rightfully mine. Women are ever more eager for the loud-sounding noises of authority than are men. Is that not known to you? They say it is for the sake of their children they seek advancement. Therein they lie. It is for themselves. They delight to bask in the shadow of their man's authority.

"And so I left the valley—alone. Nor have I since returned to that place; nor do I wish to do so now. Yet that valley is a goodly place. Its men folk are men among men. The cattle are sleek, for fodder is plentiful; it is sweet and green. Nowhere do the crops yield so plentifully as in that valley; nowhere are the maidens more pleasing to the eye. And nowhere, *baas,* do the women folk make such strength-giving beer. But I have been away from the herd too long to desire to return now— Pardon, *baas,* if I have wearied you."

The Major did not speak, but, turning, reentered the tent and began to dress. The Hottentot, after a moment's hesitation, busily occupied himself with preparations for the morning meal. He seemed strangely clumsy. His movements were lethargic. Several times he sighed loudly.

"Jim!" the Major called presently.

"Yah, *baas?*"

"When we have had scoff, we trek south. And we go to visit your *kraal,* Jim, in the valley."

"It is an order, *baas,*" Jim assented mournfully, but his face beamed with joy.

THREE WEEKS later the Major and Jim came within sight of the valley—Jim's valley. For the past week the trail had led between—and sometimes over—groups of *kopjes* and now, from the top of one of these stony hills, the Major saw a green oasis surrounded by a barren country.

"It is indeed a country to boast of, Jim," he said softly.

And Jim, his broad, homely face all smiles, assented. He pointed out the numerous *kraals* which seemed to grow mushroomlike amid the luxuriant foliage. Spirals of smoke floating lazily upward suggested peace and well-being—and the preparation of food. He pointed to the precipitous walls of the valley, which made a surprise attack unfeasible; indeed, the only entrance to the valley was a steep and winding path directly at their feet. To all intents and purposes the valley was cut off from communication with the outside world, ignored by the white men by reason of the miles and miles of non-productive, almost waterless land which surrounded it, and protected from warlike tribes by its sheer inaccessibility.

"And do no white men come here, Jim?" the Major asked incredulously. "A storekeeper in this place would quickly grow rich."

Jim scowled.

"The police come, *baas,* once a year to collect taxes. And that is not altogether just. Look you—why should my people pay a tax for what is already theirs?"

There was an answer to this, and a good one, but the Major knew Jim would not appreciate it; so he made no reply, but, looking keenly at the Hottentot, smiled a little at the expression on his face.

"I think I'll open a store in your valley, Jim," he said presently.

"That you must not do!" Jim said fiercely. Then, rather ashamed of his outburst, he added: "Nay, *baas;* do not do that. My people would not understand. They know very little of the white men—when the police come for the tax, the women are all sent away. Only the men remain in the *kraals.* Once, long ago, a white man came and set up a store, and my people trusted him. But he betrayed that trust, and so he died. Since that time the valley has been closed to white men. No white men may dwell there, and in that the police have aided us. We pay a tax, but in all other things we live as we lived before the white men came to this land."

The Major nodded absently and returned to the place where he had pitched camp. Jim, with many a backward glance at the valley below, reluctantly followed him.

"Put pack-saddles on two of the mules, Jim," the Major ordered, and climbing up into the covered wagon, he watched as Jim sullenly went about his task.

"It is finished," said Jim presently, and led the two mules up to the wagon.

"Yes; it is finished, Jim," the Major echoed sadly.

Rousing himself, he opened one of the chests containing trade goods and handed its contents to Jim.

"Load them on the mules, Jim."

"But the *baas* does not mean to trade, surely?" Jim protested.

"And if I would—must I ask thy permission?" The Major's voice was stern. Never before had he spoken to Jim like that, and Jim flinched.

"It is an order, *baas,*" he said humbly.

BUT IT was with no enthusiasm that he loaded the mules with a weird assortment of knives and mouth-organs, alarm-clocks and bottles of cheap scent, whistles and patent medicines, colored beads and canned foods, gaily patterned cloths, shirts, opera-hats, cheap toys—such as monkey-on-a-stick—and corsets.

And, last of all, the Major handed Jim an old carbine. It was useless, but Jim took it with great awe and handled it gingerly as if it had been a piece of dynamite due to explode at any moment. The Hottentot was notoriously afraid of firearms, although he was wont to boast to any chance-met native that he was an even greater marksman than his *baas.* As a matter of fact, he had fired but two shots in his life. The first had been quite involuntary; on the second occasion he had been forced to chose between tackling a lion barehanded or firing his gun. And Jim had chosen the braver course.

"Are the pack-saddles full, Jim?" the Major asked.

"Aye, *baas*. There is no room for more."

"Then take these also."

The Major counted out into Jim's battered helmet one hundred gold sovereigns.

"For me, *baas?*" Jim exclaimed. "But why?"

"You are going to your people, are you not? And shall the servant of the Major go empty-handed? No! Now get you gone—you and your brothers, the mules."

"Baas! Inkosi!" Jim's voice boomed out into happy salutation and thanks. Without further word he turned and, with boisterous cries, urged the mules in the direction of the path leading to the valley. He had not gone very far, however, when his footsteps lagged and, turning, he came running back to the Major.

"But will not the *baas* come with me?" he asked.

"Nay. Have you forgotten the law concerning a white man entering the valley?"

"It is true—I had forgotten. But how shall I see my *baas* again? Where shall I find him?"

"Five days I will await you here. After that, you will not find me. I shall go my own way."

"Have no fear, *baas;* I shall return before five days have passed. I am old—not very old—yet in some things I am as a child. It is only that I wish my people to see me as I am." And Jim, all bedecked in a cast-off white-duck suit of the Major's, strutted peacocklike. Suddenly he sobered. "There is something, *baas*," he said wistfully, "which makes me forget the ten years I have spent with you. I forget that I am Jim, the Major's servant, and think only that am Mytata, the son of a chief."

"Then go, Mytata. *Hamba gaghle*—may thy path be smooth."

"Aye! *Shlahla gaghle*," Jim replied absently. "Remain in peace." And he hurried after the mules.

A few paces, and again he stopped.

"First suffer, *baas*," he called back, "that I prepare thy evening meal."

"Not so," the Major answered. "Shall the son of a chief do the work of women?"

Jim's right hand shot up in salutation, and he hesitated no longer. A few minutes later he disappeared from sight over the brow of the hill.

The Major was an expert camp-cook; men who had hunted with him spoke in awed voices of his skill. Yet, somehow, that night the buck kidneys tasted like leather to him, the coffee bitter.

IT WAS long after sundown when Jim, the Hottentot, tired but happily excited, came to the *kraal* which stood sentrylike at the foot of the step trail leading from the hills into the valley. As he came nearer to the cluster of beehive-shaped huts, he broke out into the joyful song of the home-coming. It seemed as if the world held no sound but Jim's joyful paean of praise. As he sang, he leaped high into the air—he was a dancing goblin, a moon-worshiper. He flung stones at the mules, urging them to better speed.

Then suddenly he ceased singing—he was quite close to the gate of the *kraal* now—and listened for sounds of life within, expecting to hear the voices of men, the barking of dogs, the cries of children and the soft lullabies of women. But all was silent save for the timid bleat of a goat and the lowing of a motherless calf.

Jim hurried on, stilling his half-born fears with the thought that it was late, that the men folk were asleep.

And so he came to the gate of the *kraal,* entered unchallenged and came to the large clearing before the hut of the headman. There he stood undecided—astounded. The place was strangely deserted. On hands and knees he entered and explored several of the nearby huts—risking an *assegai*-thrust—anxious to greet and be greeted. But the huts were empty; the fire-ashes were cold.

One of the pack-mules brayed mournfully, echoing Jim's bewilderment, and the Hottentot, as one in a dream, unsaddled his animals, turned them into the cattle corral and then sat down beside his wealth, endeavoring to reason out the cause of the *kraal's* desertion. After a little while, assuring himself that the morning would bring its explanation, he slept.

He was wakened by the scent of cooking food and the consciousness that he was watched.

Springing quickly to his feet, he saw four women seated at the entrance of a hut just across from him. Two of them were monstrously fat, a third tall and ludicrously thin. The fourth was neither fat nor thin—a meek, self-effacing woman who shrank behind the other three as if for protection.

"*Sauka bona, abafazi,*" said Jim, making a Major-like bow.

"*Eh bor—sauka bona,*" the four replied tonelessly, then waited expectantly.

Jim continued bravely,

"My eyes are blinded."

"The rays of the sun are very bright," the four replied, simpering at Jim's compliment.

"Where are the men folk?" Jim asked.

"They are not here." The tall, thin one's voice was strident and shrewish.

"They have gone to the head *kraal.*" The two fat women spoke as one.

"And all the people have gone with them," said she who was neither fat nor thin.

"Then why are you here?"

"Because we are women of no name, we are women who have been put to shame. Our husband left us. He—"

"Of what need to tell a stranger that?" interposed the fat ones. "His going was your fault, O noisy stick of flesh!"

"Not mine but yours—fat, lazy cows that you are!"

And then ensued a heated altercation which only ceased when Jim exclaimed:

"Peace! I am hungry. Let us eat."

Quickly order was restored, and food and beer was set before him.

"And why," asked Jim, his hunger appeased, "have all the people gone to the *kraal* of the headman?"

"Because the chief is dead, leaving no man child, and another must be chosen ere the sun sets this night. Would that Mytata were here!"

"Mytata!" Jim was startled.

"Yes. Our husband. Do you know of him?" The voice held a note of suspicion.

"I have heard the name," mumbled Jim, but he started excitedly to his feet and, catching the mules, feverishly began to saddle them.

"I go to the *kraal* of the chief," he said, in answer to the women's questions.

"And what will you do there, stranger?" mocked the shrewish one. "Meet death, belike. Better that you stay here with us—we have brewed much beer."

"Nay!" Jim exclaimed impatiently. "I go not as a stranger. I go as Mytata to take the place that is rightfully mine."

"Mytata! Art thou indeed Mytata?" the fat ones exclaimed breathlessly.

"Without doubt," Jim said proudly. "And you—you cows are my wives. So now be at peace."

"At peace—yes; after I have had my say." The thin woman advanced threateningly, her hand upraised in anger. "For ten years we have been scorned because of you, and now you shall pay."

"Yes! Now you shall pay!" One of the fat women picked up a knobkerrie and struck viciously at Jim. Only a catlike leap saved him from a broken skull.

He looked about him despairing for an avenue of escape, for the women were closing in on him on all sides.

"This is folly!" he cried. "I die now, and you remain women scorned forever! Let me but go to the *kraal* and assert my right, and the long years of waiting will be forgotten in the homage that will come to you, O women of the chief!" The women hesitated. "Besides," continued Jim craftily, "I have brought many wondrous presents for you."

The thin woman nodded.

"Let him go his way, sisters," she said. "Let him take the place that is his. After that, we shall know how to deal with him."

"Then hasten, Mytata," said the fat ones. "We will come also."

"Aye," Jim assented relievedly, "that is your right. But you must be dressed in a manner befitting the wives of a chief. See!" He took from the pack-saddles an assortment of colored cloths and beads. Other trade "truck" quickly followed, and soon the four women, richly clad, were ready for the journey.

Mafuta, one of the fat women, wore pink corsets about her massive calves, Macabe, the tall, thin one, had suspended an alarm-clock from the lobe of her ear. Mabele, the other fat one, wore long white stockings upon her arms. Inyoni, the fourth woman, was content with the beads and a headdress of vivid scarlet cloth.

Jim looked them over with the eye of a connoisseur, then, shouldering his carbine, led the way out of the *kraal*.

TWO HOURS later Jim and his retinue arrived at the chief *kraal* of the valley.

By virtue of his evident wealth, his carbine and his name—which the four women shouted continuously—he was permitted to enter the large hut where the old men of the tribe were holding solemn conclave.

But the women were forced to remain outside. Their claim for reinstatement had not yet been upheld; this man who called himself Mytata might be an imposter—that was for the council of headmen to decide. So the women took their stand beside Jim's mules and their burdens, surrounded by the envious women of the *kraals*.

As Jim entered the council-hut, carrying his carbine over his shoulder, Tomasi, the chief of the headmen present, was loudly espousing the claim of his nephew, Jhentsi.

"If there is any man," Tomasi was saying, "that is better fitted than Jhentsi to dwell in the hut of the chief, let his name be spoken."

"There is none other," chorused the headmen. "The choice is a good one. We are well content. Let us proclaim his name to the people."

"Wait!" cried Jim. "What of Mytata? Is he not the lawful chief?"

"Mytata has gone from us; he is dead to me," Tomasi said sternly. "And now, having answered your question, stranger, tell what you do here—and take heed to your answer. Death walks close on your heels. Speak quickly—before I summon warriors to take you away."

"Softly! Softly! I have another question. Look on this"—Jim aimed his carbine at Tomasi—"and see how death has almost caught up with you."

"Au-a!" It was a low-breathed note of astonishment. The headmen were astounded that the white man's "fire-stick" should be in the hands of one of their own people.

"What else would you know?" Tomasi's voice trembled.

"If Mytata were here, would there be any question of his chieftainship?"

"Nay."

"Then look no further—for I am Mytata!"

JIM SPOKE the words with all the pride with which he was wont to say, "He is the Major, and I—I am Jim, his servant."

The headmen crowded round him, peering at him closely—recognizing him, yet not quite sure that they recognized him. In ten years a man changes, and Jim's dress confused them.

"It is truly Mytata," said some.

"He is an impostor," said others.

Sensing the cause of their bewilderment, Jim doffed his helmet, quickly stripped himself of his ill-fitting clothes and stood before them clad only in a loin-cloth—not all the garments of civilization had ever induced Jim to part with that. And then the doubters doubted no longer.

"It is Mytata!" they cried.

"A word!" cried Tomasi. And, because he was an old man and full of wisdom, they listened to him. "What claim has Mytata on the people of the valley? He left us of his own will, and has been gone from us these many years—wandering wheresoever he wished, serving, without doubt, many white men. He apes their ways; he is marked with their evil. He is soft and knows not the ways of the hunt. Our tongue is strange to him. He has forsaken our customs. And now, when he returns, broken, a beggar, you would do him honor—putting to shame a warrior who has been ever faithful. He—"

"Peace, old one," Jim interposed hotly, "before I forget that you are old! I have served a white man—yes. But only that I might gain some of the white man's wisdom. Having gained my end, I put the white man on one side—he was nothing to me. I am soft, you say? Bah! What say you to that, headmen? You used to be proper judges of men."

"This is no weakling, Tomasi," murmured one of the headmen, as he expertly eyed Jim's barrellike chest and felt the mighty muscles of his legs and arms. "We have no warrior who could stand against him. He could take up that nephew of thine in one hand and throw him further than the width of this hut."

"No; I am not soft." Jim laughed, and, taking hold of the pole which supported the roof of the hut, he raised it from the ground. The roof-poles creaked and groaned, and the headmen cried out in alarm:

"Let be! You will have the hut fall upon us!"

"Let be!" echoed Tomasi. "At least you are not soft."

"And I am no beggar," Jim continued, as he let the pole down to the ground. "This"—he patted the carbine—"is worth more than all the cattle in your *kraal,* Tomasi. Some day you shall see me kill a lion with it, old man."

From his pockets he showered gold pieces upon the floor of the hut—a hundred of them in all.

"That will pay the taxes for the people of the valley," he continued. "Outside, on *my* mules, I have gifts for all you headmen. Is it permitted that I order them to be brought in?"

"It is permitted!" shouted the headmen gleefully.

At Jim's command, warriors took the packs off the mules and brought them into the hut. Then, with a lordly air, the air of a paternal autocrat, Jim distributed his gifts. The weighty matters of public welfare were forgotten as gray-bearded headmen blew lustily upon mouth-organs, twanged upon jew's-harps or stuck opera-hats upon their heads and posed delightedly.

Even Tomasi seemed to be appeased as, squatting in a corner of the hut, he examined with childish awe a gaudily painted monkey-on-a-stick.

That same night the council of headmen announced Mytata as their choice for chief, although he would not actually assume authority until the night of the full moon—five days hence.

Many of the people received the news with great enthusiasm, for they remembered Jim of old. But many others grieved, for Jhentsi was a man well liked and would have made a good chief.

THE NEXT two days passed very swiftly for Jim. He lived in a state of perpetual excitement and intoxication. The women of the *kraals* had brewed much beer in anticipation of the festivity accompanying the choosing of a chief, and for once Jim was able to drink his fill.

In all things his slightest wish was instantly gratified. Was he thirsty? A comely maiden presented him with a calabash of beer. Was he hungry? Food was set before him. Anon he wished to sleep, and even the dogs ceased their noisy clamor.

And so Jim—eating and sleeping and drinking, waited on, hand and foot—gradually assumed an intolerant air of arrogance, came to believe that he possessed all the virtues the people attributed to him. And constantly he boasted of his prowess as a hunter.

"No man," he said, "no, not even among the white hunters, has killed as many lions as I have."

"Show us the manner in which you slay *Silwane,* O Great One," the warriors demanded.

And Jim, staggering to his feet, aimed his carbine at some imaginary beast.

"Bang!" He said. "That is all, my children. The lion is dead."

"Au-a! A mighty hunter! Bang! And the lion is dead."

Jim slowly reseated himself, nodded his head in solemn gravity and explained further,

"But you must understand that the voice of this fire-stick is louder than all your voices—it can be heard above the loudest thunderclap."

"Then let us hear its voice," sneered Tomasi—he had broken his monkey-on-a-stick—"or is your voice only the voice of a braggart?"

"Have a care, old one! Once before I said that death was close at your heels."

"You are not yet chief," retorted Tomasi. "Until the full of the moon my voice is greater than yours."

Jim nodded.

"That may be. But talk not too loud unless I remember your words when the time comes."

"I care not what happens to me then. I do not care to live under the rule of a boaster and a drunkard. Woe is me! Jhentsi, my nephew, should be sitting in your place."

"Brave words!" shouted Jim. "Thou art a man after my own heart. You think I am a liar because I speak of my prowess with the fire-stick. I would let you hear its voice, but the huts would be shaken to their foundations—they would collapse, your ears would be deafened. Yet, if you still doubt my word, I will—"

"Nay!" protested the other headmen. "We do not doubt you, O Mytata! Pay no heed to this fool. The sweets of authority have turned sour in his mouth. Let us drink, O Great One, and forget this ancient babbler."

But there was a fly in Jim's ointment of happiness—four flies, to be exact—four women, who tried to order his outgoings and incoming—four women who constantly nagged him and squabbled with each other.

And of the four, Mecabe, the shrew, was the most persistent. In order to silence her, and also as a warning to the other three, Jim refused to acknowledge her as his head wife—and that she was—threatening to divorce her if she gave him more trouble.

This, to a certain extent, stopped Mecabe's noisy tirade, but it also made her exceedingly bitter toward Jim. News of the dissension in Jim's family having come to Tomasi's ears, he at once sent for the disgruntled Mecabe, bidding her come secretly to his hut.

AS SHE entered, Tomasi rose quickly to his feet.

"Hail, woman of the chief!" he said. "To the ears, the eyes and the mouth of the man who will be chief, Tomasi gives greeting."

Mecabe smiled bitterly.

"You do me too much honor. I am nothing. Mytata has put me on one side."

"That is not possible! Mecabe jokes." Tomasi's air of astonishment was well feigned.

"I do not deal in jokes of that sort. But why did you send for me?"

"Because a whisper had come to my ears of the things you have just told me. I could not believe."

"And now you know that the whisper was true, what then?"

"Doubtless Mecabe mourns because she has not found favor in the eyes of her lord? Doubtless she would do much to regain that which she has lost?"

Mecabe's eyes flashed angrily.

"I only desire," she said, "to see him put to shame. Perhaps he would then regret that he had put me on one side."

"If Jhentsi were chief, he would see to it it that you were given your right place."

"But Jhentsi is not chief."

"Yet he would be—were Mytata not here."

"You mean that I should kill him?"

Tomasi nodded assent.

"Death is not too great a punishment for his treatment of you," he said.

"That is true—but there is a better way. If he died, many many men would murmur; but if he were to become a thing to laugh at, then—" She hesitated.

"Then," Tomasi finished, "Jhentsi, my nephew, would become chief."

"That might be done," Mecabe said slowly.

Tomasi's eyes gleamed.

"Yes, that might be done," he assented. "But how?"

"He has continually spoken, has he not," Mecabe said slowly, "of how he can shoot with that fire-stick of his? Yet it comes to me that he is lying, that he is afraid of the thing."

"I had thought somewhat that way," said Tomasi.

"Aye!" Mecabe was all eagerness now. "But you have not heard him speak, as I have, when the sickness of much drinking was upon him. He is afraid of it, I say; and he is afraid that the time will come when he *must* use it."

"And—"

"And I would hasten that day."

"Words, of wisdom!" scoffed Tomasi. "But how?"

"Are there no lions in the valley?"

"Of a truth, yes."

"Then arrange a lion-hunt, O Tomasi! Let your warriors show their prowess before Mytata, and see that he is there to witness it. Let the beaters drive the lion up to where Mytata stands, and then, when it is time to make the kill, let the warriors forsake him. Not one must cast an *assegai*. Then shall we see how great a hunter is this man Mytata."

"Much wisdom is truly thine, Mecabe!" Tomasi cried joyfully. "It shall be done. Tomorrow shall be the time of the hunt. Tonight I shall make all things ready. And rest assured that men of my *kraal* will form the body-guard of Mytata. This is a way to my liking. I have no desire to set brother against brother and *kraal* against *kraal*. If Mytata comes through this test, I will no longer work against him."

"And you will not forget me?"

"Nay! If Jhentsi becomes chief, you shall be his head wife. If the test fails—should Mytata prove to be no boaster—I shall still see that you are rewarded."

With that, Mecabe was well content, and would have left the hut, but Tomasi stayed her.

"There is one other thing: Last night a white man was captured by warriors of my *kraal;* by guile they captured him. He rode a black devil of a horse. My warriors would have killed him, but he claimed friendship with Mytata. Therefore they brought him to me secretly, that I might pass judgment. Has Mytata spoken of this man?"

"What manner of man is he? Is he round of face, beardless, with gray eyes that see all things? Does he laugh often? Does he in some things seem womanish—yet is all man? Does he wear a thing that glitters in his eye? Does he—"

"There is no need to say more," Tomasi interposed. "It is the very man. What know you of him?"

Mecabe laughed scornfully.

"Through the long hours of the night hath Mytata wearied us with talk of this man. He is as the rising and the setting of the sun in Mytata's eyes. The man who would be chief was the white man's slave. In his drunken cups he told me how he debased himself before the white man—cooking his food, drawing water and the like—performing all manner of tasks which are only fit for women."

Tomasi nodded.

"What shall I do with this white man?"

"Bring him before Mytata and let us see if that man will keep the law which says, 'Death to the white man who enters the valley.'"

"Again you counsel wisely. It shall be done," said Tomasi.

JIM WAS seated before his hut, watching the departure of the young men who were to "drive" the lion to the kill.

A little distance to the right of him, armed with the sharp-stabbing *assegais,* were the warriors who had been selected to kill the lion when the beaters had driven it to them; they were the African matadors. At Jim's left sat a group of the headmen. Tomasi was among them.

At length the last of the long line of beaters passed out of the *kraal* gate. Already their shouts and the din of tom-toms sounded faintly in the distance.

Jim stirred uneasily, looked at the pot of beer before him and sighed, looked at his carbine—and shuddered.

"Is it time for us to be moving, Tomasi?" he asked.

"There is plenty of time, O Great Hunter! First, we would have your counsel concerning a weighty matter—"

"Let that wait until I have been proclaimed chief," Jim said irritably. "Why bother me now?"

"It is a matter which will not wait. It concerns a white man taken prisoner by the young men of my *kraal.*"

"A white man?" There was a note of apprehension in Jim's voice. "I warned him not to enter the valley," he muttered to himself. Then, aloud, "What manner of white man?"

"You shall see for yourself."

Tomasi shouted an order, and four warriors emerged from a nearby hut. They carried the Major, bound hand and foot, between them.

"You know the law?" Tomasi questioned.

"Aye, Tomasi; I know the law," Jim answered despondently.

"And know that it cannot be changed?"

"Aye. I know that, too."

The four warriors put the Major on the ground at Jim's feet. Jim looked at him with lackluster eyes—eyes which held no look of recognition.

"What make you in this valley, white man?" he asked sternly, almost fiercely.

"I am looking for my servant," the Major answered. "Have you seen him?"

"What manner of man is he? What is his name? Yet think not that that excuse will serve."

"He is somewhat of your build. A man of no great worth—given to much drinking, full of vain conceits and a great liar. He—"

"I know not the man," Jim interposed hastily.

"His name is Jim," the Major added, as an afterthought.

"Jim? I know not the name. What say you, Tomasi? Shall we let this man go?"

"No!" The old headman sprang to his feet. "The law may not be broken. He must die."

"You hear, white man? Have you anything to say?"

"Only this: Should you, at any time meet the man Jim, tell him that you killed his *baas.*"

Jim was overcome with confusion but, recovering quickly, ordered the warriors to take the Major back to the hut.

"I will deal with this white man tonight, he said "And now, O Tomasi, let us go to the hunt."

Shouldering his carbine, he led the way out of the *kraal,* followed closely by the body-guard and the councilors. The four warriors who had carried the Major to the hut also followed after a little while.

The Major, bound hand and foot, lay on the ground of the hut, cursing the curiosity and the anxiety to learn of Jim's welfare which had caused him to enter the valley.

He wondered at Jim's attitude—astonished that his old-time devoted body-servant should have evinced such a cold-blooded indifference to his *baas's* fate.

The Major had not openly appealed to Jim for mercy—that was not the Major's way. Besides, he knew that Jim's hands were probably tied in a matter of this sort and that any attempt to show leniency would be fatal to Jim's chance of becoming chief. The warriors who had captured the Major had told him all about the choosing of a new chief.

Still the Major could not but reflect on Jim's ingratitude—at the same time excusing it. The call of race and color is strong; a man quickly reverts to the traditions of his people.

But this was a rotten way to die! He strained at the sinews which bound him.

"They've done a bally good job," he reflected aloud. "Believe there's no way out, unless Jim gets a change of heart—and that's not likely."

He looked longingly at his rifle and belt of cartridges which his captors had hung on the wall of the hut. A knife was hanging from the belt. He tried to reach it, but, bound as he was, it was impossible.

He looked round the hut, hoping to find some sharp instrument—a stone, even—with which he might cut himself free. But his search was unrewarded.

By careful maneuvering he managed to work his monocle out of his tunic pocket and let it fall to the ground. But it broke into pieces far too small to be of service to him.

Then, and it was with difficulty he restrained from shouting with joy, he saw a thin wisp of smoke—it was almost imperceptible—rising from the charred log, the remains of the morning cook-fire, in the center of the hut.

He rolled painfully over to it and blew very cautiously, endeavoring to fan the few visible sparks into a flame.

The wisp of smoke thickened; the glow of sparks brightened, and soon a little yellow flame flickered feebly.

An ill-judged puff put it out again, but he persevered, and shortly the flame appeared again. Turning his back—his hands were tied behind him—he held his wrists over the flame. The sweat poured from his face; he bit his lips to hold in check the moans of pain that sought utterance. He felt the strands give, and in a little while—yet it seemed an eternity of agony—his hands were free.

The rest was easy.

Then, crawling on hands and knees, his rifle slung at his back, the cartridge-belt at his waist, he cautiously left the hut.

Luckily the women folk and such men as were too young or too old to join the hunt were taking their noon-day siesta; so he reached the gate of the *kraal* and the bush beyond unseen.

But his difficulties were not yet over. He had yet to gain the trail which led from the valley, and to do this he would have to pass through the ring of beaters. That he could do this he had no doubt; but it would entail bloodshed, and the Major was adverse to that. After all, he was a trespasser. Jim had warned him not to enter the valley.

If he had his horse it would have been different. The warriors then would be unable to get close enough to him to be a serious menace. But he did not have his horse, did not know where the stallion was. So he determined to wait in a nearby corn-patch for night and darkness.

Entering the patch, he came to a clearing fringed with Kaffir-orange trees. He retraced his steps a little way, then lowered himself wearily to the ground. He was conscious now of a dull pain in his wrists. They were badly swollen and blistered. After a little while he slept.

He was wakened some hours later—it was nearing sunset—by the shouts of natives and the beating of tom-toms—a very pandemonium of noise. And, dwarfing all other sounds, the angry snarls of a lion at bay.

"THE LION comes, O Mytata!" said Tomasi.

Jim grunted.

"It is well," he grumbled. "There is not a blade of grass in this whole valley on which I have not trodden this day. 'The lion will go there,' you said, and we went there. 'He will come here,' you say, and we have come to this place. I am thirsty. I will get me some fruit."

Jim walked to one of the orange trees which fringed the clearing.

The cries of the beaters sounded nearer. There was a crunching sound, a smashing-down of corn-stalks, a menacing snarl.

"Wait!" screamed Tomasi. *"Silwane* comes, Mytata!"

As he spoke, a splendid black-maned lion sprang from the corn-patch at Jim's right and crouched, head on ground between his massive paws, not ten yards from where Jim stood as one transfixed.

"Now is the time," said Jim, speaking slowly and distinctly, "for the young warriors to prove their mettle."

"Not they!" scoffed Tomasi, and his voice came from a height. Jim knew—he did not have to turn his head—that the old headman had climbed a tree. "Show us how you kill a lion with that fire-stick of yours," Tomasi's mocking voice continued, "or die. What need has such a mighty hunter of the spears of warriors?"

"No need," said Jim slowly.

He realized now that he had been trapped, that Tomasi had planned just this. What a fool he had been to boast of his prowess with the carbine!

The shouts of the beaters had stopped. Jim felt that every inhabitant of the valley was watching him.

The lion, its tail lashing savagely, was creeping nearer to him inch by inch, as a cat stalks a bird. A few more feet and—

Jim had two ways open to him. He could turn and make a dash for one of the orange trees with a bare chance of reaching its lower branches in safety. But if he did that—and lived—his name would be a byword. He would be treated with contempt, would be driven from the valley—forced to run the gantlet of all the men folk, and each one would strike at him with a *sjambok*. He would, perhaps, be killed. That way did not appeal to him.

On the other hand, if he stayed where he was, the lion would surely kill him; but he would die as a brave warrior should die, and his name would always be spoken of with reverence by the people of the valley. Such a death would not be a cause for mockery. Even the mightiest warriors, the craftiest hunters sometimes failed.

All this passed through Jim's mind with one short intake of the breath. In as short a time he reached a decision.

"The way to the Land of the Spirits," he muttered, "will not be lonely. My *baas* will join me very soon. Perhaps he will forget my folly, and we shall continue to hunt, as before, in the place of the shadows."

He slowly raised his carbine—that worthless weapon—to his shoulders, determined to carry out his pose to the end. Then, shutting his eyes, he waited.

The lion at that moment leaped. Just for one flickering second Jim opened his eyes and saw the tawny form in mid-air. He was dimly conscious of a loud report which seemed to come from behind him. Then the lion was upon him, and he was to the ground before the fearful impact—the beast on top of him.

Moments passed like hours. All was very still. It came to Jim that the lion was a dead weight upon him; it was singularly relaxed and motionless.

Something warm splashed on Jim's forehead. He cautiously opened his eyes and looked full into the face of the lion. Its eyes were glazed. Just above the bridge of its nose was a gaping hole from which the blood oozed, and Jim realized that a miracle had happened, that the lion was dead, that he, Mytata, one-time servant to the Major, was a great hunter. With an effort he got from under the tawny carcass and rose to his feet—bruised but intensely happy.

With a swaggering gait he walked toward the trees where Tomasi, the other headmen and the warriors had taken refuge.

"Are you satisfied, doubters and men of little courage, that I am a mighty hunter?"

"Aye! Well satisfied," they answered in awed voices. "Never have we seen such slaying, such bravery."

"It was nothing—but do not doubt again."

The men climbed down from the trees, and the beaters hastened to the clearing and surveyed the lifeless jungle king.

They made a rough litter on which they put the carcass and then, loudly singing the praises of Mytata, all returned to the *kraal,* eager to celebrate the wondrous killing.

As for Jim, he was as one who treads on air.

BUT DURING the evening meal and during the drinking which followed he became strangely silent, and after a little while he went to his hut. There his wives quickly followed him.

"Tomorrow you will be proclaimed chief, Mytata," said Mafuta.

"Aye," he assented wearily. "What of it?"

"It is time that you selected your head wife."

"What care I who she is—so long as it is not that shrew, Mecabe? Choose between yourselves."

"The place belongs to me," said Mafuta.

"No! To me, fat cow!"

"You both lie—mine is the place," said Inyosi.

"And what of me?" shrieked Mecabe. "He calls me a shrew. Well, a shrew I will be."

"Oh, peace!" Jim groaned. "Or must I give order to have you beaten?"

But they paid no heed to him; instead, they advanced their claims in still louder voices, and soon the wordy warfare gave place to one of "tooth and nail." Several times Jim was the recipient of blows meant for one of the women, and at length, in fear for his life, he fled from the hut.

His appearance was greeted by the men of the *kraal* with good-humored raillery.

"What!" cried the warriors. "Does the killer of lions flee from his women?"

"May they be forever accursed!" replied Jim mournfully. "There is no peace where they are. What say, Tomasi? Can I not put them on one side when I am chief?"

"Have you forgotten the custom of the valley? Have you any just cause for putting them on one side?"

"Their voices are like the screams of the 'Go-away' bird. They jabber incessantly; they are continually fighting—the one with the other. They give me no peace."

"That is no cause," said Tomasi.

The warriors laughed.

"That is the way of all women, O Mytata!" they cried.

Jim made no reply. He was looking with bewildered eyes at his hut, from which came the sound of women's voices raised in heated altercation.

"To live with them," he muttered, "is not to my liking. Rather would I have been killed by the lion."

And now came a warrior running.

"The white man!" he gasped. "The white man has gone, Mytata!"

"How could that be?" said Tomasi. "He was bound hand and foot; warriors were left to guard him."

"The warriors went to the hunt, O Tomasi! And as for the ropes which tied him—here they are!"

The man handed the charred sinews to Jim, who took them and examined them closely in order to cloak his feelings.

He was conscious of a great relief. The Major, his *baas,* had escaped. He, Jim, would not have to see him die. But—what a fool he was! He had known long before the warrior came with the news that the Major had escaped—had known it back in the clearing at the moment the lion charged.

He smiled happily; then his face clouded once more. He was conscious that he was unutterably lonely; he thought of the long years of stagnation, of inaction which were before him. He— But what was this Tomasi was saying? Ordering warriors to go on the trail of the white man!

"How now!" Jim shouted wrathfully. "Whose voice gives orders? By the fire-stick and the lion I killed, you go too far!"

"Your pardon, Great Hunter," the old headman replied humbly. "I thought that—"

"Do not think, gray-head," interposed Jim. "Bring hither the horse of the white man—or has that gone, too?"

"Nay, Mytata. It is in the cattle-*kraal.*"

PRESENTLY A warrior led the black stallion, bridled and saddled, to where Jim waited impatiently.

"I go to find the white man," Jim announced, as he mounted the horse, "in order that the law of the valley may be fulfilled. Let no warrior follow the spoor. This is my *indaba*—is it understood?"

"It is understood, O Mytata! But how can you take the trail on the back of that black devil? The valley is in darkness."

"I am a hunter," boasted Jim. "I will find that white man though the valley were as dark as the country of the wicked dead. I shall not return without him."

"But if he kill you, what then?"

"Let Jhentsi be chief in my place if I do not return, and see to it that the lazy cows, my wives, are treated as becomes the widows of a dead chief. But have no fear. The killer of lions will not be killed by the white man."

He rode slowly away. Coming to the gate of the *kraal,* he turned in his saddle and shouted,

"*Shlahla gaghle*—remain in peace!"

"Aye!" They cried after him. "*Hamba gaghle*—may thy path be smooth!"

He waited just a moment longer, then urged the horse to a gallop and was quickly swallowed up in the darkness of the night.

WHEN THE MAJOR, his clothes and flesh torn by the *Wachenbitje* thorns, tired, bruised, hungry and sad at heart, came to his camp at the top of the *kopje* overlooking the valley, he was astonished to see a camp-fire burning brightly. Savory odors came to his nostrils. As he neared, a form sprang up from beside the fire and uttered one pregnant word:

"*Baas!*"

"Ah! Is it you, Mytata?" The Major reeled for very weariness.

"Nay, *baas!* Not Mytata, but Jim."

"Jim?" The Major laughed—a hollow laugh. "I once had a servant—closer to me than my shadow he was—named Jim. But he became a chief and forgot his *baas.*"

Jim led the Major to the fire and seated him in the camp-chair he had placed close by. He gently bathed his *baas's* cuts, removed his boots and gently rubbed the swollen ankles where the ropes had cut in.

"I am hungry," said the Major. "I have not eaten since yesterday's sunup. I must get food." He rose from his chair, but Jim gently pushed him back.

"The food is ready, *baas,*" he said, and brought him a plate of buck soup.

"Nay!" the Major protested. "It is not seemly that Mytata, the chief, should wait on a white man."

"But Jim may, *baas,*" the Hottentot pleaded.

The Major flashed him one of his old-time looks.

"Yes—Jim may," he assented.

"I have been a fool," said Jim happily, as, with each spoonful of the soup, strength came back to the Major.

"Yes, Jim?"

"Aye, *baas*—a very big fool. I thought that I would be happy having full authority over many people. I became puffed up with pride; I thought that my glory was greater than that of the sun."

"And is it not, Jim?"

"It is less than that of the firefly, *baas*. Does the *baas* feel stronger now?"

"Aye. All my strength has returned to me."

"Then take this, *baas*"—Jim handed the Major a *sjambok*—"and beat me with it."

The Major took it and, rising to his feet, raised his hand. Jim waited expectantly, but the blow did not fall. Instead, the Major threw the *sjambok* to the ground.

"No! Not that, Jim. All is forgotten. Tomorrow I go my way, and you—you shall return to your people. I will give you more goods—all that I have—and you shall be richer than any chief in the country."

"But I shall not return. I go with you, *baas*. The *kraal* is a fair place, but it is oversmall. The beer is impotent; the women folk are shrews— all of them. I have no place with the people of the valley. I go with you, *baas*. You know me for what I am—they sing my praises now because they think *I* killed the lion. But I know that but for you I would now be dead."

"It is not well to boast," commented the Major. "You no doubt said that you went all powerful with the fire-stick?"

"Aye," Jim confessed. "They tested me—and because you were there, unseen, I seemed to prove my worth. That was a good shot, *baas*."

"Not bad," said the Major in English. "Not half bad." Jim grinned. "And so, my dear old chap, you would renounce the pomp and ceremony of authority?"

"Aye, *baas*. Damme—yes!"

"Having learned," the Major continued, "that a gaily painted drum makes a deuce of a row but is quite empty."

"Empty—yah, *baas*."

The Major felt in his tunic pocket for his monocle and exclaimed, "Oh, what a bally nuisance!"

"What is it, *baas?*"

"We trek early tomorrow morning, Jim?"

"Yah, *baas*." Jim's face beamed.

"Yes—very early, Jim. I must get me a new monocle—a platinum-rimmed one, I think. They must be jolly topping."

"Golly, yes, *baas*."

"I'm going to sleep now, Jim. Good night."

The Major climbed up into the wagon and in a few minutes was fast asleep. But Jim sat by the camp-fire. Sleep was far from him—he was too happy.

"Au-a! What a man!" he ejaculated softly. "And I thought, like a fool, that much beer, my wives and the flattering tongues of men could take his place. *Au-a!* He is a man among men, and I—I am Jim, his servant."

BLUE CLAY

I T WAS generally believed that Whispering Smith—he was more often called "Whip"—was in the confidence of all the criminals in South Africa.

Captain Breen, late of the Kimberley Police, was even more radical in his statements and infinitely more positive. At the same time, he frankly admitted that he had no definite proof to back up his statements which were to the effect that Smith engineered every robbery, planned every murder, and was the chief gainer in every illicit diamond buying deal.

Captain Breen was never given the chance of proving his statements for, shortly after they were given publicity, he was transferred to an outlying district and his official duties, from that time on, were strictly confined to native affairs.

As for Smith:

It was his habit, for he was a methodical man, to keep strict office hours. From nine to five he sat at his desk in a little room leading off the bar of his saloon. It was a neat, efficiently appointed office; it contained no superfluous furniture. A roll-top desk, one chair, a large safe, sundry letter files and a copying press—that was all. In the small, pot-bellied stove a fire was always burning no matter how hot the day. Smith believed that fire was the best destroyer of secrets entrusted to paper.

Most of the time at his office he spent working at his books— wherein names appeared with greater frequency than figures—or reading newspapers from every part of the world. He was an accomplished linguist.

Occasionally as he read he chuckled softly to himself, occasionally a muttered curse would pass his lips, and occasionally he would cut out an item and paste it in one of his books.

These clippings were nearly all accounts of missing men—wanted men; absconding cashiers, bankrupts, embezzlers, men who had made one step from the straight path of honesty and lacked the moral courage to face the music.

Such accounts as included a portrait and full description of the missing man, Smith pasted in a special book. This he, with delicious irony, had labeled "Black Sheep to be Redeemed."

All "wanted" men seemed to gravitate to South Africa—to Jo'burg or Kimberley—in those days, and Smith paid a bonus to any of his satellites who could indentify among the constant stream of newcomers to the diggins a man, or woman, whose dossier was in his file.

No one liked Smith; all feared him. Not a physical fear—he was undersized and notoriously afraid of firearms—but the instinctive fear which many men have for snakes. He had ways to make men come to heel—ways of treachery—and the men who haunted the underworld of South Africa acknowledged him as their superior, and jumped to obey the whip-like urge of his whispering voice.

This morning Smith seemed to be in a good humor and, as he hastily, yet thoroughly, examined the pile of foreign newspapers on his desk, the scissors and paste were in constant requisition. His chuckles were staccato, like the reports of a rapid-fire gun. Then, the newspapers having been attended to, he stamped loudly on the floor—twice.

The door behind him, leading to the bar of the saloon, opened instantly and closed behind a tall, gray-haired wreck of a man. "Yes, sir?"

Smith did not turn his head; did not move.

"Tell Solly and Brimmer I want them."

The door quickly closed again behind the gray-headed one.

Smith opened his "Black Sheep" book and turned the pages slowly, stopping occasionally to read an item or to closely scrutinize a portrait. He was still engrossed in his task when the door opened again and two men entered.

One, he who answered to the name of Solly, was a horsey-looking fellow, wearing a loud-checked suit and a bowler hat which was cocked jauntily over one ear. His face was unhealthily pale, save for the boiled lobster scarlet of his prominent nose. His fingers were long and slender—the fingers of an artist. They were the tools of his trade; with them he filled his pockets with other people's money.

His companion's well set up figure suggested military training. His alertness and general bearing was in striking contrast to Solly's slinking posture.

The average man in the street would have accepted Brimmer as an honest man, but a close observer would have noted his bloodshot eyes and the furtive look of fear which was in them.

Both men waited in silence, exchanging uneasy glances, then, believing that Smith was unaware of their presence, Brimmer shuffled his feet by way of announcement.

Smith turned over another page of his book. The minutes passed.

Then Solly, prefacing his words with a dry, apologetic cough, said, "We're here, boss. Ba said you wanted us. We—"

He stopped short as Smith whirled round in his chair.

"You talk too much," he said. His voice was barely above a whisper, yet Solly and Brimmer quailed. "Come here," he went on, and pointed to one of the portraits in his book.

"Got anything on this Johnny, yet?" he asked.

"No. He won't gamble and he keeps to himself, boss." This was Solly's contribution.

"And you, Brimmer?"

The man shook his head. "Not a thing."

"Well—" Smith sighed—"What do you suppose I keep you in the police for? I want him badly. Go and get him for me—both of you. Here—"

From his desk-drawer he took a medium-sized, uncut diamond and handed it to Solly.

"Same as usual boss?" asked Brimmer.

Smith nodded.

TWO HOURS later, at the sound of voices raised in anger, Smith leaned back in his chair and smiled contentedly.

"Don't you let him take you, cully!" That was Solly's whining voice. "The police are all crooks; he wants to frame you."

"Come on now," it was Brimmer speaking, "young feller."

"I tell you I won't." The third speaker was evidently excited and a little bit afraid. "I've done nothing. What do you want me for?"

There was the sound of a scuffle then Smith went to the door and opened it.

At the far end of the room, Brimmer was arguing with a stranger, and Solly was standing close by urging the stranger to resist arrest.

Excepting these three, and the barmaid who watched the men with incurious eyes, the barroom was empty.

As Smith entered Solly yelled, "Go and tell Whip Smith all about it, Kid. He'll settle this—in his place; he'll help you out."

"What's all this about, officer?"

At the sound of Smith's voice Brimmer turned and said apologetically, "I was trying to persuade this man to go quietly with me."

"What's he done?"

"He's an I.D.B. He tried to sell a stone to Solly."

"You'd better go quietly," Smith advised the stranger. "No good making a fuss—it'll only make the case look blacker against you. Besides, I won't have any scrapping in my saloon—it gives the place a bad name."

"If he wants to take me, he's got a fight on his hands," the other replied hotly. "I'm no I.D.B., and I'm not going with this man until I can find some friends to go with me. I've been warned that some of the plain-clothes men are always trying to frame a man."

"You'll either come quietly," Brimmer began threateningly, "or—"

He glanced significantly at his revolver which he had drawn from his hip pocket.

"Now don't be impatient," Smith said complacently. "Suppose you both come into my office and talk it over."

He turned and entered the room, followed, after a moment's hesitation, by the stranger and Brimmer.

The policeman softly closed the door.

"Now," said Smith—he had seated himself in his chair and, leaning back, his finger-tips pressed together, had assumed a judicial air—"what have you against this man, Brimmer?"

"As I said before, he's an I.D.B., Mr. Smith. No doubt of that. I saw him try to sell a stone to Solomon.

"It's a lie," the accused man said hotly. "I was having a drink at the bar with Solly—don't know why he asked me to come in; hardly know him—when this chap came up and made his ridiculous accusations."

"Lies pretty, don't he?" Brimmer said mockingly.

"Have you searched him?"

"No, Mr. Smith."

"Well—suppose you do that now. If he hasn't the stone on him, he's free. If he has—"

A shrug of the shoulders completed Smith's sentence.

"That's good sense, Mr. Smith," Brimmer said as he advanced to carry out the suggestion.

The man backed into a corner.

"I tell you I won't let you search me."

"Then suppose I do it?" Smith suggested. "You don't suspect me of crooked work, surely?"

"All right," the other assented reluctantly.

Methodically Smith went through the suspected man's pockets and placed on the desk the articles he found there—a watch, penknife, a handful of coins, the photograph of a buxom, motherly-looking woman, and a bundle of letters.

Finally, from the top vest-pocket, he extracted a medium-sized, uncut diamond.

The expression on his face was one of pained surprise, but Brimmer cried exultantly, "There! What did I tell you?"

The stranger looked at the diamond in amazement.

"It's a frame," he cried angrily. "Someone put it there. I—"

"Are you trying to say that I framed you?"

"Er—no, Mr. Smith," the other faltered. "I watched you closely while you were searching me. You found it in my pocket—I'm sure of that. But that man," he pointed at Brimmer, "must have put it there."

"That's what they all say," scoffed the policeman. "Come on, young 'un."

He jangled the handcuffs suggestively.

The "young 'un's" muscles tensed and he seemed about to make a break. Then, suddenly, he relaxed and held out his hands.

"All right," he said submissively. "I'll go quietly."

All fight had left him, and when Brimmer fastened on the hand-cuffs he seemed about to break down.

Smith eyed him keenly and, as the policeman was about to leave the room with his prisoner, he said, "Wait a minute, Brimmer. I'd like to have a talk with this chap—alone. I believe he's innocent."

Brimmer hesitated.

"It's not the usual thing," he said, "but I guess he's safe enough with you."

Smith nodded.

"I'll be personally responsible for him. Go and order yourself a few drinks. Tell Lizzie they're on the house.

"And now," he continued as the door closed behind Brimmer, "we'll have a nice little confidential chat. Just we two. You say you know nothing of the stone?"

He picked up the diamond which Brimmer had carelessly left on the desk.

"I saw it for the first time when you took it out of my pocket," the other said earnestly.

"Humph! Do you know, I'm inclined to believe you. But can you prove it?"

The other shook his head.

"I don't see how I could—it's my word against Brimmer's."

"And mine," Smith added softly. "Of course if he called me as witness, I'd have to tell the truth."

The other agreed glumly.

"And the penalty for I.D.B. is a long term of hard labor on the Breakwater. You know that?"

"Yes, I know that."

"It's a pity," said Smith sorrowfully. "Yes, it's a great pity—Mr. Tom Burton."

The other's eyes opened wide, his jaw dropped.

"What—why—?" he exclaimed. "How did you know my name? What—?"

"What else do I know? you would ask. I know a great deal. For instance—what do you think of this?"

He turned to his book—his Black Sheep book—and read slowly:

"Police Circular. Number 19785
"Reward offered for information leading to the arrest of Tom Burton. Age, 24. Height, 5 feet, eleven inches. Weight, fourteen stone. Brown eyes. Light brown hair."

Smith stopped and looking up, asked pleasantly, "Shall I go on? Or would you like me to read the account of the young cashier named Tom Burton who absconded with the pay-roll? Or would you like to see a picture of yourself before you grew a mustache? Or, better still, I have an account of your former social activities. You were quite an athlete, I should say— here's a touching interview with your mother."

"Stop!" The command was a hoarse croak. "What's your game, Mr. Smith?"

"My game? I don't quite understand."

"Oh, yes you do. I don't know just what, but I'm paying back the money I—I stole. In two or three months I'll have paid it all back."

"That's very noble of you—very, I'm sure," said Smith soothingly, but his smile acted like a goad on Burton.

"What's your game?" he cried again. "I don't care what it is. I've gone straight, I tell you, since I came out here."

"My dear boy, I don't want to interfere with you, but, of course, I must be honest with myself and pass on my knowledge to the police. Not to do so would make me an accessory after the fact. And as to your going straight out here—there's this to be explained, you know."

He toyed absently with the diamond.

"But," he continued quickly, "I think I can make everything all right with Brimmer about this, and forget the rest, if you can see your way clear to help me in a little deal I want to put through."

"I won't do anything crooked."

"You have no choice, my boy—not that what I want you to do is illegal. But here's how we stand: Either you promise to help me with my little job—and I warn you that people who break their promises to me don't live very happily; you'll soon find that out—or I call

Brimmer in and tell him all I know. Take your choice. Implicit obedience to me, or ten years on the Breakwater."

Burton made no comment, but maintained a thoughtful silence until Smith began to read softly:

"Mrs. Burton expressed implicit confidence in her son's ability to make good and his desire to make full restitution. She—"

"Stop!" shouted Burton. Then in quieter tones he asked, "What do you want me to do?"

Smith's smile was one of complete satisfaction and he rubbed his hands briskly together.

"I'll tell you," he said.

"TOMORROW, JIM," said the Major, "we shall do ourselves the honor of calling on our friends, the Peters."

"That is good, *Baas*," the Hottentot replied with a chuckle. "We have been camped in this place too long. Here we do nothing but eat, sleep and drink; and that is good, but of itself it is less than nothing, for soon one no longer desires to eat, or drink, or sleep. But where do we go after that, *Baas?* To the diamond town to play the game?"

"Who knows, Jim, where the wind will blow the leaf?" The Major— men who didn't know him called him that damned fool dude, but the police of South Africa knew him to be a particularly quick-witted I.D.B., an all-round athlete and a prince of good fellows—slapped impatiently at the hordes of mosquitoes which were feasting on the exposed portions of his anatomy. "What matter is it, if we are no longer to be troubled by these plagues?"

The Major was a fugitive from the law—had been longer than he cared to remember, but his crimes were, in a sense, political crimes; merely little matters of buying diamonds illegally; his protest against the unjust—at least he, and many other men thought them unjust— Draconian laws. Lately he had been spending—and for a very good reason, not unconnected with his business—considerable time in a very inaccessible part of the country near the Portuguese border, but he now felt that it would be safe to emerge. Things could be adjusted.

So he and Jim broke camp with the dexterity due to long experience in the bush, and arrived at the outlying Peters Homestead. Since the Major had, some months previously, joined Peters in checking what might have been a serious native rebellion, and been largely instrumental in saving the lives of the Dutchman's own family, he was always sure of a warm welcome from old Peters, his wife, and his charming daughter. But on his arrival this time he was quick to notice a change in his relations with the family. Peters and his wife were as cordial as ever, but the Major did not find the capable Dorothy as companionable as before. On his previous visits he and the girl had been fast comrades. They had haunted together and explored the surrounding Ropjes; had helped with the work on the farm and exchanged confidences. Dorothy could ride, shoot and follow game spoor as well as he could—and there were few men who could compete with the Major on equal terms—but now the Major found these relations changed and that a new element had entered into the Peters' household. This was a young stranger named Burton who had come to the homestead a month or so before. He had said he was a botanist and claimed acquaintance with some of Mrs. Peters' English friends and was urged to make the Peters farm his headquarters.

He rode indifferently, his shooting was atrocious, and he was as a babe in the bush. Yet, strange to say, Dorothy Peters, whose capabilities the Major knew so well, now rode, shot as badly and was even more idiotic in the bush than the young stranger. Her air of self-reliance suddenly vanished; she squealed and appealed to Mr. Burton for protection at the sight of a harmless grass snake, and began to be interested in fine needle work and other feminine arts. The Major was relegated to the position of her father's friend.

Thinking of all this, the Major, who felt a little hurt at the desertion, yet understood it, began to be very curious as to young Mr. Burton.

"What do you think of this white man, Jim?" he asked one night, when he and the Hottentot were doing a turn on guard duty over the Peters' corn-patch.

At the back of them was a precipitous *kopje* which was the home of numerous baboons, and it was from them there was danger to the corn. The Major and his servant were seated on a rough platform that swayed alarmingly at their slightest movement, and perhaps the Major had put more vehemence than was actually safe into his question, for Jim's reply was a cautious, "Careful, *Baas*. There is little between us and the ground; little but a great distance of emptiness."

Then he turned his attention to the Major's request for an opinion. "That is a hard question, *Baas*," he said thoughtfully. "At times he is in all ways worthy—save that he is a hunter and continually seeks the company of Missy Dot. Then again he seems to be a man who plans evil—or who is afraid that evil will overtake him."

"So—you, too, have noticed that, Jim?"

"Oah, yes, *Baas.* Bai Jove, rippin' damme."

Jim delighted to use the few English phrases he knew, irrespective of their appropriateness.

The Major laughed quietly.

When he spoke again it was in English and, though he addressed himself to Jim, he was really thinking his thoughts out loud. And Jim listened intently as if every word was pregnant with meaning to him.

"He's no botanist, Jim, this chappie Burton," the Major drawled. "If he's one, I'm one; and, I'll give you my word of honor, I know nothing about the flowers that bloom in the spring, tra-la."

"Tra-la! Yah, *Baas,*" Jim interposed gravely.

"What? Oh yes. Tra-la of course, Jim. Well, I'm quite sure he's not a botanist and that means he's pretending to be something he's not. Therefore he's a bally fraud. Q.E.D. What?"

Jim started violently.

"Yah, *Baas.* What? Gorblessme."

"And," continued the Major, "Miss Dorothy is—I think—in love with him; and he with her. And that won't do. Not if he's a fraud. I wonder what his game is. Could it be old Peters' gold claim he's after? I know there's a rich reef somewhere on the farm; old Peters offered to show it to me one day. I rather admire the dear old chap's refusal to work it. It might make him rich, but what a hell the miners would make of this place. It 'ud be the Rand over again. Well! On second thoughts, I don't think I'll leave too soon. I want to find out what Burton's up to. Peters is too blooming trusting; he was even ready to trust me, the Major, the infamous I.D.B." The Major smiled bitterly. "Still—"

"*Baas!*" The Hottentot interposed.

"Yah, Jim?"

"A Shenzi from over the river came to the homestead today."

"Yah?"

"Yah, *Baas.* He had a letter for *Baas* Burton."

"And you only tell me now?"

"I had forgotten, *Baas,* until this moment."

"And why do you remember now?"

"Because—look, *Baas.*"

Jim pointed across the river, a mile or more away. A tiny flame of light was discernible.

"It is a white man's camp, *Baas.* The Shenzi was sent by the men who camp there."

The Major nodded. He did not question Jim's statement. If the Hottentot said it was a white man's camp and that the Shenzi was that white man's messenger, it was so. The Hottentot had an almost uncanny intuition, deductive powers—call it what you will.

"We will pay them a visit in the morning, Jim."

"That is good, Baas. But must we stay here all night? I desire room to stretch my legs. Let us call the black dogs"—Jim was very contemptuous of the natives of the district—"who work for the Dutchman, Peters. Let them keep their brothers, the apes, away from the corn-patch. If we are to trek in the morning we need sleep."

But the Major shook his head.

"In a little while, Jim. I don't wish to hear the foolish babble of a young man and maiden, or listen to the aimless talk of the maiden's parents. When they are all sleeping, then we will go."

The Major's tone was bitter; so bitter that Jim looked at him in alarm, saying: "Does it hurt the sun if a child or a woman say, 'I like best the moon?'"

Jim stopped abruptly; his muscles tensed and he held up his hand in a warning for silence.

There was a stealthy rustling in the outer fringes of the corn-patch.

The Major took up his rifle, but lowered it as Jim shook his head.

"It is not the baboons, Baas," he whispered, "but a man—a white man."

"Can you see him, Jim?"

"Nay. He keeps well in the shadow of the corn. But in a little while—ah! There. See? It is the Baas Burton and he goes to the white man's camp across the river."

"Ha!"

The Major's eyes narrowed as he watched the tall figure of Burton emerge from the corn-patch and hasten down the hillside.

"We will follow, Jim," said the Major and climbed down the watch tower's rickety ladder.

"There is no need for such haste, Baas," Jim grumbled. "He travels like an ostrich running before a pack of wild dogs. He cannot keep a straight trail. Also, he makes more noise than a rogue elephant. We cannot lose him."

"You talk too much—come."

At a swift pace the Major led the way through the corn-patch and Jim, wondering not a little at the Major's mood, followed closely behind.

Yet, notwithstanding the speed, their progress was noiseless, and not a stalk was broken.

As they came out of the corn their attention was attracted by an excited jabbering to the right of them. There, four or five baboons were watching another which was caught in a trap. And such a trap! Only monkeys and men—some men—could be caught by it.

It was a circular hole in the hard, rocklike earth, about a foot deep and of a diameter barely large enough to admit a monkey's paw. In the bottom of the hole nuts had been placed and these the baboon discovered and, putting in his paw, had grabbed a handful, looking forward to a luxurious meal easily earned.

But his fist was so distended with the nuts that he could not withdraw it from the hole; neither would he let go of the nuts but struggled—and would continue to struggle through the remainder of the night until overcome by exhaustion—hoping to gain his freedom and the nuts, too.

"Shall I kill him, Baas?"

"Nay, Jim. He shall be our guard. The others will watch him and give him much advice. They will forget they are hungry."

"Some men are like monkeys," said Jim. "I was once caught in a trap even as that one is; ay, I had four wives. But I opened my hand and let them go and so I escaped from the trap."

The Major turned away impatiently from the chattering baboons intent upon following Burton, and Jim followed, shadow-like.

Immediately beyond the small plateau which Peters had culti-vated, the *kopje* dropped sharply, becoming, in some places, quite precipitous. The trail was little better than a goat path and, judging by the scrambling noises ahead of them, Burton was having great difficulty in negotiating it.

But the Major, despite the fact that the soles of his heavy shoes were studded with nails, experienced no more trouble than the shoe-less, sure-footed Hottentot. He had to govern the speed of his descent by that of Burton's—and Burton was very slow.

Once they had reached the foot of the *kopje,* however, they were able to make better time. Here the trail broadened, and Burton broke into a run. Every once in a while he would leap high into the air, or swerve quickly from his course.

"He sees many snakes, Baas," Jim explained to the Major. "He jumps over them!"

"Keep quiet, Jim," the Major retorted sharply. "He may hear us."

"Then his ears must be keener than his eyes, Baas," the Hottentot said with a low chuckle.

The two were running almost abreast of Burton, but were keeping well under cover of the bush which lined the trail.

After a time they came to the river. It was the dry season and, save for a small pool about which hung a heavy smell of musk, the water had vanished. The white sandy bed looked like snow in the cold light of the moon. They watched Burton cross over to the other side. Silhouetted against the glaring whiteness he seemed unreal; like a caricature shown on a shadow-picture screen. Burton, the setting, everything, seemed to belong to another world—to a world of two dimensions.

"We cannot cross here, Baas," said Jim. "They will see us. Let us cross up there."

He pointed upstream where, about five hundred yards distance, the river made a sharp bend.

The Major made a gesture of dissent and said:

"That will take too long, Jim. Much may be said in the time we take to go to that place. I will cross here; they will not see me. But you—you will go up to the bend."

"But the Baas does not mean to go on alone? He will wait for me?"

"I will wait for you under the big tree which is close to their camp. Now go."

As Jim started off on the run the Major cautiously wormed his way down the steep bank and, having reached the bed of the river, made his way across it, crawling on his belly. He felt fairly secure for, unless someone was looking for him with seeing eyes, he was practically invisible. His white duck trousers, white tunic coat and the large white pith helmet he wore, blended in with the sand. The only thing of color about him was his rifle and that he trailed behind him. At a distance, and to a casual observer, it looked like a sluggish snake.

It took him over five minutes to cross that thirty yards of sand and, a few minutes later, he was hidden in a clump of bush under the baobab tree where Jim was to meet him.

He was chagrined to find that he could not get any closer to the camp of the strangers than he now was for—and so proving that they were no novices on the veldt—they had cleared away the bush around them, the tree marking the limit of their endeavors. But, though the Major was not near enough, and could not get near enough, to overhear their conversation, he was at least able to hear disjointed fragments and could see quite plainly the faces of the strangers who were seated about the camp-fire. Burton sat with his back to the Major, the four others facing him.

Three of the four were heavily bearded and wore the nondescript garb of prospectors. The fourth was clean-shaven and was dressed in black; he wore a white collar, a "choker." He seemed to be doing all the talking and his voice boomed sonorously.

"Where have I heard that voice before," the Major reflected. " 'Pon my soul, if I closed my eyes I could almost imagine that I was in church. He sounds like a bloomin' clergyman, dresses like one, too. I wonder if it's—? Oh, it must be—Holy Joe. If it is, we'll have some fun tonight—of a sort. Wish I could get a little nearer."

He listened intently, but could get no further definite clue to the identity of the man with the booming voice.

The conversation droned on, monotonously. Isolated words and phrases occasionally registered above the drone, and the Major made a mental note of them, endeavoring to supply the gaps between. But he made little progress.

The name "Smith," "Whip Smith," "Whispering Smith," was mentioned many times. And "Peters" and "gold claim."

The Major pricked up his ears as the girl's name was mentioned and wondered when, a few minutes later the word "marry" detached itself from the drone and came floating to him.

The voices grew louder now; there seemed to be differences of opinion; threats were passed back and forth.

"You're a bloody fool—""You'll do it, or—""Whip Smith 'ull get—" "Put that knife h'up, Joe."

Then the deep voice boomed out, "Shut up, you chaps. He's all right. Leave him to me. He's just a little nervous—that's all."

Then the drone commenced again.

But the Major had heard enough. He knew that Burton, the self-styled botanist, was an accomplice of the four men—who were Whispering Smith's men—and was planning with them to get hold of Peters' gold claim. In some way, the Major reasoned, they were going to work on Peters through Dorothy.

"Probably kidnap her or something like that, and hold her for ransom," he murmured.

That was enough for the Major. With what he had seen and overheard he could face Burton before the Peters family and show him up in his true light.

"He's a bally snake in the grass," the Major reflected, and smiled at his melodramatic phrasing. "But I wonder what Miss Dorothy will do when she finds her idol has feet of clay? She's such an all round good fellow that I'm sure she won't stand for this two-faced business. But, by Jove, it's worse than that. He's the villain of the piece. And what do villains do? Why, they try to marry the beautiful heroine so they can grab the filthy lucre. So that's it—if nothing happens."

The Major sighed, then continued.

"Yes; it means the end of Mister Botanist Burton. But, somehow, I don't feel awfully chipper about it—an' I ought to be. As a matter of fact I feel rather annoyed—and I'll be still more annoyed if this business means I've got to hang around here much longer. My word! If old Peters doesn't do as I suggested about his old claim after this, he jolly well deserves to lose it.

"I wish Jim would come. He's been a deuced long time. Ha! Our friends over there are gettin' warmed up again."

The voices of the men around the fire were raised now in hot argument and above them all could be heard that of Burton.

"I tell you, I won't," he cried, and there was a note of finality in his voice.

He rose to his feet and walked slowly away.

The Major saw that the botanist's course would bring him within a few yards of his hiding place and he made ready to draw back still further into the shelter of the bush.

But this measure of caution was unnecessary for Burton had only advanced a few paces when the others sprang to their feet, as one man, and ran after him.

The man in black was the first to reach him, and grabbed Burton by his coat collar.

"Not so fast, my dear friend," he boomed. "We're not done with you yet."

Burton turned quickly, and with a wrench tore loose from the hold of the man in black and faced the four defiantly.

"I tell you I won't go on with it," he said with an air of assurance which was belied by the quiver in his voice.

That quiver, however, the Major conceded, might have been the mark of excitement.

"Well, now! So you won't go on with it?" Evidently the man in black was the spokesman of the four; the others seemed to be inarticulate. "Well—if you won't go on with it, you don't go. You stay here."

"You can't stop me." Burton was defiant. "I've played fair with you. I've warned you that the affair's all off. I might have led you on and trapped you."

"Yes, my dear boy. You've played fair with us—we're not denying that—and undoubtedly you'll get your reward in heaven. But you mustn't expect us to reward you. Oh no! And—you—stay—here!"

His hand shot out again, but Burton easily dodged it and countered with a right to the jaw which had all the force of his one hundred and seventy-five pounds behind it. Black clothes went over backward, falling to the ground with a jarring thud which knocked all the wind from his body.

It was all the Major could do to refrain from applauding the blow.

"Come on," Burton cried belligerently. "Who's next?"

Two of the men silently closed in on him—the Major wondered why they did not use their revolvers—and Burton retreated steadily before their advance. It was evidently his intention to get his back up against the baobab tree, but as soon as the men sensed his stratagem, they cast discretion aside and rushed him. The first he met and checked with a straight left, but the other got under his guard and grappled with him. Once again Burton proved his strength and the splendid condition he was in, for he lifted his assailant bodily and threw him from him, striking the third man in the chest and bowling him over. Then he turned to run, but the man in black had recovered from his fall and, leaping to his feet, rushed to the attack. Burton was forced to turn and meet him.

The man in black's fist-play was feeble, but it sufficed to hinder Burton from making his escape, and gave the other three time to join in the mêlée.

In their eagerness the four got in each other's way and, for a time, Burton held his own; the gasps and curses of his opponents punctuated his sledge-hammer blows. It seemed that Burton would win through, despite the odds against him.

Then the man in black disentangled himself from the fighters and, picking up a large stone, raised it, intending to bring it down on Burton's head.

And at that moment the Major decided that the fight had gone far enough.

Stepping out from his hiding place, his rifle at his hip, he called out, "Time, gentlemen."

At the sound of his voice the five turned to face him and raised their hands above their heads at the menace of his rifle.

"A very good mill," he drawled. "Not according to the rules of dear old Milord Queensberry, of course, but quite excitin'. And, I must say, save for the fact that you out-numbered Bruiser Bill Botanist Burton four to one, you fought quite fairly. Hitting in the clinches, of course, but that was to be expected. There was no kicking or biting. You fought quite like little gentlemen, and I'm sure you're not. No? But there was an exception I'm sorry to say. And the exception was the gentleman in black. It's Holy Joe, isn't it? I thought so. Your voice sounded deucedly familiar, dear ex-Reverend. Or perhaps you are not ex. It may be that you go on the premise that once a clergyman—always a clergyman."

"I've never been unfrocked, my dear fellow, and, let me tell you, I call this interference of yours most unheard of and uncalled for. This young man suffers from strange homicidal delusions and—er—"

"And—er—you were goin' to bash them out—and his brains in—with a stone. Is that it? Tut tut! But what I can't understand is why you didn't blow his brains out. You're all armed, aren't you? You all carry revolvers, I mean?"

"We have no desire to have the blood of a fellow creature on our hands. 'Those who take the sword will perish by the sword.' We do not wish to harm the dear boy. He is a soul to be saved."

"We wouldn't stand for no shootin'," growled one of the others. "We ain't murderers."

The Major regarded the speaker with interest.

"No? Then just what are you? Is it that—?"

He stopped abruptly and with incredible swiftness brought his rifle to his shoulder and covered Holy Joe, who thinking that the Major was off his guard had dropped his hand to his revolver.

"No. That won't do at all," the Major said in hurt tones. "Won't do at all, Joe. I don't want to have your blood on my hands, or my blood on your pure soul. So put up your hands again—quick."

The drawl was absent from the Major's voice now, and Holy Joe quickly obeyed the peremptory command.

"And now," continued the Major lapsing into the drawl again, "I'm goin' to ask Mr. Burton to disarm you all. That done we will leave you to your own sweet selves.

"But to make sure you won't be tempted to do any shootin' while he's taking up the collection, I'm goin' to show you that I'm not half a bad shot myself. Rather vainglorious of me, perhaps, but boys will be boys. Now for a mark. I think that's a hyena sneaking up to your camp, don't you, Joe? I hate hyenas. They remind me of some men; or should I say that some men remind me of hyenas? However, be that as it may, that's goin' to be my target. Of course the moonlight's deceptive, and I may miss. About two hundred yards I should say, and the bullet will go within a few inches of your sanctimonious nose, Joe, so don't move."

Without seeming to take aim, his eyes were apparently fixed on the men, the Major fired.

There was a loud explosion; the gun flew from the Major's grasp and, reeling backward, he lost his balance and fell.

Holy Joe was quick to take advantage of this sudden and unlooked for change of fortune. His hand leaped to his revolver—he was counted one of the quickest men on the draw in South Africa—and covering Burton, he shouted to the others to take care of the Major.

But they had anticipated him and, almost coincidentally with the bursting of the rifle and the Major's staggering fall, had pounced upon him. His struggles being weak and spasmodic, they quickly secured his hands and feet with their belts. That done, they carried him over to the camp-fire, preceded by Holy Joe and his prisoner, Burton. There they dumped the Major unceremoniously on the ground and getting a long *reim* from their wagon which was nearby, bound Burton.

Then, at Holy Joe's orders, they drove two stout stakes into the ground about fifteen feet apart and, turning the Major over on his face, tied his feet securely to one of the stakes. Burton they treated in a similar fashion at the other. The hands of the prisoners, stretched out over their heads, were lashed firmly together, and it would be hard to conceive of a more secure method of lashing two men. They were absolutely helpless.

Holy Joe chuckled.

"That will hold them," he said. "Dust they are and to dust returneth. But we won't take any chances. Bill, you and Jake will stay here—more to keep the hyenas and wild dogs away than to watch these beauties. You won't have to bother about them. They can't budge an inch. So you would show me how to shoot, eh, Major? That's what they call you, isn't it? Such vanity! And such a prodigious fall!"

"What hit me?" asked the Major. His voice was muffled, for he could hardly lift his head from the ground.

"Why, you fool, your rifle exploded."

"Oh! I must have got some sand in the barrel when I was crossing the river. What a bally ass I am. But it doesn't matter. I couldn't have hit the beastly hyena anyway. I don't know anything about rifles. I wish you'd let me get up. It's beastly uncomfortable stretched out on the ground this way. I'm getting my mouth full of dirt, ants are crawling down my back, and this other Johnny keeps strugglin' so that the ropes are cutting into my wrist."

"You'll stay that way for quite a while, my poor deluded fool. It'll teach you to attend strictly to your own affairs in future. Come on, Dale."

"Just a minute," said the man called Jake. "Where are you and Dale goin' to, an' wot's yer game? I don't fancy much bein' left 'ere."

"Nor does Hi. 'Ow does we know you won't play us dirty?"

"Don't be silly," Holy Joe explained. "I'd take you, but you both talk like gutter rats and that would spoil the trick I'm going to play. Dale knows when to speak and when to hold his tongue. He'll almost pass for a gentleman."

"But wot is yer game?"

"A very simple one which, D.V., I'll have no difficulty in playing. I'm going to tell Miss Peters that *Mister* Burton has been seriously hurt and needs her at once. If I know women—and I flatter myself I do—she won't stop to question the time of night, or the strangeness of it all, but will be ready to come with us at once."

"Yus—I can believe that. But supposes 'er h'old man an' woman come, too?"

"That will be quite all right. We can manage them, too. The more the merrier. Come on, Dale."

He and the man he addressed walked over to the horses which were tethered to the wheel of the wagon, saddled two, mounted, and galloped swiftly away.

THE OTHER two men, having got their rifles from the wagon, sat down on their blanket rolls which they had pulled up to the fire—the night air was chilly—lighted their pipes and puffed contentedly.

"I say, old fellows," the Major called out presently, "Won't you release us? It's bally cold, you know, and I give you my word I won't try to escape."

"You stay quiet, mister," Bill replied. "You 'eard wot Joe said. We ain't goin' ter take any chances."

"But this won't do at all, really. I tell you what. Let me in on your little game. I'll be satisfied with a fifth share—and I can help you a lot."

The two men guffawed loudly but made no reply; neither did they respond to the Major's taunts and maledictions. He had a caustic tongue and he gave it full play hoping to sting the men from their state of indifference. But they seemed deaf to it all and, finally, he was obliged to give it up. The strain of keeping his head turned toward them was too great.

He looked now straight ahead of him—full into the eyes of Burton.

"Case of when thieves fall out?" he said contemptuously.

Burton flushed, but said quietly.

"Yes. You have every right to say that. But how about you? You were offering to go in with them."

"And do you think I would?"

The answer came without the slightest hesitation.

"No. You see I've heard a great deal about you—before I came up here, and from Dorothy. But I don't quite understand. If you didn't mean to have anything to do with these men—why are you here?"

"I was followin' a sneak of a chap who was plannin' to rob his host."

The Major watched the boy keenly, but the other did not seek to avoid his gaze.

Suddenly, perhaps it was the memory of the good fight Burton had made, the Major said softly, "Suppose you tell me all about it?"

"I'd like to—from the beginning, if I may."

The Major nodded and in a low voice, without any hesitation Burton told his story. He did not whine, made no attempt to excuse his actions, but in the unbiased tone of a judge instructing a jury, told of his life at home in England; of the temptations which broke down his moral stamina leading to the pilfering of the bank's petty cash; of his escape to Africa and his remittances home which were gradually wiping out his debt.

"In another three months I would have been all square," he said, "and then Smith got hold of me. That man's a devil."

He went on to tell how Smith had framed him, threatening to have him arrested as an I.D.B. if he did not help with Smith's plans to get possession of Peters' gold claim.

"And just what part were you supposed to play?" questioned the Major.

"I was—" and now for the first time Burton had difficulty in telling his story—"I was to make love to and marry Miss Peters. I was to elope with her, if I couldn't get old Peters' assent. That's why Holy Joe's here—he was to marry us and keep an eye on me."

"But I don't see how that would help Smith. Your marryin' Miss Peters, I mean."

"Smith said that Peters would tell his son-in-law all about his affairs, and, for his daughter's sake, would give up his claim rather than let her husband be sent back to England to face trial as a thief."

"I see," the Major said reflectively. "You mean to say that Smith doesn't know where the reef is?"

"Yes. He knows where it is, but he can't work it unless Peters is out of the way, or gives his permission."

"Uh! Well, why didn't you go on with the plan?"

"I couldn't."

"Why not? Wouldn't Miss Dorothy accept you?"

The Major's eyes gleamed hopefully as he waited for the answer.

"Because she did."

"Did what?"

"Accept me."

"And you—er—dared to ask her?"

"Yes. But I told Mr. Peters first all about my trouble in England. He was a brick. He advanced me enough money to clear up that matter. Then I asked Dorothy."

"I see. And did you tell Peters about this other matter?"

Burton's face fell.

"No. Like a damned fool, I didn't. I thought if I came here tonight and told Holy Joe that the thing was all off, he would go away. I never dreamed he'd try anything like this. Now he'll get Dorothy and threaten—and perhaps do—all sorts of things to her and so compel her father to give up the claim. What a damned fool I am."

"Yes, you're a damned fool," the Major said dryly, "but I think that's partly because you are very young. Now do stop trying to get loose. They've done a deuced good job with their tying up, and the more you struggle the tighter the knots get."

Burton obediently gave up his futile struggles and was about to speak again when the raucous cry of a gray lourie sounded from the vicinity of the baobab tree.

The Major chuckled softly, and then laughed at the look of indignation in Burton's eyes.

After a short interval the cry sounded again—"Go-away!" This time the bird was, apparently, perched in the bush back of the wagon.

Again silence and then, "Go-away! Go-away! Go-away!"

The bird had flown back to the baobab tree and its cry was triumphant.

"Blast that bloomin' pest," said Bill. "I'd like to wring it's bloomin' neck. Fair gave me a start, it did. I was nearly asleep."

"Me, too. I wishes Joe and Dale 'ud 'urry back. I wants ter go ter sleep. Lumme, but h'its cold."

Jake rose stiffly and stretched himself yawningly.

He examined the two prisoners, satisfied himself that they were still fast bound and was about to return to his seat when a crimson glare just beyond the wagon held his attention. He rubbed his eyes and looked again.

Then one of the horses whinnied in fear and Jake cried excitedly, "Bill, the bush's hon fire. Come on—we got ter move the bleedin' 'orses and wagons or we'll 'ave ter walk 'ome."

He rushed over to the wagon, quickly followed by Bill, who cursed that "bleedin' fool of a Dale. Hi told 'im ter be careful where 'e frew 'is cigs."

For a while the two were busy; moving the horses and wagon away from the danger zone; beating out the flames with branches of *mapani.*

And so they did not see a dark form creep toward their prisoners from the direction of the baobab tree.

But the Major was looking for just that.

"Jim never fails," he said to Burton, who was overjoyed at the thought of the nearness of freedom. "But he's been a deuce of a long while coming. I'll have to give the old beggar what ho!"

The Hottentot had now reached them and was cutting at the *reims* which tied his *baas's* feet to the stake. Then he cut the Major's hands loose from Burton's and, his Baas freed, cut the remaining ropes which bound Burton's feet to the other stake.

"I would have come sooner, Baas," he explained, "but that lions were drinking at the pool above the bend in the river. And Jim climbed a tree—quick. Golly dam yes."

"All right, Jim. First get the rifles; they left them on their blankets, and then rub Baas Burton's ankles."

"But why do we stay here," Burton exclaimed impatiently as he took the rifle from Jim. "Let's hurry to the homestead."

"It is better to wait here. If Holy Joe's plan worked, and I expect it will, he'll be back in a little while. We can deal with him better here than on the trail. Remember he's mounted, and we don't want to shoot—unless we have to."

Burton nodded assent.

"My hands feel as if a million needles were sticking to them," he said.

The Major smiled understandingly.

"The fire dies down, Baas," Jim warned. "It was only a grass fire, and the grass was very thin. In a little while he men will return."

"Go back to the baobab tree, Jim, and wait there. Have no fear. All is well now—unless there's sand in this barrel, too," he added as an afterthought. "But a thing like that doesn't happen twice in a night."

Quickly, snake-like, Jim made his way back to the cover of the bush.

"Now, Burton, we'll lie down just as we were before. Let 'em think we're still bound. Don't want to hold 'em up until we're sure they can't break away. If they do, they'll be able to warn Holy Joe and Dale; then we'll be in a hell of a fix. And if we have to fire—the chances are Joe'll hear the shot and that 'ud put him on guard."

The two resumed their former positions on the ground and waited confidently for the return of Bill and Jake.

They did not have long to wait before the two men, muttering angry curses, returned to their camp-fire and seated themselves on the blanket rolls. They were both very tired and cross so did not notice that their rifles had disappeared.

Consequently when the Major and Burton suddenly sprang to their feet and shouted, "Hands up!" Jake and Bill, looking as if they were face to face with supernatural agency, made no show of resistance.

"It's a fair do, mister," Jake said. "And hi ain't a bit sorry. Treat hus easy. But 'ow yer got loose, beats me."

"Get their revolvers, Burton," the Major ordered and was quickly obeyed.

"Now you, Jake, get down on your belly with your feet against that stake. Tie him tightly, Burton. That's rippin'. Now you, Bill. But wait. Take off your hat and jacket first—you'll wear mine, and I'll wear yours. Fair exchange, eh? Good. Now down you get."

Bill got down and presently the two were tied as securely as the Major and Burton had been.

The Major added a final warning.

"You'd better keep quiet. If you do anything to let Holy Joe—and he'll be here soon—know how things are, you will be most frightfully sorry that your mothers ever taught you to speak. Do I make myself clear? I do? That's splendid."

The Major put on the hat and coat discarded by Bill and, moving the blanket rolls so that their backs would be toward the trail along which Holy Joe and his party would come, he and Burton sat down to wait.

After long minutes Jim, hidden in the bush near the big tree, sounded the cry of the Go-away bird.

"They're coming," said the Major. "Hold yourself together youngster, and don't go off half-cocked."

As he spoke, Holy Joe and Dale galloped up the trail and reined in close to the fire. They were leading a third horse to which was strapped a girl.

"We've got her," Joe said triumphantly as he dismounted. "She smelled a rat just as we came to the river, and we had to use a little force. Not much, of course. Just bound her lightly, and put a gag in her mouth. The little vixen nearly bit my thumb off. Come and help us get her into the wagon. Her old man's close behind. We'll nab him, too. He's walking; couldn't catch another horse. Bill! Jake! Hell, what's the matter? Wake up and give us a hand."

A loud report was the answer and his helmet flew from his head as if pulled by invisible wires.

The Major and Burton had risen to their feet and, as they turned to face Holy Joe, the Major had fired.

"Just to show you I'm really a good shot, reverend sir," said the Major. "Yes; you'd better keep your hands up—how discerning you are. You, too, Dale. Funny how the tables have turned twice in one evening, isn't it, Joe? The trouble with you is, you overlooked the nigger in the woodpile, or, to be more explicit—the Hottentot in the bush.

"Go and take care of Miss Dorothy, Burton. I'll tend to these chaps."

Quickly Burton released the girl and took the gag from her mouth.

"I'm all right, Tom," she said in answer to his inquiring look. "But you?"

"I'm all right, too. But we'd have been in the soup had it not been for the Major."

The Major—with the aid of Jim he was lashing Holy Joe and Dale to the same stakes which accommodated Bill and Jake—looked around with a smile, and for the first time in many days put his monocle in his eye. The sight of it made Jim very happy.

"Don't you believe him, dear Miss Dorothy," the Major drawled. "Burton's a regular Goliath. Why he almost licked these four single handed. I think, if I were in your shoes, I'd—er—kiss him. Really! Of course his face is very dirty, and I think he'll have one—perhaps two—black eyes, and his nose has been bleedin'—still, don't you know, dirt sometimes covers a multitude of virtues. And diamonds are found beneath mud—call it blue clay, if you wish. Not that that's blue clay which so plentifully besmears dear old Burton's face, but the idea back of it's true, if you know what I mean."

"Yes," the girl replied quietly. "I understand—and thank you, Major."

And then Peters, large of frame, sadly out of breath, came running up to them.

"*Allehmahtig!*" he exclaimed. "What is all this? I heard a shot—but first, at the river, my girl screamed. What is it you would do?"

He looked belligerently from one to the other.

"It's all right, father," said the girl. "Come and sit down by the fire and we'll make the Major and Tom tell us all about it."

When the story was told Peters turned to the Major and gravely shook his hand.

"We are in your debt," he said. "What can I do? Everything, anything, we have is yours. Is it not so, daughter?"

"Yes, father."

"Do you mean that?" the Major exclaimed.

"Surely—yes," said Peters.

"And what do you say, Miss Dorothy?"

"Yes," she replied in a soft voice, but looked at him appealingly.

"Then," said the Major triumphantly, "I want you to promise me, Peters, to do as I advise about your gold claim. Don't you see, old chap, that as long as you don't work it yourself, you'll be constantly open to this sort of thing?"

"I'll write to the Imperial Syndicate people tomorrow," the Dutchman said slowly. "But, ma-an, is that all you would ask?"

"There's just one thing more—where is this claim of yours? Everybody seems to know all about it except me."

The Dutchman chortled.

"If a man does not know where to look he would never find it. The homestead is built on the richest outcropping and, wherever there is an out-crop, there I have built stables, grain sheds—anything to hide the cursed stuff from white men like those *verdoemte* swine yonder."

"I see. Now you dear people had better toddle off home. I'm goin' to stay by these Johnnies. There are a lot of things I want to tell them."

"Let the *kinder* go," the old Dutchman said gruffly. "I'll stay and keep watch with you, my son."

THREE WEEKS later Whispering Smith was hearing the report of a failure of one of his men.

"And," Holy Joe concluded, "Peters has sold his claim to the Imperial Syndicate on condition that they don't start mining operations for five years; don't import native labor; and bar liquor selling in the district—the old fool. As for the youngster, Burton, you can't get your hands on him again. He's squared up for that business with the bank, and you know the I.D.B. affair won't hold water. It's too bad, but if it hadn't been for the Major happening along—"

"Blast that monocled dude," Smith screamed, shaken for once out of his habitual calm. "Call in the men from the barroom. The order's out to get that fool, the Major. He's butted into too many of my plans; I'm going to get him. I'm going to hound him until he'll come crawling on his knees, begging for mercy."

A MAJOR
DEVELOPMENT

IN THE early days, when the plans for a railroad between Johannesburg and Delagoa Bay were first being considered by Kruger's Government, old Oom Speys secured Government blue-prints showing the route of the proposed railroad. How he got them is immaterial, but it is worth noting that his wife's second cousin was secretary to one of the assistant secretaries employed by the committee.

These blue-prints indicated that the railroad would enter the Transvaal at the far-eastern corner of Oom Speys' farm, and that a station, and custom house, would be built on the site of the Homestead.

On the strength of this, Oom Speys found no difficulty in selling his unproductive farm land to a rich syndicate. And his price was high!

The syndicate, after greasings several palms—specially that of Oom Speys' wife's second cousin—smelled a rat and disposed of their holdings, in small lots, to worthy settlers—thirty of them—who were quick to realize the opportunities the place offered. Even if the land was poor and sparsely watered, it was in close proximity to a proposed railroad, a border station, and a custom house.

For that, they were willing to pay high—and did.

But the railroad never came. It crossed the border some two hundred miles to the east, and after a long time—years later—the settlers discovered that old Oom Speys' blue-prints had been specially drawn for him.

All of which merely explains the existence of any town at all in such a benighted, God-forsaken, man-cursed spot; explains how Speysburg came into being, sweated and groaned through the long days of drought, and shivered and cursed through the months of rain.

And the settlers, their numbers augmented with the passing years, by dint of hard work and clever planning, made a living where Oom Speys had starved.

Normally the scattered township was one hundred percent, law-abiding, and old "Snorter" Jones, the mounted policeman on duty there, had nothing to do but examine the passes of native laborers, and see that all the dogs were registered.

"Ugh! I wouldn't know how to arrest a man now if I had to. Ugh!" He used to complain bitterly.

Then, in one day, the white population of the burg was increased by four men. Two came from the west, but not together; one from the north, and the third from no one knew where. And they were all law-breakers.

Three of them—the two from the west and the one from the north—were under the direction of "Whispering" Smith, who, men said, was the biggest rogue in South Africa. At his bidding men stopped at nothing—from stealing postage stamps to murder. In his little room at Kimberley, Smith planned. His plans perfected, he sent out his instructions, and a man was killed in Cape Town, or a rebellion staged in Mashonaland; a rich and prominent man was blackmailed in Jo'burg, or a chief's son in Bechuanaland was abducted and sent to work in the mines. Smith had a wonderful organization; none of his creatures ever thought of questioning his commands, and he carried his criminal efficiency to the extent of receiving, and filing, reports of jobs done by his operatives. A man who was rated A.1 in Smith's Blue Book belonged to the aristocracy of crime.

The two men from the west were rated C minus; the third, the man from the north, a plus B.

As for the fourth man—he was the first to arrive—he had many aliases, but was generally called the Major. He was admitted by members of the various Colonial police forces to be the slickest I.D.B. in South Africa. They had all sought—were still seeking—to arrest him in possession of illicitly bought diamonds, and they had all failed. He had held them up to ridicule, good-natured ridicule, again and again. Yet they all liked him—there was something crooked about the exceptions—he was so decent, and such a damned good sort.

He reached the outskirts of Speysburg about noon and, after telling Jim, his Hottentot servant, to outspan the mules and make camp in the shade of some nearby trees, rode up to the hotel, tied his horse to the hitching-rack and entered.

The barroom was empty, save for the barmaid, and her eyes opened with amazement. Men, perfectly tailored and sporting monocles, were not common in Speysburg.

"O mi gawd!" she exclaimed breathlessly.

He looked at her blankly. "Can you tell me where I'll find Mr. Jones?" he asked. "He's the constable here, I believe."

"What do you want with old Snorter?"

"He's an old chum of my boyhood days. We used to rob the flowers of their honey together."

"Ow! You're just makin' fun of me. Old Snorter's over fifty-five, and you can't be no more than thirty."

The Major sighed. "You flatter me— really. But where will I find him?"

"You won't. Won't find him I mean. Not until sundown or thereabouts. He went out to arrest a few niggers—or so he said. But, bless you, old Snorter wouldn't arrest a fly. He's too tender-'earted. But he'll be back by sundown. He's never late for scoff, and he eats then."

"But still I don't know where to find him."

The girl tossed her head, then hastily gabbled off directions for getting to the police quarters.

"Thank you," the Major said when she paused for breath. "I'll have no difficulty in finding the place, I'm sure. And now, if you'll give me a 'local' I'll sit me down at one of these chatty little tables, and wait."

He took the beer she poured out for him, and sat down at a nearby table. Then one of the men from the west entered.

"Me name's Joe Timons, ducky," he said to the barmaid by way of introduction, and with the air of a man who is confident of his ability to charm. " 'Oundsditch Joe, or just plain Joe, me friends calls me. And what's yours?"

Before she could answer, Timons' roving eyes fell on the Major.

"S'help me," he ejaculated. "If that ain't me good friend, Percy Algernon Montagu!"

Hand outstretched, he rushed toward the Major, who looked at him, yet seemed not to see him.

Joe stopped at the Major's table.

"Ain't you goin' ter shake 'ands with me?" he asked. Then, receiving no reply, he turned back to the bar and, winking knowingly at the barmaid, ordered a brandy and soda.

"Who's the dude?" he asked in a hoarse whisper. "He's a fair out and outer, ain't he?"

"He knows how a lady should be treated, and that's more than some knows," came the retort.

Timons sipped his drink slowly, with much smacking of lips and sucking of his sandy, unkempt mustache. Joe Timons was thinking.

He knew the dude was the Major, and he was trying to recall what Smith—the whispering man in the back room at Kimberley—had said about the Major.

He finished his drink with a gulp, replenished his glass, and retired with it to a table just behind the Major. The effort of thinking seemed to be a great strain on him; his forehead was lined with deep wrinkles.

Suddenly his face cleared; suddenly he remembered.

"The Major," Smith had said, "is perhaps the clever man the police say he is. On the other hand, he may be a fool. I think he's a fool dude who has had a lot of good luck. But, slim or fool, you're to get him, if you ever meet up with him. See? He's blundered on to one or two of my affairs several times, so I want him. See? And mind you don't take any chances with his blasted luck. Play safe, but sure."

'Oundsditch Joe rose to his feet—he was big and ungainly—and started for the door. As he passed the Major he stumbled awkwardly against that immaculate one's foot, and would have fallen to the ground, had he not grabbed the Major's coat.

He quickly recovered himself, and growled, "Why in 'ell don't you keep your feet to yourself?" Then he passed out, ignoring the Major's confused apologies. Once outside of the hotel Joe scribbled a message on a page torn from his notebook and, hailing a native who was loafing against the side of the building, gave him the paper and told him to take it to the policeman—Snorter Jones.

That done, he mounted his horse and rode down the dusty street until he came to a large, galvanized-iron building—originally intended for a custom's warehouse. The large sliding doors were secured by massive padlocks. Timons had keys to fit, and, after a furtive glance up and down the street, he unlocked the padlocks, pushed back the doors, and entered. Then he closed the doors again.

SHORTLY AFTER Timons had left the hotel, "Tubby" Savage, the other man from the west, entered.

His recognition of the Major was slower than Timons' had been, but his remembrance of Smith's orders came to him instantaneously with the recognition.

The Major seemed to be asleep. He lolled back in his chair; his mouth was wide-open, and he snored loudly—the snore of a man who has drunk well, but not wisely.

Savage—his rate in Smith's book was a doubtful C—found a pretext to send the girl out of the bar; the cigars she had on hand were not good enough for him.

When she returned, a few minutes later, he had apparently not moved from his lounging attitude at the bar. But, for all his big bulk, Savage was as light as a cat on his feet and, in the brief period of the barmaid's absence, he had crossed to the Major's table, and his fat, stubby fingers had flickered for a moment about the Major's body.

He took a handful of cigars from the new box Mabel had brought, threw a gold coin on the bar with a lordly air, and hurried out.

Once outside, he, too, stopped long enough to inquire the location of police headquarters and, learning from a passing white farmer that the policeman was out of town, hastily indited a note which he gave to the farmer, then hurried down the street.

Coming to the galvanized-iron warehouse he peered through the narrow aperture between the sliding doors which Timons had not closed properly. Timons seemed to be busily engaged in knocking crates together.

"Let him do the work," he muttered. "I'm not going in there until I have to. It must be as hot as a bloody oven."

He walked on quickly down the street, mopping his red face continually with a large, much soiled handkerchief. Soon he came to Big Tim's blacksmith shop, where he had left his horse to be shod. Opposite the shop was a grass lean-to, and in the shade of that he rested—and snored.

IT WAS nearly sunset when the man with the plus B rating entered the hotel. The barroom was still empty, save for the Major and the barmaid. Real business at the hotel did not start until an hour or so later.

This man, "Sneak" Saunders—the name fitted him but it was not so apt as his native name which meant, "He roars like a lion; but his tail's between his legs!"—recognized the Major at once, and at once remembered Smith's instructions concerning him.

He affected not to notice the Major at first, but loudly questioned the girl as to the likelihood of being permitted by the proprietor to run a "Crown and Anchor" game in the bar evenings.

The Major listened to the discussion with a grin.

"The luck's running high," he murmured, "and it's running in threes. Time for me to unload before the majesty of the law appears."

Aloud he said, "Why wait until the shades of night fall, old top? Can't we have a game now. I'm frightfully bored. Don't know why I came to this beastly hole. But I set out to hunt the wily denizens of the wild tomorrow—and then everything will be all right."

The man—he was rat-faced and sallow-skinned, but he had the air of a man who is veldt-wise; he was no city-dwelling greenhorn as were the other two—turned quickly.

"Yes—er—" He appeared to hesitate. "Yes; I'll give you a game. Poker or nap or—"

"Let it be nap, old dear," the Major drawled. "It sounds so deuced appropriate to this blinkin' place. But how about cards? The bar-lady perhaps will oblige?"

"I have a pack here," Sneak said hastily, and produced a greasy pack from his pocket. "Always carry 'em with me—play solitaire a lot on the veldt. Keeps a man from going off his chump with loneliness."

"You're quite a wonder," the Major commented admiringly. "I suppose you are quite attached to those cards, in a manner of speakin'. Or perhaps you have nothing but contempt for them. The contempt, you know, which comes from gross—that's such a descriptive word—familiarity.

"Are you trying to insinuate something," Sneak said hotly. "Because, if you are—" His gesture was threatening.

"Oh, dear no," the Major protested. "Insinuate—why what would I insinuate?"

"No offense taken." Sneak was somewhat mollified, but eyed the Major suspiciously. "Well, let's play." He riffled the cards. "Any limit?"

"The blue, blue sky, my hearty. The sky—that's all."

Sneak dealt the cards—five each—and the two played the game, which is a devitalized, emasculated version of poker. It is shorn of all the skill, the excitement, the everything which makes poker the game it is. Still—a lot of money can be won, and lost, at nap.

At first the Major won steadily, won until he had one hundred pounds, mostly in banknotes, of Sneak's money crammed in his pockets. He seemed to be intoxicated by his luck and poked fun at Sneak—threatening to take that man's shirt from his back, the shoes from his feet.

And then the luck turned; the Major lost as consistently as he had previously won. He lost all restraint and plunged madly. He doubled and redoubled his stakes—and lost; he doubled and redoubled, again and again—and lost.

"I'm absolutely stony," he said after a while. "You have cleaned me out—to the uttermost farthing."

"Don't be a squealer," Sneak sneered. "You've got a shirt there I'd like to wear, and riding breeches and polo boots. Come on; let's play."

The Major shook his head.

"Can't do that, really. You wouldn't want me to appear breechless and shirtless—surely?"

"Then good day to you," Sneak rose from his chair.

"Wait!" The Major caught at his coat. "Give me another chance. You're not going to keep that money, are you? I thought we were just playin' for the sport of it. I didn't know you were playin' for keeps."

Sneak laughed, and, pushing up his eyelid with a long, nicotine-stained forefinger, asked, "See any green?"

The Major looked somewhat confused.

"I am an ass, don't you think. Of course I should have known better than to try to work that ancient wheeze on you; and it wasn't very sportsmanlike of me, either. But the fact is, I'm desperate. I had no business to gamble with that money; you see—er—most of it wasn't mine. It belonged to a—er—friend. Lend me a tenner, old man, will you, and let's play some more. Perhaps I can win some of it back."

Sneak smiled sardonically. "What security will you give me if I loan you a tenner?"

"Security? Oh, yes, I see. How about this?"

"This" was a small, uncut diamond which he held out between thumb and forefinger toward Sneak.

"Give you for that? You mean what will you give me not to tell the bobby about it. You're an I.D.B."

"Oh, no," the Major cried in alarm. "Nothing like that. Please don't misunderstand me. This was given to me by a friend of mine."

"All right. I'll give you ten pounds for it. That's twice what it's worth."

"Ten pounds!" echoed the Major in awed tones. "Is it really worth as much as that? But you're on. Here's the stone. Give me the filthy lucre. Ah—and one, yes, I think one, card."

Five minutes later the Major was penniless again.

He tried to borrow money from Sneak and, not meeting with success, gloomily left the barroom, mounted his horse, and rode up the winding, dusty street.

Coming to a little group of round, thatched huts which comprised the quarters of Trooper Snorter Jones and the native constabulary, he dismounted and, handing his horse to an orderly, he entered the largest hut.

Snorter—he was a bald-headed little runt of a man who could hold his own with bigger and heavier men—half-rose from his seat, and was about to give expression of joyful greetings. Then he seemed to change his mind, seated himself and attacked a ham bone with savage vigor.

"Ha there, old top," the Major said cheerfully.

Snorter scowled and, ignoring the Major's greeting, asked, "What are you doing here, you dolled up dude? Not but what I'm not glad to see you. I am. Your coming here, saves me the trouble of going after you."

"And you were intending to come—er—after me?"

"Yes. Soon as I'd finished scoff. Just returned—ugh!—from a long trip in this blasted heat. Thought I had a snorting case. Man reported witchcraft monkey-shines down the river; said the niggers were throwing human sacrifices to the crocs."

"And they weren't, I take it?"

"You take it right. No such luck for me. It was only that old Kawiti—he's just been converted—had decided that all his people were heading for the snorting devil, so he ordered them all to gather at the river so's he could baptize 'em. He ducked 'em all himself, and trusted to the Lord to take care of the crocodiles."

"Well?"

"The Lord didn't; that's all," the trooper replied laconically.

His attention seemed to be riveted on his food; actually, he was watching the Major very closely.

"So you were coming after me, eh?" The Major reverted to the original line of discussion.

"Yah! Soon as I'd finished scoff. Duty before pleasure I always say. And it's my duty to eat when I'm hungry."

"And it'd be a pleasure to arrest me, eh?"

"You know blamed well it would be—in a way that is, and if everything was on the square. It 'ud probably mean a commission. But at that," he sighed, "I'd hate to do it. But I will—as soon as I've finished this." He indicated the table. "That is, if you're still here."

"I'll be here all right. Listen, Snorty. Do you know that there are a lot of bad men in this peaceful town of yours."

"I'm a-lookin' at one, right now."

"No, really—no joshing. A lot of bad men about, I repeat. You ought to do somethings about it. Don't you represent the majesty of the law, and all that? Well, why don't you make this place safe for an innocent chap like me. Here I was sitting in the hotel, having a quiet little drink, when in comes a rough looking guy who insulted me. And 'pon my soul I didn't even know the man to nod to, in a manner of speaking. Then, when he saw that I was giving him the stony stare, he knocked into me—it was most upsetting. After he had left the place I discovered some Bank of England notes—only I'm positive they never saw the dear old bank—in my vest pocket. Imagine that! The beast put counterfeit notes in my pocket. I wonder why?"

"Must have had it in for you."

The Major let his monocle fall into his hand. He polished it absently and replaced it.

"By Jove!" he exclaimed finally. "That had never occurred to me. But what am I to do about it?"

"When I've finished supper I'm going to search you, and if I find the notes, I'll have to lock you up. You'll find some matches in the table drawer over there. It's getting chilly. Suppose you light a fire in the brasier. Just a few scraps of paper'll take the dampness out of the air."

The Major smiled.

"You're an old fraud, Snorty. It's hotter than Hades. But listen to the rest of my complain. Shortly after this Johnny left, another chap came in. Had I been awake I would have known him, I think. Met him in Kimberley once. Well this chap, seeing I was asleep, put a small stone in my hip-pocket—and I can't burn a diamond, Snorty," he added quickly.

Jones wiped his sticky fingers on his trousers, rose from his chair, hesitated, then resumed his seat and picked up his fork again.

"I had a note about that, too," he muttered. "Thought it was damned funny, two complaints like that coming in, and both unsigned. Course they tried to frame you or—" his brows knit in sudden doubt—"you're telling me all this just to throw me off the scent."

"You ought to know me better than that, Snorty. But I'm not finished yet. Just before sundown another chap came in, and inveigled me into a card game. At first I won quite a lot; then he began to win. But he cheated, Snorty, and so I paid my losses with the counterfeit notes the first chap had stuffed in my pocket. That was strictly honorable, wasn't it? And when he cleaned me out of those, I sold him the diamond for ten quid, and let him win that."

Strangled sounds came from Snorty. He seemed to be choking; he was red in the face.

The Major patted him violently on the back, and the policeman jumped out of his chair with a yell.

"You blamed fool," he cried. "What did you do that for?"

"Thought you were choking."

"Choking—hell. I was laughing."

"I don't see anything to laugh at, and I think that you, a policeman, guardian of public morals and all that, ought to take the matter more seriously. If you only cried, Snorty, I'd be much better pleased. But you see, don't you," he continued sternly, "how dangerous it is for an innocent man like myself to be alone, unprotected, without friends, in a wicked town like this."

"Yes—very dangerous for the others. Tell me, how much did you make on this three cornered deal?"

"Just the money I won at cards. At the beginning, when I was winning, I tucked the notes Mr. Red-head lost to me safely away. Then, when I began to lose, I played with the counterfeit money; didn't touch the other at all. Red-head didn't know anything about that. Oh—I suppose I cleared about one hundred quid."

The policeman went off into another spasm of choking, of gurgling laughter, and only ceased when the Major threatened to throw a jugful of beer over him.

"Well, what do you want me to do, Major?" he gasped.

The Major chuckled. "If it's all the same to you, old top, I'd just as soon have you forget this little affair. After all I'm square with the Unholy Three and—oh, what's the use of making trouble for oneself?"

"All right, if that's the way you feel about it. But I did want to arrest someone before I died."

"Is there anyone in the lock-up."

"No—unless they're full up at the hotel. They use it as a sort of overflow accommodation."

"Well, if there's anyone in it tonight I want you to turn them out on the cruel world."

"Why?"

"Because I'm going to stay there."

"Why?"

"Wish you weren't so beastly inquisitive, Snorty. Don't you see, it's the only place I'll be safe. First thing you know I'll be committing murder—or one of these Johnnies will be doing it in my name—and I can't palm a thing like murder off on anyone."

"I can't arrest you—you ain't done nothing."

The Major reached over and taking a tin plate from the table threw it in the air. Two reports sounded, and the plate fell to the ground—pierced by two bullets.

The Major put his revolver back in its holster and drawled, "That's malicious damage to property, Sergeant."

"That's damned quick shooting! But you're right. 'Malicious damage to property.'"

He rose slowly and placed his right hand on the Major's shoulder.

"I arrest you," he intoned, "in the name of the King for malicious damage to property and—I haven't done this for a long time. How does it go, now?"

"And I warn you," prompted the Major.

"Ah, yes. Pity you don't join the force, Major. You'd make a snorting good policeman. And I warn you that anything you say'll be used as evidence against you.

"There," he concluded triumphantly. "I did a good job. I'll take you over to the *trunk* later on. Have you had scoff?"

"No. And I'm blamed hungry."

"Then why didn't you say so before. Sit down and eat."

ABOUT AN hour or so later the policeman escorted the Major to the stone jail which, for some inexplicable reason, was located on the other side of the town.

As they passed the hotel Jones and his handcuffed prisoner were observed by three men who were lounging against the veranda rail.

And the three smiled maliciously. Each one acted as if he had done something he was proud of; something which made him infinitely superior to the others. There was a smug expression on the face of each. "I heard the cop call him 'Major,'" said one. "And he's handcuffed. He must be a fool to let that geezer nab him. Wonder what he's done?"

The other two shared the speaker's innocent wonder.

"The moon's been up half an hour," said the man with flaming red hair. "We ought to be moving. No sense in hanging on here any longer. The sooner we're over the border the safer I'll feel. Across the border we can loaf all we want to."

"I supposes your advice is good, Red, but 'ow I 'ate the thought o' trekking again. Smith 'ad no business to send me on a deal like this. Why don't you let me stay be'ind, Red? I won't be any good on the veldt, there, and if I stays 'ere I could pass off a lot o' the slippery stuff. I'll go 'alves with you."

"Stow your gab, Joe. The boss said you was to go—and you go."

"The Major's camp is pitched south of the town," the third man contented mildly, "and they say he always travels in soft style."

"We'll have a look-see. We go that way."

"I was just about to suggest that."

The three moved off, and half an hour later a light wagon, heavily laden, drawn by eight mules traveled swiftly out of the town.

Meanwhile the policeman and the Major had arrived at the jail.

"I sleep here myself," said the policeman as he ushered the Major into the small, neat cell, "when it's snorting hot. It's cooler than the huts. There's a good bed, and a lamp and some books. If you want anything that's not here—just walk out and get it."

"How can I, my good man, when I'm locked in."

"You don't want to be locked in—surely?"

"Of course. Else where's my alibi if a murder's committed? Yes; you lock me up, and make sure that I can't get out—or anyone get in."

Jones chuckled.

"That's easy. Sure you mean it? All right, then. I'll be up around scoff time tomorrow morning to let you out. You'll eat with me? Good night, Major! I'd like to stay and have a chat with you, but I promised to go out and play cards with the gang at the Lonely Mine tonight."

"That's all right, old man. Plenty of time for a good talk tomorrow. Trot along."

Jones swung the big, iron door to, locked it, shouted a final "Good night!" closed and locked the outer door with much ostentation, and a few minutes later went quickly down the street—whistling shrilly.

"BAAS, BAAS. Wake up."

At the sound of the voice the Major awoke instantly and, climbing on to a high stool, peered through the small, strongly-barred window.

In the gray half-light of breaking day he could distinguish the squat, ungainly figure of Jim, his Hottentot servant.

"What is it, Jim?"

"The Baas must come quickly!"

"Why, Jim?"

But Jim seemed to be shaken out of his usual phlegmatic calm. "What has the Baas done? Why is he here? Is it because of the diamonds?"

"No matter. Have you brought me from sleep to ask questions? But your face, Jim? Have you been fighting? And why must I come quickly?"

The Hottentot gently fingered the cut under his eye as if for the first time aware of its existence.

"It is the Baas who asks questions now," he bantered.

"It is the Baas's right," the Major countered sternly. "Answer me and without further meatless talk. Tell me all things I should know."

"It was a little after moon-rise, Baas. When three men in a wagon drawn by six mules came up to the camp. They were men whose faces were evil, and I feared many things.

"One of the men—his hair was like the flame of fire—told me that you, Baas, had been taken to *trunk,* and that you would be sent to labor on the Breakwater. He spoke the language of my people, Baas, but he learned it from the women-folk. He was a man who has much knowledge of we black ones; but he knows only the evil of us—because he himself is evil.

"While he was talking with me the other two searched the tent—taking certain things from it. Then the red-headed one told me to inspan the mules, and to put all things in the wagons. When I refused he hit me first with his *sjambok* and then with his clenched fist. The moon went behind a cloud at that moment, and I was wandering in darkness.

"When life came back to me the men had gone. Gone, too, was the tent, the mules, the horse I sometimes ride—everything. Not a thing was left save the gray ashes of the fire. There was a heavy sleep in that man's fist, Baas."

"You say everything has gone, Jim?"

"Yah, Baas."

"Why didn't you come here sooner?"

"I forgot to say, Baas, that while I was in the deep sleep, those wicked ones bound me hand and foot so that I could not move. As soon as I could I freed myself—and I worked speedily, for a hyena was watching me nearby, and he had the hunger madness."

"So the man struck you, Jim."

"Yah, Baas."

The inane, almost vacuous expression vanished from the Major's face. His eyes which had seemed blue and of an almost child-like innocence, now had a glint of steel in them—they were cold, stern, ice-blue. The firm line of his jaw asserted itself; his well shaped lips were pressed firmly together and there was nothing vacillating about them. It was strange, too, the effect absence of the monocle made—

he was not wearing it now. The monocle was, in a sense, his disguise. It was his magic ring—the ring of invisibility. Wearing it, his true-self seemed to disappear; a fool, a nincompoop took possession of his body—but not of his brain. That, under cover, worked more keenly than ever.

He used the monocle, too, at times, to cloak his emotions. No man can give way to passionate anger, or grief, or joy, while he is wearing a monocle.

"So he hit you with a *sjambok,* did he?" he repeated.

"Yah, Baas. But that is nothing."

"Nothing—perhaps that is much."

The Major's tone was tense. He judged men according to the manner in which they treated natives, and natives treated them. It was a fair and eminently safe basis for judgment. No man is wholly bad who can win the affection and respect of children; and the black peoples of South Africa are the children of this day's civilization.

He roused himself; suddenly aware that Jim was tugging at the iron-grating.

"What are you doing, Jim?"

"This one's loose, Baas," the Hottentot panted. "If the Baas will help—"

"The Baas will not help."

"But the sun rises and soon it will be too late—men will come and take the Baas away."

"Not so. This is but a game I play. Go to the police camp and tell the white *Inkosi* your Baas would speak with him."

Jim hastened off on his errand and the Major proceeded to dress himself, loudly bemoaning the absence of a mirror.

"And," he exclaimed in annoyed tones, "the blighters have taken my razor and all the rest of my toilet kit. I won't be able to shave for weeks and weeks. Not unless I get them back very soon. And, yes, I must do that."

Ten minutes later Jim returned.

"Baas," he panted, "the white policeman is not there, and the black dogs refused to give me the key to this place."

"What a nuisance," he muttered in English. "Well, I suppose I'll have to wait until Snorter comes."

He had forgotten that Snorter would not be at hand until eight o'clock, and all the time the three—with his razor and everything—were getting further away.

"Go back to the police station, Jim," he ordered, "and wait there until the white man comes, then bring him swiftly here. I'm going to sleep."

NEARLY FOUR hours later Snorter Jones put in an appearance.

"I forgot all about you, Major," he confessed shamefacedly as they were walking down to the police camp. "The boys wouldn't let me go. They said they were out for revenge and, as I was winning, I had to stay. They got their revenge, and I got every snorting penny they had to their name. You're hungry, aren't you?"

"Yes," the Major answered tersely. "And I'm goin' to trek as soon as we've had scoff. I want you to get me two pack horses, Snorty, plenty of provisions, rifle, cartridges, blankets—everything, including a fast horse for Jim."

"Phew! What's up?"

"Those three bounders who bilked me yesterday have departed for parts unknown, and my outfit has departed with them."

Jones whistled.

"They're a bad lot, Major. You should have let me arrest them last night. Must have figured you wouldn't be out of jail for a year or so. Probably thought I'd arrested you for having counterfeit money, or I.D. buying, or for bad debts." The trooper chuckled softly. "The laugh is on you after all, Major."

"Perhaps so," the Major said arily, "but is it the last laugh?"

"It'll be risky goin' after them alone, Major. I'd come with you, but they're probably heading for Portuguese Territory, and I'd be helpless there."

"I won't be alone, Snorter, I'm taking Jim; he's a whole regiment. And, anyway, risky or not, I have to go. I need a shave, and they have my razor. Will you get the stuff I want while I'm eating? Don't want to waste any time. Better pack provisions for a week, and a couple of hundred cartridges."

"You're snorting well right, I will. Got two horses in the pound—don't know why their owners haven't claimed 'em—you can have for packs. Does your nigger ride?"

"Can a duck swim, Snorty?"

"All right. I'll let him have my horse. You go on in the mess hut"—they had reached the police camp—"and the cook-boy'll see you have plenty of grub. He'll take care of the Hottentot, too—he's an ugly devil, that nigger of yours, ain't he? But strong as an ox, I bet."

An hour later the Major, mounted on his black stallion—a Basutu with a leavening of Arab—galloped swiftly from the town. He was leading a pack horse, and Jim, on the policeman's chestnut, followed close behind.

THE MAJOR and Jim, the Hottentot, were down on their hands and knees, their faces contorted, their cheeks swelling and collapsing alternately, tears running down their cheeks, desperately endeavoring to fan the smoky, wet-wood fire into a blaze.

This was the morning of the fourth day of their chase after the three men who had decamped with the Major's outfit, and it seemed that each day had brought fresh disappointments, greater obstacles.

The first day out from Speysburg one of the pack-horses had put its foot down a hole, broken its leg and had to be shot.

The next day the other pack-horse developed a bad case of staggers—no wonder its owner had not taken the trouble to get it out of the pound; it wasn't worth the fee—and, despite Jim's doctoring, died.

Some of the provisions from the two pack animals were now carried on the riding animals, but not many. The Major was traveling fast and, therefore, light.

Toward sunset of the third day—they were now well into Portuguese Territory—the spoor of the wagons they were following, had left the rough, dirt road and headed straight across the bush-veldt.

The Major had been exultant, knowing that his quarry would have to slow up, for they could not continue at the breakneck speed they had evidently traveled on the road. On the other hand, the bush would make but little difference to the speed of the horsemen.

"I fancy I'll shave tonight, Jim," the Major had boasted, "or tomorrow morning, surely."

But the sky had become suddenly overcast with clouds. White clouds which quickly changed to pearly-gray, to dirty-yellow, to inky-black. They dropped lower and lower until they seemed so close to earth that, by stretching on tip-toe, a tall man could reach them;

seemed so heavy, so solid, that the Major instinctively gasped for breath as if a heavy weight was crushing his chest.

A gale of wind blew, followed by an ominous calm.

And then, before the two men could erect a shelter of any sort, the rain came; an icy-cold rain in solid sheets, as if some gigantic vat of water had been suddenly tipped over. And not once during the night did it show signs of abatement.

The Major was soaked to the skin in the first few seconds of the downpour—Jim had removed his scanty garments—and the two men spent a sleepless, dispirited night.

Dispirited because they knew that on the morrow there would be no spoor to follow; that any further attempt to catch up with the wagons would be a haphazard affair.

Just before daybreak, the rain had slackened, then ceased entirely; the clouds retreated, vanished, at the challenge of the rising sun. The flattened bushes and long grasses straightened—almost visibly. In a little while they would be erect; a little longer they would be drooping for want of moisture. The soggy, rain-saturated earth would become like baked-clay, a spider's-web of cracks would appear—each crack a mouth thirsting for water.

But now everything seemed waterlogged, and Jim had difficulty in making fire.

Finally his efforts, aided by the Major's were successful. A tiny tongue of flame appeared, and licked hungrily at the scraps of fuel Jim carefully fed it.

"It is well," Jim announced presently. "Shall I make coffee?"

"Yes, Jim. And open a tin of bully."

While the Hottentot was preparing the frugal meal, the Major undressed and spread his clothes—steam was already rising from them—on the top of a bush. It was better to risk sunburn than fever. That done, he sat down on a rock, and waited patiently for Jim to announce that the food was ready.

He was unusually moody; he was facing failure, and did not relish it.

"It's not that I care about the outfit," he drawled aloud, and in English, as he so often did when alone with Jim. It helped him to get the right perspective on things. He asked questions in a language Jim could not understand, or only a scattered word, and answered them himself.

"No—it's not the financial loss, but the affront. If I go back absolutely empty handed—actually two pack-horses less than I had when I started—old Snorty Jones will pull my leg. It 'ud be mortifying. Don't you think so, Jim?"

"Oh damme yes, Baas," Jim replied.

"I was sure you would agree with me! Then, again, those fellows somewhere in the maze of the trackless jungle that's rather good, don't you think, Jim?—ahead of us will be sure to hear of my—er—failure, and they'll take all the credit to themselves. They'll think themselves clever, and I couldn't stand that—really. And I'm not a little curious to know why they're heading this way. Possibly—why, yes, I wouldn't be a bit surprised to find they had a machine hidden away in the bush somewhere, which turns out counterfeit bank notes. I think it's my duty, oh, absolutely, as a law-abiding citizen, to look into this. Therefore, we must go on. Don't you think so, Jim?"

"Golly yes, Baas."

"And," he stroked the stubbled growth on his chin reflectively, "I need a shave badly. And that rather settles matters, I think. Yes, I'm sure it does. They were heading due east—perhaps they'll continue to do so. Well, we'll go due east, too. We may miss 'em—the bush is damned big—still—"

He stopped abruptly.

There was a rustling noise, a breaking of twigs, a crashing down of small saplings in a clump of high bush nearby.

The Major picked up his rifle, released the safety catch, pulled out the cut-off and was ready for anything.

Jim looked at his Baas with a grin. "There is no need, Baas," he said. "It is only—"

"Quiet, Jim," whispered the Major. "Oh, what a beauty."

As he spoke an old bull-giraffe emerged from the thicket and, coming to a halt not thirty paces from the men, stretched himself lazily.

There was nothing ludicrous about him, rather something regal. It is only amid the trappings of civilization that the giraffe becomes an object of derision. Here he was so much a part of his environment one would as soon thought of laughing at an elephant, a lion, or a sunset.

Then, as if to prove that nature can be cruel as well as beautiful and majestic, a tawny form shot out from the tall grasses where it had been crouching, and leaped on the back of the unsuspecting giraffe.

The lion's spring, its suddenness and unexpectedness, brought the spindle-legged creature to its haunches.

And then the Major fired. A second shot followed so quickly that it seemed the echo of the first. The lion slid slowly down to the ground roaring feebly—a strangled, choking roar. Then it turned around several times as if seeking a place to sleep, and lay down. It shivered convulsively, then died.

And now the giraffe, which seemed like a petrified creature, toppled slowly over, and did not move.

"My first shot was too low," murmured the Major. "It's a shame, but I didn't know Snorty's rifle. My fault. I should have tried the thing out before. I feel like a bloomin' murderer. I didn't want to kill dear old long-neck."

But Jim had no feeling of sorrow, only elation.

The lion was well enough—its claws and whiskers and the tuft of its tail would make a powerful charm—but the giraffe! There were a hundred and one things he could do with its skin.

"The coffee is cooked, Baas," he said. "While the Baas eats I will take the skin off the long-legged one."

Brandishing his long hunting-knife Jim ran toward the dead animals.

"Have care, Jim," the Major shouted in warning, "the lion may not be dead, or its mate be at hand."

"The lion is dead, and if another comes, my Baas has a gun and many cartridges."

The Major laughed at the Hottentot's expression of confidence in him. Then, sitting so that he could see Jim and also had a clear view of the bush about him, he commenced breakfast. He was very hungry, so it may have been his attention momentarily wandered, at least he did not see all that happened.

He had a vision of Jim clambering boy-like on to the back of the giraffe, shouting gleefully, and then the Major had looked away—to pour himself some coffee.

"O-he, Baas!"

At the note of fear in Jim's voice the Major looked up quickly in time to see the giraffe leap to its feet. Jim was on its back clinging tightly to its neck.

"Jump off, Jim," the Major shouted between laughs.

"I—I—dare not, Baas—" the fear in Jim's voice was matched by the expression on his face. His black, ebony skin seemed to have faded to a dirty yellow; his eyes protruded from their sockets.

"Jump, Jim," the Major commanded sternly.

"I can't, *Baas,*" Jim wailed. "He is mad. He will kick me and I shall die."

"See the brave warrior," the Major said sarcastically. "What a story to tell the women. Why—"

But he did not finish the sentence. The giraffe which all this while had been pawing the ground, and striking at the carcass of the lion with its forefeet, suddenly galloped away—and vanished. A giraffe's speed has been computed at thirty miles an hour.

But that last vision of Jim, naked save for a breach-clout, clinging for dear life to the neck of his ungainly steed, was too much for the Major, and he laughed until he could laugh no more.

"My first shot must have just creased the beast," he gasped, "and he came to just as Jim was clambering over him. It must have given old Jim the deuce an' all of a shock. Must be annoying to have a beast you are about to skin come alive. Well, I'll finish breakfast. Jim'll be back presently. As soon as he's recovered from the first shock he'll know what to do.

"What a story to tell. But who'll believe it?"

The Major dressed himself, and leisurely finished his breakfast.

Half an hour passed, an hour, and still no sign of Jim.

The Major was worried now.

"He may have been knocked off, or fallen off, and broken a leg or something," he said.

Quickly saddling the horses, he mounted and, leading Jim's horse, swiftly followed the spoor of the giraffe. The trail in the rain-soaked ground was easy.

Two hours later the Major came to a thickly wooded piece of country, and in the outer fringes of it he saw a giraffe. That it was Jim's giraffe there could be no doubt—the Major could see the long wounds made by the lion's claws—but there was no sign of Jim.

The Major was mystified, and rode up to the place where the giraffe had been standing when he first sighted it, hoping to find that Jim had seized the opportunity to slide off at that place. But, though he examined the ground all about, he could find no trace of Jim's footprints. He shook his head doubtfully. There was something uncanny about it.

"I'd better back-track," he muttered. "Perhaps he dropped off on the way."

But he knew that was a false premise. He had watched the spoor carefully all the time, and he was too expert a trekker to have overlooked the imprint of Jim's feet.

Before turning back, however, he decided to explore still further into the wooded country. This decision was forced upon him by the condition of the horses.

He had not spared them in his mad ride, and the coat of the stallion was flecked with foam, while Jim's horse was black with sweat.

He unsaddled, gave both mounts a rub down, hobbled them, and turned them loose to roll or graze as they saw fit. Then, rifle in hand, he went forward calling the Hottentot's name aloud, firing several shots into the air.

As he progressed the jungle growth became thicker, the trees taller, and their heavily leafed branches interlaced overhead.

A stealthy rustling in the bush to the left of him caused him to swing round sharply, drawing his revolver as he did so. Then something hard and heavy struck him on the head, and he pitched forward on his face.

WHEN HE opened his eyes again, several hours later, it was to meet the mocking looks of 'Oundsditch Joe, Tubby Savage and Sneak Saunders.

"Where am I?" he asked feebly.

His head throbbed painfully, and he felt nauseated.

"You're in good 'ands, ducky. The three kindest men—to their friends—in South Africa are takin' care o' yer. Only, you ain't their friend."

"That's enough for you, Joe. Get on with your job. You, too, Tubby. I'll attend to the Major."

The two men sullenly obeyed Sneak who, turning to the Major, continued.

"Yes. You're almighty *slim*, you are, Major." His sarcasm was rather labored. "You ought to be tied to your mama's apron strings. What was the matter? Were you lost or just tryin' to have a game with us."

"Lost?" The Major echoed. "I don't know. I don't remember. Oh yes, of course I'm lost; I mean was lost before you fellows came along and found me. You did find me, didn't you?"

"Yes; we found you all right."

The Major tried to rise to his feet, and discovered that his feet were securely bound.

"Why am I bound like this? It's positively ridiculous, you know."

"We were afraid you might wander off and get lost again!"

"Kind of you I'm sure. But you'll be kind enough to cut me loose now, won't you?"

Sneak hesitated then coming to a sudden decision, bent and cut the ropes; first warning the Major not to move lest Joe and Savage see and insist on having him bound again.

"We've got your rifle and revolver, so you're harmless, Major; and if you try to get away, you'll find that a bullet'll travel a damned sight faster than you can."

"But why should I want to leave you, dear old pal of mine? Here I am in the midst of plenty, so to speak, and with friends. No, I'm quite content to stay, I assure you."

"It's as well," Sneak said grimly. "You couldn't travel far without shoes, anyway. I told you the other day I wanted them."

"I thought those boots you have on looked familiar," the Major murmured, "and that my feet felt beastly naked. But this is monstrous. I'll—I'll report you to the police. I'll have you arrested."

Sneak grinned.

"You won't get the chance. I don't think you'll ever see a policeman again."

"Really?"

"Really."

"But I don't understand, Mr.—er—I don't know your name."

"Saunders, Sneak Saunders. Does that help any?"

"Lots. 'Oundsditch Joe I know, and the other chap is called—wait, don't tell me—Tubby Savage. Am I right?"

"You know a hell of a lot."

"I want to know more, too. Oh, my head. I must have fallen on a rock. There's a large bump at the back of my head."

"That was Joe. He tapped you playfully on the head with his revolver."

The Major smiled faintly.

"He has a quaint sense of humor, hasn't he? Hope he hasn't any more little jokes like that to play on me! But you said something about my never seeing a bobby again. How splendid! Where are you going to take me—heaven? That means I must die, I suppose—" the Major sighed—"and that's not so splendid."

"How did you get out of jail, Major?" Sneak asked abruptly.

"Why Jim—he's my servant, you know—came and told me all about the way you had borrowed my outfit, and, he's very strong you know, one of the bars in the cell window was loose, *and* there was no one on guard, so—" The Major's shrug was very expressive.

"What made you come after us?"

The Major's eyes opened in astonishment. "I—er—needed a shave, and you had my razor."

"You weren't really lost, were you, Major? You were looking for our camp—don't lie—weren't you? Though how you picked up our trail after last night's rain is beyond me. Perhaps you are not such a fool after all."

"Oh, but I am. A most fearful one, really. And I'm a frightful liar. As a matter of fact I wasn't lost, but Jim is."

"A nigger lost in the bush!" Sneak's scorn was withering. "Yes; you're a liar all right."

"Ah, but now I'm telling the truth. You see it was like this: There was one of those long-necked beasts having a quiet little snooze, and Jim—he's a regular daredevil, you know—climbed up on him. Then the giraffe jumped up and ran away with Jim on its back. It was most amusing, really. I wish you could have seen it. I laughed until my sides ached. And I've been looking for Jim ever since."

"And you expect me to believe that? I'm no fool, Major."

"It's the truth, old chap. But I said at the time no one would ever believe it. I wouldn't believe it myself, if I were in your shoes. I mean my shoes. But turnabout is fair play. What are you doing here?" He indicated with a wave of his hands the crates which Joe and Savage were unloading from the wagon. "Going to do some mining? The crates are labelled, unless my eyes deceive me, 'Machinery Parts—

Fragile.' But mining in this out-of-the way place doesn't seem to ring true. Somehow I don't think those crates hold machinery. But rifles, now? Oh yes, most certainly rifles. Gun-running, eh? Helping our dear black brothers to kill each other off more quickly; and if they wipe out a few whites as well that doesn't matter. The profits are good."

"You're too damned clever," Sneak growled. "But now you've guessed that, you may as well know the rest. You ain't goin' to live very long anyway."

"You intimated as much before, old man," the Major interposed sweetly.

"Oh stow yer gab. You've heard of Yellow Pete?"

"There you go asking me questions again. Yes; I've heard of that Johnny. He runs amok once in a while, doesn't he? Leads quite a powerful tribe somewhere in this section, and wipes out all who oppose him. He's a sweet lad, if all I've heard's true."

"It's true, all right. He's a wicked devil. They say his favorite sport's skinning men—white men—alive."

"Then you and your handsome comrades are safe, aren't you?"

"You're not," Sneak said viciously. "He's coming here tonight for these guns. We'll sell him you, too."

"Thanks! Don't fancy I'll fetch much, though."

"But there's a way out, Major." Sneak lowered his voice to a whisper.

"Ah! Here it comes. There's always a way out, Sneak. But how, in this particular case?"

"Help me to put Joe and Tubby out of the way. They're too damned careful for me to handle alone and, beside, I want help in handling Yellow Pete. It'll be a big haul, and we'll divvy up between us. Yellow Pete's crazy to get hold of a bunch of rifles; he'll give his soul for them—and he's got hundred of diamonds, his niggers have brought back from the mines. He'll pay us with stones as many as we ask for."

"Um!" The Major seemed to be turning the proposition over in his mind. "But if that's the way you treat old friends, how would you treat me?"

"They ain't old friends, Major. I never saw them before I came to Speysburg, four days ago."

"That sounds a bit thin—if you'll pardon me. Here you are partners in a dangerous piece of work and yet—"

"We are all Smith's men—Whispering Smith. You've heard of him, ain't you? He planned this thing. I got word from him to come to

Speysburg where I would meet the other two men. He had everything planned; he'd been storing guns in the old freight house for months— three or four at a time. All we had to do was pack 'em up. Smith said I was to be leader, and God knows why he sent the other two—unless he expects me to put 'em out of the way. They're fools and, besides, I think they're planning to do for me."

"Beastly cads."

The Major fished in his pocket for his monocle, extracted it, polished it and fixed it firmly in place.

"Well, what do you say?" Sneak growled impatiently.

"What do I say? Why I say—I need a shave, very badly. Get me my razor, there's a good chap."

Sneak cursed.

"You know your choice, Major. Come in with me, or—"

"You might bring my soap and shaving brush, too."

"Don't be a fool, Major."

"And hot water and a clean towel."

Sneak walked angrily away, and started to unpack the cases. In this he was aided by Joe and Tubby, and very soon one hundred rifles were stacked in neat rows on the ground—also a large box of cartridges.

Their work finished Tubby and 'Oundsditch Joe climbed up into their wagon—the Major's—and, opening some tinned foods, com- menced to eat. As they did so they carried on a whispered conversa- tion, watching Sneak furtively.

Sneak went to the other wagon and, sitting down in its shade, moodily chewed on a piece of biltong. His eyes never left the other two, and his hand hovered continually about his revolver butt.

The Major sat up, and with the quick eye of the trained observer took in the geography of the camp and its surroundings. They were in a deep depression—the crater, probably, of some long extinct volcano—the steeply sloping sides of which were covered with large cacti. At the eastern end, where the slope was more gradual, there seemed to be a well-defined trail. It was the sort of place that a man would only find if he knew exactly where to look for it, or stumbled upon it by accident. And the Major knew that there was very little likelihood of anyone doing that. He was in a hole, and there seemed no way out.

He thought of making a dash for the rifles, but at once discarded the thought. Even if he got safely to them—and they were thirty or forty feet away—he would still have to open the case to get at the cartridges. And in the meantime—

Still it irked him to give up without a struggle. Perhaps his best plan would be to go in with Sneak or, at least, appear to. He knew that he could expect no mercy at the hands of the half-caste, Yellow Pete.

"But where's Jim," he muttered. "I hope the dear old chap's safe. I can't imagine what's become of him. Why did I laugh at him when he rode off on the giraffe? Perhaps I hurt his feelin's, and he's hiding somewhere in order to punish me. But that's not like him—and he really was funny."

At the memory the Major laughed aloud. "What do you find so damned funny, Major?"

He looked up to find Sneak standing over him. "I was just thinkin' how surprised you'd be when Jim comes here with the soldiers."

"What?"

"I sent him, you know, to the Portuguese garrison as soon as I discovered where you'd camped. They ought to be here about the same time Yellow Pete arrives. It'll be a nice little surprise party all round, won't it?"

Sneak seemed to be taken aback, but only for a minute.

"You're a liar, Major," he said tersely. "There ain't no Portuguese post within a hundred miles or more of this place."

"All right; have it your own way."

"Sneak!"

Joe's cockney twank cut the air.

"Well?" Sneak growled.

"Me an' Tubby 'ere don't like the way you're gettin' pally with the Major. Keep away from 'im, or I'll blow yer bleedin' brains out."

"You will, will you." Sneak's voice was hoarse with anger. "Why you little rat, I'll—"

His hands leaped to his revolver, but, seeing that Savage had him covered, let it fall empty to his side.

"All right, boys," he said smoothly. "I've got nothing to say to the Major that I don't want you to hear. I don't want to talk to the bloomin' dude. Tie him up again, Joe, if you're a mind to. I don't care. Only remember this when you get to talking of blowin' my brains out: You'll need them brains to get you out of this place. You'd never find the road alone."

The two men whispered together, then Savage returned his revolver to its holster, and he and Joe climbed down from the wagon.

"We're willin' to cry quits," Joe said, "but we're goin' to tie up the Major ourselves."

All this time Sneak had his back turned to the Major, and was between that man and the other two.

It was an opportunity the Major was not the man to miss. With a cat-like spring he leaped upon Sneak, and disarmed him before the other two knew what was going on.

"Hands up," he cried. "All of you."

So quick, so unexpected was his attack that it was successful.

Cowards at heart, Savage and Joe made no attempt to show fight—beside Sneak formed an effective shield for the Major—and quickly put up their hands.

"You, too, Sneak."

And Sneak, too, reached skyward.

The Major lined them up in a row and, making them turn their backs to him, quickly disarmed them.

" 'Pon my soul," he drawled, "I don't know what to do with you." His monocle was in place again; he had removed it before springing on Sneak. "There are a lot of things I'd like to do, but— No Joe, don't swear, there's a good boy. If you do I'll have to imitate your merry little game."

He lightly tapped the cockney on the head with the barrel of his revolver.

"Now don't talk—any of you—I want to think. And please continue to hold that graceful, sun-worshipping pose. It's priceless."

He moved gingerly—for the ground was hot and he was bootless—toward a small boulder, intending to sit on it while formulating some plan.

Then—and it is the little things which count—he stubbed his toe on a sharp piece of rock, and almost lost his balance. His monocle fell from his eye and, in his frantic efforts to save it, he lowered his revolver. For a moment he was off guard, and in that moment the three men—they had been squinting over their shoulders—turned as one man, and leaped on him.

The struggle which followed was furious, but brief. In a little while the Major was lashed securely to a wagon wheel, listening to the three revile each other—and him.

"To think," he said sorrowfully when lack of breath brought a temporary cessation to their cursing, "my best friend should play me false. If I had let the monocle go, I'd be going at this moment."

"Well, yer can say yer prayers, Major," Joe panted. "'Ere comes Yeller Pete."

All looked in the direction of the trail, and watched in silence the approach of a party of natives headed by one dressed in the regalia of a witch-doctor. His face was hidden by a hideous mask.

"Get your rifles and revolver and see you've plenty of ammunition," Sneak ordered. "We'll have to watch Pete pretty close."

"All right. Get it over quick, Sneak. The sooner I'm out o' here the better I'll like it."

"Yus! Hand don't forget, Sneak, to do all the talking in Henglish. Understand?"

Sneak scowled then whispered quickly to the Major, "Wha' d' you say? It's not too late, yet."

But the Major did not reply. He was watching the approaching warriors, and seemed specially interested in the witch-doctor.

When the natives were within one hundred feet of the camp. Sneak shouted in English, "Is that you, Pete?" and receiving no answer, repeated the question in the vernacular.

Now the answer came readily.

"Nay. He is behind us. He will be here by sundown. Us he sent to clear a path for him."

"It's all right," Sneak said in answer to the inquiring look of Joe and Tubby. "They're just an advance guard. They won't start anything, and neither will Yellow Pete the way I'll handle him. Go get some gin and give these niggers."

A few minutes later the natives were squatting on their haunches about the wagon, drinking from the bottles the white men gave them.

The witch-doctor, seeing the Major lashed to the wheel, seemed to be greatly excited and asked Sneak many questions.

"He says," Sneak interpreted, "that Yellow Pete will give us a lot for the Major. Need him to sacrifice—guess he means to torture him. They're bloodthirsty devils, ain't they?"

And now the natives seemed to be inflamed by the gin, and, as one man, they rose to their feet, and danced a grotesque movement—symbolical of bloody tortures.

"I don't 'arf like this," Joe muttered.

"Don't show 'em you're scared," Sneak said sternly.

"I am, and I don't care who knows it," said Savage.

And then, as if in response to some prearranged signal the warriors pounced upon the three white men, and trussed them up securely.

That done, the witch-doctor cut loose the Major.

"Great, Jim, old top," said that man. "Have a nice ride?"

The witch-doctor snatched off his mask; there was an expression of intense disgust on his face.

"Then the Baas knew? But how?"

The Major chuckled.

"A lion once wore an ostrich skin, and said, 'No man shall know me.' But when he walked abroad all men said, 'There walks a lion.'"

Jim looked crestfallen, then asked, "Is the Baas well? Is there anything he wants?"

"Boots, Jim. The red-head has them."

With no gentle hands Jim removed the boots from Sneak's feet, and gave them to the Major.

"Thanks, Jim. But who are those fellows? Yellow Pete's men?"

"Nay. They are my servants," Jim answered proudly. "They call me Lord."

"Then bid your servants—who call you lord—to inspan my mules in my wagon. Tell them, also, to load these on to the wagon." He indicated the rifles and cartridges. "Bid them hasten and, while they are working, tell me everything."

Jim shouted his commands to the natives. "An' be damn quick," he added in English. "By golly, O dear no."

"Aye Lord," they shouted, and the Major wondered at the respectful fear in their voices.

"Now, Jim."

"There is not much to tell, Baas. This morning I decided to go for a ride on the long-necked one," he looked quickly at the Major whose face was very grave, "and he traveled fast until he came to a place where the trees grow thick. And there, having ridden far enough, I caught hold of one of the branches, and let the giraffe pass from under me. Then I pulled myself on to the branch to rest awhile and lo, beside me was one of those dogs." He waved a hand airily in the direction of the hardworking natives. "He recognized, Baas, my power over animals and called me Lord—had he not seen me riding on the back of the giraffe?—and bade me go with him. And, because I thought he would show me things you would have me see, I followed where he led.

"We traveled on the tops of trees, Baas, never touching ground. He did not want to leave spoor, he said. After a long time we came to a large village, and there I learned many things—but chiefly that others had seen me riding the giraffe and all called me Lord. They told me, Baas, that the white men we followed were camped at this place, and that they were bringing guns for the man you call Yellow Pete. My servants hate that wicked one who had sent word that he would burn their village after he had got the guns from the white men. Without guns he dared not attack my people, for they are strong. And so they waited, Baas, spying upon the white men, planning to raid them when darkness came, so that Yellow Pete could not get the guns.

"And so, Baas, knowing this was a matter too great for me, I came back with these men to the place where I had left the long-necked one, thinking to find you there. The sun had traveled far, and I knew you would follow the spoor of the giraffe. And there I saw what had happened to you—the story was told in the spoor. So we came to this place.

"That is all, Baas."

"It is a lot, Jim. But where is Yellow Pete?"

"My servants—the people who call me Lord of animals—have scouts watching him. He is on the other side of the river; a mighty river. And the river is in flood. He cannot cross tonight. But see. My servants"—with each repetition of the word servant Jim assumed a bombastic attitude; he was proud of his achievement, yet somewhat afraid of being laughed at—"my servants," he repeated, "have finished the tasks I set them."

It was true. The natives had worked speedily.

The Major's and Jim's horses—Sneak had caught them at the time the Major was captured—were bridled and saddled; the Major's outfit was all packed in his wagon, the mules inspanned.

"It is a wonderful story, O Lord of all the Animals," the Major said gravely. "At another time I will question you further—if it is permitted—but now we must hasten. Tell your servants to depart, one of them driving the wagon. We will follow presently."

Again Jim's orders were quickly obeyed.

"Now," said the Major, addressing the three white men, "I don't want to appear vindictive, and I'm not, really. But there are some things which must be said. First, to your address, Joe: You shouldn't put counterfeit money in an innocent man's pocket, really you shouldn't. And you, Tubby: If you ever have a diamond you want to get rid of, throw it in the river. Don't follow Joey's bad example.

"As for you, Sneak: I never did like a man who can carry cards up his sleeve; there's something dishonest about him. Are you up on ethics? I'd like to know if I were guilty of dishonest conduct in payin' a crooked gambler with counterfeit money, and a 'planted' diamond?

"What! Didn't you three tell each other all about your little plans to trap me? Really! Oh, this is too much. And I bet each one of you wrote to old Smithy, and told him how smart you were. Oh say you did—of course you did. Why be so modest?"

The look on their sullen faces answered his question, and he rocked back and forth, roaring with laughter.

"But to continue," he said sobering quickly, "I could have forgiven everything except the beastly inconvenience you've caused me—about shaving, I mean.

"And then—notice how big trees from the little acorn grow—it is deuced bad form, oh very, to sell guns to a renegade like Yellow Pete. When small souled little toads play with counterfeit money, and diamonds, and cards up their sleeves—why, one just smiles. But when they develop into gun-runners! Ah, that's—er—a giraffe with different colored spots. So I must punish you. You'll see how in a moment.

"Tubby, I'm goin' to loose your—er—fetters so that if you work industriously, you'll be able to release yourself, and Joe, and Sneak—I purposely put Sneak last, and, if I were you, I'd untie him last—before Yellow Pete comes.

"No thanks, please!" He held up his hands. "And most certainly no curses. I'm quite deaf to 'em all.

"There! I'll cut the ropes here and there, and loosen it there, and there. You have one foot quite loose, and one hand quite.

"Work hard, old chap, you can guess what will happen to you if Yellow Pete comes and finds you trussed up—and no rifles or cartridges for him. As Sneak says, Yellow Pete's favorite sport is skinnin' white men alive. And, failin' white men, perhaps he'd be satisfied with you.

"So long! Don't curse, cultivate a placid disposition, and never take a man's razor away from him again. That's your major crime.

"Come on, Jim."

He and the Hottentot mounted and rode quickly away.

Coming to the trail leading out of the crater the Major pulled up his horse and looked back.

The sun had set, but the Major could distinguish three figures struggling together.

"Tubby worked fast," he muttered. Then to Jim, "Are you quite sure that Yellow Pete won't be here until the morning?"

"Yah, Baas. The river is big with the rains. A crocodile couldn't cross it now."

"Then I'll let 'em fight it out," and singing gaily, the Major rode on.

OUT OF BONDAGE

EVERYONE WHO knows South Africa knows Veldts-dorp. It is typical of the numerous mushroom townships which are scattered about the veldt, and which owe their existence to the discovery of gold or diamonds in the vicinity.

"Veldtsdorp" and "diamonds" are almost synonymous terms. When you think of one, you think of the other. Fortunes are made there between sunrise and sunset, and lost in the various saloons overnight. It has its share of law-breakers, has Veldtsdorp, for crooks, as well as honest men, gravitate to places where money is easily made.

Among the law-breakers present and known—"deucedly well known," as he put it—to the police at this time was the Major. The Major—the man who had for many years been the despair of the diamond-mining syndicate, the man whom the police were continu-ally trying to catch in the act of buying illicitly procured diamonds. And they seemed doomed to perpetual failure. They knew the Major was an illicit diamond-buyer—he airily admitted it—yet they could not prove it. But they never gave up trying.

And so, when Trooper Cox, of the Mounted, saw a slim-waisted, elegantly attired wan lounging on the grass near the native compound of one of the large mines, he at once rode up to investigate.

"Hello, Major! What are you doing here?" he said, as he dis-mounted. The Major looked rather peeved.

"I don't like the suspicious tone of your voice," he replied.

"Well, I like that! Haven't I the right to be suspicious?" Cox an-swered, with some heat. He was very young and self-conscious. "When an I.D.B. suspect hangs round the native compound of a diamond mine, that's enough to make anyone suspicious."

The Major's round, smooth-shaven face lighted up with a smile—a disarming smile, the smile of a frank, ingenuous, man.

"Dear old top," he drawled, "you chappies do run true to form; don't you? Here you've only been six months in the corps, and—"

"Nine months!" snapped Cox.

"My mistake—sorry! Nine months in the corps, and you're just as suspicious as old Sergeant-Major Hough. Well"—resignedly—"I suppose you want to search me." He rose lazily to his feet and held his hands above his head.

But Cox made no move. The Major's eyebrows arched in surprise.

"Why don't you search me?"

"I'm not going to."

The Major stroked his jaw meditatively. His gray eyes opened wider; he appeared puzzled. Then he chuckled softly.

"Ah! I have it. You're afraid you'll find a scorpion in my pocket. But you won't—really! 'Pon my word of honor and all that. But perhaps you're thinking of Simkins. You haven't heard about him? You astonish me, really. It was very funny.

"Simkins, you know, wanted to make me a present of a diamond—the dear old boy wanted it to be a surprise, I believe. Anyhow, he tried to put it in my pockets when I wasn't looking, but little Johnny Scorpion was—oh, my, yes!—and Simkins took his hand out again in such a hurry that he forgot to let go of the diamond. And the scorpion liked him very much—wouldn't be parted from him, in fact."

The Major, somewhat breathless, paused. He seemed to expect some comment from Cox, and getting none, continued:

"I say, old dear; I wish you wouldn't stare at me like that. It's bally embarrassing and—er—damned bad form, if I may say so. Something is troubling the old bean, perhaps?"

"I was just wondering how you knew Simkins was going to frame you, Major."

"Going to *try*, you mean," amended the other. "I don't know—'pon my soul I don't. Perhaps—er—the scorpion told me. He was an affectionate little beggar, and very pointed in his remarks. I hated to lose him. But to the question on hand—I talk quite a lot; don't I?"

"Yes. And say nothing."

"You misjudge me, dear boy. But so have many better men. And so you don't want to search me?"

"No," Cox said slowly. "Even if I found the diamonds on you *now*, they'd be bits of glass or alum before I got you to the station."

"Or they might just vanish," the Major murmured softly. "But there you go, accusing me of witchcraft. Really, this is too much!"

"No," continued Cox, ignoring the Major's levity; "I just want to know why you're hanging round here."

"The view's delightful."

The Major indicated, with a wide sweep of his arm, the level plain, ugly in its bareness, beyond the town. Cox snorted.

"It's no place for a white man who's keeping within the law."

"The man declaims riddles," purred the Major. "Meaning?"

"That native laborers sometimes manage to smuggle diamonds from the mines and sell them to degenerate white men."

"Ugh! Meaning that's my game?"

"Well, isn't it?"

"Not very complimentary, are you? And if that *was* my game, do you think I'd play it out here, where any passerby could see me?"

"You might. Being so in the open, it wouldn't occur to anyone to suspect."

"But *you* did."

"Yes, I did," Cox agreed complacently.

"How very clever! And of course you'll stand beside me now and watch the native come up to me and sell me the diamond. Then you'll arrest me. I don't see why you wait here, though. Why not send me an engraved invitation to appear at the police station with the diamond in my possession? It'd save you no end of time and trouble. Still, your idea's clever—frightfully clever. You'll get promoted for this, old dear; they ought to give you a commission. If my recommendation is worth anything, they will."

COX FLUSHED crimson. He knew that he had acted like a fool. He should not have approached the Major at all, but should have hidden in a nearby hut. Perhaps it was not yet too late. He could ride away, and then—

The Major's bantering voice broke in on his cogitations.

"You've made me feel very uncomfortable, Cox. I shall feel as if someone is spying on me all the rest of the afternoon. Even if you rode away now, I should still feel that you were watching me." He sighed. "It's silly of me to be so sensitive, but it's bally hard to be wrongfully suspected—specially when I'm on such an innocent errand."

"Just what is your errand, Major?"

"My native servant, Jim—he's a Hottentot, you know—is visiting some friends in the compound, and I'm waiting for him. If I don't, some degenerate white man will fill him up with rotgut whisky at two shillings a drink, and then some other degenerate white men will arrest him."

Cox sat down on the sun-bleached grass.

"That settles it," he said in decided tones, answering the Major's look of surprised inquiry. "I'll wait here for Jim, too. When he does come, I'll search *him*."

The Major made a gesture of resignation and sat down beside the policeman.

"Very well. I'll be glad of company. A chap gets frightfully lonely out here— Ah! Here comes Jim now. Do you mind, dear sir"—the Major was mildly sarcastic—"getting through your searching party as quickly as possible? It's getting late, and I'm most deucedly hungry."

By this time Jim, a squat, ugly Hottentot, had come up to where the two men were sitting.

Cox looked at him searchingly and smiled contemptuously at the native's attire—evidently the Major's cast-off garments. Save across the shoulders, they were ludicrously too large.

"Dress him like a white man, don't you, Major?" Cox scoffed.

The Major's eyes narrowed, but he made no reply.

"Here you boy, Jim!" Cox continued. "Don't *wena* know how to boss up before a white man. *Susa lo* hat! Quick! Before *mena sjambok wena.*" The policeman rose to his feet and raised his hand threateningly.

"I think he was born in that hat," murmured the Major. "I know he sleeps in it. And I don't think I'd threaten to beat him if I were you. I don't like that sort of thing—really, I don't."

Jim, in response to an almost imperceptible nod, snatched his hat—a battered and greasy felt, creased in the middle—from his head and threw it on the ground.

"Pardon, *baas,*" he said. "Yah, *baas?*"

Cox's answer was to examine Jim from head to foot. He made the Hottentot discard his garments and searched them one by one. He looked up Jim's nose, in his ears, in his mouth—not a wrinkle of Jim's body was left unexplored. But his search was a vain one.

"All right," he growled at length, and, turning away in disgust, mounted his horse and galloped swiftly townward.

"Dress quickly, Jim," the Major ordered. "We trek tonight."

"Yah, *Baas.*"

"I am tired of this place. It has too many eyes."

"Yah, *baas.* See everything—see nothing. That *nonquai*" (mounted policeman) "his eyes closed. Me—damned glad—golly, yes."

An hour later, after they had reached their camp on the veldt and the Major was smoking his pipe with that contentment which comes to a man after a good meal, Jim said softly.

"Does the *baas* want to see it now?"

"Aye, Jim," the Major replied absently.

For the second—no; the third time that day Jim took the battered felt hat from his head.

In the cleft of the crown—holding it in shape—was a lump of fat. Nearly all the natives wearing that style of head-gear which Jim favored used similar pieces of fat to retain the fashion-prescribed cleft.

Jim removed the fat and from it extracted a smooth pebble. This he wiped carefully on the tail of his coat and then handed it to the Major.

"It is well that the policeman did not pick up the hat," the Major commented.

Jim grinned.

"It is an old hat, *baas;* and all covered with grease. Why should a white man be interested in Jim's hat?"

The Major toyed with the pebble in his hand.

"This makes twenty, Jim," he said. "Twice the count of your two hands."

"I can get more if the *baas*—"

"No. This is enough. Get ready—we trek when the moon rises."

"Where do we go, *baas?*"

"What matters? Which way blows the wind, Jim?"

"East, *baas.*"

"Then we trek east."

IT WAS nearing sunset of the following day when Jim halted the four mules which drew the light Cape cart, in the scanty shade afforded by a stunted tree.

"Shall we outspan here, *baas?*" he asked.

"Aye, Jim. It is as good a place as any."

In an incredibly short space of time Jim unhitched and unharnessed the mules, hobbled them and turned them loose to snatch what food they could from the withered herbage, had erected the bell-tent, set up the Major's deck-chair and portable table, and then—when he saw that his *baas* was comfortably settled—lit a fire and set about preparing the evening meal. He worked swiftly. A model of efficiency, he made no waste motions.

It was an interesting comradeship, this which existed between the superdandified but very masculine white man and the Hottentot. There was something about it infinitely deeper than the relationship between an indulgent master and a devoted servant. Perhaps the eternal boy, so strong in both, the aversion each bore to the conventional ways of their respective peoples drew them together. And there was a mutual admiration of the essentials of manhood which were so strong in each; they had tested each other time and again.

And yet, despite this unity of thought and aim, the Major was always the "*baas*," the white man, the supreme creation.

And Jim—well, Jim was Jim. There was no other like him. He had forsaken his people—the ease of *kraal* life—in order that he might follow his *baas*—his *baas* who could do no wrong, his *baas* who could do all things and do them well.

It was the Hottentot's greatest joy, the time of his proudest moments, when he could declaim to a circle of mouth-open natives, "He is the Major, and I—I am Jim, his servant."

He looked up now from his task at the camp-fire.

"Someone comes, *baas*," he said.

"Where, Jim?"

The Hottentot rose to his feet and pointed toward the setting sun. The Major rose, too, and, shading his eyes, scanned the veldt to the west.

"I can see no one, Jim," he said, and resumed his seat.

The Hottentot chuckled. It was always a source of merriment to him that his *baas,* in all things else so clever, should fail to see the things and hear the things which were so plain to him. And yet there were few white men who were so well versed in veldt-lore as the Major.

"A man comes on horseback, *baas,*" Jim continued. "He rides fast this way."

"You're a bally miracle-man," the Major drawled in English.

"Oah, yah, *baas.* A mirle-man. Damme, no."

The Major laughed.

"When will he get here, Jim?" His voice was now sharp and incisive. Only when he spoke English and was concentrating on some plan of action did the Major drawl.

"By the time scoff is ready for the *baas.*"

"Then set the table for two, Jim."

HALF AN hour later a heavily bearded man rode up to the tent, dismounted and stood looking at the Major in dumbfounded astonishment.

"What the hell—" he ejaculated. Then: "Haw! Haw!"

The Major, not at all conscious of the incongruous figure he presented—a man in dinner clothes on the veldt—looked up with a bland smile and adjusted his monocle.

"You're just in time, old chap," he said. "Let my servant take your horse, and then we'll have dinner. Sit down; won't you?"

He indicated the chair which the Hottentot had placed on the opposite side of the table.

Still speechless, the man slumped down in the chair. On his face was a comical expression of bewilderment. He seemed to be moving as one in a dream, and gingerly fingered the silverware.

"S'welp me!" he muttered, and, "Strike me pink if this ain't a one-er!"

"My name's Aubrey St. John," the Major hinted.

The man looked up quickly—noted the Major's carefully brushed hair, his manicured nails, his smooth-shaven face, the monocle and his polished pumps.

"You look it," he said briefly. "My name's Smith. Bill Smith— 'Bruiser' Smith, some folks call me."

"You look it," the Major said pleasantly.

Smith glared truculently, seemed about to take offense, then changed his mind, swallowed hard, half choked, muttered something under his breath about "swell dudes tryin' to poke fun at a bloke. I'm a good mind to biff 'im one," and then resorted, in his confused embarrassment, to fingering the silverware once again.

The Major clapped his hands, and Jim, wearing a white-flannel shirt and white-duck trousers supported at the waist by a flaming red cumerbund, brought on the first course.

Smith ate noisily, but otherwise the meal was a silent one, broken only by the Major's softly voiced orders to Jim.

"I do not indulge in sweets," the Major said, when Smith looked up from the carcass of a pheasant, with a sigh of satisfaction, "but Jim will open a tin of fruit if you wish."

Smith wiped his greasy fingers on the table-cloth.

"Naw! I don't want none. That was a meal wot is a meal, Aubrey. I don't want to spoil it."

"A cigarette, then?"

"Thanks!" He lit it and, leaning back, his gnarled hands clasped at the back of his head, puffed contentedly.

"Nothin' like a fag to settle a man's stummick after a big meal," he said. "I wouldn't call the king me uncle now, guv'nor."

"I'm sure he reciprocates your sentiments."

Smith snorted.

"You're pokin' fun at me again; ain't you, mister?" He ignored the Major's expostulations and continued: "But go on—we don't tork the same languige, so I don't understand—a bloke wot blows me to a meal like that can pull my bleedin' leg all he's a mind to. S'welp me, I ain't 'ad such a blowout since I took my missus down to Brighton fer a day's houting. We 'ad fish an' chips an' winkles then. Next day I sailed fer this Gawd-forsaken country, and 'eaven knows when I'll see the old gal again."

"The missus? The old gal?" the Major repeated softly. "Your wife, you mean?"

"Yus. Lumme, she's a daisy! The best pal a covey ever 'ad. She wasn't no city gal—came from the country, she did—was a 'ousemaid in one of the big Lunnon 'ouses. Dressed and torked like a lady, she did. Then she married me, an' we lived down W'itechapel way."

"In the slums, eh? And she a country girl?"

"Yus. Lumme, but love's a funny thing; ain't it, Aubrey?"

The two men smoked for a while in silence, then,

"Didn't she want to go back to the country, Smith?"

"Lor lumme, yes! But wot could I do? There ain't no jobs fer such as me in the country. Now, Lunnon I know. I used ter work be'ind a bar, I did—tap-room man I was. I used to make as 'igh as three shillin's a day w'en trade was good. I used ter buy 'er a bunch of vi'lets days I was specially lucky. I wouldn't 'ave been any good in the country; would I?"

His voice held a note of appeal. The Major nodded sympathetically.

"But she wasn't satisfied?"

"She was until the brat came. Then she 'ad to go. Went to live with 'er folks, she did, and wouldn't come back to our plice in W'itechapel. She said it was no plice fer a kid. But, lumme, I was raised there, guv'nor, and I'm all right."

"Yes. You're all right. And so—"

"An' so—lumme, I seem ter be a-tellin' of you everythin'; don't I? An' so I sees it's hup ter me to get a plice fer us in the country—a little pub, maybe. You know the kind I mean. Wiv a thatched roof, an' chickens and ducks in the back yard. An' may be roses and bloomin' vi'lets climbin' up the walls. But a plice like that costs money—as much as two hundred jimmy-o-goblins, most like. An' where was I goin' to get two hundred pounds? An' then I 'ears as 'ow a man wot can serve nippylike be'ind a bar could get good money hout 'ere—an' hout I comes. Worked my blinkin' passage over."

"And you got a good job?"

"Yus, I did. Like 'ell I did!" The man's voice was full of self-contempt. "Do you know Jake Shiners, guv'nor?"

The Major shook his head.

"Well, if you ever meets up with 'im, remember that Bruiser Smith warned yeh to look out fer 'im. He's a sly devil; he's a lousy—" Smith's voice shook with suppressed hate.

The sun had long since set.

"We'll have a light," said the Major.

There was something about Smith which interested him. He wanted to know more. He sensed the romance and the tragedy which had come into the man's life.

"Bring candles, Jim," he ordered softly.

A GHOSTLIKE figure emerged from the darkness beyond the fire, entered the tent, and a moment later set two candles, in sticks of polished silver, on the table. They did not flicker, so still was the night air, but burned steadily.

"You were speaking of Shiners," prompted the Major.

Smith roused himself with a start.

"He hired me at Cape Town the day I landed. I was green, an' soaked in his oily talk. It sounded on the square with me; I thought 'e was a little bit of all right. 'E looked like a real gent to me. I ought ter 'ave known better, 'owever, w'en I saw the way men treated 'im down there an' on the way hup. 'Asn't got any friends, Jake 'asn't. Do you know Peterstown, guv'nor?"

"Peterstown? Let me see. Isn't that the place where they had a big gold boom a few years back?"

"Yus. That's the place. It ought ter be called 'Shinerstown.' Jake owns it—body and soul. The mining coveys there tork about another boom comin', but, lumme, it ain't never stopped boomin' fer Jake. Them coveys in Peterstown get a goodish bit of dust from the old workin's, but it ain't their'n. It's Jake's. The only way they can get food—an' some of 'em 'as wives and kids—is to buy it from Jake. An' w'en they're broke, which is most frequent, 'e let's 'em 'ave credit; but the interest 'e charges would make a two-'undred-percenter Whitechapel Jew dream of 'oly 'eaven."

"Why don't they get out of the place?"

" 'Ow can they, guv'nor? Everything they own is mortgaged to Jake. 'E owns the shirts on their backs, the grub wot goes into their bellies. An', besides, Peterstown 's a good seventy miles—bleedin', thirsty, 'ot miles—from anyw'ere; an' they ain't none of 'em got no trekkin' outfit. So they stays out, prayin' like bleedin' 'ell fer a big strike."

"But you have a horse?"

"I 'ave an' I 'aven't, in a manner o' speakin.' " Smith smiled.

"You mean?"

"This 'orse"—he jerked his thumb behind him—"ain't mine. It's Jake's. I 'ooked 'im. Stole 'im, if yeh like. See? 'Ere's the lay of the game: I've been workin' a year fer Jake. A year at twenty quid a month an' board—that's wot 'e promised me. An' I asked 'im to take care of it fer me, for, thinks I, if I 'ave it, I'll spend it—thinkin,' I does, to surprise my missus wiv a lot—all at once like; thinkin' I'd be able to go 'ome at the end of the year an' buy that little pub in the country; thinkin'—

aw! Wot a bleedin' fool I was! I 'ad no business ter think; it ain't safe ter think w'en ye're dealin' wiv a chap like Jake. An' then, w'en I asks 'im fer my pay—last week, it was—'e laughs at me an' gives me five quid—five lousy quid fer a year's work! The rest, 'e said, I'd 'ad in keep—the blighter!

"An' wot could I do but swaller 'ard an' take it wiv a smile. Jake 'e's big enough to take me up in one 'and an' throw me across the bar. And so, night afore last, I 'elps myself to wot's in the till an' rides off on Jake's 'orse. And wasn't I within my rights, guv'nor?"

The Major nodded absently.

"I thought," Smith continued, "as 'ow I could reach the railway an' be on my way to the Cape afore sundown tonight. But I got lost; I ain't no good on the veldt. An' now it's too late. Jake'll be after me in the mornin', an' 'e'll get me."

Smith shivered, and for the first time his air of assurance—the assurance of a little London sparrow—failed him. His attitude was tense; he peered furtively from side to side. He whimpered a little— the game was too strenuous for him; the vastness of the veldt and the knowledge of his inability to conquer it overwhelmed him.

"How do you know Jake's not after you now?"

The Major's question, suddenly put, helped to restore the cockney's confidence.

" 'Cause 'e went to Veldtsdorp after some supplies an' won't be back until tomorrow mornin'. I'm goin' ter give 'im a long chase, guv'nor. I'll go on again as soon as the moon comes up."

"How far do you think you're from Peterstown now?"

"Lumme, I ain't much of a 'and at guessin' distances. I rode 'ard all day yesterday an' today. A good 'undred miles, I should say."

The Major looked at him pityingly.

"You don't know much about the veldt, do you, old chap? Must have been riding round in circles. You're not more than twenty miles from Peterstown."

SMITH ROSE, with an oath, and stared into the inky darkness beyond the fire.

"Gawd! Then 'ere's where I make a break for it. I ain't goin' ter wait fer the moon to come hup. Tell your nigger ter bring my 'orse, Aubrey. Thanks fer the scoff, and the way yeh listened ter me."

"Don't be a fool. You'd be caught sooner or later—probably sooner. What you're going to do is this: You're going back to Peterstown and return the money. Jake won't know anything about it, and everything will be all right. And just to make sure you do it, I'm coming back with you."

"I'm damned if I go back!"

The Major reached across the table and grabbed him by the shoulder.

"Let me go!" A whine crept into Smith's voice. "It ain't as if I stole the money. It was mine by right; you said so. Why should I go back?"

"Because I tell you to—and here's something to back up what I say. Look!"

Smith looked at a revolver which had appeared suddenly in the Major's free hand. It was leveled at his stomach. His hands dropped as if to guard the threatened spot.

"All right, guv'nor," he said meekly. "Put that bleedin' thing away. It gives me the funks. I'll do as you say. P'raps it's the best way, after all. The missus ,'ud say so."

"I thought you'd see reason. Jim!"

The Hottentot rose shadowlike from his seat by the fire.

"Baas?"

"Inspan, Jim. We trek at once."

A GROUP of miners—hard-living, hard-drinking men, all of them—were listening to the harangue of one of their number. He, a bald-headed, rubicund little man, with an apple-cheeked, smiling face, was standing on the counter-bar of Jake Shiners' saloon, exhorting the others, with the eloquence of a soap-box orator, to break loose from the shackles which bound them.

"It's union we want," he was saying. "We ought to stand together. If we do that, we can tell this lousy Jake Shiners to go to hell." A murmur of assent came from the listeners. "Yes—you're with me now; but what will you do when Shiners comes? Will you stick by me, or will you touch your hats and bow and scrape and keep on paying him ten quid for every one quid's worth of stuff you get from him."

"That tork's all very foine and laarge," said a tall, black-bearded Cornishman. "But what be ust to do if he doan't agrees to sell to us at our price—starve? There's naught place else for us-'uns to go."

"Let him sell at our price, or—"

"Or what?"

At the sound of the voice—a harsh, sneering voice—the men melted away from the little man on the counter and seated themselves at the various tables about the room.

The man behind the bar—he had been listening open-mouthed to Tubby's speech—busily began polishing the brass taps, which already shone like gold, whistling tunelessly as he did so.

Not a man in the room looked toward the open door save Tubby, who, after shouting a contemptuous "Quitters!" at his erstwhile listeners, boldly faced the man with the harsh voice.

"Or what?"

The repeated question sounded like a threat.

"I was saying, Shiners, that we've had enough of you. You'll sell us stuff at a decent price or we'll take it for nothing."

"Allehmahtig! What is this? You would take it away from me? You yourself?"

"Me and the rest of us—yes."

"So-a—this is the way you would treat me for the way I have fed you these years past. If you don't like my way, why don't you go?"

"You know we can't leave empty-handed, Jake. We're none of us as young as we used to be. We can't make the trip without provisions, and you know none of the women could."

Shiners ignored the note of supplication in Tubby's voice.

"Does this fat sow of a man speak for you all?" he asked the others.

"No, Jake!"

"Tubby's only kiddin'!"

"We ain't grousing."

"You're all right, Jake!"

Tubby looked reproachfully at the men who had sworn to support him.

"Yes," he faltered. "I was only joking, Jake."

"Ach sis! Your joking will be the death of me—if it is not first the death of you."

He rolled up his sleeves, displaying hairy, mighty forearms.

"Come you here!" he said.

Tubby clambered down from the counter. Further than that his legs refused to bear him.

"So-a!" It was like the menacing hiss of a snake. "I must come to you. Give me that *sjambok,* Smith."

The man behind the bar turned quickly and reached for the terrible whip of rhinoceros-hide. As he did so, he saw in the mirror on the wall the reflection of a slim-waisted, broad-shouldered man.

"Stilte! Hurry, man!" roared Shiners. "Or must I get it myself and use it first on you?"

Smith turned quickly—empty-handed.

" 'Ook it, Tubby!" he shouted. "Hout of the winder—quick!"

Tubby made a quick break, but Shiners, with a catlike pounce surprising in a man of his gigantic build, caught him and, holding him by the throat with one hand, smashed him in the face with the other. His fist was drawn back for a second blow.

"Oh, really, now! How brutal! You must stop that."

At the soft, drawling voice, Shiners loosed his hold on the luckless Tubby and turned to face the intruder.

"Ach sis!" he ejaculated. "Look what talks! Look!"

The miners left their seats and crowded round the newcomer.

"So-a! You think I'm brutal, do you? By Jove, now, that's too bad!"

At Shiners' clumsy burlesque of the other's drawl, the miners burst into a roar of laughter and crowded still closer.

"It ain't human," said Tubby. "If it couldn't walk and talk, I'd say as it was a dummy."

"Dear laddies," said the monocled one, "if you've quite finished, I'd like to buy you all a drink."

"He *is* human!" shouted Tubby. "Come on, stranger; let's see if you can drink as pretty as you look."

The thirsty ones lined the bar and shouted orders.

"Wait a minute, Smith!" snarled Shiners. "I want to see the color of this dude's money before you serve drinks."

"Money? Why, yes—of course. I've money. But why do you ask, old top? Is it—pardon me—any of your blinking business?"

"Seeing that I own this place, I should say that it is my business."

"Oh, splendid! Then you are Jake Shiners—yes?"

"That's my name," said Shiners heavily. "What about it?"

"Well, you see, my name's Aubrey St. John, and you're just the chappie I want to see."

Shiners grinned, winked at the miners, who were grinning as at some secret joke, wiped his greasy hands on his trousers and then clasped the other's outstretched hand.

"I'm pleased to meet you," he said, and put all his gigantic strength into the grip.

The miners watched laughingly. They expected to see the stranger wince, to break into a sweat, to moan, to plead for mercy as many apparently stronger men had done. But the stranger only stiffened, placed his feet a little farther apart and continued to smile blandly.

Shiners' face grew crimson; his shoulders hunched up with the effort he was making.

"Let's drink," he said suddenly, with a gasp of astonishment. "We don't have to stand here shaking hands all day."

"All right," said the dude, and, releasing his hold, joined the others at the bar.

SHINERS, SCOWLING fiercely, retired to a table in a far corner of the room, and there the dude, after a little while, joined him.

"I say, old top," he began; "they tell me you know all there is to know about this bally burg. Is there any gold about here?"

"Now you're talking! You've heard about the boom we had three years ago?" The other nodded. "Well, we're going to have another boom bigger than that. She's liable to break any day. Ain't she, boys?"

"You've said it, Jake!" shouted two or three of the men at the bar. But there was no trace of enthusiasm in their voices.

"Else why would we stay here?" questioned another.

"Because we can't get away," Tubby responded, with spirit.

Jake scowled at this, but the stranger affected not to hear.

"Really?" he said. "That's top-hole, because I thought of taking up a claim. I suppose you own several, old top."

Shiners sighed.

"Wish I did. But the boys have got 'em all pegged out, and you can't get 'em to sell at no price."

"That's too bad," cooed the dude. "I was hoping to stake a claim. It must be ripping, you know, to get gold from dirt. Such an easy way of getting rich, don't you know."

This was too much for Jake, and he laughed uproariously.

"This whisky is beastly stuff," continued the monocled one. "Haven't you some fizz—champagne, you know?"

"I'll get you a bottle."

Jake, grinning widely, went behind the bar.

Smith dodged as he neared, and Jake smiled. He had not forgotten Smith's early defiance, but just now he chose to ignore it.

"I'm going to clean out the *verdoemte* dude," he whispered. "If you'll help me, I'll forget that other matter."

"All right, guv'nor," Smith whispered back. "But 'e ain't no dude. 'E's the Major. You've 'eard of 'im; 'aven't you?"

Jake looked over at the gracefully slouching figure.

"The Major? You sure?"

"Yes, guv'nor. I saw a picture of 'im once in a police notice. 'E's a crafty devil, they say, for all he looks so soft."

"*Allehmahtig!*" Shiners rubbed his fingers. They were still numb from the Major's crushing grip. "He's not soft. Yes; I've heard of the Major. And—you're right, Smith; that's him. He's *slim*" (crafty)—"yes; because the police are fools. Now he meets a man who is *slim,* too, and we shall see. He tried to fool me; he makes believe that he is a monocled fool. All right. If you help me Smith, I'll give you a quid."

"It's a go, guv'nor. What do you want me to do?"

"Fix his drink to put him to sleep—I'm going to take him into my office—and get these men out of here."

Two hours later Smith quietly entered the cluttered room which served as Jake's office.

Seated on a chair, his arms sprawled over the grease-bespattered table, his head on his arms, was the Major. His hair was all tousled. He was only partly dressed. Most of his clothing was strewn about the room.

"It's only me, guv'nor," Smith said. "Are yeh all right?"

The Major straightened up quickly and laughed softly.

"Jake made a bally good job of it; didn't he? He ought to be in the police. He could teach them a lot about the searching game."

He rose to his feet and sluiced his face with water from the bucket which stood on a rickety stand in the corner of the room. As he dried himself, he whistled softly.

"He hasn't left me a penny!" he exclaimed later, as, having dressed, he felt in his pockets. "He has even taken my cigarettes. The hog!"

"Yus. He's all that," Smith assented. " 'Ere—let me 'elp you wiv them ridin'-boots. S'welp me!"

"What now?"

" 'E's pried hoff the 'eels, guv'nor."

The Major chuckled.

"Yes; I watched him do that. It was very funny. He had the deuce and all of a job."

" 'Ow do yeh feel, guv'nor?"

"Top-hole. But what was that beastly drink you fixed for me?"

Smith grinned.

"Sour tea and powdered quinine, guv'nor. And yeh can thank yer bleedin' stars it wasn't the stuff Jake's made me fix up fer other coveys. 'E thought it was—but I 'ad the powdered quinine all ready for you."

The Major made a wry face.

"It was terrible, Smith, but it did the job. Put me to sleep in ten minutes. It was bally hard not to laugh, though, while Jake was searching me. The beggar tickled. Did you do the other things?"

"Yus. Some of the boys are hout in the barroom now, guv'nor. I told 'em just wot yeh told me to—no more, no less."

JAKE SHINERS' eyes roamed wrathfully around the Major's tent. It looked as if a cyclone had struck it, and the fact that he had been the cyclone did not lessen his ill humor.

On learning that the dude who called himself "Aubrey St. John" was really the famous—or infamous—I.D.B., Jake had reasoned that the Major must have some diamonds with him, and, when the search of the Major's person had been fruitless, he had determined to search the Major's camp.

And now it seemed that the search of the tent was also to prove fruitless.

He turned, with a furious oath, to where Jim, bound hand and foot, was lying in the corner of the tent.

"Tell me where your *baas* keeps his diamonds," he roared, "or—" He menaced Jim with a *sjambok*.

"I do not know, *baas*."

The whip rose and fell. Jim's eyes narrowed.

"Wait, *baas!* Let me think. I will tell you. But, first, you must promise to save me from my *baas's* wrath."

Shiners licked his lips greedily.

"I will take care your *baas* does not whip you," he said.

"He is a hard man, *baas*," said Jim. "I will tell you where the stones are. Look in the water-barrel, *baas*. You will find them there."

Shiners rushed out of the tent, and Jim, turning on his side, his ear pressed close to the ground, smiled happily. He heard a distant pounding on the hard, sun-baked veldt—a pounding that came ever nearer; the *"tot-a-a-tot-a, three ha' pence for tuppence"* of a horse approaching at the triple—that pace-deceiving gait of the Major's mount.

But Jake Shiners did not hear it—no white man would have heard it. The Major was, he well believed, still in the room back of the bar, sleeping the heavy sleep of the drugged.

AND SO Jake gave all his attention to the barrel. It was a big one, and filled to the brim with water. It was too heavy for him to tip over, and it was too deep for him to reach inside to the bottom, where, he was well convinced, the diamonds were hidden.

There was only one thing to do: to knock out the bung—a makeshift affair of pitch—and let the water drain out.

He pulled out the plug and then sat down, his back to the tree-trunk, and smoked his pipe with great enjoyment. He had plenty of time. The Major was safe for several hours yet. He thought pleasantly of the diamonds—wealth—which would soon be his. He indulged in day-dreams of the luxuries he could command. In order that he might visualize them more clearly, he closed his eyes. Perhaps he dozed; the day was very hot, and it was so peaceful out there under the trees—

He opened his eyes and swore. The water had ceased flowing from the bung-hole. He jumped to his feet and saw that the barrel was empty save for some six inches of water below the bung-hole. He tilted the barrel.

Carefully, yet with difficulty restraining his feverish impatience, he up-ended the barrel. The "things" rattled down the side of it and on to the ground.

One, two, three, seven, ten, twelve. How Jake's eyes gleamed! Fifteen, sixteen, seventeen, twenty. Twenty in all!

He pounced on them and picked them up. One by one he examined them closely, closer—and then, cursing, he threw them away. They were stones—not diamonds.

He rushed back to the tent. That *verdoemte* Hottentot would pay for this.

Then he stopped short, turned in his tracks, mounted his horse and spurred swiftly away. In his ears sounded the mocking laughter of the Major and Jim, the Hottentot.

"It is well that you came when you did, *baas*," said Jim. "I do not like to be beaten."

"But he did beat you, Jim." The Major indicated the weal on the Hottentot's naked shoulder.

Jim chuckled.

"Only once, *baas*. I was well paid for it. Under the flap of the tent I looked, and I saw him find the stones which were not stones."

The Major's eyes glittered steely blue; the vacuous expression of his face disappeared; the lines of his jaw seemed to tighten. And then he relaxed.

"All right, Jim," he said. "Get the bung—I'll make another—that one's too loose—and then we'll go for water."

Jim left the tent, returning almost immediately with the bung.

The Major took it with a smile, and carefully breaking it with the butt of his revolver, he picked over the pieces until he had on the table before him twenty rounded stones. Diamonds—not stones!

"We must find another place for them, Jim."

The Major was speaking English now, as he often did when alone with Jim. Not that Jim understood—save a word here and there—but it always helped him to work out his problems.

"It'll never do," he continued. " 'Pon my soul it won't—to hide the bally things twice in the same place. I think they'd be safe here for the present; don't you, Jim?"

"Yah, *baas*," agreed Jim, seeing that some comment was expected, and the Major carelessly dropped the stones into a cigar-box.

"The trouble with this bally business is the difficulty I have in finding a good market. In the course of the years, Jim, old scout, we've handled hundreds of stones between us, and they were worth thousands and thousands and thousands of pounds. And yet I'm not rich. Wonder why."

"Not rich—golly, no!"

"I suppose it's because the dealers know my trade and I have to take what they want to pay. If they don't buy I can't sell anywhere. Of course I could carry them round with me and take a chance of smuggling them out of the country. But that's a risky game, and, if I'm caught, twenty years on the Breakwater. I'm afraid I'm not made for hard labor, Jim."

"Yah, *baas*."

"Don't be a blooming pessimist, Jim." The Major sighed. "But really I'd like to go to Jo'burg for a spree. Haven't seen the dear old town for months and months. And I can't go there without lots of money. You know, Jim, if I could sell only two or three of these diamonds at half their value, I'd be rolling, simply rolling, in wealth."

"Yah, *baas*."

"I think I shall sell some of the stones to dear old Jake. He seemed very anxious to get them. I think—no; I'm absolutely bally well sure—that he would pay a very good price for them—a very good price, indeed. My price, in fact. Don't you think so, Jim?"

"Yah, *baas*. Top-'ole, yah, by Jove! Jus' what you say."

"You're a treasure, Jim!" the Major cried. "He shall pay me—oh, he'll be most willing and anxious to pay—just what I say. I wonder how much he's worth."

"CHERRIO, OLD top! Balmy weather we're having, and all that. Eh—what?"

Jake Shiners looked up with a scowl. His hand reached in the open drawer of his desk and closed on a revolver.

Since his little searching party five days previously, he had steered clear of the Major. Yet he had expected that man to come gunning for him, and wondered why he had delayed so long. And now Jake's nerves were rather ragged.

No fool with a gun himself, he knew that if but half the things he had heard were true, the Major could beat him to the draw. He wondered if he could slide the gun from the drawer unobserved. The Major would be watching the one in his holster.

Not very chummy this bright day, are you?" the bland voice continued. "Tut, tut, and again tut. I haven't come a-shooting, dear old chap. So shut that drawer—and leave the revolver inside."

The last words came with a snap, and, as if to enforce them, a revolver suddenly appeared in the Major's hand.

Jake shut the drawer with a bang.

"Well?" he snarled.

"Ah! That's much better. We'll be like two cooing doves before long—a regular Damon and Pythias and all that, you know. But perhaps you don't know."

"No, I don't. What do you want with me?"

The Major twirled the revolver in his hand, returned it to the holster, pulled up a chair beside Jake's and sat down.

"Just a little talk, old dear—a business talk."

"*Stilte!* You talk business with me?"

"Exactly. 'Pon my word, your lack of discernment is quite embarrassing. Of course you know who I am—clever of you not to show it when we first met—and I know why you searched me and my camp."

Jake mumbled something about having made a mistake.

"Oh, don't apologize. I don't blame you. I should have done exactly the same thing myself had I been you. But you shouldn't have whipped Jim. Really, you shouldn't."

Jake shifted uneasily. But the Major's soft tones carried no threat, and he replied:

"He's only a nigger, Major. A nigger don't mind *sjambok*ing once in a while."

The Major's eyes narrowed.

"I see," he said rather absently; "I see your point of view exactly. Yes, indeed! However, to return to business: I'm quite ready to forget the little affair you pulled off—quite willing if you are. I don't think you'll do anything like that again. No? Of course not! No reason to. You know now that I haven't any diamonds; don't you?"

"For God's sake, get to business, Major," Jake exclaimed irritably. "You talk like an old *Vrouw*."

"But first tell me this, old dear: Shall we let bygones be bygones, or is it the frozen mitt and the back of my hand to you?"

"I'm willing to forget all about it."

"Good! Now you must swear not to tell anyone what I am going to tell you now."

"I swear." Jake's tone was that of an indulgent parent humoring a talkative child. "What is on your mind?"

"S-sh!"

The Major put his fingers to his lips, tip-toed to the door, opened it suddenly and peered about, closed it and came back to his chair.

"I thought there might be someone listening," he explained.

"There is," Jake said sarcastically. "I am. That's all I've been doing since you came here."

The Major held up a protesting hand.

"You do me an injustice. It is essential that I be very cautious; as you shall see."

"Get to business, man!"

"Well"—the Major drew his chair still closer to Jake's—"that boom you've been talking about so long is here."

"What are you talking about?"

Jake was torn between two emotions. He wanted to believe the Major, and yet—

"Do you mean they've located a rich strike?"

The Major nodded mysteriously.

"Something like that. It's true. Look!"

HE PLACED a small package on Jake's desk, unwrapped it and exposed a lump of clayish substance.

"Do you know what that is?"

"Blue clay, fool! What about it?"

"And what do they find in blue clay? Tell me that."

The Major's whisper was dramatic in its intensity. Jake's jaw sagged. He looked in bewilderment at the lump of clay.

"What—" he began, and stopped. The look of bewilderment gave way to one of comprehension. "Why," he exclaimed suddenly, "diamonds are found in blue clay! Where did you find this?"

"Softly," cautioned the Major. "Now look at these."

"These" were ten stones—unmistakably diamonds, unlovely in their uncut, unpolished state.

"*Maan,*" cried Jake, "do you mean to say you found these in Peterstown? It means our fortunes! But why"—and suspicion took the place of joy—"do you come to me?"

"Because I can't swing a big thing like this alone, in the first place; in the second"—the Major smiled whimsically and sighed—"I'm far too well and widely known to get a diamond-mining permit. They wouldn't give me one."

"That's right; they wouldn't," Jake assented. He was beginning to see light.

"But," continued the Major hurriedly "you can get one without any trouble, and no questions asked. You do that—and we'll go half-shares. Do you agree?"

"No. I do all the work—take all the risk. I should get seventy-five percent of the shares and you twenty-five."

The Major shrugged his shoulders.

"You're a hog, Jake, but I'll accept. The Lord knows twenty-five percent will bring me all the money I want. I'll be a multimillionaire. Think of it, old top."

His enthusiasm was infectious. Jake smiled. At that moment he was scheming to retain all the proceeds. He would be the sole owner; he would be the richest man in this world. Barney Barnato and the Joels would be paupers compared with him.

"Let's shake on it, Major," he said. He held out a greasy paw.

The Major was at that moment polishing his monocle.

"I'd rather not, if you don't mind, old, chap. You have such a bone-crushing grip, you know."

Jake leered.

"It is as a girl's compared to yours, Major. But what's the next move?"

"I'm a pretty poor business man," confessed the Major; "but how does this strike you? You go for the diamond-mining permit, and I'll buy up the claims—you want to get 'em all; don't you?"

"Yes. We want them all. But you must think I'm soft to leave you up here running things. How do I know but what you'll do me out of the whole business?'

The Major looked hurt.

"You wrong me—really, you do. What good would the claims be to me without a permit?"

"That's right, too."

"And here's another point: I can buy the claims cheaper than you. They'd suspect something if you started buying. Now, me—they think I'm a fool. They'd never suspect me of anything. They'd sell me—don't you see?"

"With what will you buy the claims? Your money?"

The Major chuckled and rubbed his hands gleefully.

"Ah! Now you're joking," he said waggishly. "I had but ten quid, and you cleaned me out of that the other day. No. You're going to provide the wherewithal, Jake, dear soul."

"I'm damned if I do!"

"All right." The Major picked up the diamonds—one by one—and put them in his pocket. "I'll tell the chappie on whose claim I found these. They're legally his, you know."

He rose from his chair and walked toward the door.

"Ta-ta, old chap!" he called over his shoulder.

"Wait, *Maan!* Don't be so hasty." Jake was panic-stricken.

The Major returned to his chair.

"You're hard on me, Major," Jake whined. "How do I know you'll play square?"

"You don't. That's the funny part of it. But—don't you see?—we can't run this any other way. I'd go if I could; but they'd laugh at me. You know that. No. I'm afraid you'll have to trust me. But wait—I have it! You want some security for my good behavior; don't you? Quite natural that you should. How much would you say these stones were worth?"

"Five hundred pounds," Jake replied promptly.

The Major almost fell from his chair with laughter.

"Say six thousand, and you'd still be getting a bargain, Jake. I'm not talking about an I.D.B. price; they'll be legally mined. The smallest one there is worth more than your price."

"I'll say five thousand," conceded Jake. "But what of it?"

"Wait a minute! At how much do you value your property, including cash on hand?"

Jake turned to his desk and did some unnecessary figuring—at any moment Jake could have told to a penny just how much he was worth.

"There's four thousand pounds in cash."

"By Jove! So much?" the Major exclaimed in tones of admiration.

"Don't believe in banks," Jake explained. "Keep all my cash where I can put my hands on it."

The Major nodded understandingly.

"Four thousand pounds in cash," he said. "Yes—go on!"

"I don't know what you're driving at; but I value the property—mules, horses, wagons, everything, including the bad debts—at one thousand pounds."

"High valuation, Jake, old dear! But that's the way to get rich. Five thousand in all—eh?" Jake nodded. "Very well, then. Don't you see that you can't lose? You take the diamonds with you when you go for the permit. At your own valuation they are worth at least as much as your property and cash together. As a matter of fact, you know they're worth a bally sight more." Jake's eyes gleamed as he nodded assent. "All you have to do, then, is to give me power—er—power of attorney, I think they call it, to buy the claims for you. That makes it sure that whatever I buy will be yours—that I am only acting as your agent. See?"

Jake hesitated a moment.

"All right," he said finally. "Give me the diamonds."

"The power of attorney first."

Jake picked up a pen and began to write.

"That's fine!" said the Major a few minutes later. "How's your man, Smith? Can he keep his mouth closed?"

"He'd better," growled Jake.

"Fine! We'll have him in to witness this. Here are the stones."

Jake took them greedily.

"When will you start, Jake?"

"Tomorrow. I'd go tonight if there was a moon. You'll be careful; won't you? Don't want any of the —— to tumble to our game."

"They'll not," said the Major airily. "They're such bally idiots they would not believe there were diamonds on their claims if I told them. You'll be back inside of ten days; won't you?"

"Yah."

"Fine! I'll have all the claims for you by then. When you signed this paper, Jake, you made our fortunes."

Jake grinned. He was thinking that he had, indeed, made his fortune; but he replied:

"Call in Smith if you want to, Major, and get him to witness that paper. I'm going to bed then. Got to make an early start tomorrow morning."

NEARLY A month elapsed before Jake Shiners again rode over the veldt toward Peterstown.

Instead of returning as soon as he had procured his mining permit, he decided to stay a while and enjoy the pleasures that wicked city had to offer. Jake was no cheap sport where his own selfish pleasures were concerned; besides, he knew the capital well—it was his native town—and his tastes ran high. Also, Jake was a poor card player and the town was—probably still is—full of card-sharps, confidence men and the like.

In one day Jake lost all the money he had with him, but he had not lost his taste for the night life and, in order to pander to that taste, he offered the ten diamonds for sale. The only dealer who would talk business with him was one who was not above buying from an I.D.B.—and Jake was suspected of being that. In fact, he rather posed as such among the habitués of the gambling-houses, thinking thus to ward off any possible chance of someone following him back to Peterstown. The dealer's highest offer for the stones was eight hundred pounds—"Take it or leave it."

Jake took it, and left it with certain expert card players.

Broke at last, Jake set his steps Peterstownward—broke, but happy. The diamonds were gone; but he cheered himself with the thought that there were plenty more where they came from.

Most of the time during the tedious journey home—the train trip to Veldtsdorp, and the two days' trek on horseback from that place to Peterstown—Jake spent in thinking up suitable schemes to oust the Major from the partnership.

But as he rode into Peterstown he had many other things to think of. The place was deserted! Not a soul was to be seen—the houses were empty—uninhabited.

Jake began to sweat, and it was not wholly due to the heat. Spurring his horse to a mad gallop, he came to his saloon. It, too, was empty; the table and chairs, the long counter and the bottles on the shelf, were covered with dust. The brass taps were tarnished; mice scampered about the floor.

A letter was sticking in the gilt frame of the mirror behind the bar counter. It was addressed to him.

Wonderingly, fearing he knew not what—but fearing—Jake took it down, opened it and read:

DEAR JAKE:

The night after you left I held a meeting of the miners and was astonished to find that they were more than willing to sell their claims, and, I flatter myself, I bought them dirt cheap for you.

The miners are jolly old chappies; aren't they? And very accommodating. All they asked was fifty pounds each, a release from their debts to you, provisions and conveyance to Veldtsdorp. Bally reasonable—what? I agreed to their terms of course, and the next day we sent off the first batch in your wagon. It was a merry sight to see the old codgers and their wives going to a decent, civilized town. They all gave three cheers for you—that should brighten your generous heart. Of course I did not tell them why you wanted the claims.

Well, well! To cut a long story short, the next ten days we were busy—oh, very busy!—sending parties off.

Quite some job, old chap!

When the last batch lined up, ready to depart, Jake, I decided to go, too. It would have been terribly boring here all alone, and worse still when you returned. And then I remembered that Jim—the Hottentot, you know—owned two claims, and as you said you wanted all the claims, of course I had to buy Jim's. And the beggar held me up! There was just fifteen hundred pounds of your ready money left, and the heathen made me pay it all. He wanted a lot of tobacco, too, and a mouth-organ and some scent. I refused him the scent, so he took a felt hat instead. The hat cost more than the scent, but, as you now have *all* the claims, I'm sure you're satisfied.

I am.

Cheerio, old top!

Your ex-partner,
THE MAJOR.

P.S. I forgot to say that Mr. Bill Bruiser Smith helped me a great deal, so I paid him fifty pounds for his services. He said that you owed him a year's pay, and also a quid for mixing a certain drink. He seems to be a truthful chappie; so I paid his claim. I think the blue clay I showed you came from Veldtsdorp; I know the diamonds did.

P.P.S. Jim says that you did not hurt him very much when you hit him with a *sjambok*. The weal has quite disappeared, and Jim says he likes the tobacco very much and is sorry he couldn't have the scent. I'm not. My people are calling. I go now, like a modern Moses, to lead the Peterstownites out of the House of Bondage—out of the House of Shiners, in a manner of speaking.

Keep a stiff upper lip, dear lad, and don't swear too much.

BUT JAKE SHINERS—sole owner and inhabitant of Peterstown—did swear. He cursed loudly and continuously—cursed until he was exhausted and could curse no more.

But his curses fell on empty walls; there was no one to hear them, and, having no place else to roost, they fell on his own head.

A PERSONAL
INTERVIEW

"**W**HISPERING" SMITH—SOME men called him "Whip"—was in a vile temper and as he stalked up and down the little room which opened into his saloon bar, he read and re-read the letters he held in his hands.

A South Africander once said that Smith reminded him of a tyrannical, evilly sarcastic bully of a schoolmaster whose pupils had a greater fear of his softly spoken innuendoes than the whip used as a threat. And never was the comparison so apt as now.

"The dolts!" he exclaimed. "The fools!" With an impatient gesture he brushed back the wisp of hair which had fallen down over his low, receding forehead. As he did so the dazzling sunbeams which streamed into the room through the one small, narrow window, were split up and reflected in rainbow hues by the diamond rings which covered his fingers. The rings were Smith's weakness—his only deviation from the attire ordained by good taste.

"The fools," he repeated, and his accents were those of a cultured man, "I'm through with them. They need not come whining to me for protection any more."

The other occupant of the room, a big Dutchman, shifted uneasily on his feet.

"If I ever get my hands on them," Smith continued, speaking rapidly and riffling the papers with his white, well cared for hands, "I'll tear their hearts out!"

The big, slow-witted Dutchman, Piet Deemster, scratched his head, greatly puzzled. Somehow he was afraid of this man with the soft voice who cursed so venomously.

"Allehmahtig!" he muttered. "I could take him up in one hand and throw him out onto the *stoep*. And yet—" He shook his head. "I'm glad I wrote him not those letters I brought him! I wonder—"

"What's that, you oaf?" Smith wheeled suddenly and faced the ungainly, full-bearded Dutchman. "You wonder what's in these letters, do you?"

"No," the Dutchman stammered. "I would only say I'm sorry they give bad news. If I can help you, Whip—"

"You help!" Smith sneered. "You—oh, get back to your kennel and don't let me see you in the *dorp* again, you mongrel!"

The insult penetrated the Dutchman's thick skull and for a moment he seemed as if he were about to express his resentment but, thinking better of it, he backed slowly out of the room—banging the door behind him with some force, however.

Instantly, with a catlike leap, Smith sprang to the door, opened it and called to the Dutchman, "Come back here, you, and close the door quietly."

Sheepishly the Dutchman obeyed and then went out into the street again.

Just outside the saloon he bumped into a man as tall and broad as himself and with a bellow of rage he lashed out and hit the stranger full between the eyes with his mighty fist, knocking him off his feet. Deemster—he had been known to knock down bullocks with similar blows—did not wait to see if the man would get up and show fight but lumbered on his way up the street.

Meanwhile, Smith had seated himself at his desk and was preparing to file the letters which had caused his outburst. Before adding them to his files, which were partly explanatory of his hold over the criminals of South Africa, he glanced through them once again.

The first, an illiterate scrawl, read:

> Dear Whip:
> I was first at this bloomin' berg. The majer was at the Hotel. i remembered wot yew said you wanted dun with him. I slipped some of the greasys into his poket. Then i rote a leter to the poleeseman hear and told him the mejer had some counterfeet banknots. The bobby arested him tonite. He'll het ten yrs for that.
> > Yrs respect'ly
> > Joet Timmons.

The second letter was much briefer.

Dear Whip:

Saw the Major here at the hotel. I framed him with a diamond and notified the police he was an I.D.B. He was arrested tonight and I don't think he'll trouble you for a long time.

Yours,

Savage.

The third was a lengthy epistle. The most interesting part, the part which caused Smith's mouth to tighten, read:

The Major was staying at the hotel here and I managed to inveigle him into a game of cards. I cleaned him out; and when he didn't have any money left I gave him ten quid for a good-sized "stone" he had. And I won that, too, of course. The joke of it all is, the money he played with wasn't his and tonight the bobby arrested him. Don't know what for—something to do with the money, I expect. Anyway, he's done for. You were right, Boss. The Major's a fool.

Don't think much of the two chaps you've told off to go with me on this trip—they're greenhorns. What do you want done with them? Put out of the way?

We leave here as soon as the moon's up and I'm going to help myself to the Major's camp stuff. He won't need it where he's going. Ha-ha!

We ought to be able to deliver the guns and be on our way back inside a week.

I'm sending this, as per instructions, through Piet Deemster.

Yours,

Saunders.

"He's the biggest fool of the three," Smith muttered. "If he'd kept his hands off, the tricks of the other two might have done the job. Might have—but I think not. The Major's got more brains than I've given him credit for. He shall have a file all to himself! I'll show him that he can't interfere with my plans—and remain happy!"

He spread the fourth and last letter on the table before him and examined it closely. It had not come to him via Piet Deemster, but had been even longer en route.

"He's an Oxford man, judging by the scrawl," Smith reflected. "Wonder what he did over the other side. Something big, I imagine. If all the stories they tell of him are true, he must have made thousands in the I.D.B. game. And yet he's never been back home and he's going under an alias. I'll set some men looking up the Major's record. If he's wanted for something on the other side, I'll find out. And that'll make things so much the easier.

"It's strange, now I come to think of it, that I've never seen the chap. But then, they say he hates the *dorps;* poses as a great outdoor man. Bah! We'll see."

He picked up the letter again. He read it aloud and, as he read, a drawl crept into his voice—the drawl affected by Cambridge University men. Occasionally he smiled—not unpleasantly. The letter ran:

> Most dear and honored sir:
>
> I've recently had the dubious pleasure of making the acquaintance of three of your business associates. They're charming fellows—oh, really! And so naïve. They've probably told you about the presents they wished to give me and how I, not desiring to give them offence, returned them—secretly as it were.
>
> And then, because I didn't want to hurt their feelings, I asked the well-known and mighty representative of the law to put me in *'trunk'* for the night. Your friends rather expected that, and it gave them no end of joy. The merry wags ran off with my camp kit and, of course, I went after them! You understand that, don't you, or you will when I add that the beggars had taken my razor and I needed a shave very badly.
>
> I came up with them just in time to persuade them not to sell rifles and ammunition to a renegade native named Yellow Pete—a most frightful fellow. I'm sure you'll approve of my action. It is deuced bad form to sell weapons to the natives, don't you know? And, oh yes, to make sure your three wise laddies wouldn't be tempted to do a little gun running contrary to my well-meaning advice, I took all their stock away from them and sold it to Yellow Pete myself. But first, dear old man, I removed the firing pin from each rifle, and the charges from all the blinking cartridges. It was a deuce an' all of a job, let me tell you.
>
> The last I saw of the three, they were conversing loudly but not exactly amicably. Well, boys will be boys, and one can't handle pitch without getting one's hands all messy—and they all worked for you. That explains a deuce of a lot.
>
> I've heard a lot about you of late, Smithy, dear heart. You seem to be quite a little devil and I'd like awfully to know you better.
>
> Until then, to be quite brutal, I thumb my nose at you.
>
>   Ta-ta,
>   The Major.

With one final devastating curse, Smith put the letter in a folder on which he printed in large letters: IN ACCOUNT WITH THE

MAJOR. That done he opened a large scrapbook and looked carefully through the items pasted there.

This book was a complete Rogues' Gallery, containing the photograph and dossier of every rogue operating in South Africa—and each one was under Smith's orders. His hold over them was uncanny. Never infringing the criminal code himself—at least nothing had ever been proved against him—he was the prime instigator of every Major, and many a minor, crime executed in the colony.

Like a spider in the midst of an enormous web, Smith sat in the office of his Kimberley saloon and waited for things to come his way. The newspapers of the world—he was an accomplished linguist—were his threads of information; and almost daily he read of a potential victim who would respond to his invitation couched in true Mother Goose spider style.

Smith set his traps chiefly for first offenders; they were more easily moulded.

He wanted those who, by force of circumstances, environment, apparent opportunity and their own inherent weaknesses, had stepped over the narrow line separating legal and illegal practices. The fraudulent, bankrupt bank clerks who had gambled with the bank's money, shoplifters and governesses who, under the stress of the moment, had forged their employer's signature—all these, were fair game to Smith. And the majority of these, if they could succeed in dodging arrest, made a break for South Africa. Extradition warrants were hard to get there.

Of these, some few succeeded and made good; others were located by the police at Cape Town and sent back in irons; but most of them were located by agents of Smith and, when faced with the option of helping him in one of his many nefarious schemes or being handed over to the police, invariably decided on the easiest path. And Smith, once he got a hold over man or woman, never let go.

The book he was now consulting was marked "Sheep Found." Close by was another and larger volume which bore the label "Black Sheep to be Redeemed," which contained the photos and dossiers of people his agents had not yet succeeded in locating.

Slowly Smith turned over the pages of his "Sheep Found" book, stopping occasionally to scrutinize closely a photograph or read the account of the subject's offence against the criminal code.

He turned back several times to look gloatingly at the photograph of a pretty, dark-haired girl, whose wide-open eyes held an innocent, baby stare.

Finally he leaned back in his chair and rubbed his hands briskly together.

"She'll do," he exclaimed at length in well satisfied tones.

Just then a timid rap sounded on the door.

"Come in!" Smith said.

The door opened slowly and two men entered, closing the door slowly and quietly behind them.

Smith looked at his watch, scowled fiercely, but did not turn to look at the two men who had entered. A small shaving mirror on his desk obviated that necessity.

"You're late," he snapped. "Ten minutes. Why?"

The two men came forward and the taller one, an alert, soldierly looking man with furtive eyes, said, "I was ordered out on special duty, Boss. And I couldn't get back any sooner."

"That's a hell of an excuse. What do you think I got you appointed plain-clothes man on the force for, if you're not here when I want you? Why couldn't you get someone else to take the duty for you?"

"I would have, Boss, only I don't think you would have wanted me to." The man's round face flushed with embarrassment and his eyes wandered aimlessly about the room. "You see, Boss, some of the 'black coats' have been squealing to the chief that 'Cat' has been selling booze to the niggers and I was detailed to go out there and get evidence. I thought I could do better than any of the others, so I went."

A shadow of a smile flitted over Smith's face.

"Sometimes you show smatterings of intelligence, Brimmer. It's just as well you didn't back out of the job. Did you get anything on Cat?"

Brimmer grinned broadly.

"Not a thing, Boss. I was there four hours and I didn't see Cat serve one drink—don't believe he's got any stuff on the place at all. He says he's never sold a nigger liquor and I believe him. Cyanide knocks 'em out quicker and it's got a bigger kick—and it's much cheaper."

Smith waved his hands.

"All right. That'll do for you. But how about you, Solly?"

He turned swiftly on the other man.

"I waited for Brimmer, Boss. Thought you wanted to see us both together."

"Thinking again, eh, Solly? How many times have I told you not to? Your hands are your brains, Solly, and I'll grant you that they're exceedingly good in their line. I always keep my eyes on my watch and purse when you're around. But outside of your hands, Solly, you— Well, don't think, Solly, that's all. And Brimmer!"

"Yes, Boss?"

"Next time you see Savage, or Houndsditch Joe or "Sneak" Saunders, arrest 'em—then let me know. I'll supply you with enough evidence to keep 'em in jail for the rest of their lives. See?"

"All right, Boss," Brimmer said with forced cheerfulness, but he and Solly exchanged uneasy glances. Always when Smith notified them that he had withdrawn his protection from this or that man, they wondered when their turn would come.

"What have they done?" Solly asked timidly.

The question aroused Smith's anger again.

"Done? It's what they haven't done. They had a chance to get the Major. And the fools fell down. Not only that, but he beat them at their own game and upset the slickest gun running scheme I've ever planned. I've had my fill of that monocled dude—do you hear? He's upset my plans three times—and that's three times too many."

"Do you want him croaked, Boss?"

Smith looked at Brimmer pityingly.

"No! That's too easy—and there's always a danger of them pinning it on the chap who did it. And when a chap's neck is in danger he won't think twice about squealing on me. Not that anyone knows a great deal—not even you, Brimmer. Remember that. No! I'm going to find out what the Major's done on the other side; I want to know why he's hiding out here. And once I know that, I'll have him where I want him. But until then, Brimmer, I want him in a safe place so that he can't get in my way. And what place is safer than jail, eh?"

Smith rubbed his hands together and chuckled softly.

"That's easy, Boss," Brimmer said quickly. "Frame him with diamonds. Solly here can slip a couple in his pocket and I'll arrest him."

Smith shook his head.

"I don't want you or Solly to figure on any deal I make with the Major. I want some of his friends on the force—and there's plenty of 'em, I hear—to do it. Then again, if you or Solly have anything to do with it, there's sure to be talk of a 'frame-up' and the Major may get away—and then good-bye to the Major. He'd steer clear of this *dorp* in future and I'd have the devil's own time getting hold of him."

"Then how about sending him a 'stone' by registered mail, Boss, and tipping the cops off?"

Smith considered this plan of Solly's for a moment, then shook his head.

"No! I don't think that's any good either. He's too *slim* to be caught by that old trick. I've a good mind," he continued reflectively, "to ask him to come to see me. Perhaps we could do business together. I need a man like the Major."

"Then you don't think he's a damned dude fool, Boss?"

"What's that?" Smith said sharply. "No—he's no fool. Just because he wears a monocle, drawls and wears swagger cloths—that's no sign he's a brainless idiot like you two. And he's a gentleman, remember that."

"But you always said—" Brimmer began.

"However—" Smith disregarded the detective's interruption—"he's played his last hand against me." He pointed to the photograph of the dark-haired, baby-eyed girl. "Is she in the *dorp* now?"

"All the chaps on the force are moony about her. They've all proposed to her and she promised to be a sister to them." He snickered. "She aims higher than poor troopers. She's setting her cap at—"

"Never mind all that," Smith exclaimed impatiently. "Is she in town now?"

"Yes, Boss."

"All right. Go and get her. I'm ready to gamble that she won't refuse *my* proposal."

"Very good, Boss. Solly had better come with me. She may be stubborn."

"Take him, then. Has the Major moved camp, yet?"

"No, Noss. His nigger's sick—had a dose of malaria; and when niggers do get it, they get it bad. The Major was a Cat's place when I was there."

Smith's eyes suddenly dilated, then narrowed to pin-points and, rising from his chair, he paced up and down the room several times. For the moment he seemed incapable of speech. At last a torrent of invectives came from his scarcely parted lips, sounded all the more evil because his voice was soft, almost womanish.

"Why didn't you tell me this before?" he snarled finally.

"I forgot," Brimmer stammered. "And—and you were talking and I didn't want to interrupt."

Smith reseated himself.

"What was the Major doing at Cat's place?" There was a note of suspicion in his voice. "Do you think the missionaries hired him to get evidence of liquor selling to the niggers?"

"No." Brimmer scoffed at the idea. "He's just fooling away the time, waiting until his nigger gets better. He was feeding the pigeons while I was there. Had his pockets stuffed with corn and was feeding it to them. He said they were his lady loves! Cat said that's all he does; said the Major's a great bird tamer."

Smith waved his hands impatiently.

"All right. Go and get the girl. And look smart about it."

THE MAJOR stood at the entrance to his bell-tent, looking down at the homely face of Jim, the Hottentot, who, wrapped in many blankets, was lying on the camp cot.

"It is folly to keep me here, *Baas*," Jim pleaded. "The fever has left me and I am strong. It is not fitting that the *baas* should wait on me."

"It is most fitting, Jim," the Major replied with a whimsical smile. "But, yes, today you shall get up. And tomorrow, if some strength has come back to you, we will trek. Now I will leave you for a little while. You shall get up when I return."

"Where does the *Baas* go? To the *ivinkeli*—to the store?"

"Yes, Jim. To feed the pigeons."

The Hottentot moved uneasily.

"I do not like that place, *Baas*. It is not wise for you to go there alone. Yesterday, while you were away, one of the 'boys' from the mines told me many bad things about the store of the white man you call Cat."

The Major laughed.

"I have eyes, Jim. I have ears."

"True, *Baas*. But the bullet which kills is not seen—and it has no voice."

"There will be no killing, Jim. I have no enemies in this place."

With a final word of warning to Jim not to move from the bed during his absence, the Major let fall the flap of the tent and strode off across the veldt toward the store buildings of Cat Perkins, half a mile away. As he walked he whistled a cheery tune. There was a snap in the air despite the heat; the veldt smells were sweet and refreshingly reminiscent of an English spring.

Halfway between the tent and the store he passed a group of native laborers returning home to their *kraals,* having completed their two years' contract of servitude in the mines. At the sight of them the Major's whistle died away on a plaintive note; he no longer felt gay. They were typical examples of the way in which the vicious element of South Africa's white population degrades the natives.

When they had come to the mines, naked, possibly, save for a loin cloth, they had been magnificent in the physical perfection, their eyes had been clear, their gait buoyant and, somehow, royal. But now they were hollow-cheeked, round-shouldered and emaciated. Accustomed to active, outdoor life and simple living, the forced labor in the diamond mines had exacted a heavy toll of them. Their natural dignity of carriage had been replaced by a slouching, shuffling walk and they were objects of derision by reason of the ridiculous hodge-podge of white men's garments they wore. They had sold their heritage for a mess of pottage.

They leered drunkenly at the Major as he passed them; flippant, obscene jests, learned from white men at the mines, were ready to their tongues—though these jests did not find utterance. There was something about this tall, white man of round face and glittering eye which shamed them. His erect carriage, the manliness and evident sympathetic understanding of them, demanded the respectful homage they were accustomed to pay to a chief. And this homage they gave— almost automatically, as it were.

The monocle he wore, his dudeish attire, the vacuous and almost inane expression which masked his face, did not blind *their* eyes to the real man under the veneer of effeminacy. Service in the mines had not completely destroyed that sense which the Spirit of the Universe has given to all children—the ability to measure a man's true worth.

Whatever he might be, judged by the white man's superficial understanding, they recognized in him a man of keen wit, eminently just and of great strength and sincerity of purpose. They saw that he was a man who demanded and received instant obedience; who could do all things and do them well.

So they doffed their hats and greeted him with: "*Sauka bona, Inkosi*—Greetings, Oh Chief!" And by their attitude they seemed mutely to apologize for their drunkenness; each wishing that he had shield and spear in his hand that he might salute the white man in a manner more worthy.

He waved his hand in acknowledgement of their salute and passed on.

But now his face was stern, his gray eyes were cold, hard, glittering, and as he increased his pace a little he clenched his fist.

Drunken natives—drunk on the vile concoctions sold to them at exorbitant prices by men like Cat—always affected him this way; but his anger was directed against the white men.

Presently he saw three men—white men—ride from behind the store and gallop swiftly toward him. He wondered a little, wondered still more as they thundered past him without word or greeting. Not that he knew them, but it was customary for men meeting on the veldt to exchange courtesies.

He turned and stared after them, saw the band of natives he had met scatter in all directions, saw the white men attempt to ride them down, striking right and left with their *sjamboks* and heard the curses of the whites and the frightened pleas of the blacks.

"The rotten devils," the Major exclaimed, and ran swiftly back, prepared to shoot, knowing now that the three white men were scum of the diggings, knowing that they were men who preyed upon native laborers as they were returning to their *kraals* and robbed them of their hard earned money. It was easy game. The natives had few, if any, legal rights in those early South African days.

As the Major drew nearer, the white men dismounted. The natives had suddenly capitulated and were kneeling down on the veldt, their hands raised before them in abject surrender. The whites, intent on searching the natives with methodical brutality, did not notice the approach of the Major until he was quite close. And then it was too late.

Their hands leaped to their revolvers—and one, a big heavily-bearded Dutchman, had his gun half-way out of the holster but, seeing that the Major had him covered, followed the example of his two companions and held up his hands.

The natives looked inquiringly at their deliverer and in response to his command, "*Hamba, wena,*" rapidly departed. The attack had completely sobered them and in a few minutes they had disappeared from sight.

Still, for a quarter of an hour or more, the Major kept the three in their sky-reaching attitude, indifferent alike to their threats and curses, laughing at their invitation to go in with them on equal shares.

"You're such charming birds," he drawled scathingly. "Wife-beaters are angels—comparatively, that is to say. Well, you can go your own way now. I fancy your erstwhile would-be contributors to your general fund—having learned their lesson—will not linger by the wayside and you won't catch them again. It's much easier to find a needle in a haystack than to find a native on the veldt. That is, when the dear old aborigine doesn't want to be found."

With a schoolboy gesture he stubbed his toes, sending a cloud of red veldt dust over them, put his revolver back in its holster and with a snort of contemptuous disgust turned away.

For a moment the three gazed after him, speechless, not daring to move, fearing he meant to trick them. Then with a bellow of rage and fists flying the Dutchman sprang after him, followed by the other two.

"Leave him to me," the big man yelled. "This *verdoemte* fool is my game!" The others, nothing loath, grinning with joy at the anticipated slaughter, stood by and watched.

His round face wreathed in smiles, the Major turned, lightly evaded the Dutchman's wild rush and succeeded in reaching his chin with a right as the big man lumbered by. The blow, which would have knocked out many a man, served only to sting the Dutchman to greater fury.

Turning clumsily, he came once more to the attack. The usual bovine expression of his face was replaced by a murderous look of madness. His eyes, almost hidden by the thick beard which grew high on his cheek bones, glinted piggishly; his lips were parted and drawn awry, showing uneven, discolored teeth.

Making queer, grunting, animal noises, he came on and this time the Major made no attempt to dodge but, stepping inside the swinging, flail-like blows, beat a rapid tattoo on the Dutchman's stomach, blows which traveled hardly six inches, but each one made the Dutchman gasp and shook him visibly.

Then before his opponent could come to a clinch, the Major broke away, whipping home an uppercut to the jaw as he did so.

"You're in deuced bad condition, Dutchy, old chap," the Major chortled. "Too much bad booze and nigger baiting. That's the trouble with you."

With the back of his hand the Dutchman wiped away the blood, which flowed from the corner of his mouth.

"Stand still, man! Stand still and I will come to you!"

With his huge, gorilla-like arms stretched out before him, fingers wide-spread but curving slightly, the Dutchman slowly advanced. He was horrible to watch. He seemed to be feeling his way—was groping like a blind man. There was something elemental, indomitable, about him; nothing could stop him.

The Major, realizing this, retreated warily, watching for an opening, knowing that if he stopped one of the Dutchman's sledgehammer blows he would be stopped and out, knowing that if they came to grips he would be lost.

He found himself regretting that he had been drawn into such a brawl. He thought of using his revolver to extricate himself from the predicament, but at once vetoed the idea as a confession of weakness. He would play fair, would match his science and great strength against the almost superhuman strength and brute-like indifference to pain of the Dutchman.

And so he retreated slowly, his eyes watching the Dutchman's feet, always keeping just beyond reach of the ever-menacing hands, ready to leap to the right, to the left, or backward at any moment.

The Dutchman followed.

One of the watching men giggled hysterically. The other, creeping softly up behind the Major, gave him a push which sent him headlong into the Dutchman's arms.

"Cuddle him tight—cuddle him tight, Deemster," he screamed, and laughed shrilly.

Deemster did not need the advice. As the Major came to him his arms closed automatically and strained his foe to him. The Major's arms were pinned to his side and, though he struggled desperately, he could not move. As well try to break loose from iron bands as from that mighty grip. Slowly his head was forced back by the pressure applied to the middle of his back.

He knew that soon he must relax, if only for a moment, and that moment would be the beginning of the end—if not the end. He tried to trip the giant, but Deemster, his feet set wide apart, seemed to be rooted to the ground.

The pressure increased. The Major's face was purple, blue-black; his eyes protruded from their sockets; he gasped and his head fell forward limply. He had reached the limit of his endurance. In another moment, he thought, his ribs would cave in. Colored lights flashed before his eyes and a wild pounding, like the drumming of surf on a rocky shore, sounded in his ears.

He heard—or rather seemed to be subconsciously aware of—a fresh, girlish voice exclaiming, "Oh! Make that terrible man stop, Sergeant. He's killing the other one!"

That voice was echoed by a man's—the one who had giggled at Deemster's advance.

"Stop it, Piet—here's a bobby!"

And then a big wave seemed to come up and cover the Major, beating him down, smothering him, and he wandered in great darkness.

WHEN HE came to, he was conscious first of a great soreness, and then wondered at the softness of the ground under his head. Opening his eyes, he looked up into the face of a dark-haired, dark-eyed girl. His head was in her lap.

The Major, though no woman-hater, knew little about the fair sex, and immediately considered her a personification of all the feminine virtues.

A woman would at once have remarked that her hair was several shades lighter at the roots and would have made scornful criticisms anent her bizarre attire—a lacy, frail blouse, khaki riding skirt, silk stockings and high heeled shoes. The Major mentally voted it A.1.

He did not move for several minutes. Then, becoming suddenly embarrassed, he struggled to a sitting position.

"What happened?" he asked feebly. "How did you manage to—"

"Oh, I didn't do it all," the girl interposed quickly—and there was a babyish lisp in her voice. "I was riding with the sergeant and we saw you fighting with the beast of a Dutchman—and the sergeant stopped him from killing you. What was it all about? Why did that big, naughty man try to kill you?"

The Major fumbled in the breast pocket of his tunic coat and sighed with relief to find his monocle unbroken.

"Why—er—it was about this," he stammered, bringing the monocle out and fixing it in his eye. "The beggar made some rude remarks about it and, do you know, I'm as blind as a bat without it. Besides, I feel so beastly self-conscious unless I wear it." He rose to his feet, suppressing a groan. "And where is the sergeant now?"

"Oh, he's gone off after those men," cooed the girl. "He said they were probably I.D.B.s—whatever that means. So he rode away and forgot all about poor little me."

"But I'm here, dear miss," the Major said gallantly.

She looked at him archly.

"Yes—but I don't know you."

"My name's Aubrey St. John." He pronounced it Sinjun. And bowed.

"And mine, Mr. Sinjun—well, does it matter? Call me Martha."

"Martha. It's a pretty name but, dear Miss Martha, surely you are not troubled by many things?"

She gazed at him uncomprehendingly.

"Martha—er—of the Bible, you know," he explained lamely.

"I don't know," she said somewhat tartly. "But I must go. The sergeant told me to wait for him at Cat's. What's Cat's?"

The Major smiled and pointed to the store.

"Cat's the name of the man who owns that. They call him Cat because when he fights he—er—scratches."

She giggled.

"Won't you let me escort you there?" the Major continued. "It's not a nice place for a lady like you to wait alone."

She hesitated.

"But you—are you all right?" She touched his arm timidly.

"Yes. Quite all right, dear miss." He caught her horse which was grazing nearby and led it up to her. "I was going to Cat's anyway," he added, as she still showed signs of hesitation. "I go every day to feed the pigeons."

"But you must ride." She stamped her foot impatiently as he shook his head. "You've been hurt," she added, "and if you don't ride—I'll—I'll cry."

"If I ride," said the Major, becoming suddenly bold, "you must ride, too."

She clapped her hands gleefully.

"All right," she cried. And after the Major had gingerly climbed into the saddle she lightly sprang up before him.

"It would be dreadful if Sergeant Brimmer saw us like this," she murmured. "He's terribly jealous."

The Major frowned a little but made no reply. He was thinking very deeply.

In this way they came to Cat's store. The place seemed deserted save for some heat-weary, dispirited pigeons. And the girl, jumping to the ground, looked curiously at the Major.

His face was very pale and he swayed in the saddle.

"Better get down," she said sharply, "and sit over here in the shade."

She indicated a wooden bench set against the side of one of the store houses. The house's tin roof had a sharp pitch to it and, because water was scarce and every drop of rain carefully hoarded, was well provided with gutter spouts which emptied into a pipe leading to a large cistern.

The Major leaned back and wearily closed his eyes.

"I'll go inside," she said presently, "and get you some brandy. That will fix you up."

"Thank you, dear miss," he murmured. "You are awfully kind to a chappie. Please don't bother."

But she had already run across to the large hut and, after a moment's hesitation, entered.

The Major cautiously opened his eyes and whistled softly. The pigeons became suddenly interested in life and flew to him, some perching in his shoulders, other fluttering in the air just above his head.

"You're greedy creatures," he said. "Always hungry. Well, I've lots of corn for you."

From his pockets he very carefully took a handful and threw it on the roof of the hut just behind him. A second and third handful quickly followed the first.

It pattered like hail on the tin and with a whir of beating wings the pigeons left him and were soon pecking away on the roof, seeking to get the corn he had thrown before it all rolled down into the eaves and so—because of the steep pitch—into the cistern.

The Major watched them for a few minutes and then, resuming his seat, closed his eyes.

Hardly had he done so when four men of the mounted police came out of the hut the girl had entered and with revolvers leveled shouted, "Hands up, Major."

The Major opened his eyes wide in astonishment but, because in his long career of I.B.D. he had been many times in a similar situation, he lost no time in obeying the peremptory command. But he looked reproachfully at the girl who had also come out of the hut and was peering over the troopers' shoulders. She was flushed but triumphant.

And now the Major's face was masked with a bland, innocent expression. He looked more than ever like the "silly ass," of the stage; and his voice, when he spoke, heightened the illusion.

"What's it all about, old dears?" he drawled. "Why the well known whatness of the which, eh? And why the little poppers?"

The troopers laughed. They all had had encounters with the Major before this, and knew that he was never so dangerous as when playing the part of a dude fool.

"I'll tell you, Major," said the senior trooper confidentially, "we think we have the goods on you this time and we don't intend to be drawn into an argument with you here."

"No, old dear? Then what? But first may I put down my hands?"

"No! Keep 'em up. We're not taking any chances."

"Very well," said the Major in resigned tones. "If you must have your little joke. But I think you're bally cruel, Fenwick."

"Give you half a chance," growled one of the other troopers—he did not know the Major very well, "and you'd be shooting the daylight out of us."

"You misjudge me, really," murmured the Major.

"Yes, he misjudges you," continued Fenwick. "I don't. Just the same, I'm not taking any chances, Major. You know what getting the goods on you means to us. Promotion for us all."

The Major looked at him quizzically.

"But you wouldn't care awfully much for promotion earned that way, would you, old top? Sort of Judas money, isn't it? I suppose you're goin' to frame me?"

Fenwick flushed.

"No!" he said hotly. "We are not going to frame you. You ought to know me better than that. You know damned well what we think of you on the force—the ones that know you, at any rate—and we wouldn't stand for framing. But this is a straight tip—*and* I'm going to play it straight. You've had your inning—and a pretty long one. Now it's our turn. Didn't think you were a squealer."

"I'm not," said the Major hurriedly. "I'm sorry if I've hurt your feelin's, old man. Didn't mean to, 'pon my sacred aunt, I didn't. So you've got the goods on me, eh?"

"Yes," Fenwick said complacently. And despite his undoubted friendship for the Major a note of triumph crept into his voice.

"Well, dear boy, goodness knows I'd like to be the first to congratulate you—yes, and be deucedly happy to offer my poor, unworthy, as it were, self on the altar of your blinkin' ambition. But let us meditate a while dear lad. Don't want you making an ass of yourself. Like you far too well for that. Tell me your little story. I suppose it has to do with diamonds?"

"Of course. I happen to know that you have a dozen or so stones on you right now."

"Oh, don't Fenwick. Don't joke this way. Remember my heart—it's very weak—and the fate of Annanias."

"Annanias didn't work on the Breakwater," the tall, thin trooper said. "But you will, Major."

The Major chortled.

"Very neat, Longshanks, deucedly neat, if I may say so. But you were saying, Fenwick, that I had a few score diamonds in my possession—and having diamonds is against the law. Therefore, not withstanding and so forth—eh, what?"

"Exactly."

"But suppose I came by the diamonds—er—honestly?"

"I never did like fairy stories, Major."

"No. Then you'll never be a good bobby. Too bad. Then suppose I say I haven't any diamonds."

"Ah! But we *know* you have."

"How do you know—and won't you let me take my hands down?"

"No. Keep 'em up. How do we know? Why this little lady, Miss Martha, just told us that you showed them to her ten minutes ago. No! She didn't mean to give you away."

"I see!" The Major spoke sadly. "But she did all the same."

"Oh, look here, don't be a cad, Major! It happened this way. Miss Martha came running in and said she wanted a glass of brandy for a poor man who had been hurt in a fight. We asked her if he was a 'sundowner' and she said, 'No! He must be awfully right. He showed me a handful of diamonds. He carries them around loose in his pockets.' That's how we came to know. Miss Martha doesn't know anything about I.D.B."

"I see," said the Major. "But how did she know they were diamonds? Oh, but of course, I told her. Well, if Miss Martha says I have diamonds on me—I suppose I have. Too bad. But somehow— Well, never mind. What are you goin' to do. Search me here?"

"No. We are goin' to truss you up, hand and foot, and then take you into headquarters. We'll do all the searching there. And I give you my word, Major, there'll be no 'frame-up.' If we can't get you without that—all right."

"That goes for us, too," the other troopers added.

"Then I've nothing more to say, old dears. Only this. I wish you'd take me first to my camp—it's just over the way—where my servant Jim is recovering from an attack of fever. I want to give him a few instructions. Also, I'd be awfully glad if one of you fellows would remain at my camp—sort of keep guard, don't you know? You will, Longshanks? Oh, that's rippin', positively rippin'. Well, let's go."

ABOUT HALF an hour after the departure of the troopers with their prisoner the girl who called herself Martha was joined by Brimmer, the Dutchman, Solly and the man who was called Cat.

"Well, did it work?" Brimmer asked eagerly.

The girl laughed scornfully.

"Like a charm," she said. "He never suspected until it was too late. I don't think he had it right, even then. Tell your boss, Brimmer, to give me something hard to do next time. I know all about monocled Johnnies. Plenty of 'em in London. And how I hate them!"

"The boss should have let me settle the *verdoemte* fool in my own way," growled the Dutchman. "He loosened a tooth, look you! But I had only to tighten my arms a little more and—"

His gesture was very expressive and the girl shrank away from him with a little cry of fear.

TEN DAYS later Smith was listening to the report of his henchman, Brimmer. And Smith's face was not a pleasant sight. It was contorted with rage and, all the time during the policeman's recital, curses and blasphemies burst out of Smith's mouth.

"Something went wrong somewhere, Boss," Brimmer concluded—and looked apprehensively at Smith.

"You're damned right something went wrong. How about the girl? Did she play square with me?"

"Yes, Boss. There's no doubt about that. She's been carrying on worse than you about it. She slipped the stones in his pocket all right!"

"And the search was on the level?"

"Yah! The chief searched the Major himself. And then he called in one of the compound managers—Schmall it was—and you know how Schmall searches. He's never let any niggers get away with stones from his compound! No! The search was on the level—and they didn't find anything."

"Well, he must have got rid of them when they were bringing him in."

Brimmer shook his head.

"He couldn't, Boss. They tied him so tightly he couldn't move an eyelash."

"Was he alone any time? Before they arrested him, I mean?"

"The girl went in to spill the beans to the troopers—left him about two minutes. Be she could seem him all that time, she said, through the window!"

"What was he doing?"

"Threw a couple of handfuls of corn to the pigeons, that's all."

"Then, you damned fool, he—"

"No, Boss. I thought of that. Had every bloomin' bird on the place killed and examined their crops myself. Not a bloomin' sign of a stone. And if there had been, it wouldn't have done us any good. That 'ud be no evidence."

"I know that, you fool. But, at least, I wouldn't have been out any. Oh, get out of here. Suppose I'll have to handle him myself. Get out! And if you fall down on the next job I give you, I'll see to it that your chief is told certain little things about Sergeant Brimmer."

Brimmer hastily left the room and Smith, opening one of his books, turned the pages slowly.

"If I could get him with me," he murmured once, "I could—why, there's nothing I couldn't do. Think I'll ask him to pay me a call."

Sunset and the gathering darkness found Smith still at his books, recording, as words came in, the successful carrying out of certain crimes, the planning of others and the assigning of tasks.

When it became too dark he lighted an oil lamp. Then, just as he was about to turn to his work again, a pane in the little window which looked out into a narrow alley was broken and the muzzle of a rifle appeared in the opening.

Smith looked at it in terror. He had always meant to have that window walled up and now—the Nemesis he had so long feared had overtaken him. He was notoriously afraid of firearms.

He was reassured somewhat by a low, drawling voice.

"I'm coming in to see you, Smithy, and this is just to warn you not to try any little jokes. Jim—he's a Hottentot, you know—and my servant—is holding this rifle an' he's quite a good shot at close range. So, if you move—why, there'll be a big red blotch on your book, old top."

"Come on in, Major," Smith whispered. "I've been wantin' to see you for a long time."

"All right, Smithy. Watch him closely, Jim. If he moves only his little finger, shoot. You understand?"

"Yah, *Baas*."

There was silence. Then, after a while, the door behind Smith opened, closed again.

But Smith did not move. He watched the rifle with unblinking eyes. He seemed to be beyond speech.

"I'm here, Smith," the Major said cheerfully, "and 'pon my soul I don't think much of the place. It needs ventilation, if you will pardon me. You ought to get out in the fresh air more, Smithy. But I'm in a hurry. Just wanted to pop in to see the master mind, as it were. Just a little joke with you, and then I pop out again. Why are you so unkind to me, Smithy?"

"I want you to work with me, Major, and—"

"And you thought by framing me on a charge of illicit diamond buying to win my everlastin' gratitude. Oh, come now, Smithy, that won't do."

Smith looked at the Major out of the corner of his eye and sneered slightly at the man's impeccable attire. But he did not speak. He was under a disadvantage. While he was covered by the rifle he seemed incapable of connected thought and, being too clever to expose his weakness, sought refuge in silence.

"Sulky?" went on the Major. "Fie, for shame! Well, I'm deucedly fond of talking. Too much so, sometimes. At least my friends tell me so. Have you any friends, Smithy? No; I thought not. I don't like you Smithy. I don't like the way you do things—the little I've seen of your work gives me a very poor impression of you. Oh, very! And so I'm just goin' to spoil your little games whenever I run across them—if I can, of course. I've done rather well so far, eh, what? Four scores to me, I think.

"And now, because I don't like a man to be puzzled over simple things, I'm goin' to tell you what happened to those diamonds Miss Martha put in my pocket. She is very clever—oh, very clever—and quite fooled me. I'm very susceptible to women, you know—bless 'em. But Martha isn't the sort of woman who would make some man a good wife, is she? Too self-centered, I should say.

"Well, about those diamonds. You see, dear old pig, I'm very fond of pigeons and so I always used to feed those of Cat's. And—well, it was so easy to throw the diamonds up on the roof at the same time I was feedin' the birds. But, ah! Verily and forsooth! What then became of the diamonds? Did the birds eat them? Nay, verily no. What then? Why, dear old chap, they rolled down the roof into the gutter. I had thrown them aloft first—before the birds got on the wing. And they rolled down the gutter until they came to the pipe which leads to the cistern. And they rolled down that pipe—fell down expresses their speed better perhaps—until they came to the—

"Ah! your eyes light up! What a clever Johnny you are! But—and I'm greatly distressed—I must disappoint you. No! They didn't fall into the cistern. Your assistant, Mr. Brimmer, would have found them had that been the case. No, dear old Fagin Smith. I had fixed a wire mesh across the inside of that pipe, about six inches from the end, weeks ago, so that the grain wouldn't be wasted. And that caught the diamonds as they fell down. And there they were when the police chappies let me go. Of course they're not there now. Clever of me, wasn't it?"

Smith grunted savagely. His eyes did not waver from the gun barrel.

"You're not very sociable, Smithy, I must say. But to finish the story. Of course I felt that I had no right to keep those diamonds, and I hardly thought you would want them, so to make everything all right I gave them—or rather the money I got for them—to the Mission

Fathers. They're goin' to use it, I believe, to put places like Cat's out of business. I gave the money in your name. Won't Cat be pleased? Well—ta-ta, old chap. One gets terribly tired of hearin' one's own voice. And you're not very pretty to look at. Oh, Jim!"

"Yah, *Baas*."

"Keep a close watch. If he moves—shoot."

"Yah, *Baas*."

The door of the room opened, closed, and Smith was left alone again.

FOR AN hour Smith sat watching the menace of the gun muzzle. Outside in the barroom he could hear the clink of glasses, the songs of drunken men, the peace-seeking voice of the barmaid.

Then his pen dropped from its lodgement behind his ear and involuntarily he stooped to pick it up. Still bent over, he looked up somewhat fearfully at the window. The gun still there, but it no longer covered him.

With a catlike leap he sprang to the window and caught the barrel in his two hands. He met no resistance and, wonderingly, hauled the "gun" into the room.

It was a mock of a gun. It was not loaded and could not have been fired had it been loaded. He had been held up by a dummy.

At that moment Brimmer burst into the room.

"The Major leaves tomorrow, they're saying down at headquarters! Do you want me to go out and tell him you'd like to see him before he leaves, Boss?"

"See him!" snarled Smith. "Why in hell do you think I want to see that damned dude?"

"But," stammered the luckless policeman, "I—thought, Boss, you said you wanted a personal interview with him, and he—"

He would have said more, but the look on Smith's face frightened him and he left the room even more precipitately than he had entered.

CONCESSIONS

JIM, THE Hottentot, crouched miserably by the camp-fire, his hands outspread to its warming blaze. It was nearly sunrise and the heavy, low-lying clouds were fast disappearing; but there was a chill in the veldt air and the Hottentot shivered despite the heat from the fire and the thick blanket which enshrouded his muscular figure.

Several times Jim gazed uneasily, conscience-stricken, at the white bell-tent; and his bleared eyes, red-rimmed, held the half frightened look of a child who has been stealing jam.

He started suddenly at a noise from within the tent—the sound of a man lazily awakening from a deep sleep—and discarding the blanket he rose and industriously made preparations for the morning meal. In a very little while the billy was on the fire ready for coffee and some "veldt-bricks" were baking in red embers raked from the fire.

"Sun is up, *Baas*," Jim announced presently in dejected tones and, a few minutes later, a white man came to the opening of the tent.

He was naked save for a towel about his middle, *veldschoens* on his feet and a monocle in his eye. He yawned widely, stretched himself, and expanded and deflated his mighty chest. The muscles of a trained athlete rippled under his white, satiny skin.

Then, ignoring the Hottentot, he silently made his way to the river, a hundred yards away, kicked off his shoes, carefully placed his monocle on a nearby rock, dropped the towel from him and dove into the water. So graceful, so effortless was the dive that he seemed for a moment to be arrested in mid-air—hovered like an eagle preparing to swoop on its prey. There was hardly any sound as he struck the water, no splash.

He swam leisurely upstream, deaf to Jim's frantic cries of, *"Baas, Baas!* Come out! Crocodiles will get you, *Baas."*

Reaching a bend in the river the white man turned and, churning the water to a white, yeasty foam, swam back with great speed, climbing out onto the bank just as a rotten, moss-covered log on the opposite side of the river suddenly came to life and vanished noiselessly under the surface. It appeared again a few seconds later at the spot where the white man had left the water; and the vicious snapping together of two powerful, teeth studded jaws spoke eloquently of a hunger unsatisfied. Then the crocodile backed leisurely to the center of the river and became a rotten log once again, moving sluggishly to the swirl of the current. But its cold, basilisk-like eyes were focused unwinkingly on the spot where its food had escaped.

"Gave me a scare," chuckled the white man; "but I mustn't let Jim know. The bally old fraud."

He rubbed himself briskly, making his skin glow healthily pink, then carefully adjusted his monocle, slipped his feet into the shoes and returned to his tent.

He did not appear again until Jim announced, "Scoff ready, *Baas."*

Then he came out fully dressed. His riding breeches were spotlessly white, his polo boots highly polished, his white shirt open at the neck, immaculately ironed. And, somehow, the clothes had changed the athlete into a dude. In build he seemed to be slightly obese; his bland, round face helped to create that impression; and his eyes, light blue, were mild and vacuous looking. "A good-natured, silly ass," the casual observer would have judged him; "concerned only with his own pleasure, capable of no greater exertion than that entailed in caring for his own person."

He sat on a campstool and silently, fastidiously, ate the food Jim brought to him. He was apparently unconscious of or indifferent to the look of appeal in the Hottentot's face.

"The *Baas* is angry with me," Jim said mournfully when the meal was finished. "He does not look at me; he does not speak."

The expression in the white man's eyes changed instantly. The inane, vacuous look vanished; they became cold, keen, steel gray. The loose lines about his mouth tightened; one became suddenly conscious of his jaw. It was a fighting jaw.

"If a man has a dog and that dog disobeys him, bites him, does he pet it?"

"Nay. But—" Jim's eyes flashed angrily—"I am no dog, *Baas,* but a free man. I come when I please; I go, when I please."

"True," the white man said curtly. "And, for a time your way was my way—my way, yours. Now—" He rose slowly to his feet and, with a gesture which embraced the tent, wagon, horses and span of twelve mules, said, "Take what you will; choose the way you will travel and—go!"

"*Baas,*" Jim said quietly, "that is not just. That is—" He stopped, hesitated a moment and began again. "Once, *Baas,* a man came to my father's *kraal* and asked for beer. It was given to him. But the calabash containing it was old, the outside of it was dirty. *'Au-a!'* said that man. 'This beer is bad.' Yet he had not tasted the beer. Now I say, and who can know better, that the beer was good." Jim smacked his lips and added, "Very good."

A smile broke the sternness of the white man's face.

"Well, read me the riddle, Jim."

"It is easy, *Baas.* Sometimes a lion will share his kill with a hyena; but that does not make him a cur."

"Neither does it make the hyena a lion, Jim," the white man countered swiftly.

"The *Baas* does not see because he will not see," the Hottentot said reprovingly. "Listen more, then: three days ago the *Baas* sent me to the *dorp* for *gwai* (tobacco) and when I did not return that night he came seeking me, forgetting that I was Jim and full of wisdom."

"Remembering," murmured the white man, "that when you are full of drink you are empty of wit."

The Hottentot ignored the interruption.

"And so," he continued, "when the *Baas* found me last night and I was a little drunk—"

"Very drunk, Jim."

The Hottentot accepted the amendment.

"Very drunk, then, *Baas*. The drink was strong. And the *Baas* brought me back to this place and says, being very angry and seeing only the outside of the pot, that Jim is no good, is a liar, a drunkard and no true man."

"Well?"

Jim grinned.

"A liar I am, *Baas;* but I have never lied to you. A drunkard I am whenever there is *puza* in plenty to be had and the *Baas* has given permission."

"I did *not* give permission this time."

"Had I returned asking for it there would have been no drink left by the time I had come again to the feasting place. At a wedding there are many thirsty mouths."

"So-a! It was a wedding, eh?"

"Yah, *Baas*." Jim chuckled. "A chief's son was married."

He looked quickly at his *baas* and, as that man evinced no undue interest, continued, answering the last of his *baas's* accusations.

"And I am a true man. The *Baas* knows that. It is not seemly to speak of bygone things. Yet how many times could Jim have gained many head of cattle by saying, 'My *baas* is the Ma-jah?'"

"That I have never forgotten, Jim," the Major agreed. "But you were drunk on *puza* given to you by men who have no love for me—men who would give ten times a hundred head of cattle to see me working on the Breakwater."

"True, *Baas*," the Hottentot said complacently. "They asked me many things concerning you and promised, if I told them, to give me great wealth. And so, I told them all that they wanted to know."

"So?" The Major's eyes flashed.

"Yah, *Baas*. All that they wanted to know."

"Then, if you are a true man, a vulture is the most noble of birds," the Major said heavily. Yet he wondered at the tone of Jim's voice and the mischievous gleam in his eyes.

"*Baas*," the Hottentot said banteringly, "have you ever heard a child cry because his mother said that what he called a lion was only a rock?

And did not that child continue to cry until his mother said, comforting him, 'It is true. That is a lion. My eyes are getting old, oh man child, and at first I did not see clearly. Indeed it is a lion. And see—' she will point to other rocks—'there are three other lions.' Then the *umfan* will stop crying because he has been told what he *wants* to know and can again play his hunting game."

"I'm beginning to see, I think, Jim."

"And truly you should, *Baas*. These men said, 'Your *Baas*, the Ma-jah, he is here to buy diamonds.' And when I answered, 'No,' they kicked me and hit me with their fists. They asked the same question again. So then I told them many things: that the *Baas* had not come to buy, having caused a tunnel to be dug from this place to the mine-pit. And this they believed, *Baas,* and gave me gold."

"That is rich, Jim," the Major said in English and chuckled at the thought of a mile-long tunnel by which he was supposed to enter the well-guarded mine and help himself to any diamonds which might be lying around.

"Rich! Oh, golly damme yes, *Baas*," Jim, too, spoke English, of a sort!

"What then, Jim?" the Major asked, reverting to the vernacular.

"Somewhat they spoke in the white man's tongue and I did not understand them. But the servant of Brimmer, the policeman, told me afterward. He was drunk, *Baas*, and could not control his tongue. They will watch for many days until the *Baas* has taken plenty of stones. Then they will take them from him—all but one or two."

"I see," the Major mused. "And the one or two will pay my passage to the Breakwater. Very neat! Oh, very! It's a priceless plan."

He smiled forgivingly at Jim who said reproachfully, "You have not asked about the wedding, *Baas*."

"The wedding? Ah, yes. I had forgotten that. That was where you got drunk. What were *you* doing at a wedding?"

"Had there been no Jim, there would have been no wedding," the Hottentot said with dignity.

The Major raised his eyebrows and the monocle fell from his eye into his hand which opened instinctively to receive it; his mouth gaped in incredulous astonishment.

"You—you haven't taken another wife, Jim?" he asked in alarm.

Jim guffawed derisively.

"Many evils come to a man unbidden—shall he, then, knowingly add to them?"

"Many do, Jim. So the race lives."

"But not Jim, *Baas*. No. Thus it was: you remember Marka, son of Tomasi?"

The Major nodded. Tomasi was one of two petty chiefs of a district nominally under Portuguese jurisdiction. The Major had once helped Tomasi overthrow a revolt headed by the old chief's degenerate son. Marka—degenerate because, having come in contact with the white man's civilization, he had taken to himself only the evil of it.

"Marka was at the *dorp, Baas*. The white men were keeping him, he told me, because when his father dies and he becomes chief he has promised to let no white men but them enter his country."

"Concession hunting, eh?" the Major murmured. "Didn't know there was anything in Tomasi's land worth having,"

"And so," Jim continued, "hearing that, I went to the white men. I was drunk, they had given me gold, therefore, I was their friend, and I said, 'Marka is a liar and a fool, but he is a man. If he wants to go from this place, he will go; you cannot stop him. He will make promises to other white men and forget the one he has made to you.'

"And those men saw, *Baas*, that my words were true words.

" 'What shall we do then?' they asked me. And I said, 'Is there not a maiden greatly desired by Marka?' This I said, knowing that he had looked with foolish eyes upon Sar-rah, a half-caste who worked for one of the white men. 'Yes,' they answered. They, too, knew of Sar-rah. 'Then,' said I, 'Marry her to Marka. She will see that Marka does not leave her and will do as you bid.'

"And those white men, *Baas*," Jim concluded triumphantly, "seeing that I spoke true words, did as I advised. That is all, *Baas*."

The Major looked at Jim in admiration.

"That is all, you say? That is much!"

Leaning back against the trunk of a marula tree he began to laugh; at first silently and then, as the meaning of it all became clearer to him, loudly. He laughed until the tears ran from his eyes and holding his sides he slid helplessly to the ground, and continued laughing. Jim, too, began to laugh, boisterously. The horses looked in dismay at the two men; a mule brayed loudly.

"This is too much," the Major gasped, at length, wiping the tears from his eyes. "What a deuced clever Johnny you are, Jim, old top. You're perfectly top hole."

Jim grinned in full agreement. Not that he understood that much English, but the tone of his *baas's* voice was sufficient for him.

"Clev-ah! Oah, yess," he parroted. "Deuced clever—I don't think."

"Just the same. Jim, you old reprobate, you disobeyed; and for that there should be punishment. Also you were drunk, beastly drunk. Yes, you must be punished. But how?"

The Major was silent for a while and when he spoke again it was in the vernacular and the drawl had left his voice.

"You will dig a hole here, Jim."

He pointed to a place just before the entrance to his tent.

"To what end, *Baas?*"

"You will build a tunnel. Is that not understood? You would not have men call you a liar?"

"Better that, *Baas*," Jim replied lugubriously, "than to attempt such folly. Also the sun is hot."

"The sun is hot, yes. But to build a tunnel is no folly. Further, the digging will sweat the poison from you."

"The poison does not bother me; I am content to keep it and would that I had more of it," Jim grumbled; but nevertheless he took a spade and pick from the wagon and commenced on his task.

While he was thus engaged the Major hobbled the horses and mules and turned them loose to graze. Then he loaded all his equipment onto the wagon, packing it neatly. That done he took his rifles and shotguns and busied himself with giving them a thorough overhauling. He handled them as if they were living things and once, when he put a rifle up to his shoulder and squinted along its barrel, it seemed to become a part of him.

But, despite this apparent preoccupation with his arsenal, the Major kept an eye on Jim, encouraging him to better effort, deriding him at times, especially when the Hottentot sat wearily on the edge of the hole he was digging.

"If you had not been drunk, Jim," he called out, "the digging would be easy."

"If I had not been drunk, the *Baas* would not know many things he now knows," Jim retorted.

"True," the Major conceded.

"And," Jim continued, quick to seize an advantage and drive home a point which had been on his mind for some time, "I am no fool. I would not swim in this river and become food for crocodiles."

"Sometimes your *baas* is a fool," the Major said penitently.

Jim's face lighted-up and, singing a wild chant of his people, he attacked his work with renewed vigor.

A few minutes later the Major climbed down from his seat on the wagon, measured the height of the water-barrel, standing nearby, and then sauntered over to the tent and examined the hole Jim had dug. It was about four feet deep and two feet in circumference.

"That is enough, Jim," he said. "Now help me with the barrel."

Jim looked at him with dull, uncomprehending eyes—the hard and long labor seemed to have sapped his vitality. He thought his *baas's* actions were strange, a little mad, yet he knew that at other times the Major had done peculiar things—but always had a reason for them. And so, undoubtedly, now.

"Come, Jim," the Major said, and with Jim's help lowered the barrel into the hole. It came within a few inches of the top. Then they made several trips to the river with water-buckets and half-filled the barrel with water.

"Now you shall rest, Jim," the Major said with a chuckle, "The remainder I will do."

Nothing loath, but with wide-open, wondering eyes, Jim squatted on the ground close to the hole and watched his *baas* throw spadeful after spadeful of dirt into the water until the barrel was full of oozy, yellow mud.

The Major then stretched an old piece of canvas across the top of the barrel and on that strewed more dirt until, when he had finished, the ground above the barrel did not differ, to the casual glance, to the veldt surrounding it.

And now Jim's wondering astonishment gave place to a full understanding and he broke into peals of uncontrollable laughter. "You must not laugh," the Major admonished him gravely. "I have only hidden the entrance to my tunnel. In-span, Jim. We trek in a little while."

He entered the tent and when he emerged, about half an hour later, Jim had harnessed the twelve mules and had hitched them to the light wagon; the Major's horse, a coal black stallion, was saddled and bridled while the other horse was tethered to the rear of the wagon.

The Major and Jim quickly cleared the tent of its contents, stepping gingerly over the "planted" ground, and packed them in the wagon. Then the Major mounted his horse and Jim clambered up into the driver's seat.

"Which way do we trek, *Baas?*" he asked.

"To Tomasi's *kraal*," the Major answered.

With loud shouts of "Ah, there, *schelm!*" and the rifle-like reports of his long whip, Jim got his team away at a fast canter, wheeled them smartly—missing a hut-sized anthill by a fraction of an inch—and headed due east.

A few minutes later the Major followed.

THE BARROOM at Whispering Smith's place at Kimberley was crowded with men and women. Some had that hardened, immobile expression of criminals; these, the riff-raff of the world, had flocked to the diamond fields, and the gold mines at Jo'burg, attracted by the easy pickings to be had from the pockets of honest, harder working men. Some were well dressed, some flashily dressed, others were ragged, down at heel, and their faces, drawn and haggard looking, gave plain evidence of the privations to which they had been subjected.

Some, blatantly at ease, indulged in loud banter and ordered drinks with a lordly air; others huddled together in the corners of the room, whispering nervously, plainly unaccustomed to the company in which they found themselves. Yet others sat despondently at the round tables which were scattered about the room, sipped their drinks moodily or, dabbling their forefingers in the slops, traced intricate, meaningless designs on the table-top.

But all present glanced furtively from time to time at the little door at the far end of the room as if expecting a summons ordering them to pass through that door. And none looked forward to that.

Beyond that door was the office of Whispering Smith. He was more often called "Whip," because of the whip-like urge of his whispering voice. He was the man who boasted that he held the liberty of every criminal in South Africa in the hollow of his hand, the man who watched the activities of criminals, through the foreign press, the world over, and set traps to catch such as fled from the lawmakers of their own country to seek a haven in the crowded gold fields. First offenders were Smith's special pets; they were easier to handle than the old-timers; and, under his expert, driving tutelage, they were not first offenders very long.

Smith was very crafty; more, his intelligence was of a high order, his education thorough and all embracing, save in the use of firearms. Of them he was notoriously afraid. So, despite the fact that he was the prime instigator of every big crime and directed most of the smaller ones pulled off between the Zambezi and the Cape, Walfisch Bay and Lorenço Marquez, nothing had ever been proved against him. The police suspected many things, but they were powerless to act. In that, Smith and his chief antagonist, the Major, were on a par. Both were suspected of a multitude of crimes, both had so far escaped conviction. But there the resemblance ends. The Major's many crimes all came under one heading—I.D.B. That is, the buying of unregistered diamonds. Often his buying, although legally illicit, was honorable; sometimes he bought diamonds he knew to be stolen. But, in each case, his activities were regarded by many prominent, law-abiding citizens as a just protest against the monstrous I.D.B. act.

Smith, on the other hand, was incapable of a decent deed or thought; his crimes were of the gutter, beastly. Robbery, blackmail, murder.

The Major was universally liked and respected, even by the police who essayed to entrap him. Smith was hated and despised, even by the men in his closest confidence.

Smith was wise and very cautious; he'd confess to the stealing of a stamp in order to win a confession of murder, well assured that the murderer would not, dared not, report the stamp stealing.

Yet, despite the great hold he had over all his henchmen. Smith's liberty had recently been endangered. Someone had turned informer and it was only by introducing much perjured testimony that Smith had escaped the threat of a life sentence.

But freedom, discharged "without a legal stain on his character," was not sufficient for the man with the whispering voice. He wanted revenge; he could not rest with the informer at large, unknown, capable of working further mischief. To that end, he carefully went over his books; he was a methodical man and, by a process of elimination reduced the hundreds of names on his roll-call to forty-odd. Forty-odd men and women among whom was numbered the informer, or inform-ers. These men and women he "commanded" to appear before him that he might personally interview them, interrogate them, in his inimitable way and endeavor to discover the guilty ones.

And no one thought of disobeying Smith's commands. His arm was too long, the penalty too great, the chance of successfully evading his wrath practically nil. By ones and twos they had passed into Smith's inner office—and out again. Some had faced him more than once. The man and the girl who were now being interviewed had been in five times.

The barroom was terribly hot; mosquitoes *pinged* a savage obligato to the drone of mumbled conversation.

Suddenly from the inner room a woman's voice shrieked.

"My Gawd! Don't, don't!"

Her voice trailed away into silence.

All conversation in the barroom suddenly stopped. The hum of mosquitoes rose to a shrill note, ominous, foreboding. The barmaid, blue of eye and blonde-dyed hair, her mouth agape, kept her hand on the tap indifferent to the fact that the beer was splashing her much be-frilled lace blouse. Everyone turned to his neighbor, as if seeking the answer to a riddle; but they already knew the answer!

The door of the little room was suddenly thrown open and Whispering Smith stood silently in the opening.

They all rose, stared at him and past him and waited for him to speak.

Behind him, wraith-like through the swirl of tobacco smoke, they could see two men holding a third, a rat-faced little man, by the arms.

" 'Putney Nell' and 'Gentleman Joe' had a little quarrel," Smith said quietly, softly, but everyone in the room heard him distinctly.

"Joe said Nell had passed him up for a Dutchy. So, he knifed her. She's dead. Of course—" he waved his soft white hands, loaded with sun-reflecting rings—"the police have arrested Joe. I'd have saved him if I could; but he's guilty. And so he'll hang. That's all. You may go now. Thank you for coming. And don't be too sorry for Joe and Nell. They both talked too much; a damned sight too much."

He smiled sardonically as the men and women quickly, as if fleeing from a plague spot, left the room.

"The rats!" he muttered. "And some of 'em were Joe's pals; some of 'em were Nell's."

THAT NIGHT a tall, hatchet-faced man entered the barroom. He was grotesquely thin and his skin was drawn tightly over his prominent cheekbones. He looked very tired and his clothes were powdered with the red dust of the veldt. He seemed jaundiced, bloodless and, one judged, had just returned from a long sojourn in a fever infested country.

He ordered and drank four tots of dop in quick succession and when the barmaid sweetly suggested that he show the color of his money, he snarled, "Tell Smith 'Rake' Barnby's here."

"Oh!" the frightened girl exclaimed. "He said you were to go into his office as soon as you came, sir."

Barnby leered at her and raised his hat, somehow making the act of courtesy an insult, and passed on into the office.

Smith was seated at his desk, scowling at the other occupant of the room, a youngster just out from home, judging by his fresh pink and white complexion.

"At the old game, Whip?" Barnby sneered as he sat down on the corner of the desk. Smith occupied the only chair in the room. The latter indicated the door with a jerk of his thumb to the youngster, who quickly left the room, evidently happy at the interruption.

"He's a good penman," Smith explained as the door closed behind the boy, "but—er—a little obstinate."

Barnby nodded understandingly.

The two men were silent for a while; Barnby stared curiously about the room; Smith scrutinized his well-kept hands, looking up once or twice, as if about to speak, then shuddering as his eyes were drawn, as if by a magnet, to a bulge under Barnby's thin coat, a bulge made by a revolver holster.

"Well," he asked at length, "did you get the concession?"

Barnby shook his head.

"Why not?" The purr in Smith's voice had given way to a menacing rasp.

Barnby shrugged his shoulders, an act which so infuriated Smith that he rose to his feet, his face white, his eyes blazing.

"I asked you a question," he said hoarsely. "I want an answer."

"You'll get it, but in my own way and my own time, Smithy. Sit down; and remember that I'm no mother's pet just out. I shoot pretty well, Smithy and—"

He laughed as Smith dropped back into his chair, breathing hard. "That's better," Barnby went on. "Now we can talk. I'm not likely to kick over the traces. You've got too much on me." He smiled bitterly. "Just the same, don't try to ride me."

Smith's eyes narrowed, but he did not speak.

"No," Barnby continued, "I didn't get the concession and no other white man will get one from that black—Tomasi."

"I thought you knew all about niggers?" Smith sneered.

"I do," Barnby said confidently; and his statement rang true, not boastful. "That's why I say no one can get a concession from him. No one can offer him a big enough bribe."

"What are you talking about? They say Rhodes got his concession from Lobenguella for a hundred quid a year."

"Maybe. But Tomasi isn't Lobenguella. Gold doesn't mean anything to him. He's got everything he wants: cattle, wives. What else does a black want?"

"Whisky, tobacco, trade goods—"

Barnby laughed.

"You don't know Tomasi. He belongs to the old order. Civilization doesn't mean a hoot in hell to him."

"So you failed."

"Yes. There's only one thing to do. Wait until the old chief dies and Marka is chief. He'll be an easy proposition. But—"

"But, what?"

"I don't know where Marka is. No one knows."

Smith chuckled. "I know, I've got him safe."

"You have? How did you get him? Where is he?"

"You're not my only iron in the fire on this deal. Don't you think it. I've other men who know the niggers as well as you."

"Who?"

"Brimmer. I had been thinking of letting him go; he's such a blundering fool. But he turned this trick all right. Showed more brains than I've been giving him credit for."

"Brimmer, eh? That's the plain-clothes sergeant, isn't it?"

Smith nodded.

"How did he get hold of Marka? And how's he going to keep him where he can lay his hands on him any time you want him?"

"That's my business," Smith said sharply. "You fell down on your end of it. Don't butt in on another man's end."

"All right. Only wanted to see if I could help you out. Just wanted to warn you, that's all. Marka's a crafty devil and he'll give you the slip if you don't keep your eyes peeled. But perhaps Brimmer has him in *trunk*—a prisoner. Has he?"

"Sort of," Smith answered with a chuckle, then added, "Brimmer is a damned fool about some things, though. He got hold of the Major's nigger the other day, filled him up with rotten whisky and then pumped him. The nigger told Brimmer that the Major had dug a tunnel from his camp, over a mile away, to one of the mine-pits so that he could help himself to all the diamonds and make a clean getaway."

"You mean to tell me Brimmer believed that cock-and-bull story," Barnby asked incredulously.

"Yes," Smith laughed softly. "And he was so damned sure it's true that I promised to go out with him tonight, after the moon's up, and investigate."

"How about the Major? He's quick on the draw, they say."

Smith flinched.

"Brimmer will handle him. The Major, blast the monocled dude, never resists a policeman. I have a feeling, though, that the laugh will be on Brimmer and I want to be there to see it. Want to come?"

THREE HOURS later three horsemen cantered swiftly down the dusty main street of the town, passed out through the Commonage gate to the open veldt, and headed for the white bell-tent which, in the bright moonlight, stood out ghostlike against the dark background of the veldt.

About twenty yards from the tent they reined in their horses, dismounted and went cautiously forward on foot.

"Where's his trekking outfit?" Barnby whispered.

"I don't know," Brimmer answered. He was a soldierly built man, his spiked mustache upturned; his eyes, however, were furtive. "Perhaps he's visiting some farm, nearby."

"And leave his tent like this," Smith scoffed. "Hardly. He's no fool."

"He's not here now, I tell you," Brimmer said positively. "See, here are the ashes of his camp-fire. They're cold,"

"He may be hiding in his tent."

"We'll soon find out about that," Brimmer replied and, drawing his revolver, fired several shots at the tent while Smith, cowering, covered his ears with his hands.

"What in hell did you do that for," he screamed as the report of the last shot died away. "Do you—do you want a crowd from the *dorp* out here?"

Barnby and Brimmer exchanged sly winks and then Barnby quickly cut a bunch of the long, tinder-dry veldt grass, rolled it into a loose ball which he lighted and tossed into the tent.

It blazed there brightly for a moment, lighting up the interior of the tent.

"If he's there, we would have seen a shadow of him on the canvas," Barnby announced curtly. "We didn't; so he's not there. Say, Whip—"

But Smith was no longer by his side. He had run forward. His keen eyes had spotted a little mound of dirt just before the tent opening and he was hoarsely shouting, "By God, you were right, Brimmer. He's been digging. He—"

His words ended in a wild shriek of surprise, of fear, as the ground suddenly seemed to open at his feet and he sank up to his armpits in slimy, yellow mud.

"What the hell are you standing there for?" Smith yelled hysterically. "Come and pull me out!"

Brimmer checked his laughter with an effort, remembering that he was the indirect cause of Smith's predicament, and ran quickly to the aid of the embogged man. He nearly fell into the trap himself. One foot did go in, sending a shower of mud into Smith's face and increasing that man's anger.

Barnby, still laughing, now joined Brimmer and the two men caught hold of Smith's outstretched hands and, after much effort, pulled him out of the mire.

For a brief interval the three lay resting on the veldt. Brimmer was the first to move and he silently rose and stealthily made his way to his horse. He dared not stay to face Smith's wrath because of his mishap; and he was afraid, too, that he would be questioned regarding the matter of the concession. He had not told Smith that the plan by which they intended to keep Marka under observation had been suggested by Jim, the Hottentot.

The sound of Brimmer's departure brought Smith and Barnby to a sitting posture and from Smith's mouth came a stream of curses, blasphemies and invectives, leveled at Brimmer, as he gingerly cleared the mud from his face and scraped it off his clothes. In this Barnby helped him, his shoulders shaking with suppressed mirth.

"Get my boot," Smith ordered curtly.

"Boot? Where is it?"

Smith pointed to the mudhole.

"It came off while you were pulling me out. I'll break Brimmer for this!"

Barnby shook his head.

"No. I'll not go fishing in that. It stinks too much. You'll have to ride back without it. I'll bring your horse to you, so you won't have to walk at all."

"All right! Let's go now; I've got a lot to do tonight. Better have a look in the tent first, though. Might be something in there."

Rising, Barnby carefully entered the tent and emerged a few minutes later.

"Nothing there," he said. "It's empty, except for this." He gave Smith a large piece of white paper, folded neatly. "It was nailed to the tentpole," he explained.

Smith took it, a look of disgust on his face.

"Another of the Major's letters, I suppose. Well, I needed an example of his handwriting."

"Read it aloud, Smithy," Barnby urged.

Smith shook his head. "I'm not interested in what the blasted fool writes."

But, just the same he read it carefully, every word showing startlingly clear in the bright moonlight; and he mumbled curses as he did so.

Then, he read it aloud, imitating with bitter irony, the Major's affected drawl and intonation, he read aloud:

> This is to your address, Brimmer, old horse, because I dare not flatter my unworthy self that our dear old bosom friend Smitty will fall into my little trap. That was a wonderful story Jim told you. He's a bloomin' marvel, isn't he? And I felt, 'pon my word, that I ought to do something to back it up. So we dug a little, Jim and I, really thinking, don't you know, that by perseverance we might have the tunnel finished for your inspection. But it was not to be; dear me, no! Such hard work. So we filled the bally hole with a barrel and filled the barrel with mud and—well, you know the rest. Quite a nice, chatty little booby-trap,

what? I wish I could see you. But then, a chappie can't have everything. No? By the way, I've just heard that the season is now open for concession hunting up Tomasi's way. I haven't a bloomin' license, but I'm goin' up, dear heart. And I may bag something. One never, or hardly ever, knows.

Cheerio, dear lad. It might have been worse.

The Major

Barnby laughed; and a hyena nearby added its raucous clamor to Smith's outpouring of wrath.

"Let's go," he said at length.

"AND NOW for business," said the man with the whispering voice.

It was hard to believe that Smith, in the midst of the soft luxuries with which he had surrounded himself, was the same man whose iron rule made hardened criminals jump to obey his bidding; most certainly he did not seem to be the man who was embogged in the Major's booby-trap not two hours previously.

If Smith prided himself on the Spartan simplicity of his office furnishing, he was even prouder of this house of his on the outskirts of the *dorp*. It was luxurious; the dwelling place of a sybarite. It suggested beautiful, veiled women; it was a house of whispers.

A fountain splashed merrily in the courtyard, although, at his saloon, Smith charged ten shillings for a bath; water was very scarce.

At his "office" Smith's attire was quietly modest; he generally wore a black serge suit, of clerical cut, only his be-ringed hands giving evidence of his love for the ornately beautiful.

Now, in the privacy of his home, he gave full play to that desire. He was wearing gold brocaded slippers and a long, blue silk dressing-gown, across which dragons, golden-colored, crawled or contorted themselves into weird, fantastic knots.

Yet, in the midst of all this oriental display, Smith's death-pale face, his black hair brushed back from his high forehead, his eyes glowing somberly through sunken sockets, his lips thin and tightly compressed, seemed to be the face of an ascetic.

"Business," he repeated impatiently. And Barnby let go the day-dreams in which he had been indulging and, coming to with a start, stared blankly at his host for a moment.

"Ah, yes," he said. "About the concession. I've already told you there's only one thing to do, Smithy—wait until old Tomasi dies. You say you've got Marka safe—"

"Yes," Smith interrupted irritably, "I've got Marka where I can put my hands on him at any moment. How long do you think Tomasi will live?"

Barnby shrugged his shoulders. "He's pretty old. He ought to go off in the next five or ten years."

"And do you think I'm going to wait that long?"

"Don't see what else you can do, Smith. But why trouble? You're rich," He glanced around the room meaningly.

"I'm poorer than hell, Barnby. A big percentage of the hauls goes out in bribes."

Barnby knew that was a lie; but he made no comment.

"Besides," Smith went on, "that has nothing to do with the case. I want that concession and I'm going to get it *now.*"

"Why specially now?"

"Because the Major's after it. That's enough for me."

"Perhaps he was only bluffing."

"He never bluffs in letters. Listen, Barnby: I'll confess to you that the Major has me puzzled, for the simple reason that I can't afford to waste time in going after him myself. That's the only reason, you understand."

"Why bother with him at all?"

Smith snarled.

"He's butted into too many of my little schemes—and he won't join me; I've offered him the chance. All right then, he goes out. Now, if you can suggest a plan that will get me the concession and at the same time get rid of the Major, I'll give you all the papers I've collected, dealing with the murder of an American broker and the strange disappearance of the murderer."

Smith leaned back in his chair and watched Barnby through half-closed lids.

"Do you mean that, Smith?" Barnby asked. "You'll give me *all* the papers? You'll not keep some back?"

"You shall have them all."

"And you'll forget everything?"

"Yes. I promise."

Barnby thought a while.

"That means I'll be free," he muttered. "I would go back home. I wouldn't have to be afraid any more. I'd be free!"

Smith caught the last words.

"Yes. You'd be free," he whispered softly.

Barnby rose and passed restlessly about the room.

"I've got it!" he shouted suddenly in his excitement, "Listen to this."

TOMASI'S *KRAAL* was a scene of great excitement. The men were testing their weapons, whetting the broad blades of their *assegais* to a razor-keen sharpness and looking to the lashings of their shields. The women were busily engaged in preparing quantities of food and the young maidens passed constantly among the pushing, gesticulating mob with large gourds of beer balanced on their heads.

It seemed to be a preparation for war. And it was just that. A war against a lion, a man-eater, who had become overbold, even to the point of entering the *kraal* and taking a baby from the side of its sleeping mother.

It was in vain that the Major begged for permission to kill the tawny one in the white man's way—with a bullet, soft-nosed, aimed as he knew how to aim it. But Tomasi would not hear of it. Tomasi's people would not hear of it. The lion had attacked their honor; they, and they alone, with spears, meeting the "snarling one" face to face, could adequately wipe out that stain.

And the Major, who had been at Tomasi's *kraal* over a month, knew the black people so well that, once Tomasi's word had been passed, he did not argue further, save to ask permission to accompany the hunters.

It was high noon.

At last the feasting was over, the songs of the hunt had been sung, the beer pots emptied and, at a sign from the old, gray-bearded Tomasi, those who had been appointed beaters moved out to take up the positions designated by the scouts.

Half an hour or so after the departure of the beaters, the hunters, the picked men of the *kraal,* feathered headdresses nodding bravely in the sun, shield in left hand, a bundle of *assegais* in the right, marched proudly out to the beating of tom-toms and the excited shouts of women.

With the hunters marched Tomasi, the chief, the Major and Jim, the Hottentot.

They came soon to a steep knoll, to the top of which all but twenty of the party climbed. The twenty encircled the base of the knoll, facing outward. They were the men who had been chosen to do the killing.

From the knoll the Major was able to view the country for miles around. It was flat, low-lying, the barren veldt being broken by patches of tall elephant grass, clumps of *mapani* bush and mounds such as the one on which they were standing.

Far to the east, blued by the distance, was a high, truncated-cone shaped *kopje*, and at its base, the Major knew, was the *kraal* of Jhentsi, who was Tomasi's rival for the absolute chieftainship of the district.

To the west the veldt seemed unbroken. But not five miles away a mighty river ran between high, precipitous banks, forming a natural boundary and a very formidable barrier. In the wet season it was unfordable; and, in the dry season, only at the fords could passage be made.

"Look, *Baas!*" Jim said suddenly, "There is the lion."

He pointed to the east, but the Major could see nothing save the line of beaters, a half-mile or more away, forming a wide circle about the mound. Their nodding plumes made him think of surf breaking upon a rocky shore.

But if the Major could not see the lion, Tomasi and his warriors could, and their eyes sparkled with anticipation of the hunt.

"See, *Baas*," said Jim again. "Near to the anthill." He pointed to one midway between the beaters and the mound. "See, he moves."

And then the Major saw a tawny, slinking form—and then lost sight of it as it moved forward and vanished into a clump of elephant grass.

A perfect bedlam of noise ruptured the stillness as the beaters slowly narrowed their circle, yelling, beating tom-toms.

Nearer and nearer they came, the lion retreating before them. Often he was in full view of the men on the mound, often he was hidden by bush, rocks, or the tall grass. Once, when the Major lost sight of him, the lion was crouching on a bare patch of red veldt, not a hundred yards distant. Once the lion attempted to break back and through the ring of beaters. But his attempt was foiled; the threatened spot was quickly reinforced and the ground vibrated to his baffled snarls as he turned again.

Nearer, nearer!

There was a stir among the men at the foot of the mound. One of them, a mightily muscled man, standing half a head taller than his fellows, stepped a few paces to the front of them and in the direction in which the lion must come. He carefully examined his shield and, selecting a short, stabbing spear, discarded the others, then waited silently, motionless.

Now the lion's snarls were continuous, punctuated by sharp, hacking coughs and they could see the tawny beast crouched belly down, not twenty yards away.

The other men at the foot of the mound formed in a compact body behind their leader.

The snarling and coughs ceased. The lion froze. Everything was quiet. Nothing moved.

Then the beast's tail waved gently, slow at first, then quicker and quicker.

The beaters bettered their previous efforts. The din was deafening. They mocked the lion, screaming curses at him, called him a coward and an eater of children.

And then the lion charged, head down, his slobbering jaws almost touching the ground. He came on swiftly. Almost instantly he was on top of the waiting man who thrust shrewdly with his *assegai* and then went down before the force of the impact, covering himself with his shield, the lion on top of him.

Quickly then, with hoarse, bellowing shouts, the other hunters closed in on man and beast. Nineteen *assegais* flashed in the sun and, with a sharp *ghi-sh*, sank into the body of the lion.

The beast turned his mighty head and angrily tried to bite at the spears. Then he shuddered convulsively, roared once—a faint, muffled roar—and collapsed.

For a moment all was silent. And then the hunters beat upon their oxhide shields, shouting joyfully. Their shouts were echoed by the beaters, who now came forward with a rush, and by the men on the mound who leaped and pranced excitedly as they made their way down the incline.

The Major and Jim remained with Tomasi, who watched the scene from the top of the mound, Tomasi restraining the white man's desire to go down and tend to the wounds of the man who had met the lion's charge.

"Let be," said Tomasi. "It is the custom. He is not hurt. The shield was between him and the lion."

"But he has not moved," the Major pointed out. "The lion is still on top of him."

Tomasi smiled.

"He only waits for the song of praise. When that is sung, then you may go down. Listen."

As he spoke the noisy, clamoring babel changed suddenly to a measured chant which terminated in a mighty yell of "Kawiti!"

And then the man crawled from under the body of the dead beast and, rising slowly to his feet, grinned broadly, pivoted slowly so that all could see that he was unmarked. The others crowded around him, cheering him; Tomasi, the chief was forgotten. At that moment Kawiti, the man who had met the lion's charge, was greater than all chiefs.

"We will go down now, Jim," said the Major, "That one—Kawiti—is indeed a man and I would talk with him."

He turned toward the Hottentot when Jim did not answer. But Jim was staring intently at something on the veldt at the back of the mound.

The Major followed his gaze then, with a cry of warning, he leaped forward, intending to push Tomasi on one side. In this he was frustrated by Jim who dived at his *baas's* knees, bringing him to the ground.

At that moment a vicious crack of a rifle hushed the clamor of the hunters; and Tomasi tumbled slowly to the ground, groaning heavily, his hand pressed to his side.

"Look to him, *Baas,*" Jim cried as with knob-kerrie upraised he dashed down the mound and ran toward a stranger who, taking advantage of the confusion of the hunt, had joined the beaters and, getting within some fifty yards of the mound, had fired the shot.

This stranger yelled triumphantly and brandished a rifle as Jim and some of Tomasi's warriors closed in on him. But he offered no resistance nor made any attempt to escape. They brought him to the mound where the other warriors crowded excitedly around the Major and the body of their chief.

Tomasi's chest was torn by a gaping wound.

WAILING AND lamentations of women went up from Tomasi's *kraal* that night. The killing of the lion was forgotten. The people only remembered that Tomasi, their chief, was dead.

At the council place the elders were discussing plans of war against the people of the *kraal* at the foot of the distant *kopje*. For the man who had shot Tomasi was one of Jhentsi's men. When the discussion was at its height the Major, present by virtue of the friendship which had existed between him and the dead chief, asked for a hearing.

"Speak, white man," said one of the old men. "We know you to be wise and our friend."

"An evil deed has been done," he said slowly. "But look to it that out of evil comes not more evil. The slayer, you say, you will kill with the rising of the morrow's sun; and then, with your spears red with his blood, you will go against the people of Jhentsi.

"But, hasten slowly. The slayer indeed must die. On that I am silent. His deed was an evil one. But think on this; is it not true that you are stronger than the people of Jhentsi? Are you not better fighters? Do you not outnumber his warriors two to one?"

"True, white man. For that reason, what need have we to fear? Before the sun is at noon tomorrow, Jhentsi's *kraal* will have been put to the fire. You are talking to no purpose."

"Listen yet a little," the Major pleaded. "You know that Tomasi thought no shame in seeking my advice; you know that I was entrusted with his most sacred secrets; you know, also, that it was the man who now speaks to you who prevented Marka from making this *kraal* a place of desolation. You know, then, that my words will be true words. Good. Then answer me this: Has Jhentsi ever dared to work evil against you before this?"

"Save for the stealing of a goat or two, no."

"Then why dares he now? I will answer. He dares so greatly because new confidence, new strength, has come to him. What that is I do not know. But, and this is sure, if you go up against Jhentsi in ignorance of what that strength is, you will fall into the trap he has set for you. I have spoken."

The councillors looked at each other uneasily.

"Then what would you have us do?" one asked.

"Have the slayer brought before you. He will tell you many things, if you promise him life."

"He will tell all, if we show him death," Kawiti, the lion killer, said grimly. "But the word is good. Let the slayer be brought in."

The order was quickly obeyed and the slayer, a thin, frightened-looking man, sullenly defiant, guarded by two warriors, was brought before the council.

"He is your meat," said Kawiti to the Major. "See if you can open his mouth. If you fail, then we will question him. And we shall not fail." He gave orders that a fire be lighted.

"I shall not fail," said the Major. Then to the prisoner, "What is your name?"

"Semoukwe," the man answered sullenly.

"Then tell us, Semoukwe, why you, a warrior, a fighting man and well skilled in spearplay, killed with the white man's weapon."

"It was an order."

"An order? How? Not the Chief Jhentsi's order. What does he know of the white man's weapon? Nor is that his way of doing things. He is a man; and I thought you were a man, also."

Semoukwe shifted uneasily, but remained silent.

"So, then," the Major continued, "Semoukwe is a liar and a coward. He kills from afar with the white man's weapon because he is afraid to meet his enemy, not even an old man like Tomasi, face to face with an *assegai,* as a good warrior should. And he covers his cowardice by saying, 'It was an order!' Bah!"

Semoukwe flinched at the biting scorn in the Major's voice and answered hotly, "It was an order, white man, I do *not* lie."

The Major laughed.

"And do all the warriors of Jhentsi carry 'the thing which kills from afar?' Or is Semoukwe alone favored? Listen! I will tell you of the cause of things. A white man came to your *kraal* and won Jhentsi's ear, showed Jhentsi how Tomasi could be killed, promising to make Jhentsi chief of all this land. And Jhentsi, because he wanted to believe, believed and appointed you to do the deed. He promised you, belike, fifty head of cattle—"

"Nay! A hun—" he began, then stopped, overcome by confusion.

The Major and the others laughed.

"A hundred, you say. Great riches! But of what good are cattle to a dead man?"

Setnoukwe's somber eyes glowed, filled with almost fanatical light.

"To a dead man cattle are no good, it is true. But to a dead man's children they are much good. And it is no small thing, look you, that my name, because of this deed, becomes a great name. Because of the thing I have done, the people of Jhentsi will become a great shadow in the land. Death is nothing, death is less than nothing, for my name—Semoukwe—" he uttered the name with an almost religious fervor—"lives. Semoukwe, the Slayer!"

He uttered the last words in a piercing, triumphant yell. It was a battle-cry, a brave man's challenge.

There was a silence for a while and then Kawiti commented, "He is a man. It is a pity he must die."

"Truly," the Major answered sadly, "He is a man; yet is he a fool. Yes, you are a fool, Semoukwe, and Jhentsi is a greater fool. The white man uses you for his own purpose. For some reason he wanted Tomasi killed; well, Tomasi is dead. And now, what of you? What of Jhentsi? Tomasi's people thirst for blood. They outnumber your spears two to one. Tomorrow your *kraal* will be a place of desolation. The smoke from its ashes will blot out the setting sun; rivers of blood will flow; your menfolk will be killed, your women will become the slaves of this people and people will spit when mention is made of Semoukwe, the Fool! I weep for you."

The Major averted his face.

Semoukwe was silent for a while, pondering on what the Major had said. Then he laughed exultantly.

"You know not whereof you speak, white man," he cried loudly. "Let the people of Tomasi go against my *kraal*. They will find the people of Jhentsi waiting for them. And each warrior will hold in his hand the fire-spitting stick. Some few they have now; and this night, or at least before the rising of the morning's sun, a white man who is our friend comes with many more. Even now our warriors are waiting for him at the ford."

Semoukwe's voice rose to a triumphant shriek.

"Take him away," ordered Kawiti. "We have learned enough."

Semoukwe was silent as the guards hustled him away. He had had his great moment; all feeling of exultation now left him and he was a broken, frightened man.

"So you see," began the Major, "I was right. Semoukwe was just the dog of an evil man. Kill the dog and the evil still remains."

"You are right. But what now? Must we submit to the dog's master?"

The Major shook his head.

"I think not. But this is my *indaba*. With the black one, my servant, I go presently to the ford and do there what seems best."

"But why not take the warriors with you?"

"Tchut! Can they run as fast as a horse?" Then, as they made no reply, he continued, "Also it seems best to me that they do not go from this *kraal*. Who knows? Semouwke may, perhaps, have lied. It may be a trap. So wait here lest, if you go out and leave this *kraal* unguarded, the people of Jhentsi take it unawares and put it to fire."

"It is good council," some of the old men muttered, "Tomorrow, or the next day will do. There is time enough to deal with Jhentsi. Now we will be cautious."

"Good!" the Major approved. "Now one other thing before I go to the ford. Who, now Tomasi is dead, is chief of this *kraal?*"

"Marka, his son."

"And he is well deserving of the honor? He is well liked by you all?"

There were mutterings of anger.

"You know that is not so, white man. Marka is a fool, a boaster, a liar and coward."

"Somewhat I had thought of that. Who then is chief should Marka be dead."

"Kawiti. No other."

"And he is well worthy?"

"You know it, white man. Worthy in all ways."

"I know it."

"But Marka is not dead. Why this talk?" asked Kawiti.

"No, he is not dead," the Major said slowly. "But he has taken to himself a wife, a woman of no great worth. A little white blood she has in her veins; and therein a white man sinned greatly!"

This was received in great silence, and then one asked, "Is this true, white man?"

"True. If you doubt send messengers to the white man's *kraal* where Marka now lives."

With that he quietly left the place, leaving them to their excited discussion of the strange thing he had told them.

AFTER LEAVING the council place, the Major was joined by Jim and a few minutes later the two mounted and rode swiftly from the *kraal*, heading for the river about a mile above the ford used by Jhentsi's people.

The moon was at the full, flooding the veldt with its white light.

Both men rode unusually well, the Major sitting upright, graceful; Jim slouching forward in an almost jockey-like posture. They avoided the many pitfalls in the shape of ant-bear holes with uncanny precision.

They rode in silence and so, after an hour or more, they came to the river and, tethering their horses, made their way cautiously downstream toward the ford, taking advantage of every bit of cover.

"The *Baas* is not wise," Jim said softly. "Twice today he has acted foolishly."

"Yes, Jim?"

"Yah, *Baas*. This morning at the lion-hunt he tried to put himself in the way of the bullet meant for Tomasi."

"Ah! I meant to speak to you of that. You were guilty of great impertinence, Jim. Because of you, Tomasi died."

"Because of me, you live, *Baas*. Tomasi had lived long; his time was at hand. But you are young—you are my *baas*."

The Major made the clicking noise of impatience.

"We will let that pass now, Jim. But you said I was twice a fool this day. Speak then of the second time."

"The *Baas* is a fool to have taken upon himself the quarrel of the *kraal* people. Let them eat their own dirt. What are they to us? Out of this doings methinks death will come."

"Better that two men die, Jim, than that two *kraals* should be blotted out. But look—"

They had come now in sight of the ford and on the bank of a river, not two hundred yards in front of them, three or four hundred warriors were encamped. Their *assegais* flashed as they caught the moon's rays.

"Now will the *Baas* give up this folly? It is clear that we cannot cross at the ford, those warriors of Jhentsi would see us."

"But we must cross, Jim."

The Hottentot shrugged his shoulders.

"Where, *Baas?*"

"Here, foolish one."

"The water is very deep."

"We can swim."

"Aye, we can swim. But, above and below the ford there are crocodiles."

"Bah!"

"Their jaws will not go 'bah!' when they bite into the *baas's* body."

The Major laughed and sitting down on a nearby rock pulled off his riding-boots.

Jim eyed him with consternation.

"Is the *Baas* in earnest?"

"Truly."

"It is folly," Jim grumbled. "Yet wait a little while and I will come too."

Jim took two of his *assegais* and, breaking them in two, lashed the blade ends together so that he had, in effect, a two-bladed spear, about two feet long.

"At least," he said grimly as he tested the strength of his weapon, "one crocodile will be well fed. I am ready now, *Baas.*"

Silently they slipped into the river, with Jim slightly ahead and on the upstream side of the Major.

The current was strong and the river wide at that point; but, save that Jim took alarm and struck at a log which floated near him, the swim was devoid of incident.

"You are an old woman, Jim," the Major chuckled as they clambered up the steep bank. "You see evil where no evil exists."

"I am content to be an old woman, then, *Baas.* It is only by avoiding the evil that is not, yet might be, that young maidens live to be old women."

The current had taken them downstream, despite the fact that they were both strong swimmers, and they were now a little below the ford, not far from a large patch of *mapani.*

They made their way toward this and, a few minutes later, found refuge from observation in its cover.

"We will wait here, Jim," said the Major, "until our little friend the gun-runner comes along."

"Yah, *Baas.*"

"But I wish I weren't so deucedly wet."

"Damme yes. Wet, top-hole."

"Your English is improving, Jim, old horse, and—"

"Hands up!"

It was a curt voice, impelling obedience and, as it was echoed by two other voices of a like nature, one of which repeated the order for

Jim's benefit in the Hottentot dialect, the Major and Jim did not hesitate in obeying.

A sergeant and four troopers of the Mounted, rifles in hand, now rose up from their place of concealment.

"You must be getting old, Major," said the sergeant with a laugh. "Never thought you'd walk so prettily into our hands like this."

"I don't understand," the Major gasped. He was the dude now, and there was no trace in him of the man of action. "But, I say, old dears, before we talk business, do you mind if I lower my hands. I'm absolutely unarmed; and so is dear old Jim, if one accepts that twobladed thing which he says is good bait for crocodiles. He says that if you put that in crocky's mouth, why, crocky can't hurt you. But I digress. I'll give you my parole. Now can I take my hands down."

"If you'll promise not to play tricks," the sergeant said doubtfully.

"What? Oh, yes. I promise. You have my parole, you know."

The Major and Jim lowered their hands; and the Major, taking his monocle from his pocket, fixed it in his eye and blandly scrutinized the troopers.

"That's better," he exclaimed. "I can see you much better. And, bless me, if it isn't our friend 'Fatty' Wimple, accompanied by Stevens, Thompson and— But I don't know the other two Johnnies, do I? Well, I will anon. We're all good friends. What's troubling the old bean, Fatty?"

"Gun-running, Major. You can consider yourself under arrest. The evidence will be along in a little while."

"Gun-running! I don't understand. Why, Fatty dear, that's a terrible crime. You don't accuse me of that, surely?"

"Oh, stow it, Major, You can't fool me with that innocent talk. Trouble with you is you write too many letters."

"White? How?"

"Well, when the chief at headquarters received a letter from you saying you were going to pull off a little gun-running down this way and challenged him to catch you, he had a message relayed to my post, and here we are."

"So I see," the Major murmured. "So I wrote a letter telling the well known and honored chief all about it, did I? What a fool I must be."

"That's what we all thought. But—" reproachfully—"this isn't like you, Major. I.D.B., now, that's nothing. Everyone has done a little bit of it at one time or other; that's all square and above board—unless we catch you at it. But this gun-running business is damned rotten!"

"I quite agree with you, Wimp, old boy. But suppose I say that I know nothing whatever about it?"

"Then I'd call you a liar. You wrote the letter, Major. There's no mistaking your scrawl. And, besides, the chap who sold you the guns turned king's evidence and gave the game away."

The Major shrugged his shoulders.

"Then where are the guns?"

"That's what we are going to wait for. You came on ahead to make a deal with the natives. You made it all right, I take it. They're all over there—" he indicated the waiting natives on the opposite bank of the river—"waiting for the guns your confederate's bringing along."

"Still," expostulated the Major, "even if all this is true. I don't see that you have any evidence to convict me. Even you don't claim that I've actually sold guns to natives."

"Don't quibble, Major. The intent is there. We can prove that."

"Perhaps," the Major murmured.

"He's coming, sergeant," cautioned one of the troopers.

The rattle of wheels and the pounding of hoofs sounded on the hard, sun-baked veldt.

"Get to your post, men," the sergeant ordered. "Come along, Major—or shall I handcuff you and the Hottentot to a tree?"

"No, far otherwise," the Major said hastily. "I want to see all the fun. Give you my word that I'll be good."

The troopers took up positions behind rocks lining the road leading to the ford. The sergeant and his two prisoners lay down in a clump of long grass.

Presently a swiftly moving wagon came into view, drawn by mules who were galloping at a breakneck speed.

"God!" one of the troopers exclaimed. "They're running away!"

It was true.

As the wagon came nearer, swaying perilously from side to side, threatening to capsize any moment, the watchers could see the driver, his face white, feet braced against the front board, swaying desperately with the reins.

"He's going to have a terrible spill if he doesn't halt 'em before he hits the ford," said the sergeant and, running out into the road, brandished his arms wildly.

But the mules, mad with fear, seemed not to see him. Not for one instant did they falter in their stride but came on at that same mad gallop and it was only by a quick side leap that Wimple avoided being knocked down and trampled underfoot.

The wagon rattled down the gully leading to the ford and, a moment later, without any visible slackening of speed, the mules splashed into the river.

"The ford is very narrow," muttered the Major. "If he doesn't—"

At that moment the wagon lurched and capsized, luckily throwing the driver clear. He at once started to swim for the shore.

The policemen, Major and Jim rushed to the bank and saw, with horror, long, ominous shapes making for the struggling, squealing mules.

"He's a good swimmer," said Wimple. "He'll make it all right if the brutes prefer mule-meat to human flesh."

He opened fire on the slimy beasts and the three troopers quickly followed his example. And at the first volley Jhentsi's warriors fled, and considered not the order of their going, thinking the shots were meant for them.

Good shooting was impossible in that deceptive light, but the troopers' object was to create a barrier of shot between the swimmer and the crocodiles. In this they seemed to be successful. The man was now only twenty feet from the bank and swimming strongly.

"Ah!" the Major exclaimed suddenly. "A man-eater!" And snatching the two-bladed weapon from Jim he dove into the river.

So swift and unexpected was the Major's move that Wimple thought, for a moment, he was making a mad attempt to escape. Then the sergeant saw that one of the crocodiles had left the mules, now still and silent; churning the water to a foam with his powerful tail, he was rushing fast at the wagon driver.

"The fool!" gasped Wimple. "The splendid fool! He can't do it."

All watched anxiously, fearfully.

They saw the Major meet the wagon driver, heard him encourage the man to better speed; they saw the Major swim on, right into the path of the oncoming crocodile.

They saw the beast's mighty jaws open, saw the Major thrust his hand into the cavernous opening. In the Major's hand was the weapon Jim had made.

Followed a tremendous bellowing as the crocodile backed, lashed the water with his tail, then swam round and round in frantic circles. Twice, three times, he leaped right out of the water, hitting the surface with a resounding *smack* as he came down. Then, with one final bellow, he sank out of sight.

"God! He did it!" one of the troopers half-sobbed. "But where is he?"

"Here, old chap," The voice sounded from below and, clambering down the steep bank, they hauled the Major, and the man whose life he had saved, ashore.

"Three times you've been a fool this day, *Baas*," Jim cried excitedly. "But that killing—that killing of the slimy one! *Au-a!* Even I could not have bettered that!"

"I SAY, old top," the Major asked the wagon driver, who called himself Rake Barnby, "just what started your bloomin' mules on the merry-merry? They were goin' L for leather, you know."

"Lions," Barnby said tersely. "Two of 'em sprang out at my leaders. After that there was no holdin' 'em."

"This is bad lion country," Wimple commented. "I remember once—"

"Oh, shut up, Fatty," one of the troopers interrupted rudely, "and pour me out another cup of coffee. Your Hottentot's a good cook, Major."

They were all seated around a large camp-fire. The Major and Barnby were wrapped in blankets, borrowed from the police, while their clothes were drying. Jim, after foraging amongst the troopers' kits, had produced a warming, savory meal.

And so the men, full and well content, lounged lazily by the fire, smoking and exchanging stories of their thrilling experiences with natives and beasts.

There was no thought now of hunter and the hunted, as applying to the police and the Major. An atmosphere of good fellowship had them in its spell.

"Well," Wimple said presently, "I suppose we'll have to talk business again. Of course, Major, this gun-running charge won't stand, now. The evidence is at the bottom of the river and I'm not going to ask Barnby, here, to turn evidence."

"I wouldn't—" Barnby began hotly, then finished lamely, "I couldn't."

The Major looked at him with interest.

"As to that," Wimple continued, waving his pudgy hands—they were very powerful hands, just the same, "I'm not so sure. At any rate, Major, we've no case. You're free to go any time. But—"

"Yes? But what?" drawled the Major as he absently polished his monocle.

"I wish you hadn't started this business, Major. It's rotten. It even makes me forget that thing you did a little while back."

"Oh that," the Major flushed. "I—er—just wanted to try Jim's little croc-teaser. As for the bally gun-running! I never have done it and I never will! Please believe that, dear lad."

Wimple's laugh was echoed by that of the other policemen.

"We'll say we believe it, if you want us to, Major. Still, knowing what we know about—"

Followed a silence. Then the Major, looking intently at Barnby, said, "Can't you persuade these chappies differently? You're supposed to be my confederate, you know. You ought to know something. Really, I feel this accusation most strongly."

Barnby coughed and pulled the blanket closer about his thin, attenuated figure.

"Yes, I know something they ought to know," he began in a low voice.

Wimple looked at the four troopers inquiringly and, satisfied with the message their eyes conveyed to him, said, "Don't tell us anything that'll incriminate the Major."

"You've said it," put in Stevens, "If he does, I'll throw him back to the crocs myself."

"It won't incriminate the Major," Barnby said with a wry smile. "On the contrary. But first I'd like you to promise me one thing."

"What is it?"

"When you send in a report to headquarters, say I was drowned. Will you?"

"Why?"

"Because I want to get away from Whip Smith, and," he added bitterly, "I can only do that by dying."

The sergeant was silent for a moment.

"Where will you go? I take it you're wanted badly, somewhere, or you wouldn't be in Smith's clutches."

"Yes. I've been wanted for ten years or more. Someone else is involved, too, or I'd go back and face the music. But that's something else. Where will I go? Oh, I'll lose myself up-country, somewhere."

"Suppose you come with me for a while, Barnby," the Major suggested.

Barnby considered this for a moment. Then, "That's white of you, Major, but, no, I can't do that unless you ask me again after I've told my story. What do you say, Wimple? Will you report that?"

"By God, yes. As far as we know you're in the belly of a croc right now."

Barnby smiled faintly.

"Then listen to my ghost talking: I came up here for Smith and tried to get a concession from Tomasi."

"Concession? For what?" interposed the Major.

"Gold. There's a rich reef over there." He waved his hand in the general direction of Tomasi's *kraal*. "Didn't you know?"

"No. Wouldn't know gold quartz if I saw it."

"It's there. It'll make the Rand look like a 'pocket.' Tomasi wouldn't give or sell me the concession but, when I returned with the news to Smith he told me that he had succeeded in getting one from Marka, Tomasi's son. But Smith didn't want to wait until the old chief died a natural death. He was in a hurry to get at that reef. Also he wanted to get even with you, knowing that you had left suddenly for Tomasi's *kraal*—and specially after he fell into the booby-trap you set for Brimmer."

"He did? Oh, that's too, too rich. But go on. I'll tell you chappies all about it, later."

A smile lighted up Barnby's face, but was quickly replaced by a frown.

"So, Smith put the screws on me—promised to give me certain papers which meant freedom, if I got rid of you and Tomasi at the same time. And I planned well. We knew that you were on your way out here, so one of Smith's men who can imitate you pretty well and looks something like you, in the dark, bought a consignment of rifles and ammunition and announced that he was going to sell 'em to the blacks out this way. Another of Smith's men wrote a letter to the

Chief of Police—it was a clever bit of forging—and that started the wheels moving. In the meantime I had sent a message to Jhentsi—Jhentsi is an old ally of mine—and told him to wait for me here at the ford on the night of the full moon and promised him that, if Tomasi was killed, accidentally or otherwise, I'd give him enough rifles to wipe out Tomasi's *kraal* and make him chief."

"But I don't see," the Major murmured, "how this affects me."

"Wait! I know natives. Few white men have studied them more closely. I knew that whoever Jhentsi appointed to kill Tomasi would allow himself to be captured so that he could crow over Tomasi's warriors and boast of the superiority of his own people. I ran no risk. They say you understand native psychology, Major. You ought to know my plan was sound."

"Yes, it was sound," the Major murmured. "A native would rather die, knowing his name would be handed down with the traditions until it, too, became a tradition, than live possessed of great wealth. And so—"

"And so, knowing you, it was sure you would question him, if he had not already volunteered all he knew, and find out about the rifles; finding out, it was sure you would try to stop me from delivering them. Now do you see?"

"A little, a very little. And that is too much. I'm glad now that you didn't accept my invitation. Poor old Tomasi is dead."

"That's why I refused. Major. I'm not proud of that. But it was Tomasi's skin against mine. And Tomasi was old; I'm not—not very—and I'm fond of life."

"Get on with your yarn," the sergeant said irritably. He wanted to follow the example of his four troopers who were dozing peacefully, for food, the warmth of the fire and the low-toned conversation had a somniferous effect.

"Yes, go on," the Major urged gently, "Supposing the mules hadn't run away and—er—all the rest, what then?"

"There was one little error, I didn't think you'd come over this side and wait for me; also the police came a little sooner than I calculated. But, even so, it would have been all right. Don't you see? You would have held me up; I'd have shown no fight; and you'd have taken charge of the wagon."

"It's plain now," interposed the sergeant.

"Then we'd have come on the scene and arrested the Major. And there would have been the rifles—and there the natives—and Tomasi dead, and—"

"And the Breakwater waiting for me, eh, what? Oh, a very jolly little plan."

"Damned dirty, I call it," growled Wimple.

"But you'll keep your promise?"

"Yes," grudgingly. "But don't let me run across you again. Get dressed and make your getaway. Take Stevens' horse. We'll get another for him at Tomasi's *kraal* first thing in the morning. Suppose I'll have to stay there until this thing blows over."

Ten minutes later Barnby rode silently away from the camp-fire, heading north, determined to keep to a new trail which would not cross that of the man with the whispering voice.

Presently, when the sergeant's snores added volume to that of the others, the Major dressed quietly.

"No lions would come near *them*," Jim said contemptuously.

"They have trekked far, Jim. We will keep watch."

ABOUT THE same time that he heard of Tomasi's murder and death, by drowning, of Barnby, Whispering Smith received a very brief note from the Major.

It read in part:

> There's a mounted police post here now and Kawiti has been rec-
> ognised as chief by the powers that be, and all that. So I wouldn't
> advise you to press your concession claim. It's not worth the paper it's
> written on. Really! Pay a visit to someone who knows native law and
> tell him the facts, the whole truth and nothing but the truth. Tell him
> that the heir apparent married a woman not of his tribe. And, when
> you're foaming at the mouth after hearing the news, remember, dear
> lad, that Jim, my servant, you know, suggested to Brimmer that he
> find a wife for Marka. Jim's quite a gay little Cupid, isn't he? Oh, yes;
> I have the concession. But I don't know where the reef is.

Smith lost no time in consulting an authority; he consulted three, in fact.

In each case the answer was the same.

"What happens if a chief's son of that tribe marries out of the tribe or, worse still, a half-caste? Why, he loses whatever claim he has to the chieftainship and is damned lucky if he's not kicked out of the tribe altogether."

"Then this concession's worthless?" Smith asked weakly.

"Absolutely."

Then Smith, remembering the last sentence or two of the Major's letter, foamed at the mouth with rage and sent messengers with instructions to bring the hapless Brimmer before him.

"I'll make the fool smart for this," he raved, "And as for the Major—"

A BUCKETFUL
OF DIAMONDS

WHISPERING SMITH—SOUTH AF-RICA'S Fagin—reluctantly admitted to himself that he had made a great mistake in withdrawing his protection from Sergeant Brimmer. He made a still greater mistake when he mailed, anonymously, to the Crown Prosecutor such evidence as he had of Brimmer's unlawful operations. That evidence had been sufficient for a jury to convict Brimmer on no less than ten counts, any one of which carried a penalty big enough to keep the erstwhile police sergeant laboring at the Breakwater at Cape Town for the rest of his natural life.

Smith's regret was a selfish one: "Whip"—as he was often called because of the lash-like urge of his whispering voice—felt no feeling of sorrow or pity for the man who had been his loyal henchman for so many years. His conscience did not trouble him at the thought that Brimmer was doomed to a life of hard labor solely because he had faithfully carried out Smith's own instructions. Brimmer had not executed any one of the crimes on his own initiative; every one, and many others which had not been uncovered at the trial, had sprung from the fertile brain of Smith.

But Smith was entirely conscienceless. That partly explains his great hold on the criminals who flocked to South Africa from the four corners of the earth in those early days of gold strikes and diamond finds; that partly explains his own immunity from punishment.

However, Smith was not the sort of man to cry over spilt milk. He had brains, and he was big enough to admit—to himself—that he had made a mistake when, actuated solely by a fit of pique, he had had the police sergeant put away.

Brimmer had been an extremely valuable man. As a plain-clothes detective he had been able to get inside information on many of the plans whereby the police fondly hoped to round up criminals; and Smith, by passing on such warnings as the information warranted, had been able to solidify still further his hold on the threatened men.

Then, too, Brimmer had been useful in other ways. For instance, when a man refused to ally himself with Smith or threatened in any way to kick over the traces, a frame-up organized by the worthy Brimmer never, or hardly ever, failed to bring the balky one to reason. And now this worthy and most valuable henchman was lost to Smith, and he had no one to blame but himself.

Brimmer's only error had been that he was too credulous in his eagerness to get the goods on the Major—the monocled dude who had become an even greater menace to Smith's autocratic rule of the criminal world than were the police. Because of his incredulity Brimmer had exposed Smith to one of the Major's practical jokes, and had unwittingly betrayed a carefully planned scheme which would have greatly enriched Smith and have put the Major behind bars.

After having admitted to himself that he had made a mistake, Smith set himself to rectify it. By pulling the many strings which led from his office to men who sat in high places—as well as those in the gutters—he attempted to arrange for Brimmer's retrial, complete exoneration and restoration to duty.

But, for once, Smith seemed powerless. He was compelled to abandon the attempt, for some of the strings snapped and their recoil came dangerously near to him. He didn't wish to call attention to himself; he had a big game afoot. He was playing for large stakes that would make all that he had done hitherto seem like snatching candy from a child.

He was philosophical about this defeat, when, from his dirty little office at the back of his very ornate saloon in Kimberley, he began to spin his web, inviting the members of the police force to walk into it. Spiderlike, he offered many inducements, all having to do with great wealth and a life of ease—that is, if one had no conscience to trouble him.

But for a long time, so long indeed that Smith had almost resigned himself to the fact that he would be compelled to dispense with an ear inside the police councils, the only response to his invitation seemed to be, "Not today, Mr. Longshanks; I have other fish to fry."

Brimmer's arrest and imprisonment had proved even more disastrous to Smith's plans than he had feared. With such an example before them, those of the police who were not already honest changed their old policy for the best one.

AND THEN Trooper "Rat" Snyder was sentenced to ten days C.B. for insubordination; "Silent Contempt," the charge read. For ten days the Rat was confined to barracks, deprived of everything—wine, women and song, but mostly wine—which made life in this "blawsted 'ell 'ole they calls Kimberley," worth living.

Rat spent the ten days dwelling on his grievances, in dreaming of the happy days of his youth in the slums of London, cursing the events which led to his forced departure from those happy hunting grounds, and planning revenge on the corporal who had been responsible for getting him put on the "peg."

On the eleventh day Rat Snyder hastened townward with a ten-day thirst to assuage.

Not far from the police camp he was accosted by a pretty, dark-haired girl whose wide-open eyes held an innocent baby stare.

"Where are you going, Trooper?" she asked with a slight lisp.

The Rat scowled, recognizing her at once. Photographs, full face and profile, of her were on the police bulletin board with a terse summary of her achievements and convictions on the other side. As a pickpocket she was supreme although, so far, she had not been suspected of plying her trade since coming to South Africa.

"You ortter get shut o' that lisp, kiddo," the Rat said. "It's a fair give away."

"Yeth?" she smiled. "That's what a lot of people tell me. Perhaps you could teach me how."

She placed her hand on his and looked appealingly up into his little, red-rimmed eyes; her long, sensitive fingers tapped a light tattoo on his wrist.

He shook her off roughly.

"That's not nith," she said with a pout. Then giggled.

"Wot are yer grinnin' at?" the Rat asked suspiciously.

"Becauth you're so croth. Are you afraid your beth girl will thee you?"

"Ain't got no girl, don't want one, neither. I'm in a 'urry. I'm thirsty."

"Poor boy!" She almost cooed the words. "Tho am I."

"Go an' buy yerself a drink, then. You've got plenty o' money—or know 'ow to get it. I ain't, an' can't."

She sighed. "I know."

She opened her purse and emptied a number of gold pieces into her hand and shook them.

The Rat's eyes glinted at the golden jingle. He looked around to see if there was anyone in sight. The long dusty street was deserted, and he chuckled softly. It would be so easy to help himself to the girl's money, and then arrest her for something or other. That'd be killing two birds with one stone, and the thought rather intrigued him. He hadn't made an arrest yet, and he fancied the feeling of authority it would give him.

He moved toward her, then jumped back with a sucking intake of breath; his jaw dropped. From some mysterious hiding place the girl had produced a small, but very business-like revolver which was aimed unwaveringly at the pit of his stomach; her eyes had become suddenly hard and cruel.

"Wot's the gime?" the Rat asked in tones of injured innocence.

"I'm dwy. I want a dwink. Won't you buy me one?"

"Course I will," he responded promptly. "Yer don't 'ave to pull the 'ands-up game to make me stand treat to a pretty lady. But where'll we go?"

"Whip Smith's place." The revolver disappeared beneath a sea of billowing lace.

The Rat shook his head. "I can't go there. That's out of bounds. Besides, 'e charges like 'ell. Only toffs can afford to go there."

She took his arm confidingly.

"Oh, come along," she teased. "Here's thome money, all I have is yourths."

She forced open one of his not too tightly clenched fists and dropped the gold pieces into his grimy palm. His hand closed on them quickly, as if fearing she would demand their return, put them in the canvas money belt strapped about his waist, and grinned triumphantly.

The Rat had changed subtly from a downtrodden, sulky man into a conceited, overbearing bully. The whine vanished from his voice. His apparently easy and total conquest of this beautiful daughter of joy went to his head, but then he'd always been "such a one wiv the women."

"I'll buy yer a drink an' welcome," he announced magnanimously, "but I ain't a-goin' wiv yer to no Whispering Smith's. I've 'eard too much abart that blighter. Besides, as I've told yer, the bloomin' p'lice is hout o' bounds."

She sighed somewhat impatiently. "We can thit at a nith little table in the corner and no one will thee us. What do you care for the narthy old regulations—a big man like you? I'd like to thee any corporal or thargeant twy to make twouble for you." She gave no sign that she was conscious of the Rat's sudden start and the stiffening of his muscles at the mention of his deadliest enemies—corporals and sergeants—but continued blithely. "I know you could pick one up in each hand and knock their thilly heads together. You'd be a corporal, too, and perhaps a sergeant, if they weren't tho jealouth, wouldn't you?"

"Yus," he admitted bitterly. "They've all got it in for me, they have. Allus pickin' on me."

"Oh!" The little scream and realistic shudder was very complimentary to the Rat's fierceness. "You're tho big and twong, they wouldn't dare thay anything to you even if they did thee you in Smith's."

It may have been the appeal of her voice, her flatteries, her piquant face and full, over-rouged lips; or perhaps his fears were lulled by the strong scent of jasmine—its effect was almost narcotic—with which she had drenched herself. But whatever the cause, Snyder's capitulation was sudden and absolute.

"All right," he said with gay insouciance. "I don't care if we does."

He cocked his helmet jauntily over one ear and unbuttoned the collar of his tunic to express his defiance of regulations.

"You're tho brave," she murmured as they strolled lazily toward the *dorp.*

On arriving at Whispering Smith's place Snyder lost some of his confidence, and hesitated about entering.

"It don't seem proper like for me to go in there," he objected. "I 'ears as 'ow some of the big bugs of the diamond syndicate go there sometimes." And this was true, for Smith did not allow his many criminal activities to jeopardize his reputation for purveying the best drinks in town. Nominally, Smith was an honest saloonkeeper and a respected citizen.

"Supoose you go in hand 'ave yer drink alone," the Rat continued. "I'll wait for yer here."

He held out a shilling toward her.

But she caught hold of his wrist, and with considerably more strength than he had given her credit for, pulled him in through the swing doors of the barroom.

"There," the girl said as she sat down opposite the discomfited trooper. "No one's going to thee you here. Now order me a dwink."

She clapped her hands and one of the barmaids, her nose uptilted in scornful derision, came up to them and wiped the table-top with an insulting flaunt of a dirty towel.

"Two whiskys, miss," Snyder said, his voice thick with embarrassment. This place had too much class for him. His eyes were downcast, and so he did not see the exchange of winks between the girl with a lisp and the barmaid.

Time passed quickly and the barmaid made frequent visits to the table and with each visit Snyder's voice grew more confident, much thicker, but not with embarrassment.

Then, when he became maudlinly sentimental, the girl rose.

"Where yer goin'?" he asked, grabbing at her dress.

She lightly evaded him. "I want to thee a friend over there." She nodded to a far corner of the room, but Snyder, though he peered hard in that direction, could distinguish nothing through the wreaths of smoke.

"You'll come back?" he demanded.

"Yeth, of course," and with a flounce of her skirts, which seemed to release a heavy cloud of jasmine, hastened away.

Snyder, the Rat, watched her until she was lost to his sight in the haze of tobacco smoke, then pounded on the table for another drink.

II

THE GIRL had passed through a small door at the far end of the room, and now stood on the far side of a cumbersome roll-top desk at which sat a medium sized man dressed in a suit of somber black.

"Well, Martha," he whispered huskily, stroking his long, thin nose with fingers which glistened with diamonds. "What is it?"

"I've got a policeman for you," she replied, and now there was no trace of a lisp in her voice.

He looked up with interest. "Is he any good?"

She made an expressive moue and answered noncommittally, "He'll obey orders, if you frighten him enough."

The man's thin lips tightened. "Has he brains?"

"No, but—"

"Never mind the buts," he interrupted harshly. "Brimmer had brains and tried to use 'em. See where they landed him. I want a man who can't think for himself; a man who'll be content to simply obey orders."

"Then Rat Snyder ought to please you, boss."

"The Rat, eh!" Smith's eyes glistened unpleasantly. "He hasn't the guts to run crooked. He'd squeal at the first sign of pressure."

The girl was silent. She knew that there was little chance of anyone squealing to the police about Whispering Smith. He always saw to it that his creatures had no proof to back up any accusations, which they, to save their own skins, might make. The men, and women, who had squealed in the years gone by, had not lived long. Smith had seen to that! Made sure, also, that their sudden decease was known to all and sundry.

"How did you get hold of the Rat?" he now asked.

"The same way I got the others. Only difference is, that they refused to come into your saloon. He's out there now. I've been drinking with him. God, how I hate the weak tea Betty's been serving me instead of whisky. I must have drunk a quart of it in the last hour."

Smith smiled sardonically. "You wouldn't be half as clever if you drank whisky—drink for drink—with your male friends. So Snyder's drunk, eh? Not much use talking to him in that state, is there?"

"He's not drunk—only talkative. He can hold more booze than any other man I've met."

"All right. Tell Deemster to bring him in here."

"Deemster'll need help, boss. Snyder's a big man. He's as big as the Dutchman."

"Piet can get help if he needs it, can't he? And without any advice from me?"

The girl flounced out of the room and Smith took a large scrapbook from one of the drawers of his desk, and turned the pages slowly.

This book was one of several which formed Smith's Rogues' Gallery. It contained the photographs and record of practically every crook in South Africa—no matter whether that crook had acted profession-ally in the country or not; no matter whether the man was an ha-bitual criminal, or whether he had made but one slip from grace. Smith kept a very accurate watch on the movement of all foreign law-breakers, so unlucky as to receive newspaper notoriety. Should they decide to seek immunity from arrest or a new hunting ground in South Africa, Smith was quickly apprised of the fact. His next step depended on several things, but it could be only one of three things—an invitation to join his organization, the giving of information to the police, or blackmail.

When he came to a page in the book whereon was pasted a full-length photo of Rat Snyder in a boxer's costume, he leaned back in his chair, his lips pursed, eyes half-closed, and waited patiently.

Presently there was a scuffling noise outside. The door was sud-denly thrown open and two big stolid-faced Dutchmen entered with Snyder struggling ineffectually between them.

The Rat was inarticulate with rage and fear.

Smith looked up placidly. "What's the trouble, Piet?" he asked mildly.

"Trouble enough, boss," the black-bearded Dutchman replied. "This *verdoemte skellum* tried to pass the greasy stuff."

He threw two golden coins on the desk before Smith—they made a leaden sound.

"Counterfeit, eh?" Smith said, picking the pieces up and examining them closely.

"Where did you get these, Trooper?"

"A skirt gave 'em to me," the Rat exclaimed excitedly. "A saucy little piece of fluff with a lisp, so help me!"

Smith looked at the two Dutchmen inquiringly.

They guffawed loudly. *"Allehmahtig!* What a liar!" exclaimed one.

"It's you wot's the bleedin' liar," Snyder retorted hotly. "I tell yer a girl give 'em to me, and I brought 'er in here for a drink. S'elp me, I wish I 'adn't."

"There was no girl with him, boss," the Dutchman, Deemster, interrupted heavily. "He was drinking alone. Two of the greasy pieces he gave for drinks."

"See if he has any more of them on him."

Indifferent to Snyder's struggles, practically unconscious of them, the two searched him with a thoroughness which evidenced much practise, and produced five more of the golden coins and a handful of silver.

"I tell you a girl gave 'em to me," Snyder repeated hoarsely as Smith looked accusingly at him.

"Perhaps there's been some mistake," Smith said to the Dutchmen. "I'll have a talk with this man—alone."

Without a word they silently left the room, and when Snyder, panic stricken, would have followed them, they shut the door in his face. They must have locked it, for, though he tried hard enough, he was unable to open it. Snyder was caught in the outer fringe of Smith's net.

"I wouldn't make so much noise, if I were you," Smith suggested quietly. "If some of your comrades of the force happened to come by, you'd be in a hell of a mess. First for being here—my saloon's out of bounds, you know—and then, of course, I'd have to give you in charge for passing counterfeit money."

Snyder instantly ceased his kicking and pounding at the door; his loud curses and blasphemies stopped abruptly as he turned round and glared at Smith with his shifty, rat-like eyes.

"What do yer want?" he asked sullenly.

"A little chat. It isn't often I have a chance to talk with a crooked prizefighter and a wife beater."

Smith pointed to the open page of his book.

The Rat came nearer to the desk and looked over Smith's shoulder with an expression of pride on his face. "They've got a lot to say about me, 'aven't they?" he smirked. "An' you've got it all down there? Wot do yer know about that. I've 'eard all about your book. But clubbin' yer woman over the 'ead ain't a capital charge. They can't extradite me—she didn't die. You can't scare me by 'oldin' that over me 'ead."

"I'm not trying to scare you," Smith said dryly. "But don't forget that you'd find it very hard to explain that counterfeit money."

Snyder became panicky again.

"What do yer want?" he repeated hoarsely.

"Just a little talk."

" 'Ow can I tork standin' up like this. Ain't yer got another chair a bloke can sit in?"

Smith ignored him—his was the only chair in the office. He preferred that his visitors should stand; thus they appeared before him in the rôle of suppliants.

"You've heard of Sergeant Brimmer?" he continued.

"Yus. But you ain't planning to do fer me as you did fer 'im, are yer?"

"Yes," Smith answered, and smiled.

"But, why? I never done you no 'arm, guv'nor."

"You haven't the guts," Smith said contemptuously. "What I meant was this: I'm prepared to pull the string that'll get you promoted sergeant, and as for the rest—why that all depends how you behave."

The Rat's eyes gleamed. "Lumme! Do yer mean it, guv'nor? Me a sergeant and a plain-clothes swaddy! I won't arf give that corporal wot put me on the peg 'ell!"

"But first you've got to show me that you're worth it."

Snyder's face fell. "Oh! I knew there was a do in it somewhere," he grumbled. Then brightened. "What?"

Smith looked at him narrowly before answering, "Put the Major out of the way."

"The Major?"

"Yes," impatiently. "You've heard of him, haven't you?"

Snyder grinned. "Lumme, yes. He seems ter be a little Godalmighty round 'ere. And 'e's only a monocled dude, I keeps a-tellin' them."

"You've seen him?"

"Hell, no!" The Rat spat contemptuously. "But I've 'eard them torkin' about 'im. It's 'Major this,' and 'Major that,' till his name fair makes me sick. Is that hall yer want me ter do? Put a silly-ass Johnny out?"

"Out for keeps, I mean," Smith explained.

"Yer mean—kill 'im?"

Smith nodded and Snyder's face lengthened. "'Ow! That's something different. They 'ang men for murder, an''anging's a nasty way to die."

"But if you shot him while he was resisting arrest," Smith suggested. "That wouldn't be murder, and you'd be promoted sergeant. You'd get all the easy money Brimmer used to get, and would be getting now if he hadn't played the fool with me."

The Rat's face was contorted in his effort to think.

"Do you want Brimmer's job?" Smith asked suddenly.

"Yus," the Rat answered after a moment's hesitation, "if this job o' gettin' the Major's a safe 'un."

"Safe enough, if you work it the way I tell you. The Major's up in the Vaal district now, 'resting' as he calls it. All you have to do is to get him alone and drill a hole in him. They'll have to believe your version of the affair because you'll make sure there are no witnesses—see?"

The Rat was a coward as most bullies are—as all wife-beaters are—but he had no foolish compunctions about murder, in theory, at least, and as long as his own neck was safe. The objection he now made was rather the fruits of his indolence than his reluctance to kill.

"Wouldn't framing him with a diamond and gettin''im sent to the Breakwater please yer just as well?"

"No!" Smith snarled furiously. "Don't you go try any monkey business of that sort. That's how Brimmer got in wrong. It'd take a much smarter man than you to frame the Major properly. I'm the only man who could do that, and I haven't the time or the inclination. No!" He consulted his book again. "You've got the reputation of being a good revolver shot. That's your line. Get as close as you can, the closer the better. And no shots in the back. Your story'll be that he drew and fired first. You can fix up the necessary evidence afterward. Do you see?"

Snyder nodded. Everything seemed so far away; he could have agreed to anything at that moment. Yet he wondered, vaguely, nor troubled to deny it, how Smith got the information that he was a good revolver shot.

"That's all right then," Smith exclaimed. "But mind, now, no tricks. And, if you fail, there'll be these to explain."

He toyed with the golden coins on his desk.

"I shan't fail," the Rat said confidently—he'd take good care to get up very close indeed. Then, struck by a sudden thought, he added, "But 'ow am I to get near the Major w'en 'e's hup in the Vaal district?"

"You'll apply for a transfer in the morning. They'll be glad to get rid of you."

"Lumme! Fink of everything, don't yer? But 'ow am I goin' ter know 'im w'en I see 'im. 'Ave yer thought o' that?"

"Here." Smith took down another book which, as he placed it on his desk, fell open at a much bethumbed page covered with the photographs of a tall man with a smooth, round face and high fore-head, immaculately dressed and wearing a monocle. Apparently he was a dude; his face was vacuous, inane almost. But even these poor snapshots did not altogether fail to register something stern, yet intensely likeable about the man.

The Rat, seeing only the foppish clothes and on them basing his judgment, swore mirthfully. "Is that the man that's led the perlice such a 'ell of a chase all these years?"

Smith smiled caustically. He had crossed wits with the Major too often to be misled by exteriors.

"Lumme!" went on Snyder, proving that he was not entirely un-observant. "Momma's pet's got a fightin' jaw on 'im. I bet it's a glass 'un, though. One biff on that—" he made a vicious swipe with his big fist at an imaginary opponent—"'ud kill 'im as easy as a bullet, an' it wouldn't be so messy like."

Again Smith smiled and turned the pages, showing a lot more photographs of the Major in various disguises—as a trader, as an old prospector, as a half-caste (this a truly marvelous get-up) and as a drunken miner.

"Let me 'old the book a minute, will yer, guv'nor," the Rat asked breathlessly. "I want ter 'ave a good squint at that bloke. I wants ter know 'im w'en I sees 'im."

Smith hesitated a moment and then, with a shrug of his shoulders, gave the ponderous tome to the Rat.

"Go and sit down in that corner over there," he said with a wave of his hand, "and see that you don't get the pages dirty." Mumbling something about, "bein' treated like a kid," the Rat lowered his lanky frame to the floor, leaned back against the wall and concentrated on the photographs of the Major.

"I fink I'll know 'im w'en I see 'im," he announced presently. "Once I sees a man's photo, it's funny-like, but I can always remember wot 'e looks like an' can recognize 'im—no matter 'ow long after I've seen 'is photo."

Smith looked up with interest. The Rat was showing some glimmerings of intelligence. Of course he was boasting, still—

"Is that so?" Smith commented. "Then you had better look at some of the other photographs. No telling when you may run across a man—or woman—who's listed in that book. And when you do, *remember this*. Report his whereabouts to me. I'll deal with him. See?"

"Yus, guv'nor," the Rat said meekly, but his eyes glowed avariciously.

III

"JIM," DRAWLED the Major, "I'm getting terribly bored with this bally hunting trip. I feel the urge for music, laughter and excitement."

"Yah, *baas*," assented the Hottentot gravely. " 'Citement—dam true."

The Major chuckled. "What an old fraud and all you are, Jim. You look so deuced wise and yet you don't understand a word I'm saying, do you?"

He shouted the question and Jim, looking up with a start, almost dropped the white silk shirt, on which he was sewing a button, into the red dust of the veldt.

"Golly! No, *baas*," he stammered. "Und'stand? Yes. Do you?" Then in the vernacular, he added, "The *baas* was saying?"

"The *baas* was saying," the Major replied, also in the vernacular, "that he is tired of talking to himself and of doing nothing. Tomorrow we start on the trek for the big *dorp*."

Jim's face registered dismay. "Only a little while ago the *baas* said that he was tired of the *dorp* and the talk of men who could only speak lies."

The Major sighed. "I know. I must be getting old, Jim."

"Au-a! In Chaka's time a man no younger than the *baas* would have been counted old enough to be a warrior, and not until a man had lived four or five years longer than the *baas* would he have been permitted to take a second wife. No. The *baas* is not old, yet."

"Very old, Jim, for do not old people always cry for what they have not?"

"So do children."

"But I am no child. Therefore, tomorrow we trek for the *dorp*."

"The *baas* has spoken. But here—" Jim's gesture embraced the boundless bush veldt, the patches of waving elephant grass, the distance-blued hills, the smoke from the cooking fires of distant *kraals*— "here, *baas,* there is room to breathe; here a man can walk freely."

"True, Jim. And here a man grows old before his time, because tomorrow will be like today which is the same as yesterday. Here nothing happens."

"Au-a!"

Jim's expression was one of intense disgust, and his eyes wandered to the skin of a lion pegged out nearby; to the bulky carcass of a kudu bull; to the fawn which was roasting at the fire. The three animals had fallen that morning, and the Major had only used three cartridges. The lion he had dropped not thirty feet from where he and Jim had stood waiting the charge. Surely, Jim thought, that was enough excitement for any man. Even he, veteran hunter though he was, had experienced a thrill, fearing that his *baas* was delaying his shot too long.

The Major shook his head. "The shot which killed the fawn would have killed the lion, Jim," he said. "What difference?"

"Great difference, *baas*. If the *baas* had missed the fawn he had only to whistle and the fawn would have stopped its flight and the *baas* could have shot again. But, had the *baas* missed the lion, he would never have whistled again."

"True, wise one. But I did not miss."

The two men were silent for a little while. Then the Major said with a bantering laugh, "Soon the sun will have set, Jim, but I do not see the mounted policeman who was to have been here. Your ears are lying to you, your eyes see things that are not. You, too, are getting old, Jim."

Chagrined, not a little alarmed, Jim sprang to his feet and, with wide-open, unshaded eyes looked directly toward the setting sun.

"I had forgotten, *baas,* all about that man. He has not come, no; but he was coming, yes. My eyes and my ears are still my servants; they did not deceive me. I heard the beat of his horse hooves, I saw the dust. And he was riding this way—fast."

"But I saw nothing, Jim, I heard nothing."

And is that strange, *baas?*"

"No, not strange."

The Major had never ceased to wonder at the marvelous development of the Hottentot's senses. His eyes had an almost telescopic vision; his ears were attuned to the faintest whisper. From amidst a herd of cattle, Jim could distinguish the lowing of his *baas's* beasts; when following game, an apparently casual examination of the spoor was sufficient to tell Jim the number of animals in the herd they were following, specie, approximate size of the leader, the distance they were ahead. Indeed, the secrets which the veldt and the animals of the veldt guard so carefully from the majority of men were an open book to Jim.

So the Major had not questioned the Hottentot when he had said, earlier in the afternoon, "By sundown a mounted policeman will be here," but had ordered Jim to cook extra food—policemen are always hungry. Yet it seemed, now, that Jim had been wrong. If not, then the man should by now have been visible to the Major.

"I made no mistake, *baas,*" Jim muttered. "He was riding fast this way. It was the same policeman I saw at the ivinkel yesterday. When I heard him speak your name I would have spoken to him, but he turned away as one not wishing to be seen. Later I saw him on a gray horse. It was that same man I saw riding this way when I said that a policeman would be here before sundown."

"But you could not see the color of the man's horse, Jim, surely?"

The Hottentot chuckled.

"Nay, *baas*. Even Jim's eyes are not so good. But the man was a poor rider and so his horse could not make its proper gait. *Ta-tot tot tot, ta-tot tot tot* it went."

"But the man is not here, Jim; no man is in sight. Neither can we hear the beat of a horse's hooves."

"No, *baas,*" the Hottentot agreed absently.

He turned slowly so that he was facing north, and idly glanced at the veldt beyond the camp. Presently his brows knit in a puzzled frown, his nostrils dilated and, as the Major was about to speak, he held up his hand for silence.

The Major relaxed and watched Jim with mirthful curiosity. "I suppose the old fraud's goin' to find some plausible explanation to cover his error about seeing and hearing the policeman," he muttered, "and I must pretend to be convinced or he'll be terribly hurt."

"The *baas* is very tired," Jim said suddenly.

"Not very, Jim."

The Hottentot nodded his head vigorously. "Yah! Very tired, *baas*. You will lie down behind this—" he pointed to an outcropping of rock four or five feet away.

The Major looked in dismay at his spotlessly white, faultlessly creased duck trousers.

"They can be washed, *baas,* and the need is great. Besides, see, I will put down a blanket."

"Is it a game, Jim?"

"Of a sort, *baas.* Now come. Remember, you are very tired."

The Major rose slowly from his camp stool, yawned and stretched himself lazily, then slouching over to the outcropping of rock, lay down on the blanket which Jim had spread for him.

"And you, Jim, what will you do?"

"I go down to the river for water, *baas.* Do not move until I give the word. The *baas* promises?"

"I promise," the Major said with portentous gravity. "But do not be too long, Jim. This is beastly uncomfortable."

"In a few days the *baas* will be at the *dorp.*" Jim said sarcastically. "There he can sleep on feathers and have a roof over his head. Then he can forget all this," Jim gestured expressively with his hands, "nothingness. Now I go. The *baas's* rifle is close to his hand, and it is well to kill the snake which crawls toward one."

He picked up a canvas water bucket and, singing a barbaric chant, strolled leisurely down the native path leading to the river. He quickly clambered down the steep bank onto the hard sandy bed. It was in the dry season and, save for an occasional pool, the river was dry.

Jim's actions from this time on would surely have astounded his *baas;* who long since had schooled himself to accept all that Jim did without question. Certainly had he seen Jim drop the water bucket and run upstream with great speed, he would have thought his companion of many a daring escapade had gone suddenly mad.

Even so, the Major was greatly puzzled by Jim's last statement. "Wonder what the old chap is drivin' at," he murmured. "Kill the snake which crawls toward one. Sounds like one of the proverbs I used to write in a copy book years and years ago. Is the old bounder just pulling my leg? Ah, well, it's just as well to be prepared." He reached out his hand and took up his rifle which Jim had placed conveniently near.

"Whatever it is, if it's anything," he continued, "will come from that direction." He shifted his position slightly so that by raising his head just a little he could see over the top of the outcrop and get a view of the veldt to the north.

Time passed. The shadows lengthened rapidly; in a little while the whole veldt would be covered by one large shadow, by a mantle of darkness. Already some of the lesser night beasts were disturbing the stillness with their cries. The mules which drew the Major's Cape cart, their bellies swollen with the sweet veldt grass, returned in solemn file to the camp. Behind them, kicking playfully, was the Major's coal black stallion, Satan.

As the horse neared the Major his gait became instantly sober and sedate, and he whinnied softly in answer to his master's soft chirruping noises. A bell-bird *tonked* musically; a vagrant gust of wind blew the smoke from the fire toward the Major, carrying with it the pleasing odor of roasting meat and the tang of burning wood. That same breeze, too, was laden with the beating of tom-toms and the fragment of a weird minor cadence from some distant *kraal.* The heavy night dew began to fall and the crisp air was filled with the scent of freshly watered soil.

Then the Major knew that his expressed desire for the fleshpots of the city was only a passing whim, a reaction from an over-indulgence in Nature's most prized gifts. He had been deafened by the loud beating of a distant drum which had drowned, for the moment, the sweeter music at hand.

"But I'll let old Jim stew for a while longer," he mused. "I won't tell him until the morning that we're not going back. I wonder what little trick the old swanker is planning to play on me. It'll be dark in a few minutes, and I'm bally hungry. If he doesn't come soon that buck will be done too much.

"I wonder what ails Satan and the mules!"

The animals were all facing toward the north and were obviously very uneasy.

"Must be the snake, at last," muttered the Major and, as suddenly and completely as if he had taken a mask from his face, the inane, vacuous look vanished. His eyes hardened, seemed to change color— from light blue to steel gray—his lips tightened, his fighting jaw became more pronounced. But there was no other change, nothing to indicate that he was ready for anything to happen, and prepared to meet the charge of a rogue elephant—or man. His muscles were all relaxed, his breathing was normal and he seemed to be void of all motion, save that the first finger of his right hand toyed with the trigger of his rifle.

Then the raucous cry of a Go-away bird sounded three times.

"That's Jim! How did he get there?"

Again the cry of the bird sounded, it seemed, from a patch of elephant grass not far to the north of the camp. And then silence, a heavy silence.

After a time the Major cautiously raised his white helmet on a stick above the rock. It reflected strangely the last ray of light from the setting sun.

The silence was broken by the vicious *crack* of a revolver, and a cloud of dust flew up about five feet to the right of the Major.

The shot was echoed by a bedlam of noise from the direction of the nearest clump of elephant grass; the wild fighting yells of Jim, the Hottentot, mingled with the oaths and blasphemies of a white man.

The Major sprang to his feet, and ran with deer-like speed toward the noise of conflict. He discovered Jim struggling with a tall, loose-limbed white man dressed in the uniform of a mounted policeman.

"Hands up," the Major ordered curtly as the policeman, having succeeded in throwing Jim with a well executed "flying mare" stooped quickly to pick up the revolver which he had dropped during the scuffle.

The man hesitated, weighing the chances of making a dive for his weapon and securing it before the Major could aim and pull the trigger of the rifle which he was holding so carelessly.

The Major, reading the other's thoughts, continued in a soft, lazy drawl, "I'm not a bad shot, really. And I can shoot just as well from the—er—hip as from the shoulder. Perhaps you don't know, and you ought to know, but this rifle has a hair trigger—if you know what I mean. For instance."

There was a report and the policeman's helmet flew from his head as if pulled by invisible wires. Yet the policeman could have sworn that the Major had not moved.

"Mi Gawd!" he exclaimed in awed tones as Jim, who had recovered from his fall, picked up the helmet and proudly pointed to the holes in its crown. "Don't do that again, mister."

"I'm sorry, old man," the Major said in tones of mock apology. "Of course I should have called my shot, and I would have done just that but, don't you know, I'd look such a silly ass if I missed. Pick up the revolver, Jim, and perhaps you'll lead the way back to camp. The fawn must be cooked by now, and as our long expected guest has arrived we'll have scoff at once."

This last was in the vernacular and as Jim handed the policeman's revolver to the Major, he said with a grin, "My ears and my eyes did not lie to me, *baas*," then returned to the camp.

"You will follow him if you don't mind, dear heart," the Major said. "And I hope you won't object if I rest my rifle—it's so frightfully heavy—against the small of your back. An' I hope you don't stumble, or I don't, because my finger will be on the trigger all the time. It's a hair trigger, you know. But I think that I've already told you that. No?"

"You don't 'ave to keep me covered all the time like this, guv'nor," the policeman expostulated. "I'll go quietly."

"Um! One would think that I'd arrested you, and, judging by the way you said, 'I'll go quietly,' I should venture to say that you really have been arrested more than once or twice. Well, let's toddle along. We'll have plenty of time for talk after scoff. Oh, by the way, what's your name?"

"Snyder," the other said sullenly. "Rat Snyder, they generally calls me."

"Ah! I see. Well, suppose you call me the Major. I've nothing to do with the army, you understand. That name's just a little *nom de veldt*, as it were."

A few minutes later the Major and his unwilling guest were partaking of a bountiful meal, efficiently served by Jim. Several times Snyder attempted to explain his action and blusteringly demanded the return of his revolver, threatening to have dire vengeance on the Major. But that man would not listen to him.

"Not now, laddie. Let's enjoy our buck roast *sans* a garnishing of lies and what not."

And so the Rat was obliged to eat his meal in silence—silence, at least, as far as speech went—and gave himself up to idle conjectures as to the true side of his strange host's character. Certainly this bored, monocled dude sitting opposite him, eating with the dainty fastidiousness of a woman, could not be the same man who had shown such lightning-like dexterity with a rifle a little while back. And there seemed to be no thread connecting his drawling, inane chatter with the curt, "Hands up" of half an hour ago.

The man was a fool, Snyder finally concluded. That shot had been a lucky one—"Extra lucky fer me. 'E might 'ave killed me!" He didn't know anything, and he'd be easy enough to bluff. There was still a chance to win Smith's reward.

At last the meal was finished. Jim cleared away the dishes, and was seated by the fire satisfying his own hunger. And Jim scorned plates, knives and the other implements civilization has made essential to the proper eating of food.

"Now we can have a pleasant little chat-chat," the Major said softly, and, lighting a cigarette, puffed contentedly. "I think you have quite a little to explain, Trooper Snyder, I suppose you really are a trooper, though how you passed the riding and shooting tests is quite beyond my feeble intellect."

"Never mind that," the Rat snarled. "But lemme tell yer this, Major: You can't go takin' a man's revolver away from 'im and treatin' 'im as you've treated me."

"But, ah, beg pardon, I have."

"Yus, you 'ave. And now you are goin' to give the revolver back ter me an' let me go. If yer do, per'aps I'll forget 'ow you, an' that nigger of yours, 'as man'andled me."

"I'd be only too charmed to, really. But I'm afraid it wouldn't be safe for me—or you. Suppose, however, you tell me just what your little game is."

"Little game, mister," the Rat said in astonished tones. "I ain't got no little game."

"Then why did you fire at me?"

The Rat's eyes opened wide, expressing injured innocence.

"I didn't fire at you, mister. I didn't know anyone was a-campin' 'ere. I thought as 'ow I sees a buck an', as I was 'ungry an' didn't 'ave no rations wiv me, it bein' too late fer me to get back to the station for scoff, thinks I, I'll shoot that buck an' cook it. So I fires. The next I know is that your nigger jumps on me like a crazy man. You know the rest. But now you've given me scoff—an' a bleedin' good meal it was—I can ride on. So give me my popper an' I'll wish yer good night."

He held out his hand for the revolver, but the Major shook his head.

"I can't do it, really. Not because I don't believe you, but because I do. How do I know that you wouldn't mistake me for a buck again?"

The Rat's laugh was a trifle forced. "Don't be a fool," he said. "Mistakes like that don't 'appen twice in one day."

"True, just the same, and I'm sure you'll understand my position, I daren't take the risk. So I'm going to ask you to stay the night here."

Snyder began to bluster, but was silenced when the Major patted the revolver which now hung in its holster at the back of his chair.

"All right," he assented sullenly. "Too late to go on now, any'ow. But you'll 'ave to send your nigger fer my 'orse 'an', I warns yer, I shall report yer to the sergeant at the station."

The Major beamed. "That 'ud be most awfully jolly of you. It would save me the trouble of paying the old bird a call. But suppose we go into the tent now, and I'll tuck you up nice and comfy. Early to bed, you know, and all that. Yes," he took the revolver from its holster, "as you remark, I'm bringing my little persuader along with me.

"You know," the Major continued as they entered the tent, "I'm getting most attached to you."

"Like 'ell you are!"

"Yes, really. On the whole you are a dour, silent fellow, but, when you do speak, your remarks are forceful and to the point. So I'm going to keep you with me for a few days—until I've taught you how to distinguish a man from a buck."

"I'll see yer in 'ell first."

The Major gurgled with approval. "There, that just proves what I was saying. Forceful and to the point."

Then, in anxious tones, "You have handcuffs? Ah, yes, I see you have. You must be a really truly policeman. Well, hold out your little hands, there's a nice boy. I'm going to handcuff you to this pretty iron cot. You'll sleep much sounder—knowing that there's no danger of your going buck shooting in your sleep—and so will I."

And the Rat, because he could do nothing else save to utter lurid curses, permitted himself to be handcuffed and, throwing himself down on the bed, made himself as comfortable as possible.

"Nighty-night," said the Major, as he passed out of the tent.

"Go to 'ell," growled the Rat.

"AND NOW, what is the story of it, Jim?" the Major asked as he joined the Hottentot by the fire.

"The tale is soon told, *baas*. I knew there had been a man riding this way, and yet that man did not come. Then, when we were talking about him, *baas*, I heard a horse neigh up there—you could not hear it. I remembered that the man's face was evil, and that he had asked men of the *baas's* whereabouts. The rest, is it not plain? He turned from the trail and crossed the river farther up, to the north, intending to creep up upon us unawares. So I went down to the river, first making sure that the *baas* was behind cover, and ran upstream until I came to the place where that man had crossed. I followed his spoor, came to the place where he had tied his horse, followed his spoor until presently I saw him before me, creeping on hands and knees.

"Not once, *baas*, did he look behind him; he is a fool. And so, *baas*, after a time we two came to a place where the elephant grass thinned and could see the camp. It was just after I had sounded the call of the Go-away bird, and even then he did not turn.

"Then the man pulled out his gun just as the *baas* raised his head above the rock. That was folly, *baas*."

"My head was not in the helmet, Jim."

"*Au-a!* I should have known. And then the man fired, but before he could fire again I had leaped upon him. The shame is mine that he fired at all."

"No shame, Jim. You played your part well."

Jim grinned his acknowledgement of the compliment. "Here nothing happens, *baas*," he said banteringly. "Tomorrow we go to the *dorp*. Is it not so?"

"Aye. Bring the policeman's horse here, then you can sleep. Tomorrow we trek for—somewhere."

IV

THE MAJOR broke camp very early next morning. Breakfast, coffee and veldt bricks, was eaten in the gray half-light of breaking day, while the grass was still wet with dew and the chill in the air made the warmth from the camp-fire very desirable.

Before the sun shot up above the horizon Jim, who had already loaded the camp equipment onto the Cape cart, inspanned the mules. The Major, tersely ordering the Rat to climb onto the driver's seat, jumped up beside him.

"Already, Jim?" the Major called.

"Yah, *baas*," replied the Hottentot, who was riding the policeman's horse, and leading Satan.

"Argh, there," shouted the Major in boyish glee and cracked the long whip.

The well trained mules broke into a canter, swinging round in a half-circle in response to the Major's guiding hands on the reins, and headed due east.

"This is jolly, isn't it?" chuckled the Major, turning to the Rat, his round face beaming with joy. "Nothing like trekking before sunup, is there? Everything so fresh—nice smells, fresh air, cool, everything positively ripping."

The Rat grunted disdainfully. He had not slept very well. He had been tormented through the night by a weird nightmare; he had been shooting rabbits when one, wearing a white helmet and a monocle, jumped up and bit him. Then the rabbit, its face was like Whip Smith's, had said with a lisp, "You don't taste a bit nith!" There was more to it, but he had been conscious chiefly of the fact that the bite hurt, yet had never gained complete wakefulness to move slightly so that the pressure of the handcuffs on his wrist would be removed.

"Rather grumpy, what?" the Major continued cheerily. "That's too bad. And of course you can't appreciate the beauties of that." He pointed with his whip toward the eastern sky where the glory of the rising sun seemed to be setting the world on fire; tongues of flaming color—rose madder, lavender and gold predominating—shot upward, dispelling the gray clouds of dawn.

The Rat sniffed.

The Major looked at him in disgust, "But of course you can't," he continued, "You're blind. You are a rat, a sewer rat. You can't look up."

"Wot I'm interested in," the Rat said thickly, "is just wot I'm a-goin' ter do wiv you w'en I gets a chance."

"Ah! You mean you want to go buck shooting again, laddie?"

"Naw! My 'ands are good enough ter do wot I wants to do wiv you. You just take these 'andcuffs orf, an' I'll show yer."

The Major looked at him with interest. " 'Pon my soul," he murmured, "the Rat's got guts. I've half a mind to accommodate him. But no; Jim 'ud never understand."

Aloud he said, "Tut, tut, don't be so fierce! You're having a nice ride, and I'm preventing you from committing murder. You're not as appreciative as you might be."

"So yer yeller, eh?" the Rat sneered. "Yeller like all bleedin' dudes."

The Major's eyes narrowed and the Rat was conscious of a sudden qualm, of a feeling that he had misjudged his man. Then the Major laughed softly, fixed his monocle firmly in place and looked rather sorrowfully at the Rat.

"Yes," he said softly. "It was always the curse of my boyhood days that my mother would not allow me to fight; weak heart, you know. But then fisticuffs is so degrading. Why, I've heard that men make each other's noses bleed and get their eyes blackened. How beastly! By the way, have you ever ridden behind eight mules before?"

"Naw. An' I ain't likely to again. They're too slow fer me."

The Major whistled softly. "Why, dear Rat," he exclaimed, "you haven't lived. We must rectify that."

He hooked the reins over the back of the seat and, taking the long-handled, long-lashed whip in his two hands, braced his feet against the front board.

"Hold on, Rat," he said.

Then the long lash flew out over the mules with a rifle-like report and gently curled about the ears of the leaders. Again and again the whip cracked and each mule felt the smart of it.

Their speed increased—faster, faster.

The Major called to them, urging them to still better speed, spoke to each one by name. Soon they were going at breakneck speed, stretching themselves out in a maddened gallop, and the Cape cart bounced crazily from side to side.

"Get the reins, mister," the Rat cried. "They're running away. Look hout! You'll 'ave us over."

The Major turned toward him and laughed. "You'd better get back of the seat," he advised, "and hold on."

A heavy jolt as they passed over a large rock decided the Rat that the Major's advice was good, and he quickly followed it. He reached out with his manacled hands with the wild idea of taking the reins and pulling up the mules, but the Major brought the thick butt of the whip down on his hands and the Rat subsided, whimpering frightened curses.

"We've only just begun," the Major shouted, that his voice might be heard above the rattle of the wheels. "Now watch."

And Snyder, the Rat, yellow with fear, watched a most astounding feat of driving as the Major, using only the whip and his voice, sent the mules through a maze of evolutions; now they were headed full tilt toward a large anthill, and when it seemed that they would surely crash into it the mules swung sharply to the left. For a breath-taking moment the Cape cart tilted at a precarious angle, then righted itself and bounced jauntily on. The Major made the mules zigzag, missing large rocks to the right and to the left by the barest fraction of space; he headed them between two baobab trees where it seemed that there was not room enough for the Cape cart to pass—and the Major himself breathed with relief when the hazard was safely passed. Up hill and down hill, over a rock-strewn gully, he drove, and not once did the terrifying speed lessen.

And all the time the Major, his monocle firmly in place, bare-headed—his helmet was bouncing on the floor of the Cape cart—played with the whip so that it seemed to be a live thing in his hands, obeying his slightest wish. Occasionally he would expound to the unappreciative policeman the technique of certain of the "cracks."

"This one," said the Major, "is beastly hard to do with this whip—one needs the kind the Australians use. They call it, I believe, the Sydney 'double crack.'"

He snapped the whip, ever so slightly, and the lash uncurled itself with two loud reports.

"And this, this would cut a pound of flesh from your hide, Rat."

As far as the Rat could see, not that he cared about seeing anything, the Major made the same motion, but the report was deafening.

"There's a horsefly on Skellum's ear and Mafouta's getting lazy, don't you think?"

"I don't fink anything," the Rat moaned. "But I wish you'd stop. You'll kill hus."

"Oh, I haven't started to play with 'em yet," the Major said with a chuckle. "But watch this one; I'm rather proud of it."

The long lash flicked gently forward and killed a large fly on the off-leader's ear. Then it coiled quickly back on itself and a little cloud of dust arose from the rump of the near-wheeler.

And now Jim, who had been riding close behind the cart, yelling like a mad man, called out, "Ohhe, *baas!* The policeman's horse can not keep up the pace any longer."

The Major looked behind and saw that the gray horse was white with lather. Then he grinned at Jim, and pointed to the Rat who was lying prone upon the floor of the swaying Cape cart, a victim of something suspiciously like seasickness.

Turning again, the Major put away the whip, and taking up the reins, called soothingly to the mules.

Instantly their pace slackened and a few minutes later they were trotting sedately along a well made dirt road.

Shakily the Rat sat up. "Oh, migawd," he moaned, "it was orful."

Presently they came to a gate in a five-strand wire fence which stretched to the right and to the left as far as eye could see. As Jim dismounted to open the gate, a white man rode up on the other side of the fence to meet them.

"Hello, Major," he called gleefully. "I might have known that you were the only man who could drive a team of mules like that. Man, it was stupendous. How the hell can you do it?"

The Major looked confused; he actually blushed.

"I was just actin' like a bally fool, Loring. Showin' off like a blinkin' school brat, don't you know. I ought to be horsewhipped; the poor devils are all tuckered out. Can you give us scoff?"

Loring, he was a short, plump little man with a jaunty, well-waxed mustache and sparkling black eyes, snorted.

"Can we? You're going to stay with us for a week or so—oh, yes you are. Helen said only this morning that it was about time you paid us a visit.

"But who's your friend?" Loring looked at the Rat with interest. "You are not under arrest, are you? If you are, I think I can take care of that gentleman."

The Major laughed. "Thanks. But there's no need of the rescue act. I'm not under arrest, but my friend, Mr. Rat Snyder, is, in a manner of speaking. He's not a very jovial soul, is he? Well, I'll tell you all about him later."

"Look 'ere," the Rat burst out excitedly. "This joke 'as gone far enough. You let me go now, an' I won't say anyfing about wot yer done."

"Frightfully sorry, an' all that, but it can't be done, Ratty, old top. I must have a little talk with your commanding officer first."

The Rat appealed to Loring. "I call hon you, sir, in the name of the Lor, to 'elp me. I calls on you to witness that this —— is 'oldin me against me will."

Loring looked at the Major and winked. Then, toying with his mustache, he said. "I'm afraid I can't see anything out of the way,

Trooper. You appear to be enjoying a very pleasant ride—that's all."
Then to the Major, "Let's go up to the house, shall we?"

The Major nodded agreement. "You go on with Jim," he said. "I'll
follow with Mr. Snyder. I must explain a few things to him, you know;
impress on him the fact that he must be on his best behavior—that
is, if he wants me to release him from the handcuffs. And I suppose
he does."

Loring laughed understandingly. "Come on, Jim," he called in the
vernacular, and as they cantered off continued, "now tell me what is
your *baas's* play with the policeman."

Jim grinned. "It's only a matter of shooting a buck, white man."

"You mean your *baas* has been shooting buck without a license?"

"Nay! The policeman did the shooting; my *baas* was the buck."

V

THE BIG Man was talking about you the other day," Loring
said, changing the subject from stories of hunting.

"He was?"

Loring nodded. It was after the noon-day meal and they were
seated on the spacious stoop of the Loring homestead. The Rat, sitting
in a chair close to the Major, was apparently bored and disgruntled.
Mrs. Loring, a gracious, dark-haired, blue-eyed woman, was swinging
in a nearby hammock.

"Yes," Loring continued. "He said that he wished you'd leave the
Syndicate alone for a change and get after the men who endanger
the future of the country."

"But I haven't done any I.D.B. for the deuce and all of a time," the
Major expostulated. "I'm absolutely out of practise. Don't think I'd
know a bloomin' diamond if I saw one. I'll have to pull off a deal just
to show 'em I'm alive."

"Don't, Major. It's not worth the candle. You know it isn't. Besides,
granted that the Big Man's coining money because of a monopoly
which you disapprove of, and has passed laws to protect that monopoly which you think unjust—you've got to admit that he's doing
big things with his money."

The Major nodded. "He's following a wonderful vision; he's making
a nation."

"And he's not altogether to blame for the fact that his underlings abuse the power he's given them?"

"Perhaps not. But then, old chap, I've no quarrel with the Big Man. I admire him heaps—really!"

"Doesn't the end he's aiming for justify the means, Major," Mrs. Loring put in softly.

"Yes, I think it does, Helen. But why does he want me now, Loring?"

Loring looked triumphantly at his wife before answering. "A group of men, headed by Whispering Smith, have formed a Syndicate of their own and threaten to smash the Big Man unless he takes them in and gives their representative a voice equal to his own. And you know what that 'ud mean—ruin for hundreds, thousands."

The Major whistled softly. "But he can smash 'em, surely."

"He could if he had time—another week, say—but you know how his money all goes to developing the country up north."

"And Smith has set a time limit, you say?"

"Yes. Thursday noon."

"Um! And today's Monday. And how's Smith going to do the Big Man?"

"By selling all the stones his crowd have collected at a ridiculous figure. You can imagine what that'll mean—flooding the market so that diamonds 'ud be as cheap as glass for a time. It 'ud take years for things to get back to normal—perhaps they never would."

"Clever, oh, very clever," murmured the Major. "It 'ud cause a panic on the Exchange; the Syndicate wouldn't be able to give shares away. Why, it 'ud be worse than the South Sea Bubble. Clever of Smith, oh, very. But I don't see what I can do, do you, Helen?"

"Not unless you stole—er—borrowed Smith's stones. The end would justify the means, surely."

"Ah, yes. But I'm afraid that's impossible." Then he said, not at all apropos, "I suppose I'd better turn the Rat loose."

Loring nodded sorrowfully, feeling that he had failed miserably in enlisting the Major in the fight against Smith's organization.

The Rat looked up quickly, and as Mrs. Loring now met his gaze, she shivered slightly at the malice which gleamed in his eyes. Her forehead wrinkled in thought, and she felt strangely panic-stricken.

Rising suddenly she announced, in answer to her husband's look of inquiry, that she was going for a little walk.

"Well, Snyder," the Major said after Mrs. Loring had passed out of sight, "you heard what I said, eh? Here's your revolver, but really, old man, better practice a great deal before you use it again on a buck. You can go, the sooner the better."

The Rat took the revolver, it was in its holster, and fastened it to his belt, then leaned back in his chair, a triumphant leer on his face.

"I don't know as I want ter go, fanks hall the same. I'm comfortable here."

Loring and the Major exchanged puzzled glances. "But you don't understand, Ratty dear. We are tired of your bloomin' presence. Shoo! Get out!"

"I ain't a-goin'. Has I've said, it's nice and pleasant 'ere. Fink I'll leave the perlice an' stay wiv my friends Mr. and Mrs. Loring fer a w'ile. I likes Mrs. Loring. 'Elen's a bloomin'—"

"Shut up, you," Loring said angrily, "and get out before I have you *sjambok*ed."

Snyder's red-rimmed eyes contracted to pin-points and, as the Major put a restraining hand on the impetuous Loring's shoulder, he said, sneeringly, "You'd better go slow wiv that sort o' tork, mister. It'll only cost yer money. An' I'm much obliged ter you, dude, fer bringin' me 'ere an' puttin' me in the way of makin' heasy money."

He laughed boisterously.

"Just what's the joke?" the Major asked quietly.

"W'y, I was finking 'ow I was goin' ter live 'ere in style wiv 'Elen waitin' on me 'and hand foot, an' that little blighter givin' me a quid or so w'enever I asks fer it—w'ich'll be most frequent. You see," he added confidentially, "I 'appens ter know somefing that 'Elen and 'er bloomin' 'usband 'ud give a lot ter keep quiet. I 'appens ter know that 'Elen's a crook."

With a hoarse cry of rage Loring leaped from his chair and rushed at Snyder, who rising coolly from his chair, easily dodged the charge and countered with a heavy right to Loring's jaw. The little man went down like a ninepin but, immediately regaining his feet, again rushed to the attack, apparently oblivious of the shower of blows the Rat rained on his face and which shook him visibly.

And now the Major, standing up, caught Loring by the collar and dragged him away, shouting in his ear—for Loring seemed to be anger-deafened—"Leave him to me; he's sixty pounds heavier than you and knows how to use his fists."

Loring subsided into a chair, sobbing with rage at his helplessness.

"Now come on," the Major said and, as the Rat—anxious to wipe out the indignities he had suffered at the hands of this monocled dude—greedily accepted the invitation, gave that man a lesson in feinting, footwork and hitting which far surpassed anything he had seen in his checkered ring career.

"Ugh!" he exclaimed presently as the Major's left again got home on his flabby stomach muscles. "Let's tork. I ain't got no cause ter fight wiv you. Let's tork."

"All right," the Major said cheerfully. "I knew you were yellow, Ratty. Well, talk it is. And you, Loring, you leave this animal to me. I was responsible for bringing him here, I'll send him away. Better go and put a piece of raw beef on that eye of yours and bathe your face before Helen sees you."

Loring hesitated a moment, then vanished into the house.

When he came out again, fifteen minutes later, it was in time to see the Rat vanishing in a cloud of dust down the driveway.

"Well," he asked as he seated himself disconsolately, "what did the rotter know?"

The Major lighted a cigarette before answering slowly, "He knew all about Helen's little fall from grace in London."

"You mean the—er—shoplifting?"

The Major nodded.

Loring cursed. "And you let him go?"

"You couldn't hold him here forever, dear chap. The situation would have beer intolerable."

"Better that," Loring said bitterly, "than that all Helen's friends— and my enemies—should know about it. Explanation will only make matters worse. Oh, why didn't I stay out here and settle the thing with him myself. Poor Helen!"

"I don't think the Rat will say anything about it. I've arranged things all right."

"You mean you've paid him to keep quiet?"

The Major nodded.

"How much?"

"Five thousand pounds. I gave him two hundred—all I had with me. I'm going to give him the rest on Thursday; going to meet him in Kimberley. He's on his way there now to spend the two hundred.

'Ter 'ell wiv the perlice,' he said, 'I'm a bloomin' civilian from now hon.' He's a pleasant animal!"

Loring frowned. "Do you think he'll keep quiet?"

"No, not if I know the breed. He'll bleed you for all you've got, Loring."

"Then, by God, Major, why did you give—?"

"Gently, gently, old hot-head. I want to deal with the worm in my own way. You see, he tried to murder me. Of course, Whip Smith put him up to that, and I must have a little chat with Whip about it. Can't have that sort of thing going on, you know. So, it would seem, the Rat was one of Whip's creatures and he's been looking through Whip's infamous books—you've heard about them?"

Loring nodded.

"Very well. That's where he saw Helen's photo and read about her little adventure. He boasted about it; he seems to have a good memory for faces."

"But if he's one of Whip's men, won't he tell Whip all about it?"

"Was one of Whip's men, old chap, not is. All the difference in the world. Having fallen down on the first job Smith gave him he's afraid of the man and has decided to play his own game. I helped him decide. You see, he told me that he had recognized several other women whose photos appear in that book of Smith's—and blackmailing is a very well paying profession. 'And why share the profits with Smith?' I asked him. 'I'm damned hif I'm goin' to, mister,' he answered, 'but I'm goin' to make them women sit hup an' be very nice ter me.'

"So, Loring, for the sake of the other women—as well as Helen's— I must positively settle with the bounder in my own way. Don't you see?"

"How?"

"I don't know yet. But I'll probably think of a way as I ride into Kimberley. I shall leave Jim here—do you mind?—and ride on alone. Let's have an early dinner; I want to start as soon as the moon's up."

"All right, Major," Loring said huskily. "You're a damned good pal for a chap to have. But what shall I tell Helen? She's expecting you to stay a day or two?"

The Major hesitated, then, "Oh, tell her I'm going in to see the Big Man. Now let's go and join her. I'm afraid the dear girl suspected the Rat of something. You'd better be specially nice to her, and not a word of all this."

"But how shall I explain this?" Loring pointed lugubriously to his eye.

The Major laughed. "My dear chap," he said, "you don't expect me to do your lying for you, do you?"

VI

THE RAT returned to Kimberley on foot, at least the last mile or so of his journey, and at night. His horse he left free to roam on the veldt. At a small kaffir store just outside the township proper, he purchased a suit of civilians which he immediately donned. And then, with a three days' beard on his face—he had not shaved since the day before he was captured by the Major—he slunk covertly into the town, taking care to give the mounted police camp a wide berth, well convinced that no one would recognize him because no one was looking for him.

He put up at a hotel far removed from Whispering Smith's place, and proceeded to spend his money with the regal air of one who has always had plenty, or has come by what he has dishonestly.

It was quite evident that the Rat's wealth was newly acquired, and in Kimberley furtive appearing men of no apparent occupation, yet well supplied with money, attract the attention of the eagle-eyed men who guard the output of the diamond mines.

But the Rat was ignorant of many things, so that when one of his chance-met acquaintances flattered him by continually seeking his society, he took it as a tribute to his own good qualities and two-fisted generosity.

His self-esteem would have been badly shaken had he known that his new found friend was on the pay-roll of the Syndicate.

Then, too, the Rat grossly underestimated the long arm of Whispering Smith. That he had not been sent for seemed proof enough that Smith did not know of his presence, and would not know.

But, within twenty-four hours of the Rat's return to Kimberley, Smith was apprised of his presence from two sources. One, a letter, which read:

> Dear Whip:
> I must say that your henchmen are pretty poor specimens. As pickpockets, pea-and-thimble riggers and so forth and what not, they are probably top-hole. But really, when you send out a man to murder

me—what a beastly word "murder" is, isn't it?—I wish you'd choose someone a little more proficient than Rat Snyder. I'm saying this for your own guidance; for myself, I'm perfectly satisfied, quite. But, still, I'll have to chastise you some way. Of course you want to know all about it, yes? First of all then, Ratty couldn't hit a bloomin' haystack, as the dear old rustics say; quaint old chappies, aren't they, in their smocks and what not?—and when he fired at me, an' missed, the silly blighter got the wind up and confessed all. It was most touching! How could you have the heart to lead such an innocent astray. He gave me a lot of interesting information about you and your jolly old books; gave me so much information, in fact, that I felt in honor bound to pay him. You see, I think I can make use of it myself some day.

The last I saw of Ratty he was headed for Kimberley where, he informed me, he was going on a bleedin' razzo, an' ter 'ell with Smitty an' the perlice!" He's quite coarse, isn't he?

Toodle-oo, old Spider. Hope to see you again some day.

Murderously yours,

The Major.

Hardly had Smith, his face white with rage, finished the letter when a trim little girl, who lisped when following her profession, came into his office.

"Boss," she said breathlessly, without any preamble, "Rat Snyder's in town. He seems to be in funds. He's staying at the Colonial."

Smith glared at her, speechless with anger. At last he said in a husky, whispering voice, "Tell Holy Joe to get him."

"You mean—?"

She drew her forefinger daintily across her slim white throat.

"No," he snapped irritably. "Diamonds—Breakwater. Get out."

And Martha got out.

So it happened that that same night the Rat, as he turned away from the cigar counter at the hotel, collided with a fat-jowled man dressed in clerical garb. This man, on recovering from the encounter, felt hurriedly in his breast pocket and then raised a cry of, "Police!"

The Rat's "friend" stepped up quickly, showed his badge and asked what the trouble was.

"Why," replied the clergyman in a deep, booming voice, "this poor misguided fellow has taken my wallet. I felt his hand go into my pocket as he bumped into me."

He looked sorrowfully through the strong-lensed glasses he wore at the infuriated Rat.

"It's a lie," yelped the Rat.

"That'll be all from you," said the detective, and the Rat quickly subsided. "Will you come to the station and make out a complaint, sir?"

"Well, the clergyman hesitated. "I don't want to be hard on the man. It may be his first offence and I should be deeply distressed if I thought I had helped to send him along the broad path which leads to destruction. All I ask is the return of my wallet."

"Come on," said the detective, tightening his grip on the Rat, "hand it over."

"I ain't got it, I tell yer. I ain't got it."

The Rat squirmed in his endeavor to free himself.

"I'm afraid you'll have to come to the station, sir. I can't search him here," the detective said apologetically.

"Very well. But dear me, this is very distressing."

Five minutes later the three were in the office of the captain in charge of the town police.

"Will you describe the wallet, sir?"

"Assuredly. It was of plain, brown leather and contained nothing of value to anyone save myself; a few letters, that is all."

"Search him," ordered the captain.

Quickly the detective ran his hand over the Rat, who made no protest. Things were happening far too rapidly for his brain to grasp.

"Is this yours, sir?" the detective held up a wallet which he had taken from the Rat's coat pocket.

"Yes," the deep voice boomed and the clergyman reached eagerly for it. "As you see, Captain, it contains nothing but private letters. Allow me to thank you for the courtesy you have shown me. A very good day to you both. And, as for you, young man," he paused opposite the Rat, "I hope that this will be a lesson to you, and that you will see the error of your ways before it is too late. Remember the way of the transgressor is hard—very hard."

As the clergyman passed out of the room, the Rat attempted to follow him, but was held fast.

"Lemme go," he whined. "I ain't done nothing. There's no charge against me."

"No. Not yet," replied the detective, "but I'm curious to know where you've been getting all your money from."

He searched the Rat again, a more thorough examination this time, and extracted from the Rat's vest pocket a small diamond in the rough.

"Ah!" murmured the detective happily. "That's your little game, is it? I.D.B."

"I don't know wot yer mean," the Rat cried.

"You'll have a long time to think it over, won't he, Captain? Five years, at least, I should say."

The captain nodded, and consulted his calendar.

"Get him up for trial tomorrow, Thursday, morning. It's a clear case, but you can call me as witness, if you like. We ought to be able to get him off on the one o'clock southbound. He'll enjoy the view at the Breakwater, don't you think?"

The detective chuckled as he led the bewildered Rat to a cell.

VII

IT WAS nearly Thursday noon and Whispering Smith was in an evil temper. Even with Holy Joe's account—and he had told it very comically—of the Rat's trial and that miserable man's tearful exhibition on being sentenced to ten years hard labor for I.D.B. The detective had been too optimistic!

Again and again Smith consulted his watch. It was after eleven.

In a little while he would know whether he and his partners were to be admitted into the Big Syndicate group or whether he was to flood the market and ruin the diamond industry—and, incidentally, ruin the prospects of a young country.

Smith, with his love for the theatrical, had set the stage very cleverly for his expected interview with the Big Man. In his colossal egotism he had insisted on his office being the rendezvous; the Big Man should come to him. On an extra table which had been brought in for the occasion, were black, velvet lined trays, and on the trays—arranged by shape, weight, color, quality—were diamonds; hundreds, thousands of them—the property of the men he represented. Two expert appraisers, the only men he could get to work for him, had taken over three weeks to sort those diamonds, arranging them for marketing.

It was a wonderful plan, this of Smith's; it was without a flaw. Given time, he fully realized, the Big Man could smash him. But that was where Smith's plan was strong. He would show no quarter. He was prepared; the Big Man was not.

Smith should have been happy. That he was not was due to the fact that the Big Man had so far completely ignored him. That hurt his pride.

At half-past eleven his partners crowded into the little office— fourteen of them. They looked inquiringly at Smith, then, huddling together, conversed in furtive whispers. They smoked furiously until the room was blue with smoke and it was almost impossible to distinguish the face of a man across the room. They continually consulted their watches, and the snapping of "hunter" lids sounded like the distant firing of rifles.

At ten minutes of twelve one of the men Smith had placed on guard outside the office opened the door to admit a tall man, his height accentuated by the high, silk hat he wore. He was dressed in a braided morning coat, gray trousers, spats and carried a cane. His black beard, pointed, was neatly trimmed; his mustache well waxed. He loomed up as a giant in the fog-like swirl of smoke. He looked very English, but Smith, and the others who knew their South Africa well, recognized in him a Boer who, having tasted English life, had decided to go his tutors one better.

"Which is Mr.—ah—Smith?" he asked. "I have a letter for him."

His speech was crisp. That and the peculiar way in which he clipped his vowels completely confirmed the accuracy of the impression the men had formed of him.

"I'm Smith," Whip growled. "You from the Big Man?"

"Yess."

He handed a letter to Smith, who opened it and read aloud:

"I hereby authorise the bearer, Mr. Piet du Toit, to act for me this day.

(Signed)"————————————

He passed the letter around.

"Is it genuine?" he asked.

"Yes, Whip," said one. "I'd recognize his scrawl anywhere."

Several of the others also identified the well known signature.

"Well, Piet," Smith said familiarly, "I suppose you're one of his 'young men?'"

"I have the honor to be his personal representative," the other said curtly. "But shall we talk business, not?"

"All right. But there's not much to say. I suppose the Big Man will agree to our terms?"

The other shook his head. "He wants you to give him two more days."

Smith's laugh was echoed by some of the others.

"Not—likely," he said. "Time to smash us, eh? No. You've got," he consulted his watch, "five minutes to accept our terms, or—" He shrugged his shoulders.

There was silence for a little while, broken by the dry nervous coughs of Smith's partners.

Du Toit suddenly took up the coal bucket which stood beside the pot-bellied stove, and said slowly, "I've never seen a bucketful of diamonds, have you, Mr. Smith? And I'd like to. Then here's my proposition. If they," he nodded toward the trays of diamonds, "fill this, we'll buy them at *your price*. If not—" his shrug was equally as eloquent as Smith's had been.

Then with lightning speed he tilted tray after tray into the bucket while the others watched him as if hypnotized, not fully comprehending what he was doing.

"Look!" he cried, shaking the bucket exultantly. "They barely half fill it."

He darted to the door, opened it. Then he turned again, and a monocle gleamed in his right eye.

"Ta-ta, Smithy, old top. As a murder-organizer you're poor, but as a diamond merchant you're absolutely rotten."

The door slammed behind him.

With a bellow of rage Smith leaped to the door, opened it and yelled, "Stop that dude! He's the Major. Stop him!"

Then he saw that the barroom was filled with troopers of the mounted police who were dancing hilariously, and who managed to get in the way of Smith's men and thus prevent them from carrying out his orders.

Of the frock-coated, silk-hatted one there was no sign.

Smith savagely re-entered his office and sat down in his chair muttering. "The blasted dude again. I'll—"

Then he was conscious that his partners were regarding him with hostility. Apparently they had come to some decision, or had had one thrust upon them, during his brief absence.

"Well?" he barked. "What's the trouble with you?" He glanced at his watch. "Time's up! We put these on the market and smash them."

Some of the men laughed and one said in relieved tones, "We were fools to think of coming in with you, Smith. The game's up and I, for one, am glad of it."

Smith stared at him. "What do you mean, game's up? We can carry out our plan, can't we? Flood the market and sell Syndicate stock on the Exchange? We'll clean up big."

"And what dealer'll buy stones in that condition?" The other man pointed to the bucket. "They'll all have to be sorted again before we can market them. And you know how long that'll take. No," he picked up the bucket, "we've going to the Big Man and offer them to him at his price. He'll treat us square."

He moved to the door and passed out into the barroom, followed by the others.

Smith heard him ask some of the troopers to act as escort, then the door closed and he was left to his thoughts.

The others had not lost anything: they still had their diamonds. But he, using his brains, his capital, his enormous criminal organization, he had schemed to win great wealth and the power that wealth brings. And he had lost everything!

"I need a rest," he told himself brokenly, "I'll go north for a while to see what's doing in the Big Man's country. And when I come back," his eyes flashed with their old-time fire, "I'll go after the Major myself.

"The Major!" He repeated the name over and over again. It seemed to lash him to an insensate fury. A stream of invectives came from his thin lips. "I'll get him myself."

MUFTI

IT IS hard to believe that there could be any connection between Sir Lionel Tupper, K.C.B., P.C., etc., etc., and the love-affair of one Trooper Harry Briggs, late of Whitechapel, London. Yet—

"Either you get a suit of civilian clothes or Hi don't walk hout wiv yeh no bloomin' longer."

"But listen, Gertie," the young trooper of the Rhodesian Police expostulated; "'ow am Hi goin' to get a suit? You know wot my pay is; besides—"

He stopped short. It wasn't quite the thing to remind a girl that he had mortgaged his pay for months to come in order to pay for the ring which graced her third finger.

"There's no 'besides' to hit, 'Arry Briggs. And, wot's more, it won't do yeh any good to come ter see me in borrowed clothes. Yeh got to 'ave a suit of yer own, hand it's got ter fit."

Harry Briggs squirmed. He had a lively recollection of the time when, in order to make a hit with his "little bit of all right," he had borrowed garments from his comrades.

The trousers had represented Andrew's contribution, and Andrew was tall and skinny. The coat was "Fat" Bussy's; Briggs was short and slim. No one at the camp had a hat which fitted him, and Briggs was obliged to choose between going bareheaded or wearing his police helmet.

He selected the latter as the less of two evils, but on seeing the scorn in Gertie's eyes, he wished that he had risked sunstroke.

"You don't want me to be a laffin'-stock of the dorp, do yeh?" Gertie continued in a remorseless voice. "Mrs. Jennings' nurse-maid syes Hi 'm a fool ter throw myself away on a mere trooper. Her bloke's a sergint; 'e ain't 'arf swell, I can tell yeh!"

"P'raps yeh better get a sergint," said Briggs bitterly. "Hi ain't got no love for 'em meself."

"Well, I never! Hi suppose yeh finks Hi can't. Sergint Blake asked me to go a walkin' wiv 'im next Sunday."

"What did yeh say?"

"Like to know, wouldn't yeh?" Gertie retorted. "Hi told 'im Hi would let 'im know tonight."

"Wot are yeh goin' to tell 'im?"

"That depends. Hi'll go wiv you if you get a suit of civies. If not—"

"But 'ow can I?"

"Other chaps at the police camp seem ter 'ave plenty of clothes."

Briggs snorted indignantly.

"Why wouldn't they? They're mostly remittance-men. At any rate, they 'aven't—"

Again Briggs stopped short. It was the second time he had been on the brink of mentioning the diamond ring. Though he controlled his tongue, he could not prevent his eyes from casting reflective glances at the ring—it represented the price of several suits—and Gertie, with feminine intuition, read his thoughts.

"Hif it's this, Mr. 'Arry Briggs," she said haughtily, "yeh're grievin' abart, yeh can take hit back. Hit's got a flaw hin hit—same as you."

He waved aside the proffered ring in alarm.

"No! Let me put it back. There's no call fer yeh to carry hon like that, Gert. Hi know it ain't worthy of you, but hit's the best Hi could do."

Slightly mollified, she allowed him to replace the ring, and giggled as, with a show of gallantry, he clumsily raised her hand and kissed it.

" 'Ow yeh do carry hon!" she smirked. "Listen! There's the missus callin'. Hi've got ter go hin. Goo'-bye."

He caught her by the hand, pulling her toward him.

"Wait 'arf a mo'! Hare yeh goin' hout walkin' wiv me next Sunday, or the bloomin' sergint?"

"Hi tell yeh wot," she said hurriedly: "Hif yeh call fer me in civies, Hi'll go with yeh. Hif you're in huniform—hit's hall off."

SIR LIONEL TUPPER was an abject outsider. But Sir Lionel was wealthy. Sir Lionel had contributed freely and generously to the party funds, had at all times obeyed the slightest injunctions of the party whips. Sir Lionel had—and this was most important of all—the backing of several widely read, saffron-sheeted journals. They called him the "people's David."

Consequently, when Sir Lionel hinted that he would appreciate a Colonial appointment as a reward for his services, the Big Men who run things in the Tight Little Isle sat up and took notice.

Sir Lionel—he had his eyes on the big things of the world—modestly mentioned the viceroyship of India.

As a compromise—the underclerk who suggested it was given a responsible berth in the diplomatic corps—an office was created for Sir Lionel. He was given the title: "chief agent-general" and sent to South Africa.

"He can't possibly do any harm there," said the Big Men, "and perhaps he'll get malaria and die."

Sir Lionel's powers were very limited; the Big Men had seen to that. But he had unrestricted powers of clemency, and one of his first acts was to pardon a native, convicted of the brutal murder of a white woman, sentenced to death by the chief justice of Rhodesia.

Sir Lionel's explanation was that it would he an inauspicious way to begin a new era of justice in the country—as foreshadowed by his appointment—by signing the death-warrant of a native.

"We must cultivate," he wrote, "a love for our black brothers, not allowing the question of color to stand in the way of justice."

And the Rhodesian judge was the squarest of men!

But, as has already been said, Sir Lionel was an outsider.

He was deluged with letters and telegrams from Rhodesians who, well versed in the psychology of the natives, feared the effects of his ill-advised clemency.

"They don't understand," he complained peevishly to the blandiloquent members of his staff.

His aide-de-camp offered this advice;

"Why don't you go up there, Sir Lionel? You could make them understand. These Colonials have had their own way too long."

So the chief official of Rhodesia received the following telegram:

> Will be with you on the 28th, inst. Desire to explain reason for pardons. Arrange to have group of influential men meet me at luncheon. Suggest a guard of honor composed of the Rhodesian Volunteers.
> (Signed) TUPPER,

Chief Agent-General.

The chief official tore his hair, cursed, and then called in his assistant.

"What do you think of that, Davis?" he said, handing over the telegram with a gesture of disgust.

"He's a stinker, Chief—what? I suppose we've got to play pretty for him—put on our best bib and tucker and all that, you know."

The chief official groaned.

"I suppose so. Get out the luncheon invitations and call up Colonel Baker of the Volunteers and arrange with him for the guard of honor. Better have a mounted escort, too."

"Colonel Baker reports, Chief," said the assistant the following day, "that the Volunteers refuse to turn out."

"What?"

"It's true, Chief. Baker added that he'd be able to furnish a firing party if you wanted one."

The chief official groaned.

"The escort'll be up to the police, then. Better notify Captain Scudder. Have you sent out the invitations?"

"Yes; I sent out a hundred. That, I think, ought to be sufficient to allow for refusals."

Four days later, and only three days before the coming of Sir Lionel Tupper, the chief official received the last of the replies to the invitations.

That of Dr. Lewis, one of the first settlers in the country, is fairly typical of them all.

"I'll be damned if I'll come," he had written.

The chief official was in a quandary, and he was decidedly annoyed.

"It's no laughing-matter, Davis. Sir Lionel has a strong backing at home, and he can make things warm for us. If we had time, we could explain to these chaps that their refusal to meet Tupper is an insult to the crown. It wouldn't hurt them to meet the blasted fool. There's no harm in an ass's bray."

"What are you going to do, Chief?"

"I wish I knew."

"Why not invite the police to attend the luncheon and pass them off as influential men?"

"You've hit it, Davis! Tupper would never know the difference. All he wants is someone to listen to him blurb. Get Scudder on the 'phone and put it up to him."

"Scudder wants to know, Chief," said Davis later, "if it will be all right for the men to attend in uniform."

"Of course not, you ass! They must be in mufti."

"That's what I said, but Scudder says there's not a trooper at the camp that has a suit of civilians."

"Bosh! I know for a fact that's a lie. Aren't they always sporting round the town looking like Bond Street fashion-plates?"

"I know, Chief. But Scudder says they all swear that they are destitute of clothing save that prescribed by the police regulations. And, of course, Scudder can't force 'em to wear what they swear they haven't got."

Davis smiled sweetly and waited for the explosion.

He was not disappointed.

When the chief official's wrath had subsided somewhat, he spoke curtly and directly to the point.

"Davis," he said, "you will arrange with Hamley and Cox to supply each and every trooper at the camp with a suit of clothes, hat, shirt, collar, tie, boots—a complete outfit, do you understand? You will inform Captain Scudder of this, and tell him that I shall expect all of his men present at the luncheon—and in mufti. Is that perfectly plain?

"He can tell them what he pleases, so long as he leaves no loophole for the blighters to wriggle through. He can appoint them all plain-clothes detectives if he pleases, and order them to be present in order to watch the silver. I don't care what he tells them—but they must be there, and they must be in mufti."

Davis whistled.

"And what's this expenditure to be charged to?"

"Entertainment of chief agent-general, of course. Now, get out of here before I go mad and bite someone."

All of which explains why Sir Lionel Tupper failed to see wherein he had not been a success—he resigned on grounds of ill health shortly afterward—for the true story of the famous Rhodesian banquet was carefully kept from his ears.

"I think, they recognized," he would declaim pompously, "that I was a man of my word, and respected my motives. And here's a strange thing—an incredible thing, but true: Every man at the luncheon wore a brand-new suit. Fancy that! Wasn't it a signal mark of honor."

AND BRIGGS? Why, yes; of course. This is really his story.

The day after the banquet in honor of Sir Lionel being Sunday, he hastened to keep his appointment with Gertie.

In speechless amazement she gazed upon the richly appareled youth.

"Ow!" she exclaimed. "Hi 'ardly knew yeh, 'Arry. So yeh did get 'em after hall. My! But that soot is 'andsome. Hi allus did say that a navy-blue suit and light-brown shoes bespoke the gentleman.

"Yeh know," she confided a moment later, "Hi was honly teasin' yeh about the sergint. Has hif it matters ter me wot yeh wears! As a matter of fac', Hi fink Hi likes yeh in the huniform best."

www.ingramcontent.com/pod-product-compliance
Lightning Source LLC
Chambersburg PA
CBHW051638050726
47502CB00011B/1174